CAGED

A HOLLOWAY PACK NOVEL

BOOK 3

J.A. BELFIELD

CAGED
A HOLLOWAY PACK NOVEL

Published by J.A. Belfield
www.jabelfield.com

Copyright © 2019 Julie Anne Belfield

Cover art by Aimee Laine.

First Printing: 2012
10 9 8 7 6 5 4

ALSO BY J.A. BELFIELD

BEGINNINGS
CALLED
LURED
HEREDITARY
UNNATURAL
ENTICED
CORNERED

THE THERAPIST

HER MANE ESCORT

CAGED

For ... you

1

"... from the Shropshire area. Following Carly McDowd's disappearance on the fourth, and Andrew Doherty's on the seventh, this is the third incident this month ..."

I turned from the square-jawed newswoman on TV to Dad, where he sat in his corner armchair.

His attention remained on the screen, a frown across his brow.

"... the duo of friends were first reported missing late last night by their parents, after they discovered neither of the teenagers ..."

As the newscaster's voice infiltrated once more, images of a couple of lads flashed side by side on the screen. The one on the left had the appearance of any late teen, with shaggy overgrown hair and the twinkle of mischief in his expression.

From the other image, brilliant blue eyes stared out at me from beneath a shock of pale blond curls.

"Oh, shit!" I pushed to my feet, took a step forward. "That's ..."

"Nineteen-year-old Gabriel Lewis was believed by his mother to be staying at Colum Delaney's since Friday evening, while Colum's parents ..."

Dad stood, his fingers retracting his mobile from his jeans pocket, as I worked my own out. He paused, nodded to me. "Go on, Son. You make the call."

Shelley Lewis's number had been saved in my phone book since the beginning of the year, right after we met for the first time. I'd promised to support her—a lone parent, a female no less, raising a werewolf son with no guidance. So far, I'd delivered on that promise.

I hit dial and paced to the window. September sunshine, of the early morning variety, blinded me as my phone rang.

It took only a few trills for her to answer. "Ethan?" Her voice held hope, as well as a heavy weariness and the thickness of tears.

"Is it true?"

The sob hitting my ear gave confirmation enough.

"Hold tight, Shelley. I'm on my way."

"I'll come with you," Dad said, as I hung up and spun toward him. "Shout Sean, too—in case we need to do any scouting. I think I heard him stir upstairs."

"What about Connor's lot?" The Larsen's made up the other half of our eight-wolf pack, but lived separately to us, on the south side of the forest.

Dad shook his head. "I'll update Connor while you deal with Sean."

"And Jem?" I asked with a lifted eyebrow.

Dad's lips twitched, but he continued as though he hadn't noticed my reference to his buck-passing. "Just the three of us will go. Connor and his boys can spend the morning here and stay close to Jem and your mother, unless we need them."

"Oh, come on." Jem waddled after us down the driveway to the truck, her outstretched arms doing a crazy windmill dance. "Let me come." She turned to Sean, my brother—her mate. "Baby, let me—"

"No, Jem." He stepped forward, sweeping a hand across her swollen mound of a stomach. "Gabe is the seventh werewolf to go missing since middle July. Seven in seven weeks. You expect me to allow you out in public while this is happening?"

"Jem?" Mum called from the doorstep. "Let them go."

The set of Jem's jaw clammed her lips together as she turned. "You're not helping, Beth."

"That's because I agree with them." Mum descended the steps. "And don't think I won't be keeping a close watch on you this time." The previous time Jem had been left in Mum's care, she'd snuck out to come find us; Mum had not been amused. She linked her arm through Jem's. "Let them go."

Jem's mouth opened and closed. She went back to Sean and tugged on his arm. "Don't be long, okay?" The resignation of losing the battle showed in her tone.

"I won't be." Something stirred within me, as Sean squatted down and placed a kiss against her navel. "Take care of our boy."

"Or girl," Jem murmured.

Sean smiled. "Our bambino."

We arrived at Shelley's just before nine am. Like she'd been looking out for us, the front door to her house opened, the moment the truck drew to a stop. I didn't have to get close to see the panic in her eyes and the deep blush of unrelenting emotions in her face.

The slam of my door drowned out her delicate steps along the path to greet us. Her hands reached out, as if she considered us her lifeline, before she pressed her fingers against her lips. "I can't thank you enough for coming." A shiver jerked her tiny shoulders as she spoke, while three singular tears rolled down cheeks still red from an earlier batch of crying.

"Come on." I slid my arm around her and drew her to my side. "Let's go in."

Her crown barely reached my armpit as she leaned into me and allowed me to guide her toward the house. Behind us, Sean and Dad's feet hit the path.

The brightness of the day gleamed through the window, bathing Shelley's magnolia-coloured home in warmth and light. Four dirty mugs sat beside her mobile and house phones on the coffee table. A burgundy throw, which matched the deep shade of her hair, lay scrunched into a heap on the sofa, as though Shelley had spent the night there on constant vigil.

I walked her across the room and sat her down, but she pushed back up.

"Please don't make me sit." She worried at the nail on her thumb. "I'm so sick of sitting and waiting for everyone else to do their job." Her gaze met mine. "Do you think it's like those others?"

"When did you last see him, Shel?" I asked.

"Friday." Her fidgeting feet brushed over the carpet, as the two armchairs creaked beneath Sean's and Dad's weight. "Friday dinnertime. Is it like the other disappearances?"

I frowned. "Friday was four days ago."

"He was staying at his friend's. He wants more independence—doesn't like me hassling him all the time. I thought he'd be okay." Her eyes beseeched as she stared up at me. "He promised they'd be indoors before dark. Col's parents were away the weekend—"

"Colum Delaney?" *The other kid from the news.*

Shelley nodded.

"Is he ..." Rubbing a hand across the crick forming in my neck, I lowered myself onto the sofa and took Shelley's arm to draw her down with me. "Is Colum a wolf, too?"

Her head shook as she balanced on the cushion's edge.

"Human?" Brow lifted, I twisted toward Dad, who frowned, and turned back to Shelley. "And there's no sign of him, either?"

"No. Dave and Lisa ... Col's parents—they came back last night from their break. That's why Gabe stayed over—they had the house to themselves, had plans to ... I don't ... but Dave said they came home to the back door wide open, the coffee table smashed, take out trashed on the carpet ..." She sucked in a deep shuddering breath, wringing her hands together.

"So they rang the police." My jaw tightened as the scenario formed in my mind. "Figures they would. Why didn't you call us?"

"I hoped they'd show up, I think. It all seemed so definite when the police knocked on my door and made the report. I was about to call you this morning ... then ... on the news ..." The panic cleared from her eyes a little as her gaze bored into mine. "Is it like the others? Tell me the truth, Ethan. Is it the same as the other disappearances you warned me about?"

As much as I wanted to lie and ease the blow, I couldn't. "Except for the missing human?" I gave a small nod. "It looks that way."

"The others haven't been found, have they?" she asked. "They haven't shown up—"

"Yet," Dad cut in. "Doesn't mean they won't."

Shelley turned to each of us. "How much do you know about the disappearances?"

"Nowhere near enough," Dad said.

"You must know something, or you wouldn't have called me last week to keep a close watch on Gabe."

Dad's gaze met mine—Sean's, too. The worry over how much to share with her seemed to cross all of our minds.

"You're not going to tell me, are you?" she asked. "I get it," she said with a small nod, as we all turned back to her. "I'm not part of your pack, so why—"

"I was contacted," Dad said, leaning forward, "the evening before Ethan called you, by Jack Brosen—he's the Alpha of a pack who runs here, in Shropshire. He wanted to know if I'd followed the news, and to ask for the favour that if I knew anything, I share it."

Lines creased Shelley's brow, but she didn't say anything.

"His son has gone missing—just like Gabe," Dad continued. "But he kept it off the radar. The ones on the news are the ones officially reported. We have no idea how many more have been taken. Just as we have no idea where they're going, or who's taking them, or why. Jack's also worried it's more than just werewolves that have gone missing."

"What do you mean, Nathan?"

"Five of the reported disappearances have been female," Dad said. "If there were that many female werewolves nearby?" His shoulders lifted with his shrug. "Trust me, I'd have heard about it."

"So ... so, they *are* taking humans, too?" Her brows rose higher with each word, but Dad shook his head.

"I don't think they're human, either."

2

Shelley's tiny hands clasped mine. "Thank you so much." Even with the doorstep allowing her a five-inch advantage, she still had to tip back her head to meet my eyes.

"You sure you're going to be okay, on your own?"

The small nod she gave contradicted the hesitant glance over her shoulder toward the empty house. "Gabe might come back, right?"

I fought the urge to shrug. "Right."

"Someone should stay here ... just in case." She sounded more like she needed to convince herself than me.

"Yes." I didn't need persuading. Someone should stay, for that very reason.

"Okay." She released my hands. "Okay."

I turned to leave and found Dad and Sean's attention on our exchange from inside the pickup.

"Promise you'll ring," she said, "if you hear anything."

"Sure," I said over my shoulder, and strode off down the path.

Sean and Dad tracked my route, my climb into the truck, and my reach to insert the key in the ignition.

"You two got something going on?" Sean asked from the rear seat.

A twist of my wrist, and the engine grumbled alive. "Nope."

"But you like her."

I stared straight ahead, rolling my shoulders. "Where to now?"

"Just drive," Dad said. "I have a phone call to make."

After sending Shelley a quick smile of assurance, I pulled away from the kerb.

"You been getting jiggy with Shelley when you visit?" Sean asked, as Dad fiddled with his phone.

"Nope." I shifted from second to third gear.

A ringtone echoed from the passenger seat. I glanced across, as Dad lifted his hand to his ear.

"I don't believe you," Sean said.

I shrugged. "I don't care."

"I thought your visits were to support Gabe, not his mum."

I blanked him as Dad's phone call connected, and a deep bass of a voice answered, "Yes," the word reaching my enhanced hearing with ease.

"Jack?" Dad said. "Nathan Holloway."

"You have news for me?" Jack asked.

Dad gestured for me to take a left. "Nothing good."

I flicked the indicator up, swung the wheel hard enough to sway Sean, and chuckled when his head hit Dad's seat.

Dad glared at me as he gripped the dashboard, but I pretended I hadn't noticed. "Can we meet?" he asked into the phone. In answer to Jack's 'when', he added, "Now. We're already in Shrewsbury."

A pause followed as though our proximity caught him off guard. "You know the Battlegrounds?"

Dad turned to me, but I shook my head. "You have an address, Jack?"

"You'll get to it from the A-forty-nine. I'll meet you outside the coffee shop. Twenty minutes."

Trees hugged the uneven car park on three sides, blossoms dying on the cracked tarmac below them. Four cars dotted the unmarked spaces, but none of them as large as the X5 in the far left corner. Genetically big creatures by nature, werewolves tended to opt for the bulkier vehicles, if only for space comfort. Sean's girlie Porsche made him an exception to the rule. Guessing the sleek grey wheels belonged to the other pack, I parked as far from it as possible.

All three of us inhaled upon stepping from the truck. A host of scents greeted me. Dissecting the wildlife from the flora and cooling engines, I discovered four two-legged mammals carrying the underlying scent of wolf.

Four against three. "You sure this is kosher, Dad?"

"I made the request," he said. "So I'm sticking to the arrangement."

A path wound up and behind a line of trees. Dad headed that way, Sean and I falling into step at his shoulders. The higher up the incline we walked, the stronger the other pack's scents grew.

Low brick columns supported the entrance. Beyond those, the man I presumed to be Jack Brosen sat on a far wall, as though enjoying the morning's rays.

Only someone looking for it would spot the tightness of his jaw, the tension in his body language. Just as only one who expected to see it would notice the weariness in his expression—caused, I presumed, by his missing son.

He nodded to us, as we passed the entrance, but made no effort to approach. A few metres to his right, a second male leaned against the exterior of the coffee shop. Behind the wall Jack occupied, a third and fourth skulked about in the trees.

Had an outside pack asked for a meet on my territory, I'd have brought adequate backup, too.

When we neared, the two tree-huggers rounded the wall and flanked Jack. As the other one pushed up from his casual stance and took a few steps closer, my gaze shifted to keep watch on him. If he'd stayed that close to begin, he must have had a higher priority than the other two in keeping the head of the pack protected. Another son? His hair, what I'd tag as nondescript brown, matched that of the mature wolf.

Dad halted a few feet before Jack, yet neither offered a hand in greeting. "Thanks for meeting with us."

"There's been another?" Jack asked.

Dad nodded.

Jack's eyes seemed to retract at the knowledge. "The kids on the news?"

The hairs on my arm bristled as nondescript-brown came too close for comfort. I glanced at his flared nostrils and lifted an eyebrow. "Personal space. You ever heard of it?"

"Kid," Dad said. "His friend's human."

"Aw, shit," Jack said.

I turned back from the werewolf's smirk.

"It's escalating," Dad said.

Jack's stare hardened as he lowered the hand he rubbed over his hair. "It escalated weeks ago."

I shifted forward. "What do you mean?"

Jack's attention flittered to me for a split second before reengaging with Dad. "Let's take a walk. Just the two of us."

My shoulders stiffened as it took every effort not to intervene, to allow Dad to speak for himself. Let him wonder off on his own with an unfamiliar wolf? Only a moron would consider it. I caught the alteration to Sean's stance in my periphery—a sign that he shared my concerns.

"If I come, they come," Dad said like he'd sensed our distrust. "Otherwise, we walk away, and this discussion will never take place."

"That many of us together will draw attention," Jack said.

"Not as much as continuing to argue about it outside the coffee shop." Dad shrugged. "Besides, with everything that's going on, I'd rather keep my sons where I can see them."

Tension tightened Jack's jaw, as though he tried to work out if Dad's words had been a personal insult. I knew they hadn't been—Dad had more class than that—but it took Jack a couple of seconds to nod and push up from his perch.

He inclined his head to the left. "We'll take the path. Should be quiet at this time of day."

Sean fell into step behind the two Alphas, hanging back a little. My personal minder matched each of my strides, which kept him as a permanent side fixture in my view span.

Branches from trees on our right embraced those of their neighbours on the left, creating a green hued tunnel of shadow that dappled the ground. I caught the twitch of Sean's shoulder muscles beneath his shirt as 'Odd and Odder' took positions left and right, boxing him in from all sides. As I created one of those barriers, and Dad half of another, I decided the situation could have been worse and tuned into the conversation up ahead.

"Which of the names from the news wasn't human?" Jack asked.

"Gabriel Lewis."

"Race?"

"Werewolf."

Jack's steady pace faltered for a moment as he turned to Dad. "With which pack, as he's living on my territory?" A hint of outrage underlay his tone.

"None," Dad said. "Kid's not with a pack ... yet."

"Yet?"

"We made him an offer."

I'd made the offer and confessed to Dad two days after the event, but that titbit got omitted.

"He's thinking it over," Dad said.

"You crossed the border to my county and poached on the locals?" The outrage became more than a hint.

"I had my reasons." Dad's tone of indifference dismissed the discussion. "What did you mean when you said it escalated weeks ago, Jack?"

A brief pause ensued, as though Jack warred with the urge to continue his pride-primping. "The twelve that have been reported?"

"Twelve?" Dad's steps ceased as he turned to his companion again.

I halted, too, but jerked forward when my shadow knocked my shoulder. My lips drew back with the low snarl I sent his way.

The mouth of the brown-haired wolf curved up at the corners.

"You like me," I murmured. "I get it. It's an effect I have on all the ladies." As the two leaders continued their walk, I resumed mine, my lips twitching at the quiet growl that followed.

"... two females in Yorkshire as well as two males were reported," Jack said up ahead. "I think those were the earliest ones. If there were others, before Yorkshire, they've escaped my notice, or stayed below the media radar. Then disappearances started in Lincolnshire. Only two reported there, but I've heard there were at least double that. From there, they moved into Derbyshire—"

"They?" Dad cut in at the mention of our patch. "There's a team?"

"Stands to reason. Races are still going missing in one county when they begin in the next."

Dad nodded like that made sense to him. "We only had one go missing on my territory, and I haven't a clue what he is, just what the news said."

"Only one was reported," Jack said. "Doesn't mean it was the only one."

The disadvantage, I guessed, of isolating ourselves as a pack had finally caught up with us.

"From your domain," Jack continued, "they moved across to Worcestershire. Two females from there— neither of them wolves, to my knowledge."

"Then, how do we know they're connected?" Dad asked.

"Because they were taken on the same evening, with the same disrupted signs left behind, as two pack wolves from the area. The wolves didn't make the news."

"And now?"

"Now they're here." Jack stopped walking and rubbed a hand across his face before settling it upon his hip. "They took another of mine two days ago."

Dad mirrored his stationary pose, bringing the rest of us to a standstill. "Besides your son? Why haven't I heard about this, Jack?"

"Because I hoped he'd turn out to be with his mate. But he didn't, and with the blood traces we found at his home, it doesn't look promising."

Dad blew out a slow breath. "Name?"

"Samuel Toulsen."

A few moments of quiet followed, as though they both needed the gap to absorb all the information.

"I'd like your permission to search in Shropshire," Dad said.

"We have no idea where they are. They could be anywhere."

"But this is where they're currently hunting. So this is the best place to hunt for them right now. I don't want to trespass, Jack, but I will if I have to. Do I have your permission?"

He met Dad's stare, holding it for seconds, before he gave a slight nod. "I'll let my boys know."

3

Dad and Jack shook hands for the first time since our arrival. "It might be a good idea for us to have a picture of your son and your missing pack member," Dad said. "That way, we'll know who they are, if we stumble upon anything."

"And the missing pup who's spurred you to sit up and take notice?"

"I'll get you one of him in return." Dad folded his arms over his chest, hardening his stare. "But for the purpose of identifying him only."

Jack matched his expression, before a smile tugged at the corner of his mouth. "You're invested in him?"

What did he mean by that? Although, I had grown close to Gabe over the eight, or so, months since meeting Shelley.

Dad didn't answer.

I twisted to peer at my assigned muscle, who still hadn't removed his attention from me. "You've taken a real shine to me, haven't you?"

Nondescript-brown stayed mute, but continued to smile.

"Sorry, pal." I lifted my palms. "You're just not my type."

"You'll hear from me if I get any news," Jack said.

"I'll be in touch." Dad's footsteps hit the path, drawing me back.

He collected Sean on his way past, and when they reached me, I turned to follow.

"It's Ethan, right?" my new best friend said.

Hesitating, I twisted back to him.

"I've heard a lot of stuff about you."

I gave a slow nod. "Good." A deep chuckle rumbled at my rear, as I stalked away.

****

***

"Do we have a plan?" I asked, as we pulled out of the Battleground onto the A-road.

"Not really," Dad said. "We search until there are no more places left to look."

"And you're starting in Shropshire?" Sean asked.

I glanced in my mirror at him. "You ask that like you won't be with us."

"He won't be," Dad said. "He'll be no use if he's constantly worried about Jem at home. Best all round, if he just stays there with her."

"You made this request yourself, Sean?"

Meeting my reflected eyes, he nodded, then glanced away as if to disguise his discomfort at asking to step down from the action. His need to protect his mate would far outweigh any responsibility he may have felt toward Gabe, though, and I couldn't have agreed more.

"Good move, I think. Keeping Jem happy and relaxed will also keep Mum happy and relaxed."

"And leave you with no one to watch your back," he said.

"The Larsen's are more than capable, Sean. You'll be a father soon. It won't hurt to get used to your shift in priorities. I'd be exactly the same in your shoes. Especially with all this shit going on." I thought about Jem and Mum, about the short time they'd been around, about how—badly—I'd cope if they got swept up in the issue at hand. I glanced across at Dad. "He'll have backup, right? Cover all angles. Those at home need—"

"I agree," Dad said. "Already considered and arranged. Josh and Danny are taking the first home-watch with Sean. He'll be too distracted." He pointed a thumb over his shoulder. "And, as I don't think any of us should do anything without at least one backup, he can have them both. That should leave the females more than adequately supervised, and will leave us with even numbers for doubling up to search."

***

Mundane tasks devoured another four hours. Home had been our first stop, where we swapped Sean for Connor and Kyle, much to Jem's relief. Josh and Danny hadn't even complained, when they learned our plans involved minor exploits, and we left them all with Jem's barrage of questions and an update from Sean.

From there, we'd driven the familiar route back to Shelley's.

"You have a couple pictures of Gabe?" I asked, once we'd told her how little we'd learned.

"Sure." She nodded. "The printed ones are old, but the digies ..."

"If you send them to my phone, I can call in somewhere and get them printed."

Her hands wrung as much as they had that morning, and her eyes looked no less swollen. "What do you plan to do?"

"At the moment?" I brushed a hand across my hair. "Canvassing and searching like crazy is all we can do."

She nodded, though her harried stare intensified.

"And I need the address for Gabe's friend. If we circle out from there ..." I shrugged. "Who knows? We might get lucky enough to pick up a trail—depending how far they took them on foot."

We didn't get lucky—hadn't really expected to when we'd only been clutching at straws. We caught Gabe's scent leading up to, or from, his friend's house. Other than that, any others' we picked up held only traits of human odour. As I doubted anyone without abilities could take down the number of werewolves that had gone missing, we dismissed them as Colum and his family.

The nearest A-road to their home took us as far as the M54, where we spun off to the left to circle back around. Our lack of knowledge of the area meant we had to rely on an atlas and Sat-Nav to mark out a grid to work from. It would, however, take some time to produce, so the road coverage kept us mobile until then.

Back at Brickton Heath—Shelley's town—we parked up and climbed from the truck. Dad sent me and Kyle off in one direction, taking himself and Connor in the other, both teams armed with images of the missing 'people'.

We stepped into the path of one passer-by after another, showed the pictures, and asked, "Have you seen this kid?"

The answers remained a consistent 'no', except for the odd one who recognised Gabe from the news before saying they couldn't help.

My stomach grumbled, with good reason, when eight p.m. arrived along with the dulling of daylight. I hadn't eaten since breakfast.

At the ring of my mobile, I hit the connect button and held it to my ear. "Dad?"

"Wrap it up. Meet us back at the pickup."

I glanced ahead, spotted Kyle's auburn hair, as he showed yet another pedestrian the photograph, and strode toward him.

The woman's perfume hit me harder than her knock-'em-dead looks, the flowery nastiness making me wonder how Kyle could stand to remain so close. Her head lifted as I reached them, introducing me to the darkest eyes I'd ever seen—eyes that widened when they focused on me.

I paused in my step and held up my palms in the hope of easing her alarm. "Kyle?"

He turned, inclining his head toward the stiletto-footed blonde beside him. "Thinks she might have seen something."

My brows lifted as I perked up. "Really? That's ... great."

"It's not much." She averted her gaze. "Just, I thought I saw the blond kid with some guy. Only remember the teen because of the picture, but the guy with him?" Her toned shoulders shrugged, drawing my eyes to the defined lines of her collarbone and the low cut of her dress. "I didn't take that much notice of him, if I'm honest. Sorry I can't be more help."

"You mind if I give you my number?" Kyle asked.

Her eyebrow twitched. Mine, too—at Kyle's smoothness.

He shook his head and breathed out a chuckle. "I meant in case you remember anything else about the guy you saw him with."

"'Course you did," I muttered beneath my breath.

Her quiet laugh arrived as a mellifluous tinkle of music. "Sure, I'll take your number."

As the flip of her hand at the wrist pumped out more of her artificial scent, I rubbed at the tickle in my scrunched-up nose, taking a step back, as Kyle handed over one of the construction company's business cards he'd had personalised.

"That's my mobile." He pointed to the number like she couldn't figure it out on her own.

I refrained from rolling my eyes and gave him a nudge to his shoulder. "We really need to get going."

"I'll call you." The woman's lips curved into an impressive pink-framed smile as she started walking away. "If I remember anything," she added over her shoulder with a wink.

Kyle's grin almost split his face in half, as we stared after the sashay of her slender hips in her figure-hugging dress. "She's ... really ... hot."

"And Dad's going to be ... really ... pissed ... if we don't get a move on. He rounded us up five minutes ago."

Kyle cocked his head for us to turn, and we started the trek back toward the truck. "Think she'll call?" he asked, as our long strides carried us.

I smirked. "Sure she will."

4

With a couple of pizza boxes balancing on my left palm, I knocked on Shelley's front door. A backward glance showed Dad and the other two watching me like they had nothing better to do. I shrugged my shoulder, as if to say, 'Why the hell you all just sitting there? Leave already', but they didn't move.

I understood Dad's insistence. If one of them had asked to be dropped off elsewhere, no way would I have pulled off until they'd entered the building.

Didn't stop their presence irking me, though.

A door closed somewhere upstairs within the house, followed by the descent of footsteps. I turned back, at the catch twisting from the inside.

The front door swung inward, and Shelley blinked up at me, frowning when her gaze shifted toward the pizza boxes. "I'm not really that hungry."

"Maybe not." My head ducked down to hers. "But I am."

Confusion moved into her eyes.

"You shouldn't be alone, Shel. You going to let me in, or leave me to keep an eye on you from the doorstep, where I'll have to eat my pizza like some homeless person?"

She breathed out a sigh and took a step back, widening the gap between door and frame.

As I spun to wave my faithful observers on their way, Dad's hand lifted in salute, and my truck rolled away, as I entered the hall.

"You didn't have to do this," Shelley said, closing the door.

"Try telling that to Gabe."

The TV showed one of the regular soaps as I ducked into the living room. More empty coffee mugs littered the table-top, once again with Shelley's phones set amongst them. My eyes fell on a third phone—one that hadn't been there before.

I opened my mouth to ask, but closed it again at an approach from upstairs.

Shelley's eyes darted toward the door, as it burst open into the living room, and a young girl with raven black hair slipped inside.

"Who was it, Shel—" The girl halted, her eyes widening.

"Ethan, this is—"

"Mia," I said, realising how idiotic I'd been to believe Shelley would have no one around without me. I nodded to her. "Nice to meet you."

Her eyebrows winged up. "You know who I am?"

"Sure. You're Gabe's ..." *Mate?*

Her lips curved a little, warmth pushing aside the consternation in her expression. "He tell you about me?"

"All the ... um ... time ..." My hand brushed across my hair as it dawned I'd probably said more than Gabe would have liked. "Pizza?" I lifted my food offering toward her.

She pointed to the box. "Pepperoni?"

I smiled. "Of course."

"Sweet."

"I'll get you some plates." Shelley turned for the kitchen.

"Make sure you get yourself one, too, Shel." Mia lifted the top box from my hand and rounded the sofa with it. "Woman has to eat sometime, right?"

In that one statement, I saw what attracted Gabe.

Not much conversation passed during our meal. Even if the air of despondency hadn't sullied the mood, the fullness of my mouth would have hindered my chatter. I almost couldn't get the damn pizza in fast enough—until I caught the two females staring at me, remembered my manners, and made a mental note to slow down.

Mia hopped up the moment I aimed the last slice toward my mouth and cleared away the plates. The easy way she moved about the house, from room to room, without an ounce of discomfort, led me to believe she stayed over a lot. She cut back through the living room and disappeared into the hall, the stairs creaking as she headed up.

"I'll fix you a drink," Shelley said.

I climbed from my position on the floor and followed her into the kitchen.

As though unaware of my pursuit, she paused in front of the window. Her hands rubbed across her face before they found support on the countertop, and a long, slow breath exhaled past her lips.

"We'll get him back, Shel," I said.

She turned and met my eyes with her almond-shaped greens. "I trust you to find him."

I nodded—could think of no other way to respond to someone who had more faith in me than I held in myself.

"Why don't you grab some glasses?"

I moved across to the cupboard, my hip brushing against Shelley's and nudging her. "Sorry," I mumbled, reaching out a hand to steady her.

"It's okay," she said as she continued past to the fridge.

The glasses had been kept in the same cupboard for months, so I knew where to find them. They clinked together as I picked up two, the fridge closing with a whoosh and a *thunk* behind me.

"Will Mia want one?" I turned to find Shelley with the bottle balanced between her denim-clad thighs while she twisted the corkscrew into the top. "Why don't you let me do that?"

"I can manage." Her tone held a brimful of determination, yet her grunt negated the words. A few more twists of her wrist penetrated the cork further. "I'm not as weak as you all think, you know."

"I don't think you're weak."

Her gaze lifted as she fought with the bottle and the opener. "No?"

"No. Just ..." I smiled. "... feeble."

She glowered for a second, but then she straightened and waved the offending item at me. "Fine. You do it, then."

I swapped the glasses for the bottle, grabbed the corkscrew handle, and tugged. The stopper slid out with a gaseous plop, and the richness of red wine scented the kitchen.

Shelley held out the glasses.

I poured a generous glug into each, set the bottle down on the countertop, and turned back to tap my drink against Shelley's. "Here's to ..."

What the hell did we have to drink to? The woman's son had gone missing, for goodness sake.

"Getting Gabe back," she said.

I tipped my face down to her, as she gazed up at me, forcing my head to nod while attempting to keep my worry at bay.

Fire sparked a glower into her eyes, and her free hand fisted as she leaned toward me. "You can take that look out your eye, Ethan Holloway."

I stared at her. "What—"

"You can take it out right now."

My brow knitted. "What—"

"That damn look of defeat." She poked me hard in the chest. Wine slopped over the rim of her glass, splashing at my feet.

I skimmed my drink across the counter and grabbed for her hand. "I'm not—"

"You don't give up." Her fist reformed, and she thumped it against my shoulder as I tried to pry her glass from the vice-grip of her other hand.

A low growl escaped as I freed the drink and set it down. "I haven—" I turned back to a double slam against my chest.

"It's not your style."

My jaw clenched. "I haven't given up ..."

"Don't you let me down, Ethan."

I snatched for her arms, as she lunged toward my face, ducking with a snarl when I missed. My hands tightened—more against the verbal than physical assault.

"Don't you dare let my Gabe down!"

"I've barely even started!" I snapped as my fingers circled her wrists coming at me. "Dammit, Shelley, give me a chance, will you?"

We stared at each other, chests heaving. With a sob, she jerked away from me, fisted her hands into her fringe and dragged them over her face.

Emotion effected Shelley's eyes with a high shine, her cheeks with a deep blush that glowed beneath her hair. She averted her eyes, seemed to seek self-control with long, deep breaths.

The blood passing through my carotid artery slowed its surge as I waited for her to turn back to me, fully regulating itself only once she had.

"I'm sorry. I'm not mad at you." Her fingers folded over my forearm, before she whipped her hand away and wrung it with her other. "I'm taking this out on the wrong person."

Before I could stop myself, I reached out to sweep her mussed hair back from her face. "Who else would you take it out on?"

I went to pull back, but her hand covered mine, holding it against her face. With a shallow sigh, she pushed onto tiptoe, placed her lips to my cheek. "Thank you."

I expected her to move away, but her breaths continued to warm my skin. As her fingers wove into my hair, a slight twist of my head showed me her eyes with half-lowered lashes. "Shel?" My voice came out deeper than intended.

"Just ..." Her breath shuddered out, and the tremor of her body hit my chest. "Just hold me, okay?"

I slid my arms around her back, lifting her when I realised it would be easier than stooping. She didn't protest, as I pulled her close against my body, nor did she seem to mind when my nose nestled into her neck to inhale her sweet scent.

Her fingers within my hair twisted a little, and her face came to rest mere inches from my throat. I closed my eyes as her breaths drifted over me, as her other hand folded around a scrap of my clothing, and held her even tighter when a damp patch began to expand across the fabric of my shirt.

"I'll find him, Shel," I murmured into her ear. "I promise I won't stop searching until I have."

Her face shifted, and I pulled back. As our gazes met, my heart damn near stuttered its rhythm.

Teardrops decorated the cheeks of her elfin features, like diamonds, redacting the light beneath the glistening emeralds that stared back at me. They all merged into one rainbow of beauty as I ducked nearer.

Shelley didn't flinch from my clumsy head thrust, or from the tentative sweep of my lips across hers. Instead, her face tilted, our noses brushed, and her lips parted as they pressed against mine.

A rumble brewed deep within me as the sudden tightening of my jeans announced an arousal I hadn't expected. With a dart of my tongue, I tasted the faint spiciness of the meal we'd shared. As her left leg lifted, my hand swept down, hooked beneath her thigh, and my step back brought me into contact with the counter.

Her fingers grasped onto my shirt, hauled it taut across my shoulder. One quiet sigh followed another as her tongue met with mine.

I spun, nudged her rear onto the breakfast bar, and slipped between her knees. My fingers grabbed her hips, tugged her forward against my erection, and at her gasp, I gave a low growl.

The fingers within my hair entwined with the strands. A small yank encouraged me to keep going. Another tongue dart, another sample, and the thrum vibrated throughout my entire body, shivering along my spine. My pelvis pushed forward, my lips devouring the delicious fullness of hers, until the urge to clamber up on the work surface and bring forth even more of her erotic scent overwhelmed me.

A click arrived from the living room, followed by the sweep of the door across carpet, and Shelley shot back from me like I'd zapped her with a thousand volts.

Her chest rose and fell as her hands flew out. She stared at me for a second, her wide-eyed expression one of total shock, before the scramble of her legs sent her sprawling past me to the floor. Her cheeks held high colour as her head whipped up toward Mia in the doorway.

I kept my groan silent, rubbing my face.

"I, um ..."

My hand dropped at Mia's stutter. I found her staring my way, while Shelley fussed with her blouse.

Mia thumbed over her shoulder. "I only came down to tell you I'm going to bed."

"Me, too," Shelley mumbled, and she ducked past Mia into the living room.

As I frowned after Shelley, the young teenager tracked her passage, before she whirled back toward me with narrowed eyes.

I thought about explaining myself, even went as far as opening my mouth.

"G'night, Ethan," she said through compressed lips. With a final look that could only be interpreted as a warning, she spun and shot off up the stairs after Shelley.

Alone, I let my groan free and slipped a hand into my boxers to adjust my bulging discomfort. As my fingers wrapped around my stiffness, the temptation to relieve my frustration crossed my mind for a split-second, until a headshake cleared my thoughts.

I held out my waistband, peered into the depths of my underwear as I tucked him to bed. "Settle back down, buddy." I blew out a breath, rolling my shoulders. "Not meant to be."

5

White stippled paint greeted me upon waking, just as it had bid farewell before sleep. The arm hooked beneath my head had folded at a funny angle against the sofa back, the tendons running down from my shoulder pulled taut to snapping point.

I tugged it out, stretched my fingers toward the ceiling, withdrawing my other hand from beneath my waistband. Massaging life back into my deadened limb, I swung my legs around to sit.

Gurgles drifted through from the kitchen, followed by a quiet click. I turned toward the sounds and inhaled, catching the scents of the two females. Even though the pouring of liquid and the comforting aroma suggested coffee could be on offer, I hesitated over joining them.

For hours, I'd replayed my stupid actions and chastised myself for making the move on a distraught woman. She wouldn't understand I hadn't intended to take advantage, that I really did like her. I'd seen the look of horror on her face once she'd come to her senses, but I'd also been witness to her response when I'd kissed her.

Females—the damn species mystified me.

I rubbed my hands across my face like they'd somehow remove all traces of my discomfort and fatigue. With a deep breath, I pushed up from the sofa and padded into the next room.

Mia stirred the contents of one of two mugs in front of her. Dressed in nothing more than socks and a huge sweater I'd seen Gabe in a few times, she peered across toward me. "Coffee?"

"Thanks." Leaning against the doorframe, I turned toward Shelley at the breakfast bar, pushing aside the memory of what I'd imagined doing to her on there. "Hey."

"Hey." The greeting arrived weak. Her gaze flickered away, before returning to me as she cleared her throat. "Sleep okay?"

I slid my hands into my pockets and crossed my ankles. "Sure."

She stared hard at me, like she could see right through the lie. The dark smudges beneath her eyes suggested I'd not been the only one still awake in the early hours.

"You?" I asked.

Mia passed Shelley her drink, before tossing a curious glance my way.

Shelley looked about to shrug, but instead, she eyed the brown liquid beneath her nose. "Sure," she murmured.

"You want sugar?" Mia asked me.

I nodded. "Two."

"One it is, then." She winked, seemingly amused by herself as she spooned in the white granules and stirred. "So ..." She crossed the room to me. "What plans do you have today?"

I took the coffee from her with a nod and sampled it. "I'm waiting on Dad. But my guess is, we'll expand the search and head back out to look again."

"Can I come?" Mia asked.

I studied her a moment and shook my head.

"Why not?" she asked, as I took another sip of my drink.

"Because ..." Struggling to come up with grounds that didn't sound as sexist as the truth, I raised and lowered a shoulder. "Just ... because." I ducked back into the living room to avoid the conversation that would surely follow.

The sofa groaned beneath my weight as I sat. In the kitchen, Mia mumbled to Shelley about her interpretations of my excuse for telling her no. Although Shelley placated that I probably didn't mean it that way, Mia had it spot-on.

Elbows resting on knees, mug between my laced fingers, I stared at my mobile. Maybe if I did it for long enough,

Dad would pick up the vibes and ring to get me out of there.

When the buzzing rippled it across the table, I almost spilled my drink. I snatched up the phone as I stood, hit connect and placed it to my ear in one fluid movement. "Dad?"

"You ready?"

I marched into the kitchen. "Are you here?" Straight across to the sink, I set my half-full mug down on the counter.

"Yes—just pulling up."

"I'm on my way." I spun as I disconnected and found two sets of eyes on me. "Dad's here." My long legs carried me to the doorway in four strides. Another sent me through it.

"Ethan?"

I halted and looked back at Shelley, as she took a step toward me. Her mouth opened but closed again.

"I'll call you if we find anything," I said. "Okay?"

Although the tightening of her eyebrows suggested creases hid beneath her fringe, she nodded.

I sent her a head bob of my own, returned to my route, and bolted out the front door.

The morning smelled fresh compared to the scent of humiliation that had stifled the house. Nostrils flaring to accommodate the deepness of my inhalation, I jogged along the short path and rounded the truck as though about to embark on a high-speed chase.

"Where's the fire?" Dad asked, as I leapt in beside him.

"Didn't want to keep you all waiting." I peered into the back, noticing for the first time the others' absence. "Where's—"

"Working out a better grid." He pulled off from the kerb. "We'll continue the search, and meet with Connor and Kyle before lunch. Need to remember to eat today."

Leaving it so long the day before had left me weakened—something we needed to avoid at all costs. "Where are we headed?"

"I've had a change of direction in my thoughts."

He took a corner, and I waited until he'd picked speed back up to ask, "Which is?"

"What are the chances of them still being this close to the last ones they took?" He glanced at me.

I thought about his question. "More than what are the chances, what would be the point?"

"Exactly." He nodded. "They've taken one from this area. The odds of finding another here, when Gabe isn't part of a pack, are pretty much zero. If they've done enough research to know where to go in the first place, they'll know how many are where."

"You've thought this through." More than I'd done. Only topic on my mind had been Shelley. "So, we're combing which area?"

"I rang Jack for suggestions. He believes witches are the source of the females that have gone missing." He flicked on his indicator for the turn off the island we rounded. "So, we're going north ... to Witchurch."

My eyebrow lifted. "Jess lives in Witchurch." I'd had a brief moment with Jem's older sister at the beginning of the year.

Dad nodded. "She's also a witch."

"You're telling me we're going to Jess's?" I hadn't seen her since I'd knocked back her amorous advances.

"We owe her a warning, Son." He stopped at a red light and turned to me. "Or would you like to tell Jem your pride got in the way of giving her sister a heads up?"

Staring back at him, I thought about suggesting he go on his own. Instead, I shook my head. "No, I don't." She'd played a big part in helping the pack over the previous New Year. "We do owe her."

Heading from one awkward female moment to another hadn't been how I'd envisioned my day, but it looked like it was happening whether I wanted it to, or not.

"Good," he said, and sent his attention back to the road.

Smugness coated Jess's lips as a sparkle invaded her eyes. Her confident strides carried her across the floor of the local job centre where she worked. Each step matched the swing of hips I'd once wanted to feel beneath my palms.

Three times, I'd made excuses to the pack and ducked off to meet with Jess late last winter, but we never went much farther than first base. Of course, it'd bugged the crap out of her, because I'd been the one to stall it every damn time. Though, if I'd clicked to the reason why sooner, we wouldn't have done *that* much. Because Jess's base scent matched Jem's way too closely, a sisterly vibe—which made the appeal seem *off* on a whole level of incestual-don't-go-there.

"Well, well, well." Jess came to a wide-legged standstill with one hip jutted out and her hands at her waist—not unlike the females in one of my magazines. "What brings Ethan Holloway to my doorstep?"

"Nice to see you, too, Jess." I spotted the interest from her work colleagues in my periphery. "I need to speak to you."

"Sorry, but I've moved on already."

"This is important ... I wouldn't ..."

"Be here otherwise?" The twinkle faded from the hazel of her eyes, and I knew the business-not-pleasure aspect of my visit had sunk in. "What's happened?"

"Any chance you can take a break?"

A few seconds of visual penetration preceded her nod. "Let me square it with my boss. Meet me outside."

She walked away in her tight skirt and heels, brown hair bouncing with each step.

Did she really hold a grudge over my deflection?

As she rounded the corner, I snapped my attention away, catching four females, all seated at desks—all of whom smiled my way.

With a rough hand-brush of my hair, I spun and made my second escape of the day.

Clouds had nudged across to block the blinding sun and left the car park's surface a dark shade of grey as I stepped outside.

Dad's face greeted me through the windscreen. At my nod, he climbed from the truck and shut the door. "Did you see her?"

"Yes." I slid my hands into my jeans pockets and rested against the front bumper of the pickup. A quick inhalation reminded me I hadn't washed since the morning before. "She's coming out to us."

As Dad joined me, arms folded across his chest, Jess pushed out the door, heels exchanged for flip-flops. The smile that played on her lips vanished as her gaze landed on Dad. "Has something happened to Jem?"

"Jem's fine," Dad said.

"Then, why isn't she with you?"

"She's better protected at home," he told her.

"Better *protected*?" Jess's gaze flittered between Dad and me, like she could catch us out if she only moved fast enough. "Better protected from whom, Nathan?"

"Anywhere decent to eat around here?" I asked.

Her mouth opened for a second. "What?"

"I missed breakfast. I'm starving. Is there anywhere—"

"A bakery at the bottom of the hill." She pointed off to the right behind her.

"Excellent." I pushed up from the truck, started walking that way. At lack of noise behind me, I glanced back to see irritation in Jess's eyes, and my lips curved as I spun to walk backward. "Walk and talk, Jess. Come on. You know you want to."

Her head shook as she smiled and took the first steps. "I guess I could murder one of their lamb and mint pastries."

"There you go." Chuckling, I changed direction again and trod the path with Jess and Dad brushing my sides.

Dad explained the situation, while I stuffed my face with one lamb pastry, followed by a second. I scrunched up the paper wrapper, opened a third, and shovelled in a mouthful.

"So ..." Jess brushed crumbs from the corners of her lips. "You came to see me about this, why? You need my help?"

She may as well have added the *again* on the end, with the tone she used.

"Actually, we just thought you deserved the warning," Dad said. "And—"

"Thought there might be more." Jess's skinny arms folded over her chest.

"*And,*" Dad repeated, "we thought, as you're the only witch we know, you'd do the honours of passing the caution onto any others in the area ... or anywhere, for that matter, as we don't, or won't, know when these ..."

"People?" Jess offered.

I shook my head. "No way humans could take so many werewolves down."

"So, what are they, then?"

I looked at Dad, then back to Jess at his nod. "We've no idea. Other werewolves, we presume."

"Not necessarily," Jess said. "They could be anything. You do realise that, don't you?"

"Such as?" I asked on another bite of my meal.

"Hmm, let me think." A sardonic tone tinged her words. "I don't know, maybe shifters. Or vamps. Half-demons."

My eyebrows shot up. "Half what?"

She sent a glance toward Dad before giving me her attention again. "You lot are as much in denial as Jem. You're not the only species out there, you know."

"Race," Dad said. "And we're well aware of that ..."

My gaze whipped toward him. First I'd heard of it. Didn't need to tell Jess that, though.

"... I'm just unsure how broad a range the different races cover."

"Probably more than you imagine." Jess faced Dad for seconds before her lips pursed. "Okay, you haven't heard this from me, but ..." She blew out a breath. "There's a close-knit group of vamps in the area."

Dad and I exchanged a quick glance. "You know these vampires?" I asked.

She nodded once. "Word on the street is a couple of new ones have been spotted in town."

"New vampires?" Dad asked. "Strangers?"

Jess gave us the same positive acknowledgement. "Look, I need to get back to work before my boss makes me do overtime."

"We'll walk with you." Dad fell into step on Jess's left, and I took her other side.

Between the two of us, Jess almost disappeared into shadow, and the narrow pavement meant I ended up in the road.

"Do you have a description of these new ones?" Dad asked, as we climbed the hill.

"No. There's only so much the locals share with us witches." Although her lips curved, no humour entered her eyes. "Apparently, they consider us untrustworthy."

Imagine that, I almost muttered.

"Could you ask them?" Dad asked.

"Doubt it will get me anywhere, but I'll try." It took only a few minutes to reach the car park outside Jess's work. Her hands did a double point toward the glass-fronted business. "Do you need me for anything else?"

Dad shook his head. "Just watch your back, okay?"

"Sure. And you watch yours—and Jem's." She walked away a few strides before twisting back toward us. "I take it there's a chance you might be around, then?"

"Yes," Dad and I said.

"Well ..." She shrugged, smiling with her gaze on mine. "You need a place to stay, I still have half a bed that needs filling."

"I'll bear that in mind, Jess," I told her, ignoring how Dad's head snapped round toward me.

"'Course you will." With a laugh, she spun and disappeared into the job centre.

6

Thanks to Dad's call to Kyle and Connor, and the order to meet us earlier, the supermarket restaurant bordered on empty. Only three patrons utilised the space, none of them near our spot, which allowed the four of us an element of privacy in our discussion. As I sipped on my latte, I leaned over the map of Shropshire on the table between us.

With his head lowered, Kyle's ginger hair and broad shoulders replicated his Dad beside him. Their resemblance came almost as close as that between us Holloway men. Our dark hair all matched. If not for my and Sean's eyes following the darkness of Mum's, instead of Dad's blue, we'd have passed for a family of clones.

Once Dad had relayed our conversation with Jess, and the information she'd learned from the local non-humans, Kyle's head lifted to reveal his hazel eyes. "So, we pretty much wasted the morning pouring over this damn map, then?"

"Not necessarily," Dad said. "We still need to make ourselves familiar with the areas surrounding Witchurch, in case we broaden the search."

"And these strangers Jess mentioned—they're definitely here?" Connor asked. "They've been sighted?"

I sipped at my drink. "Pretty much what Jess said—just not by her."

"By ... vampires?" Connor's eyebrow lifted. At my and Dad's nods, he frowned. "So, vampires are responsible for the kidnappings?"

"We don't know for certain," Dad said. "But this information can't be ignored. How often has Jess uncannily got her facts straight before this?"

"Every damn time," Connor muttered, as Kyle nodded.

"So, it's worth checking out, if only for that reason," Dad said.

"And we're splitting up again?" Kyle asked.

Dad's confirmation coincided with the buzz in my pocket. I stood to withdraw my mobile and peered down at the screen.

With a quiet exhale, I hit connect and put it to my ear. "Shel?"

"Hey."

I rubbed a hand across my hair, taking in the three pairs of eyes peering up as the others listened in. "You okay?"

A pause preceded her, "Sure."

I waited for her to say more, thinking she wouldn't when almost a minute passed.

"This morning ..." Her voice arrived as an emotional whisper. "Last night ..."

I spun and took a few steps to distance myself from my audience, almost sending my chair flying in my haste. "Do we have to talk about this now, Shel?"

"I ..." A quietly blown breath stifled what might have been a sniffle.

"I'm sorry, okay?" I studied the chequered floor, hoping for a hole to appear and swallow me up. "I behaved like an idiot ..."

"Ethan, that's not—"

"I'd no bloody right ..."

"But—"

"Just ... do me a favour, and pretend it didn't happen, okay?" When she didn't respond, I added, "Please, Shelley?"

"Sure," she whispered.

"I'll call you if we find anything. We got a lead to follow this morning, so we're tightening the search."

"In Brickton Heath?" Hope tinged her voice.

"No, Shel. We're in Witchurch. I can't talk about specifics, I'm in too public a place, but I'll fill you in later. I promise."

"Okay." Another quiet response. "Bye, then."

I'd barely reciprocated the farewell when she hung up. Lowering the phone, I rubbed at my hair as I stared down at it. Had I said something wrong?

The faces of the two Larsen's whipped away, when I turned back to them. With a frown, I righted my chair and sat.

"Everything okay?" Dad asked.

"Sure." I pointed to the map. "We know where we're all covering, then?"

"Connor and I will head east," Dad said. "You two are going west."

Kyle and I saluted.

"But not before we've eaten," Dad added.

Fuelled up on a full English, Kyle and I separated from the two old guys. Heading west left us with the High Street and shops to canvass first. Despite the temperature being only autumnally warm, females milled about in strappy vests and minis, and men in loud-coloured shorts as though prepared for a day at the beach.

Kyle ducked into the path of a young female with dark auburn hair, waving the picture beneath her nose. "Excuse me, do you have a moment?"

I tapped the shoulder of a spindly guy to my right and intercepted his route before he could shoot past. "Spare a moment, please?"

"Sorry, no."

I closed off my olfactory nerves to the tobacco on his breath, as he sidestepped me, hurrying on. His receding back weaved through the town's patrons before disappearing.

"Arsehole," I murmured after him.

A twist to the right showed Kyle's easy smile aimed at the same young female.

"No worries," he said to her.

She walked away, legs moving like a geisha on speed, hips doing a jig the rest of her body hadn't been invited to join. With a backward glance, she tossed a smile his way, her hand lifting in a wave.

Kyle's own raised before he turned his grin on the next candidate—another young female in shorts that showed obscene amounts of flesh.

I shook my head at his lack of awkwardness, half-wishing for some of his confidence, and switched back to our task.

Rich meaty wafts interspersed with spicy tomato and melted cheese drifted out with each opening of the door to the baker's we'd visited that morning. A small woman exited, her lowered head of wine-red hair streaked with blonde.

"Shelley?" I took a step, as she turned right, but halted when her face lifted to reveal someone whose harsh features nowhere near represented the soft lines of Shelley's face. "Damn female's warping my mind."

I spun back, mouth open to let Kyle know I wanted to head up High Street, but didn't make the full turn before something solid bashed into my left side.

My lips drew back, a low snarl rippling past them.

"Sorry." As the offending guy's hands came up, black eyes met my gaze from beneath mousey hair. He held my stare steady for seconds before his hand smacked the shoulder he'd barged with a resounding slap. "Really— I'm sorry, okay?" His tar-like gaze skimmed over me. "You hurt?"

"No." The word rumbled up from my chest as I tried to control the vibration of my lips.

He rounded me without facing away as though afraid to show me his back. Only once he'd reached escaping distance did he turn and walk in his original direction.

I followed his passage, going a dozen or so strides with nostrils flared. No scent on the air disturbed me, yet I still stared at the path he cut through the pedestrians, before retracing my steps back to where I'd last seen Kyle.

A left to right scan didn't show him. The female he'd been speaking to no longer stood where she had, either. Kyle's red hair should have been easy to spot with his six-three height, except …

"Oh, shit." I raced forward, scanning as much area as possible. A bump with a middle-aged lady earned me a glare and profanity. I hadn't time to utter more than a rapid apology before I dashed on.

Green Lane came to a T-junction. Still no Kyle. A left turn preceded a run not far off a full-out sprint. "Shit, shit. Don't do this to me."

Fifty yards down, and no sign of Kyle—I slammed on the brakes, about-turned, and charged back the other way. Straight past the road I'd recently left, I grabbed no more than a blurred glimpse of patrons moving from store to store—no red hair amongst them.

Farther along the road, trees and greenery sprang up. *The local park, maybe?*

My chest heaved as I ground to a halt. The wild scouring of my eyes bore no fruit. I rubbed a hand over my hair and dug into my pocket, fumbling in my haste to retrieve my mobile.

It vibrated against my fingers.

I stared at the screen: Kyle. My thumb depressed the connect button, and I whipped it to my ear. "Where the hell d'you go?"

"What the hell happened to you?" Kyle sounded as frantic as my breaths.

"Jesus, Kyle." I gave a rough rub to my face, releasing a heavy sigh. "Where the hell are you?"

"Right here, dammit. Where we were supposed to be. Where the hell are you?"

"All over the damn place, looking for you." I growled. "Don't move, and stay on the phone. I'm coming back."

I jogged along the way I'd come and shimmied past a gaggle of schoolgirls taking up the entire pavement.

"Which way are you coming from?" Kyle asked at my ear.

"To the right, from the lower end of where you are."

"I'm heading down to meet you." His uneven breaths stilted his speech.

"I said stay where you are, dammit."

"You think I can't hear your tone? Quit stressing, I'm already moving that way."

"Shit." I lowered the phone to save relaying my panic. As Kyle hadn't avoided kidnap nine months before, I didn't consider my concern to be unwarranted. He would never understand the void a pack separation like that could create—not when he'd been unconscious the entire time he'd been gone.

Less than twenty yards to cover, and Kyle came into view. He checked left before turning my way, lowering his phone when his gaze landed on me.

As I brought my pace to a more reasonable level, I slid my mobile back into my pocket, yet my strides remained long until I reached him.

"You okay?" He grasped my shoulder, giving a gentle shake. "You're sweating."

I shook him off. "Where'd you run to?"

"Nowhere." His frown cut deep. "I was just in the bloody doorway, right by you, showing some female Gabe's pic."

"Doorway where? Which doorway? I looked, and you were *not* there."

He flung his arm out to the right. "That doorway. Right there." He poked a finger toward me. "You're the one who ran off."

"You suggesting this is my fault?" My entire body tensed, yet I bit back the growl brewing in my chest. "I wouldn't have gone anywhere, if you hadn't disappeared."

"Like I said, I never went anywhere." Another finger pointed my way. "You did."

The growl escaped as I spun to walk off. "Next time, stay where I can see you."

His footsteps followed after me. "It's not just your body odour that stinks, Ethan."

Fists clenched, I turned back until I stood chest to chest with him. He matched my stance as well as my glare. For seconds, neither of us moved—until I realised I'd taken it out on the wrong person. My anger had arisen because of my own inability to keep him in my sights, not because he hadn't remained there.

Blowing out a breath, I pinched the bridge of my nose and closed my eyes a moment.

"Sorry," Kyle said, patting my shoulder before he herded me round to walk. "You really do smell ripe, though."

My lips twitched as I fell into step beside him.

"Even worse than you did over lunch." He sent me a sideways glance. "When was the last time you washed?"

"Don't push it," I muttered.

7

Kyle and I left High Street, hit the main B-road, and walked its length until we met the A41. From there, we headed east again, rounding back on ourselves until at the south entrance to Witchurch.

On our tour of the locality, the clouds dispersed for an hour, or two, remerging to conceal the blue of the sky. Small breaks allowed brief peeks of the warming rays, which only added more sweat to my unsavoury odour.

"You get any vibes off anybody today?" Kyle asked, as we ducked into the town.

I thought back, trying to recall all those I'd spoken to, or studied. "Nope."

"I think we're looking at the wrong time of day."

I dug my hands into my pockets. "Meaning ...?"

"Jess thinks we should be looking at vampires." Kyle mirrored my pocket-delving. "So, why the hell are we looking before dark?"

"What do you mean?"

"Vampires don't come out in the day."

I couldn't help but chuckle. "Just like we only change with our lunar cycle, and have no control over ourselves."

His step faltered for a moment, but he caught himself and matched my pace again. "You know something you haven't shared with me?"

"Not a bean, Kyle." I swiped at a trail of sweat creeping over my temple and tucked my hand back into its pocket.

"So ... what do you know?"

"Like I said, not a bean. Never met a vampire—never had reason to ask about them."

"But ..."

"But nothing." I shifted to one side of the path to allow a couple of kids past on pushbikes, shrugging a shoulder as I turned to Kyle on the other side. "Just don't make assumptions about what we don't know."

The two boys cycled like crazy, competing for speed, and reminding me how much I anticipated the arrival of my nephew. I smiled at the thought of teaching a mini-Sean new tricks.

"We walking, or gawping?"

My smile remained as I looked back to Kyle and inclined my head. "Walking. I want ice cream."

"From where?"

Our strides hit their rhythm again. "The park. I spotted an ice cream van there when I was looking for you earlier."

"Whippy?"

I caught the expectation in his raised eyebrow. "Of course."

"Excellent." He smiled, as we picked up our pace.

Fifteen minutes later, we'd each got a cone. The slight slope to the grass provided adequate seating beneath the trees, as our tongues set to work.

"I'm so freaking hungry," Kyle mumbled around licks.

"Hmm-mm." Another lap of my tongue brought me more vanilla, creamy delight.

"What time is it, anyway?"

I folded my lips over the mound of white stuff and drew a layer into my mouth before shrugging.

Kyle stood, working his phone out. "Four forty." His chuckle drew my gaze up, and he circled his lips with his finger. "Got a tosh going on there."

A lick solved that.

"What time we searching 'til, today?" He deposited his rear back beside mine.

"Until we drop, probably." I waved what I had left of my cone at him. "This should keep us going a little longer."

"Speak for yourself." He shovelled in the last of his ice cream and wiped his palms down his thighs. "Which direction now?"

"Without leaving Witchurch and without the map? Not a clue." I pushed to my feet and flicked cone crumbs off my lap. "But Dad and Connor have to be heading, or at least circling, back this way, so I say we go north."

"You made that decision based on what?"

I hit the flat grass and strode off. "Absolutely nothing."

With a chuckle, Kyle caught up. "I was thinking we should try the shops again. Different time of day means a new wave of shoppers."

"Which means more young girls in scraps of clothing. You realise the shops will shut soon?"

"Won't hurt to check them out, though." He nudged at my shoulder until I'd altered course to the right. "See? I knew you'd agree."

We somehow found our way straight back to High Street by cutting through a gulley and climbing some steps, and we joined the thinning throng of end of day store patrons.

The first female we encountered received one of Kyle's 'special' smiles. She blushed like crazy, yet she still peered back over her shoulder as she walked away.

Kyle's expression shifted from her to me. "If you smiled at them a little more, they'd probably be a little friendlier in return," he said.

"I don't need them to be friendly."

When Kyle's mobile rang in his pocket, he slid it out and stared down at the screen.

"Who is it?"

He shrugged. "No idea."

The tinkle continued. "You answering that, or what?"

He hit the button and held it to his ear. "Hello?"

I stared away while listening in, and caught movement in an alley farther down the hill.

"Oh, hello." A female voice rolled from Kyle's phone. "You probably don't remember, but you gave me your card last night …"

"I remember." Kyle's tone went from guarded to jovial in a flash. "Hi."

My ears remained on alert for Kyle's chatter, but my gaze fixed on the long-legged strip of a guy shifting about in the shadows. I took a step away, watching for further evidence as to why I had alarm bells buzzing inside my head.

"You asked me to call if I remembered anything," Kyle's caller said.

"Does that mean you have?"

At a tap on my shoulder, I peered behind at Kyle pointing to his phone with enthusiasm. I lifted my chin and turned straight back to keep an eye on the dodgy dude that bothered the hell out of me.

He'd stepped from the alley. Dark eyes stared straight back, no effort made to disguise the fact.

"I think I do." The female's voice didn't sound one-hundred percent certain, in my opinion.

"Great," Kyle said.

Holding the Marmite eyes steady, I tried to take in the rest of the guy's appearance: jeans, green cotton shirt, tall, but only half my breadth, blond hair that could do with a trim.

A gentle breeze travelled the incline. I drew it deep into my sinuses. Perfume tainted its freshness, along with subtle cologne, cigarette smoke, lager from the nearby pub, what I suspected remained in the bakery, leather, sweat, amongst a whole heap more, but nothing that told me I should have been concerned by my watcher.

"... chance we could meet up?"

My ears twitched at Kyle's request. Where had my thoughts gone that I'd switched off to his planning?

"Sure," the female said. "I guess."

"Cool. Tonight?"

If not for the step forward of the male down the street, I'd have turned to ask Kyle what the bloody hell he played at.

"Um ... okay," she said. "I have a table booked for dinner at six, but I could meet you after that. Unless ..." Her blown-out breath arrived heavy down Kyle's phone line. "Unless you'd like to join me?"

"For dinner?" Kyle sounded like he thought he'd misheard the offer.

The guy shifted forward another step. Another. His gaze had yet to leave mine.

"Sure," Kyle said into his phone. "Sounds great."

I considered approaching, almost made the move to, but he stuck his hands in his pockets, and whirled off down the hill.

"You know the Blueberry?" the female asked.

I grabbed Kyle's shirt sleeve and yanked him along with me, as I took off after the male.

"I, um ..."

As Kyle tapped my shoulder, I tossed, "Never heard of it," at him before retraining my sights on the pale hair. The guy glided as though on ice.

"It's a hotel—not far from where we met," she said.

"Brickton Heath?" Kyle asked. "Sure, I can find that."

Blondie reached the bottom of the hill and crossed the street to our side. His head turned, dark eyes relocking with mine as he stepped up onto the kerb.

"Can you make it here at six?" the female asked.

"I'll try my best."

The guy down the hill ducked off, and disappeared around the left corner.

"Shit!" I lengthened my strides, and increased my grasp on Kyle. Not that he needed me to—he'd matched me step for step while on the phone. No doubt, if I turned back, his eyes would be trained on the same spot as my own.

Almost at a jog, I passed the baker's and rounded the corner.

A handful of pedestrians trekked about, a few with plastic bags hanging from their fingers, a young couple with their hands linked as they dawdled on their uphill stroll.

I counted the heads, checking the hair colours. None of them matched the one I'd followed.

I released Kyle's shirt and took a few steps forward. With flared nostrils, I swept for hidden surprises. A quick listen assured me Kyle's steps echoed mine at my rear, and I continued on.

Only a few strides farther, I spotted an alleyway to the right. Set back from the road, its stone walls created a domed tunnel. Light stretched through, as if trying to unite with that which spilled in from the far end but didn't quite accomplish it. The shadows within held nobody I could see, yet I still turned that way.

Behind me, Kyle ended his call and closed in on my heels. As he came to my left shoulder in the entrance to the alley, I hesitated and inhaled for evidence that the guy had passed through.

Hundreds of odours accosted my senses. None stood out.

"He go this way?" Kyle asked.

"Where the hell else could he have gone?"

"We going through?"

"I am." I sent him a quick glance. "You have my back?"

"You need to ask?"

I ventured into the stone tunnel.

Step, inhalation, listen, scour, and step. No bodily odours, other than mine or Kyle's, and only our two heartbeats.

I submerged by another couple of metres.

Still nothing.

Beyond the gulley, a couple of cars dotted what I presumed to be a car park. I searched amongst them for movement, finding nothing.

Kyle's feet shuffled at my rear like my caution had him on edge. I took a deep breath, drawing in a final attempt to detect alien scents. Upon finding none, I lengthened my steps to carry me to the end of the tunnel.

Left to right, I scanned the open space. Definitely a car park—possibly the opposite corner of the supermarket where we'd parked the truck. No owners claimed the four vehicles that occupied the quiet area, yet the hackles across the back of my neck rose as though affected by static.

I heaved a deep breath, shook my head at myself, and went to turn back, when a flash of movement caught the corner of my eye, coinciding with Kyle's shout of, "Ethan, look out!"

Something clamped onto my shoulders, hauling my feet from the ground. As I flew backward, everything whizzed past in a blur.

Solid brick hit my back, stopping my flight.

A loud grunt burst past my lips, as my head cracked back to collide with the structure, and light exploded behind my eyes as the air whooshed from my lungs.

I barely had time to recapture it, before a hand closed over my throat.

8

My focus regained its sharpness, and as the pain in my skull subsided, the pale blond hair hanging over my attacker's brow identified him as the one I'd followed.

In my periphery, two more forms that appeared from God-knew-where shoulder-rammed Kyle and blocked his passage.

In front of me, ink black eyes levelled with mine, limiting my view, and as the hand holding my throat tightened, I kicked down with my dangling legs.

Hands fisted in Blondie's shirt front, my shove forward did nothing to shift him. Even an outward boot of my foot connecting with his shins had no effect.

He'd looked no more than a strip of wind when down the street from me, but the guy's body held only solidity.

Kyle's pointless nudges continued against the two inhuman rocks to my right, though I only seemed able to focus on the blond dude's eyes as the black of his irises bled into the whites.

"What the—"

"You have no right to be here, wolf." The bizarre ocular show continued, the black swirling like spiralling smoke to infuse the entirety of his eyeballs with darkness.

My heart thudded as I tried to remain calm. "I have no idea what you're talking about." My voice rasped from me. Another attempt to push him away bore no result.

"Your scent reeks like a damn beacon, you fool. You think I don't smell you? You think you're not leaving a trail across my town everywhere you step?"

I inhaled long and slow, yet caught nothing to indicate what race held me in its grasp.

"These streets are no place for a wolf still wet behind the ears."

With a low growl, I made another attempt to reach the ground with my toes and tried to uncurl his fingers from around my throat. More kicks at his legs joined in with a swing of my fist around his arm.

Although I caught his left ear, the guy merely smiled.

"What the hell are you?"

His lips pulled back and revealed his canines, where two needle-sharp fangs pierced his gums. Like ice picks, they slid down, as though finding home in an invisible sheath.

My eyes widened. My pulse lurched. I kicked down with my legs, trying to find traction against something—anything. A low growl bubbled out as my frustration mounted.

At two inches, the fangs stopped. His lips curved in a smile, as the black danced like psychedelic serpents before refilling his eyes. "I hear weres are something of a delicacy." Huskiness affected his voice, and his tongue skimmed across his teeth, toying with his left fang. A droplet of blood formed at the contact, and his smile widened—right before he twisted my jaw to the side and his face dropped to my throat.

"Shit!" I slammed my foot back against the wall at my rear and, with a roar, thrust myself forward.

The fang-wielder's eyes held shock as he flew backward. He gave a low grunt on impact with the opposite wall, and another beneath the crush of my body.

Before he could recover, I drew my head back, and powered it forward.

The instant my forehead slammed into his, pain splintered into every recess of my brain until my consciousness wavered. "Dammit!" I released him to grab my temples, made an attempt to steady myself. The vampire had a head like a fucking diamond.

With the force of a battering ram, his hands shoved at my shoulders and sent me sprawling to the ground. The base of my skull took a bashing, as did my damn ego, as the snarls ripping from Kyle told me he witnessed my fall.

A quick twist of my head to check on my pack-buddy alleviated any concern I had for his safety. The main cause of his aggravation came in the form of the wall of wiry muscle blocking his passage, as his repeated slams into their bodies earned him nothing more than amused chuckles.

I got as far as sitting before Blondie dived onto me and sent yet another blast of agony through my already damaged head.

His face pushed into mine. "Getting a warning from me is nothing—"

With a growl, I rammed my hands up against his chest, but halted as human scent entered my nose, a split second sooner than the echoing steps announced we'd have company any moment.

The vamp stiffened, too, the black of his eyes drifting aside until it settled within his irises, and Blondie's head twisted to his right as mine turned to the left.

The footsteps belonged to a young twenty-something, his pale eyes narrowed on us.

My chest compressed beneath the pressure of Blondie's hands, when he pushed himself up and faced the intruder, and the opening and closing of my mouth as I gasped in air synchronised with that of the confused human's.

"You do not want to come this way." The smooth cadence of Blondie's voice filled the air like a tonic as his eyes did their tonal dance once more.

The human turned off to the side, like he had some major decision to contemplate, before he about-turned without a word and wandered back the way he'd come.

"A pup like yourself is eas—"

I thumped my right fist against his jaw, snarling my outrage. "Who the hell are you calling pup?" No thirty-five-year-old appreciated being called pup.

The snapping back of his head lent immense satisfaction, and I followed through with a sideways drive of my left. It caught him with enough force to unbalance his stronghold, and a rapid roll reversed our positions. One hand pinned his chest as I drew the other back for another pummel.

"They'll catch up with you."

I paused.

"Then our little exchange will seem like child's play, pup."

My fist hovered above his smug face as I frowned. "Who'll catch up with me?"

"Pretending you know nothing won't help you." His lips curved into a passable smile, as his fangs retracted back into his gums. "These kidnappers aren't amateurs. Amateurs would never capture so many."

"What do you know about the disappearances?"

He gave a small laugh. His headshake suggested he considered me on par with an imbecile.

"Who's doing the kidnappings?"

My body whipped to the left with his thrust, almost bouncing off the pavement, until his hands grasped my T-shirt and hauled me to my feet.

"I know it's vampires," I said through the heave of my chest.

"Then you should know I won't bring disloyalty against my kind and offer them up to a *werewolf*." He spat the word like our race held disease.

I wanted to toss him against the bricks and batter the smugness from his insane eyes, but couldn't risk killing the first source of answers I'd come across. I suppressed my growl, gritting my teeth against my impulse. "They're not only taking werewolves."

"Maybe not." His eyes resettled until they looked close to normal. "But I heard weres are top of their hotlist. And having weres in my town is only going to attract them. So I'm giving you until nightfall to leave of your own accord. Then I'll make you leave."

I swallowed any petty retorts. "You know about them. Where have they taken the ones they kidnapped?"

"I'm done talking to you, pup." He turned and took a step away.

I grabbed his arm, tugging him back. "Where have they taken them?"

"Release my arm."

I tightened my hand. "Not until you tell me what you know."

"I don't have to tell you a thing."

My snarl erupted from within my chest, and I yanked him toward me.

Arms rigid, his hands pounded into my sternum, and an outward thrust sent me sailing.

"Get out of my town, pup!"

My legs overtook my head before the wall prevented me going any farther.

Knees hit first, followed by my chest and stomach.

From there, I headed south.

I threw down my arms, but not fast enough to break the fall, and the collision between my skull and the concrete paving infiltrated my brain with nothing but agony, damn lightning flashes, and momentary concussion.

"Final warning!" he roared.

The rest of my body slid along the wall to slump in a heap with a thud.

I shook my head and blinked my eyes open in time to see the three vampires disappear either side of the gulley exit like the bloody beings had wings.

Kyle's steps pounded the ground after them.

"Kyle!" My voice barely carried, but the breeze must have picked it up en route, because his step faltered as he went to climb the exterior wall alongside the car park.

Foot poised, hand gripping the barrier, he turned back to me.

I tried to lift my head, hiding a groan as implosion threatened my brain. "Stand down."

His frown cut deep, but he lowered his foot, and walked back.

"Stand down," I said as he reached me. "You can't beat them." That stung to say—but I couldn't allow Kyle to take the risk over hiding my admittance.

It must have shown in my face because he gave a nod. Without another word on the matter, he held out his hand for mine and dragged my sorry arse up.

"You look like shit."

I staggered a little before regaining my balance.

"You okay?"

My nod afflicted my brain like a jackhammer party. I rubbed a hand across my brow to hide my wince and headed toward where we'd parked the trucks. "I'm just peachy."

9

"It's five twenty-three already." Kyle glanced up from his mobile, as we neared the trucks. "We're not going to make it to The Blueberry."

"Sure we will."

"How? Dad and Nate aren't around yet, and the female said to meet at six." He shoved his mobile back into his pocket. "Besides, when Nate sees the state of you, he'll never let us go."

I glanced at him with a smile. "What if Dad doesn't see the state of me?"

"I know we haven't passed any mirrors on the way, but those injuries of yours are a bit hard to miss."

I could have figured that out on my own. A slow trickle of blood made a constant stream over my temple, driven by the thudding beat against the inside of my skull. My eyes didn't seem too keen on the idea of focusing, either— but not for one minute would I let that stand in the way of getting information.

"What Dad doesn't see can't worry him." I hit the remote for the truck doors then tossed the keys to Kyle. "You drive. I'll take care of the oldies."

A smile crept over his face as he traded sides with me. "We sneaking off and dumping them?"

I flipped open the passenger door. "Hell, yes."

Taking care of Dad turned out easier than expected— mostly because I informed him only of the conversation that occurred between myself and the vampire. For almost ten minutes, he tossed his musings back and forth between me, Kyle and Connor on loudspeaker: What did the vampire look like; did I believe he had nothing to do with the kidnappings; maybe he knew more than he'd shared; maybe he knew everything? His tone sounded impressed, like I'd spent an afternoon honing my excellent sleuthing skills, instead of performing unfortunate acrobatics against my will.

"We could always come back tonight," I suggested. "Try and flush them out to get some more answers."

"No," Dad said. "That's a bad idea."

"Why?" I asked.

"Because, although vampires venture out in the day, the light weakens them. Come nightfall, they'll have reached full strength."

Fuck me. That had been them weak? I caught my unspoken words reflected in Kyle's brow-lifted expression and blown out breath.

"I have a question, Nate," Kyle said as he took a right turn. "Seeing as you seem to have knowledge of vampires you could have shared with us."

He had a point. Only lesson I'd ever been taught about vampires: stay the fuck away from their teeth.

"Not much, just some." Dad seemed oblivious to Kyle's sarcasm. "Try me, though."

"Why don't they smell of anything?" Kyle hadn't detected a scent for them, either.

"They do smell," Dad and Connor said in unison.

"No—" I started, as Kyle said, "They smelled us a mile off, but we found no trace of them—not even up close. Seems pretty bollocks and unfair to me."

"What are you talking about, Son?" Connor asked.

Kyle's confused expression reflected my own. "We couldn't smell anything of them." He slowed the truck to a stop at a traffic light. "I mean, what kind of stunt is that to pull?"

"That's not possible," Dad said. "I've smelled vampires, and trust me, they stink. Are you sure these were vampires?"

I thought back to the fangs that had come way too close to my throat. "Without a doubt. I didn't know you'd met vampires, Dad. When was this?"

Kyle shifted into first and accelerated forward at the flash of amber.

"Years ago." Dad's deep bass arrived full of contemplation.

"Many years ago." Connor rumbled out his agreement.

"Before you were born," Dad said. "One made the mistake of trespassing in the forest, when Connor and I snuck off from the pack for a hunt. Damn thing blocked my sinuses up for days after I killed it."

My brows shot up, as did my already-high opinion of my father. "*After* you killed it?"

"We." Connor added a small laugh. "After *we* killed it."

"Yeah, yeah, that's what I meant," Dad said. "You pinned it, and—"

"You ripped off its ugly head." Low chuckles travelled the phone line to us. "Damn thing was a pain in the rear to take down."

"You're telling me," Dad said.

I grinned at Kyle as we listened to the old codgers reminiscing. We didn't get to hear it very often.

"And that stench?" Connor said. "Never smelled anything like it. Not since."

My confusion crept back in. "So, why couldn't we smell the ones we met today, then?"

"No idea," Dad said. "You sure you're not coming down with something?"

I rolled my eyes toward the passing sky outside the window, giving a small headshake he wouldn't see. "When was the last time I was ill, Dad?" I'd never known any of the pack to get sick.

"Or me?" Kyle said. "We'd both have to be ill for us both not to smell them. There has to be another reason for it."

"We'll think on it," Dad said. "Go, find out what you can from this female, and call me before you head home."

"Sure," Kyle and I mumbled together.

With the call at an end, I looked to Kyle. "You have any idea where this Blueberry place is?"

"No."

I reached into the glove box and grabbed the Sat-Nav for him. "Then, use this."

"Why, what are you doing?" He took it from me and switched it on, glancing between the screen and the road ahead.

I withdrew a first aid kit from the same place, before reaching up for the sun visor and exposing the mirror. "I'm making myself pretty enough to be seen in public."

"I'll be lucky if they let me in," I mumbled as we approached the hotel entrance. "I look like I've gone a few rounds in the ring."

"You did." Kyle checked me over for the hundredth time. "But I wouldn't worry about your face and head. Your getup makes them almost unnoticeable."

"What d'you mean?" Glancing down, I brushed at the dust coating my T, and poked at a hole in the knee of my jeans that hadn't been there earlier. "They that bad?"

"Nah. I'm just shitting with you." Kyle chuckled and herded me faster with a nudge to my shoulder. "Might be an idea to stay at my back, though, until we find you a table to hide behind."

I kept my head down on entering the hotel, ducking behind Kyle to pass the doorman. The effort seemed unnecessary when we reached the bar with nobody even glancing my way.

The barman zoomed in on us, stiff white collar framing his scrawny neck beneath the curled ends of his dark hair. "What can I get ya?"

Kyle thumbed at me. "He needs a drink. I need directions to your restaurant."

"Restaurant's back out the doors, then follow the tiles round to the left." The barman—Stu, according to his nametag—cocked his head at me. "What'll it be?"

"You're driving home, right?" Kyle said.

I paused in my climb onto a barstool, raising an eyebrow. "Now, I know you're shitting with me."

He patted my arm, pleading with his eyes. "Come on. How often do I get to take a hot bird out?"

"You're not taking one out now. She asked you to dinner, remember?" My eyes flicked to peer over his shoulder at movement near the door, and my lips curved into a smile. "And she must think you've stood her up."

"What?"

I gestured with my chin. "She's looking for you."

Kyle whirled round, as a smile spread across the blonde's face. She lifted a hand, wiggling her fingers and revealing toned muscles. The strapless bodice of her black dress looked like it had been spray-painted on to fit so snug.

Kyle grinned at me over his shoulder. "She's smokin'."

My lips twitched as I shook my head at his blatant admiration.

"I'll see you later."

I grabbed for his shoulder, when he went to walk off. "Just do me a favour." At the lift of his brows, I said, "Don't forget why you're meeting her, okay?"

"'Course not." His low chuckle carried back to me as he strode the width of the room to greet her.

"Are you ready to order, sir?"

I swivelled on my stool and rested my elbows on the bar. "You better make mine a water."

I didn't keep count of the number of times I hopped off my barstool to peer through the restaurant doors and check on Kyle, but it bordered on ten too many. With her back to me, his companion remained oblivious. The tiny flicker of Kyle's eyes at each of my visits, on the other hand, told me he was plenty aware of my over-cautious behaviour.

By seven, I'd worked myself into a deep enough hunger that I'd have considered changing in a nearby bush just to hunt something down if I had to wait much longer to eat.

I nodded to the barman, as he placed another water in front of me. "You do food in here?"

He reached a hand beneath the bar and handed me a card menu. "Knock yourself out."

"Thanks." I browsed the stated meals, landing on their biggest steak. "I'll take the twenty-two ounce, with chips and whatever else it comes with."

"Sure." He took the menu back from me. "Grab yourself a table, and I'll bring it over."

Leaving it to the last minute, yet again, ensured I chowed down my meal like a rabid beast. I didn't doubt the steak's deliciousness, and would have savoured it had it been allowed the chance to hit my taste buds before swallows. About halfway through my meal, Kyle's scent infiltrated the rich aroma drifting up from beneath me. I lifted my gaze and found him coming through the bar doors with the female hanging off his arm.

A second look at her brought details I'd missed on first appraisal, like the hem of her dress barely concealing any underwear she wore, and the gaping cut-out of the rear to expose hard muscle across her back. Kyle's hand against the flesh there, as he guided her to a barstool, told me he'd very much noticed it, too.

Her tight curves settled onto one of the padded cushions. She held onto Kyle's shoulder, seemed to steady herself, and trailed her fingers down his arm before dropping her hand. Her position revealed soft waves of blonde bouncing across her shoulders, and the wiggle of her butt when she adjusted once more. From the smiles that passed between them, they must have progressed pretty fast for a ninety-minute dinner.

I popped a couple of chips into my mouth and chewed, as I watched the gentle touches, the way Kyle leaned in close to her ear, and the curve of her body into him when he spoke.

He glanced my way, lips still moving, and a grin spread across his mouth. When he left her to head across to me, my eyes narrowed.

"Hey." He slid into the seat opposite me and drummed the table with his fingertips.

I speared a breaded mushroom and fed it to myself. After chasing it with a gulp of water, I stared hard at him. "Answer's no."

His palms lifted. "Come on."

Chomping on my last piece of steak, I shook my head.

"But ..." He blew out a breath, ran a hand through his hair. "She's done nothing but hint that if I had a room booked .... Come on. Do this for me."

"No." I nudged my plate across the table. The cutlery clattered as I pushed to my feet.

Kyle grabbed my arm. "Please."

"I've just eaten some mediocre meal, while you dined your rear off with Miss Loincloth over there. I haven't even had chance to call in on Shelley and make sure she's okay."

Lines etched across Kyle's brow. "You got a thing for Shelley?"

I hesitated for too long as memories of the night before flashed through my mind. If he'd asked me three days earlier, the answer would have been an easy no—before I'd gone and made everything complicated.

Kyle's forehead eased up as his eyebrows lifted. "You have."

"Did you even get the answers you were supposed to?" I asked.

"Yes. I told you I would."

"Good. There's no reason to stay any longer, then." I flicked my wrist from his grasp. "I'll meet you outside."

His quiet growl and uttered, "Fuck," hit my ears as I strode off.

More guests occupied the lobby than on first arrival. I weaved through them like a disgruntled bull.

As though he'd spotted my mood and unwillingness to remain any longer, the doorman swung open the door before I reached it, nodding to me on exit.

Coolness from a strong breeze hit my face and accompanied the first waning of light. The graze on my head prickled with the encompassing freshness. Long steps carried me, but I'd only made it to the car park border when I slammed to a halt.

"Shit!" I rubbed a hand over my face, dropped it to my hip. "You bastard, Ethan."

I spun and headed back to the entrance, tugged out my mobile, and hit number one on the speed dial. By the time I reached the door, the call connected. "Dad?" I ducked back into the building, nodding to the doorman, as he dipped his head.

"Everything okay?" Worry tinged his tone.

"What?" I sidestepped a suitcase that wheeled past in the hand of a suit. "Yeah, everything's fine, but we won't be home tonight."

"The two of you staying at Shelley's?"

My mouth opened, and I came pretty close to putting him straight, until common sense told me it would be a damn sight easier to go with the idea he'd unknowingly offered up. "Yeah," I said, the lie sitting wrong, even as I said it.

"Kyle find out anything off that female?" he asked.

"Yeah, he did. We'll update you in the morning. Drop me a text as soon as you've decided where you want us to hit up, and we'll head straight out and get started earlier."

"Good idea. Dan's taking my place with Connor tomorrow. They'll meet you first thing."

"'Kay. Speak tomorrow."

I reached the front desk with no other obstacle to hinder my path.

A blue-bloused female turned to me with a smile she'd probably been trained to give. "May I help you?"

"You have two doubles? Preferably adjoining or next to each other?"

Her gaze lowered to the screen on her desk, as her fingers tapped across a keyboard. "They're not adjoining, but they are together." She glanced back up and seemed to have to make effort to keep her gaze below the battered top half of my face. "How will you be paying for those, sir?"

Thank goodness for company credit cards.

The transaction took little time, and within minutes, I had two keys in my hand. I paused in the doorway to the bar, scanning for a moment.

Back at the stools, Kyle had taken a seat beside the blonde. He paused in the sipping of his drink and turned like he'd sensed my presence.

A jerk of my chin drew him over. "I was an—"

He slapped my shoulder, cutting off my words. "Don't mention it."

I held my palm out.

He went to shake it, until I jiggled the key balancing in the dip of my hand, and he slid a finger through the ring. "What ..."

"Room two-eleven. I'm right next door, so ..." I smiled. "... don't make too much noise—please."

He chuckled. "I owe you."

"Yeah," I agreed. "You do."

10

The lift ride up to the second floor would have been more comfortable if the car didn't have mirrored walls. Behind my own reflection, the blonde's fingers toyed with Kyle's hair, sliding around his neck to tug him to her—like they could get any closer. Even Kyle seemed to forget my presence when his nose dug in and nuzzled at her neck.

God knew how he tolerated the manky perfume she'd doused herself in again. The headache I already had worsened with each intake of fumes.

I rubbed a hand across my face, stepping forward at the ding before the doors even opened. Pausing, a quick glance left and right revealed the opposite room to be number twenty-two, and descending numbers stretching off to the east.

The copulating pair stumbled into my back. A high-pitched giggle provoked a twitch into play beneath my right eye. Before they could expect me to participate in their amusement, I strode off down the corridor.

At the end, another hallway reached off to the right. I peered down it, spotted two-eleven, and ducked that way. The inconsistent beat to the steps at my rear made Kyle and his date sound drunk.

I didn't even want to think about what the slurping suggested.

I tapped his door as I passed. "Yours." The next one along had two-oh-nine below the peephole—my room. I stared straight ahead at the numbers as I slid the key into the lock, but didn't nudge the door open.

From the corner of my eye, I watched Kyle disentangled himself long enough to insert his own key. The second he released the lock, they slammed against the wood, and the crash of it against the inner wall vibrated the length of the corridor. Only once the door swung shut at their rears did I push open my own and enter my room.

A wall of white curtain hung opposite the door, beyond a king size mattress coated in white and grey bedding. I hauled off my shirt as I crossed the room, heading straight for the dresser. My brows lifted at a bash against the wall from the other side, and I hit the switch for the TV, turning the volume up on the news in the hope of drowning the worst of them out.

After tossing my T onto a bucket seat in the far corner, I reached for the buttons of my jeans. It took less than a minute to lose my boots, denim and boxers, and send them sailing in the same direction—my mobile along with them.

"Shit!" I dived forward, caught the hem of my jeans before they landed, and rummaged in the pocket for the device before slinging them once more.

The fabric of the bed covers cooled my rear when I sat, refreshing the grimy skin of my back as I flopped down. While I searched for Shelley's number in my phonebook, I lifted my feet and propped them up on the desk, hitting dial when I found her entry.

The first ring barely reached my ear, when it connected. "Ethan?"

My heart thudded a little at the sound of her voice. "Hey. You okay?" I rubbed a hand across my chest, like I could stem the dodgy rhythm within.

"Wh-where are you?"

The thickness of her voice hinted she could have been crying again. My hand ceased its massage. "I'm—"

"I thought you'd be here by now."

An ache hit my gut. "I, um—"

"I cooked steak." The clank of pots and running water hit my ears. "Gabe says it's your favourite, so ..."

"My, um ..." I sat up, but lay back down again when I caught sight of the mess of my reflection in the mirror. "You cooked for me?" *Shit!*

"You were so hungry last night ... spending so long looking for Gabe ... I wanted to make sure you had a good meal ... to say thank you."

My jaw tightened against a growl that rumbled out.

"Ethan?"

"I can't come, Shel." I rubbed at my face, gave a low groan. "Shit!"

"It-it's okay," she murmured.

"No." I pushed up and paced across the room. "No, it's not okay. I'm stuck here in this stupid hotel room because of Kyle and his damn libido—"

"Hotel?"

"Yeah, the, um ..." Another pace across to the curtains, which I swished aside to peer out. "The Blackberry, or something."

"Blueberry?"

"Yeah, that." I watched the car park below, following the route of a couple who looked more like they belonged in a Gypsy caravan than a hotel. "Only good thing to come of it is we've now got a description of a man Gabe might have been seen with."

"You did?" Her toned perked up, tugging a smile onto my lips. "That's good news."

"Yeah, it's progress." I let the curtain drop back into place and turned to face the room. "Listen, Shel, I'm really sorry I can't come."

"It doesn't matter."

"Yeah ..." I released a sigh. "... yeah, it does."

"But you got somewhere today. You're a step closer to finding my son. I think I can forgive you."

"Another time." I brushed a hand over my head, ducking beneath my wince when it ran over a lump. "Tomorrow ... maybe."

"I'll cook." She paused before adding, "Again."

A small laugh breathed out. "Sure."

After hanging up, I headed across to my bedside shelf, but didn't get as far as putting the phone down before it rang in my hand.

The caller display flashed up at me: Jem.

I hit connect and lifted it to my ear. "What's up?"

"How's my favouritist big brother?" Unrelated by blood, her place in the pack earned her immediate sistership from me, and my title from her came in return.

However, my eyes narrowed at the sweetness of her tone. "You want something."

"Nice." Her blown out breath buffeted against my ear. "I call to tell you I'm missing you, and you accuse me of ulterior motives."

My eyes narrowed further. "So, you're just calling to say how much you're missing me?"

"Yes."

The smile that entered her tone drew my own onto my face. "I haven't been gone that long, Jem."

"This is your second night in a row at Shelley's." She'd driven straight to her point, as usual.

My shoulders tensed as I waited to see what else she had to say on the matter. Female interest in the male pack members had been known to provoke explosive responses from Jem.

"You have a thing for Shelley, Ethan?"

"Nope."

"*Jem!*" Sean's hiss in the background revealed her source, and my jaw crunched beneath the pressure of my teeth grinding.

Damn him and his big mouth.

"Because ... well ... you never said anything."

I remained silent—often the best option until I could be sure of her mood. Even more so since she'd gotten pregnant.

"Of course, it's not that I mind ..."

My left brow lifted a little as I dared allow my stiff shoulders to relax.

"Shelley's really cool ..."

My other eyebrow joined in the act.

"She'll be good for you, right?"

I opened and closed my mouth before my mind conjured words. "But nothing's going on with Shelley, Jem."

"Sure it isn't. That's why you're—"

"I'm not talking about this with you." I nodded at my assertion.

"Besides," she continued, like I hadn't spoken, "think of all the money you'll save on those prostitute bills of yours."

Sean's stifled laughter echoed out beneath Mum's call of, "Leave him be!"

My eyebrows lowered. "Goodbye, Jem."

"No, no, no, wait."

I hesitated, phone gripped tight in my hand.

"I'm right though, aren't I?" More chuckles from Sean. Another admonishment from Mum. "It will save you a fortune. No more ladies of the—"

My lips twitched despite my annoyance. "Bye, Jem."

"No wait. I was just—"

I smiled as I cut her off.

As much as I wanted to be pissed at her, I couldn't bring myself to do so. Jem had a natural lovability, which drew us all to her like moths to a flame, and none of us ever stayed mad at her for long. I certainly couldn't, not when I'd more or less got a free pass from her for Shelley— she'd never give the green light so readily if unsure. I only wished I held her certainty. The whole Shelley business still confused me like crazy.

My smile remained as I investigated the room's mini-bar and Glenmorangie stared back at me.

"Oh, yes." I reached in for the bottle. "You'll do quite nicely."

With the golden liquid transferred to a glass, I padded into the bathroom. The shower took a little fiddling to bring the temperature down to tepid. I stepped beneath the spray, almost leaping back out again when the water hit my crown and discovered yet another lump. Angling my head to the side to avoid a direct blow, I set about peeling the layer of dirt from my flesh.

Complimentary toiletries in lemon zest or lavender perfume were my only option, but I used them because they smelled better than I did. With shower gel lathered over my chest, torso and other parts, shampoo added softness to my manky hair, and the foldaway disposable toothbrush took the unwanted coating from my teeth. I weighed about ten pounds lighter when I emerged from the cubicle.

Smearing condensation from the mirror, I lowered my face and peered up to check out my head. Even in the smudged blurriness, swelling and bruising stood out, and my scab had turned into soggy stickiness, thanks to the water. I poked at it, cringing beneath the pressure, and ran my hands across my entire skull to see how many bashes I'd taken.

From the one at my crown, I brushed over a lump just above the nape of my neck, flicking wet spray from my hair as I swept over to another at the right side. My knees had taken a beating, too, on contact with the wall—along with some tenderness to my left shoulder. Luckily, only bruising would be left behind as a reminder of those.

I scooped up my glass from the vanity unit, downed the rest of the contents, and closed my eyes as the warmth of it heated my chest. Vowing to refill as soon as possible, I unwrapped the guest razor to complete my transformation from hobo to hot ... ish.

Back in the bedroom, I balanced on the edge of the bed and stared at the TV. Against my better judgement, I tuned into the room next door, breathing out a sigh at the quiet that met my ears from there. Either they'd finished for the night, or they needed to recuperate between sessions.

"And I can't believe I'm sitting here thinking about that," I muttered.

Strange surroundings always brought restlessness. Nothing smelled right. None of it looked right. After a lifetime of my bedroom overlooking the forest, even opening the window to busy streets and passing pub stragglers offered no reprieve.

The news finished on the box, and a crappy film took its place. Minutes in, some moron's arm hung trapped through a car window, and his feet skidded along the tarmac as the driver dragged his pathetic arse down the street.

I shook my head and picked up the remote to flick through the channels, clicking off a ridiculous vampire teen programme as fast as it came on. A sex documentary—I could do without that right then—came before a programme on fetish's, including men's envy over whose cock was biggest.

"Jesus, come on."

After those came, 'My daughter mutated at birth'. About the best option came in the form of a kid's cartoon, and even that bored the hell out of me with its repetitious circling of dumb animals.

I hit the standby button.

Deep silence filled the room, while beyond my walls, engines and tyres announced arrivals and departures, muted voices revealed the presence of conversation, and quiet footsteps travelled the outside corridor.

The mattress groaned a little when I pushed up. Gripping the softness of the covers, I folded them down and dropped my face to sniff at the fabric. Only cleanliness greeted me, not too overpowering, and I plumped up my pillows in satisfaction.

The footsteps from outside the room grew louder, nearer. With my knee raised to climb into bed, I hesitated when they halted outside my door. A thud resounded through the wood. I turned my head, staring at the entrance, until common sense told me I wouldn't discover my visitor if I didn't move from my position.

My damp towel lay strewn across the chair at the dresser, and I snatched it up en route, securing it about my waist. At the door, I ducked down and peered through the peephole. My brows shot up, yet my lips curved when Shelley's face came in view.

Rounded to distortion by the convex plastic, her green eyes seemed to lock onto mine through the wood.

I tugged down the handle and swung the door open. "Shelley?"

Her eyes widened. Her jaw worked a little.

I brushed a hand over my hair. "I, um ... wasn't expecting you."

Her eyes darted to the side, and she lifted her hands, entwining her fingers.

My forehead creased as I narrowed my eyes. "Is something wrong? What's happened?" I peeked around the doorframe, down the corridor. "Where's Mia? Is she okay?"

Shelley nodded. "I sent her home. She couldn't sleep at our house with Gabe gone, anyway." Her shoulders shifted in a small shrug. "I just ... I wanted to say ... thanks." A deep breath heaved her chest. "For everything ... you've done."

My brow quirked up.

"Gabe told me about the offer ..." More finger fiddling. Another eye aversion. "To join the pack." Her attention returned. "He looks up to you—a lot. You have no idea how much he appreciates the runs he gets to share with you."

"He's good to run with."

"Better than your family?" Her palm lifted. "You think I don't understand how much you give up for him, by allowing him two of your weekends every month, but I do. It's a big deal. For you to sacrifice. And for him to have you there to guide him. You're a good teacher, Ethan.

He's learned a lot from you. He respects you ..." Her lips pursed until they made a popping sound. "I just ... wanted to let you know."

I smiled, despite my confusion. "Thanks."

Her eyes flittered away again. When she re-met my gaze, her mouth opened and froze in place. "I'll see you tomorrow, then." She spun and walked away.

Frowning, I watched my source of decent company slipping through my grasp, and shaking my head clear, I stepped out from my doorway. "Shel?"

She halted and spun back.

I padded the few paces along the corridor to her and hunched down to her eye level. "You really came here just to tell me that?"

Her gaze flitted across my face. "Oh, my God." She reached up a hand but withdrew without making contact. "What happened to you?"

I'd forgotten for a moment. "I ... hit a wall."

"You need it looked at."

I thought it a question and went to answer, but Shelley continued, "I should look at that for you."

She pushed past me and re-trod her path to my room. Pausing with her hand holding the doorway, she peered back. "You coming?"

"I ..." I rubbed at my forehead, to hide my uncertainty. "I'm coming."

11

"Don't be such a baby." Shelley pressed the facecloth to my head, after my dodge rendered her first attempt a failure. "Hold still, will you?"

"You're hurting me." The scalding flannel burned the hell out of my skin, sending lava-like temperatures seeping into my wound.

She rolled her eyes as her fingers held my chin steady. "So …" Another dab, another wince from me. "You going to tell me who got the better of the invincible Ethan Holloway?"

"Invincible?" I breathed out a laugh and shuffled back in the chair Shelley had pulled away from the dresser when she ordered me to sit. "What the hell gave you that impression?"

"It's what Gabe sees in you." She guided my chin to the left. "Strong, powerful, controlled. Like I said, he holds you in high regard."

My fingers flexed as I studied her too-close narrow hips. "And you?" I tucked my hands between my knees and glanced up at her.

"Me ... what?"

"What do you hold me in?" *What does she hold me in?* My eyes did a virtual roll at my idiocy.

She wiggled the fingers of her free hand with a smile. "These, maybe?" Her expression warmed my insides enough to alleviate my discomfort, and her smile remained as she shook her head. "But that's not what you were asking ... is it?"

My gaze locked with hers for a moment. The weight of the unspoken exchange prickled at my flesh until my damn nipples hardened. With a rough throat clearing, I shoved to my feet. "Done?" My voice arrived funny.

"No." She took my arm, gesturing me to sit back down. "You have more bashes than just your head, Ethan."

The cushion remoulded to my rear when I lowered. Elbows rested across my thighs, I stared off to the corner of the room, lest she become aware of the effect her closeness had on me.

Her thigh nudged mine as she leaned around and poked at my shoulder. "This is bruised already."

I shrugged the shoulder beneath her palm and released a slow breath.

"You going to tell me what did this to you?" Her stare met mine as she came around to kneel before me.

"It's not important."

The hardening of her eyes could have set concrete.

"Vampire," I muttered. "Bastard beat the crap out of me."

Softness re-entered her green irises, along with concern. She didn't question further as she ran her fingertips over my right knee. "Just a graze," she whispered, shifting her attention to my left.

The tenderness of her touch sent tingles along my inner thigh to my groin. I almost groaned at my untimely swelling—especially as I hadn't traded my towel for anything larger—and folded my arms across my lap in a bid to conceal.

"In answer to your question?" Her eyes hooked back up with mine and contained no laughter, but a deep seriousness I had trouble deciphering. "When I look at you, I see only you, Ethan."

As my mouth opened and my almost permanent brow furrow moved in, she stood and turned for the bathroom, but I darted my hand out, folding my fingers around her wrist.

I tugged her back round. "What are you doing here, Shelley?"

"I already told you. I'm—"

"Don't ..." I shook my head. "Please ... just tell me the truth."

Her eyes flitted off to the side, but I didn't miss the slight shine that visited them as though she fought against the threat of tears.

"Shel?"

"I ..." The flesh at her throat moved, exposing her swallow, and she brought her gaze back around. "I didn't want to be alone."

"So ..." My jaw worked against my words in case hers held a completely different meaning to that which I thought. "Why not ask Mia to stay? She—"

"Mia doesn't hold me the way you did last night." Her chest heaved, like getting the admittance out had been a huge feat, and her gaze shifted away, when my shocked as hell stare refused to waver.

Seconds passed. My heart drummed inside my chest. Beneath its heaviness, Shelley's patterned my ears with a faster, more delicate tempo.

"Say something," she whispered.

I took a deep breath and reached out for her thighs, cupping my hands around the back of them. She offered no resistance as I drew her forward over my lap and settled her where I really wanted her. My hands slid up, over her hips, across the tremor that swept through them. When I pulled her close, her cheek rested against my chest, caressing my skin with her breaths, and my arms folded around to embrace her.

"Like this, you mean?" My murmur fluttered her hair.

The nod of her head swished against me. "Exactly like this."

Two beats of Shelley's heart seemed to induce a tap-tap against my chest, before mine thudded back at her—a quiet rhythm of sudden contentment.

My chin tucked in as I peeked down at her. Her parted lips allowed her breaths to seep out, and the slight flutter of her lashes explained the tickle to my flesh.

"You're so warm," she whispered. "I always imagined you would be."

My eyebrow twitched my surprise. "Always?"

Her hair teased as she gave another nod, and she lifted her face. "Did you have to keep me waiting so long?"

I took a moment to organise my thoughts beneath the intensity of her stare. "So, you weren't pissed at me for kissing you?"

Her eyes widened a little. "Is that what you thought? God, no. You ..." She expelled a tiny breath. "I spent months trying to get you to notice—"

"I've been a little blind." I twirled a strand of her hair around my finger and drew it back from her face. "My vision's a lot clearer now."

Quiet breaths passed, with Shelley's attention locked onto me, before her hand slid up from my chest. As she found the nape of my neck, she gave a tug, and my lips met with her waiting ones.

The shifting of her body as she curved into me drew her pelvis to my stomach, the denim scratching against my skin, and my hands slipped beneath her butt to hold her there.

Her fingers swept down from my neck. Both hands smoothed across my shoulders. Arms enclosed me. Fingers wove into my hair. Her exotic element of arousal infused with the sweetness of female that belonged all to her, and desire and fear tinged an underlying perspiration. My nostrils flared wide as I drew her deep into my sinuses. As her tongue and hastened breaths added her personal flavour to an already delicious kiss, my dick perked to life.

Shelley's mouth took more, demanding my response, until I strained against the restrictive fabric covering my midsection. I gave a low growl. The urge up of my hips did little to loosen the binding. Shelley's gasp only increased my body's interest further, as did the sharp rake of her fingers to my shoulders, and her catch of my lip between her teeth.

She paused, holding me captive. When her teeth released me, replaced by the softness of her tongue, my resolve snapped.

Arms encircling her back, my thigh muscles bunched, and I surged to my feet. A rolling snarl vibrated past my lips before I could leash it, as I took a step for the bed.

"No!"

I froze in place, my breaths rapid beneath the effort. "Shel?" Roughness affected my voice.

She pushed against my chest.

I sat us back down, took her face in my hands. "Shelley, what's wrong?"

"Not like this." Emotion clouded her eyes for a moment. Her fingers folded around my forearms as she stared into me. "I've never felt as useless in my life as I have since .... This ... this is the most in control I've been for days." Her head gave the smallest of shakes between my palms. "Don't take that from me."

I brushed my lips across hers. "Okay, Shelley, the reins are all yours."

A high shine visited her eyes until they glistened beneath the lamplight. For seconds, she didn't move. When she did, she took my hands from her face and lowered them to my sides. "Close your eyes." Her whisper returned, fingers sweeping over my lids until I complied. "Don't open them."

A slight shuffle of weight, and hers disappeared altogether. Cold spread through me at her absence, and my inhalations deepened, tracking her path to ensure she remained close.

One footstep, a second, created almost inaudible crunches upon the carpet. A zipper, the swish of material, the quickening of her breath, all preceded the silence of innateness and the pumped out scent of her desire.

My muscles tensed with the effort to stay put, while a gentle thrum played in my chest.

Another zipper. Rustling. The unmistakable sound of rummaging.

My left eye opened to a slit, and I peeked through my lashes. As she fiddled within her bag on the floor, Shelley's rear hovered a few feet before my knees, no more than a black strip of lace covering it. My other lid lifted, the first bead of perspiration broke out on my upper lip, and my mouth opened to share the growl rumbling at the back of my throat.

Shelley pushed up.

I slammed my mouth and eyes shut before she could spot me, made an effort to control my breaths as they threatened to come too fast.

No admonishment arrived, only a ripping crinkle of sound. More dainty padding of movement, a shuffle beside my foot, and the slide of flesh against my calf followed.

I almost jerked at her feather-light touch over my hip. A tug tightened my towel, until a second released it, and a glide of her hands exposed my readiness.

Her pulse tripled, joining my own in an erratic tune, growing louder the closer she came.

Heat spread through my thighs at her touch as she slipped back onto my lap, and across my throat beneath her breaths and tongue.

"Shel?"

Fingers pressed to my lips, and her nose nudged at mine when she replaced them with her mouth. Her whispered, "Soon," had my entire body vibrating with anticipation.

Her chest met mine, brushing with such softness I could only presume her naked.

A low groan filled the air, and I realised it came from me.

Further oral caresses graced my face, my throat, my neck. I angled my head to the side, inviting her to continue. The scent of her saturated my mind until headiness kicked in, and I searched for more. "Do you know how amazing you smell?"

Her tremor hit me, inciting my own to affect every nerve ending, before her body moved away and snatched from me what I longed for.

The density of my breaths added heaviness to my chest.

Shelley's rapid ones breezed back across my face, as moisture coated my thighs, announcing her heightened arousal.

I awaited her touch. Tension consumed every part of me, as the urge to open my eyes overwhelmed.

"Shel?" More of a rumble than a word.

Fingers encircled my hard-on. I sucked in breath through my teeth, and it burst back out as she applied pressure to the tip. One stroke down my shaft. Another. A third. Although I recognised the sound, and scent, of unrolling latex, with each fondle, my muscles tightened to implosive proportions, and risk of early explosion increased.

"*Shelley!*" My voice came out a warning.

She released me. While my body screamed out for her to return, my mind cried relief. Her rear left my lap, yet she didn't move away, only closer. With hands against my collarbone, and her breasts at my chest, her core balanced over my erection.

An upward plunge would find what I craved. My body shook against the resistance.

"Open your eyes, Ethan."

I obeyed her husked order, and could have dived headfirst into the glazed pools that greeted me.

One hand combed into my hair, pulling me to her, but she did no more than nibble at my lower lip. As she slid over my engorged head, her mouth opened on her exiting gasp, and her eyes widened.

My hands itched to grab her hips and take her the rest of the way, clenching against the effort of restraint.

With agonizing slowness, she lowered herself until I filled her. A long, low cry accompanied her journey. Her head tipped back as her eyes closed, and her nails scratched the flesh at my shoulders until my growl could no longer be tamed.

Her hips rocked back and forward, and her lids lifted to draw me back in. "Hold me."

My hands swept across her back, as hers smoothed to mine. Like silk, her flesh glided beneath my palms. With undulating thrusts, she gripped, released, each movement a sensual massage that sent shudders along my spine. Flames sparking from my groin. Tautness affected my muscles with each wave of heat that coursed through them.

I dropped my face to her shoulder and burrowed into her neck, her hair feathering across my cheek. Sweat coated her flesh, lent saltiness to my sampling of it. As I suckled, lapped, and tasted, her arms tightened, her fingers clung, and small panting cries echoed through my mind until I became deaf to all other sound.

Her contractions tugged me closer to the edge. Jolts of pleasure pumped through me at each throb. Erotic scent permeated the air to fog my mind.

My hands grasped at her hips, urged her faster. Toes flexed, spasms attempted to move into my calves, snaking higher into my thighs.

"Wait for me." Her panted demand hit my ear.

I lifted my face to see her, to watch the high shine of her unseeing stare, to study the blush of her cheeks.

A stream of gasps flew from her. Her muscles grew rigid. Her nails penetrated my flesh, making her mark upon my back.

With a loud mewling cry, her lashes lowered to half cover eyes that glistened, and her entire body stiffened, hauling me along with her.

One final tug, the pulsations of her climax, and a constriction that sparked fire into every inch of my body brought me to the point of eruption.

My body convulsed against Shelley. I fisted my hands against her back so as not to cause her harm beneath my strength. My teeth clamped against my snarl as the yearning to bite her and create my mate almost overpowered my senses.

For minutes, my body wracked in aftermath. The compressed rumble in my chest fought to get out, filling the room with a quiet thunder.

Shelley stroked my face, encouraging it back round to her from a position at her throat I couldn't recall adopting, and lids to open that I didn't realise I'd shut.

She continued to tremble as she kissed me, as her tongue darted out and pushed between my lips to find mine. "Now," she murmured with another brush of her lips, "now you can take me to bed."

12

Shelley's feet barely reached my calves, yet her body still moulded to mine like it was always meant to be there. My chest seemed mountainous beneath her delicate hands, as they continued to sear heat into my soul at their touch. Within her expression of sleepy contentment, her lips remained curved, and her sated stare could have held even the most unwilling at her mercy.

As a result, my dick refused to calm down—had been that way the whole fifteen minutes we'd been in bed.

"So, remind me what you were saying about it being Kyle's fault you're here all night." The tone of her voice matched the languidness of her body.

My gaze lifted toward the wall dividing my room from Kyle's, my ear brushing the cotton pillow beneath my head. "You really want to talk about what he might be getting up to in there?"

Her quiet laughter sent her breath across my throat. "No. But you sounded mad about it earlier."

"That was then." I returned my attention to where she lay before me and stroked my hand along the arc of her back. "I have plenty reason not to be pissed any longer."

"What reason could that be?" Amusement remained in the curve of her lips.

"I'm looking at it." My arm beneath her shoulder gave her little choice but to join the roll of my body. A nudge of my knees parted hers, allowing me room to snuggle into her warmth, as my lips found her ear. "Why the hell did I not see what was right under my nose?"

Shelley's body trembled beneath me. "You've been blind, remember?"

"That's right." I brought my face around to hers and claimed a brief kiss.

"But now you can see how amazing I am." Her smile affected her eyes with a sparkle.

"Hmm-mm." My mouth skimmed hers again.

"And how hot a babe I can be." She gave a small nod as though to emphasize her point.

My eyebrow flickered. "Hmm-mm."

"And you're realising the benefits of finding yourself an older woman."

I gave a quiet chuckle. "By a whole two years."

"They say mature women are better in bed." Her hands smoothed across my shoulders and down my back, until I shuddered beneath them. "What's your take on that?"

I smiled as a thrum began its opening chord in my chest. "In general? No idea." I dipped down to stare into her. "But you?"

The twitch of her eyebrow tugged a jerk from my dick like Shelley had the powers of a puppet master, but it didn't dampen the intensity swelling within me, as our gazes remained locked.

"No one's ever made me feel the way you have tonight, Shel."

What seemed like minutes passed without words—only the hastening of her heartbeat drumming against my chest, before the disappearance of drowsiness from her eyes gave me her response.

"So, you're not going to tell me this is a one-off?" she said at last. "There's not going to be heaps of awkwardness, when we wake in the morning and you decide this was all a mistake? You're not—"

"Mistake?" My eyebrows shot up. "Are you kidding me?"

Her eyes danced about, like she needed to gather her thoughts, before they resettled and held mine steady. "So, you're not running off at the first opportunity?"

"Only a crazy person would do that. I'm not going anywhere." I lowered in search of her mouth again, smoothing my hands up to cup her shoulders as I brought my lips to her ear. "And you damned well hadn't better, either."

"You can count on it," she murmured.

From her neck, I feathered my lips across her collarbone, heading in search of breasts I'd still to taste. Shelley urged them up to greet me as my tongue discovered their flavour, and I teased over nipples already hard.

The weave of her fingers into my hair guided me, offering encouragement, as did the gentle gasps that bristled the strands at my crown. She trembled beneath the hand I swept down the length of her torso. The lift of her thighs to circle my hips nestled me deeper into the embrace of her body, and her hands took my face until my gaze met with hers.

"Make love to me," she whispered.

"I intend to, Shel."

My upward shift reunited our lips, and I drank in the sigh that drifted from her. With a ripple sweeping beneath the surface of my flesh, I thrust into her on a snarl and took my turn for control.

At the jolt of my body, my eyes flew open.

The rush of my pulse buzzed in my ears.

Everything smelled wrong, nothing at all like my room, and I stared about through the darkness, trying to blink myself awake.

Pale walls offered no enlightenment. Only a deep inhalation and the quieting of my inner swarm allowed me to detect the human scent and additional heartbeat at my side.

I smiled as I recognised the softness of her hair against my collarbone, the gentle weight of her arm across my chest, and the contour of her shoulder blade beneath my palm. "Shelley?"

My whisper did nothing to stir her—telling me she'd played no part in disturbing my sleep.

My lids drooped back into place, and I steadied my breathing, relaxed my mind. The pillow against my shoulders murmured its welcome with the resettle of my mass. As Shelley's breaths swirled across my skin, I lifted my free hand in search of hers, in a need for entwinement.

At a quiet tapping, I froze. For a few beats, I lay innate, trying to decipher if I'd really heard the sound or it had been within the beckon of slumber.

Another tap—as timid as the first.

My lids lifted. Nothing more greeted me than had moments before.

Tap. Tap.

My eyes shifted to the left with the twitch of my ears—toward the door.

Tap. Tap.

Kyle?

I abandoned my search for Shelley's fingers and instead reached for my mobile. Hitting the keys illuminated the screen. One thirty glared at me.

I dropped it back down with a groan. "This had better be good."

Shelley whispered some incoherent mumble, as I slid my shoulder and arm out from under her. Her hands grabbed at my flesh, as though to keep me there, but reached bedding, instead. With her fingers folded over the cotton, she drew the fabric up to her chin, and curled into a ball I wished I could be the centre of.

I plucked a stray strand of red from across her lashes, tucked it behind her ear. "Back in a sec."

"'Sokay." She slurred her response as though speaking within a dream she refused to wake from.

A slight creak arrived with my push off the mattress. The soft pile of the carpet depressed with each step. I lowered my face to peer through the tiny glass window.

Dark eyes flitted from side to side. My eyebrow lifted at the mess of blonde framing them; the earlier waves had disappeared from the hair of Kyle's date. Without even knowing the reason why, my pulse increased, and my shoulders tensed.

I opened the door enough to peek around, rubbing at my eyes in an attempt to clear my sleep vision. "'Sup?"

"Sorry." Her hands lifted, and she jigged on the spot like she hadn't toileted in days. "I didn't want to wake you." Her manic whisper matched the twitch of her eyes.

"Something wrong?"

"It's your friend." Her arms swung wide in a double point toward the room next door. "I think he's sick."

"Sick?" I stared at her like she'd said something absurd. Mostly because she had. "What do you mean, sick?"

"Spewing." Her hands did some weird mime from her mouth like I wouldn't otherwise understand the word's meaning. "He's asking for you. Said to come tell you he needs you."

"Sure." I went to pull open the door, but recalled my lack of attire and nudged it back to keep me concealed. "Give me a moment to .... I'll be out in a minute."

The door gave a quiet click as I closed it, and I frowned. *Kyle, ill? How?*

My hands brushed over my head as I trotted round the bed to the bucket seat. Stale sweat tugged my nose into a scrunch before I'd even picked up my shirt. I tossed it aside a moment, concentrating on my boxers that smelled no better than my outer garments.

The scratchy slide of rough denim over my feet arrived loud against the quiet of the room. I tugged my jeans over my hips, reached for my discarded T-shirt, but paused at the rustle of bedding. I looked across at Shelley's form, smiled at the flop of her body, as she rolled to her back. Her arm stretched up and rested over her crown, like she planned on doing a few pirouettes, and lifted her right breast free of the covers.

My dick stiffened at her nipple pointing toward the ceiling. I rolled my eyes at its timing and drew my T-shirt over my head as I moved nearer.

"Shel?" Downy hairs covering her cheek leaned toward the trail of my knuckles as I brushed across them.

"Third drawer on the left," she garbled in a murmur.

My chuckle tried to escape, and I captured it just in time. I bent over her, placed a soft kiss where my fingers had been. "Won't be long."

A blown out breath responded, lending vibrations to her lips.

I padded away before I could laugh.

The female hadn't moved when I pulled the door open. A flick of the catch ensured I could get back in, and I stepped out to the corridor.

"How much did he drink tonight?" I asked.

Her hands wrung as she walked backward in front of me. "Not much." She shrugged, peering off as though recollecting and doing a mental calculation. "Three ... four ..."

"Glasses?"

She nodded, and her hair bounced with the movement, along with her breasts enclosed in the same dress she'd worn earlier. "We ordered wine—white."

I paused at the door to Kyle's room. "He eat anything that could've been off?"

Her dark eyes showed another round of concentration. "He had steak. Maybe that did it?" She shrugged again. "I don't know."

"Okay, no worries. I'll find out from him."

The handle let out a tiny squeak when I tugged it down. An inhalation on entering identified Kyle's scent. I held the door open until the female stepped in behind me and moved farther into the room, fast realising something about the interior bothered the crap out of me.

It could have been that no chair sat at the desk, like in my room next door, or the empty bed with only slight creasing to the covers. Or it could have been the lack of sexual odour that should have been present after a round of fornication.

I rubbed at the static tug to the hairs across the back of my neck. "Kyle in the bathroom?"

At the swish and click of the door, I half-turned back to her, stalling at a stab of pain to my thigh.

I peered down until my gaze fell on what looked like a dart hanging out of my flesh.

Brow creased, I wrapped my fingers around it, yanked it free, and stared hard at it before looking back to the female.

She hadn't moved from the door, but she no longer stood alone. And I instantly recognised the male beside her. He'd barged my shoulder on Witchurch High Street, and the sight of him curled my lip as much as it had then—until my eyes fell on the gun in his hand.

"Whan ..." I rolled my tongue at the unformed word.

Even the rumble in my chest that should have evolved into a growl seemed out of my reach, as grey seeped into the edges of my vision.

I took a step forward, staggering a little to the left when my foot met back with the carpet.

All uncertainty, all nervous energy, had disappeared from the blonde. Only a smile affected her features as she stood across the room.

"Wh ..." My femoral artery seemed to expand, pressurising my thigh muscles from the inside until they no longer had the strength to hold me up. My right knee hit the floor, followed by my left. "Koyer ..." As I let out a weak growl at my affected speech, the female smirked up toward the male.

Everything within the room wavered for a second, almost spiralled beyond recognition, before I refocused and caught the female's approach.

I willed my vocal chords to work. I needed to know what they'd done with Kyle. My chest heaved beneath the effort to stay alert, as heavy darkness invaded my mind and attempted to consume me. An uncontrollable elasticity softened the muscles of my torso until deep numbness set in. The sensation crept higher, spread into my shoulders, like the growth of a vine on fast forward.

"You don't need to worry, Ethan," she said.

The high-pitched tone stroked at my brain. Deciphering the words almost stole my consciousness.

"Your friend hasn't been harmed ..."

Through vision narrowed to pinpricks, I glared up at the female, watching her with great difficulty, as she dropped to my level.

She smiled. "... yet."

"You ..." My lips barely formed the word as they moved with the consistency of silly putty. "Are ..." I blinked back the shadows infecting my eyes. "Dead ..." The image of her face slanted off-kilter. "Bitch!"

My breaths spurted from me as I watched her irises bleed blackness into white. When her fangs shot down as though hammered through her gums, the pound of my pulse echoed in my head.

"You're too late." She let out a tinkle of laughter that hit my hearing like deranged chimes. "I'm already dead, wolf."

Thoughts whirled through my mind: Kyle, and where they'd taken him, or if he was okay; Shelley, alone in the next room and, stupidly, the idea that she'd be mad as all get out when she woke to find me gone; Dad, and how the hell he'd react once he found out we weren't where we should have been.

As the realisation sank in—I'd be under any second, and nobody could help Kyle because I wouldn't even be able to help myself—a surge of adrenaline pulsed into my veins.

With a quiet roar of pathetic proportions, I kicked back with my useless feet, and thrust my wasted body forward.

13

I roused to a dense thudding inside my skull, becoming aware within seconds of the dull ache in my right thigh.

At a twitch of my fingers, and a flex of my toes, the rapid pace of my shallow pulse slowed—until I inhaled, and more scents than my brain could distinguish flooded my senses.

Werewolves. Humans—yet ... not human. Other races I couldn't identify. Cat? Vomit. Urine. Faeces. Mildew. Copper—blood, I guessed. Rotting flesh. Semen? Filth and grease.

I slammed the shutters down on my olfactory system and switched to breathing through my mouth, although the surrounding vileness still forced its way through.

The lift of my lids offered no relief, either. I'd no idea what I expected, but something other than the dark stone above me would have been preferable.

I stared at it.

Maybe I hoped my vision would clear, and with that, the view would change.

It didn't.

The dark ceiling continued to loom, as did the shadows that seemed to press in on me with the hunger of vengeance.

Without moving, I took a moment to listen past the thrum of my mind.

Too many heartbeats bounced at me—too many breaths. Along with whispers, groans, murmurs, sobbing, a snarl, rattling, the quiet pad of pacing, brushing, drip-drip-dripping like a leakage of liquid.

"Pssst."

My muscles tensed. After a split-second to deduce the direction of the sound, I rolled my head. Looking to the left produced splinter-like stabs to my eyes. Thick iron bars appeared in the gloom as I focused. Between those bars, a girl's face appeared.

"You're awake." From her kneeling position, her hand lifted in a wave. "Thought you'd be out for hours yet ..."

My body didn't want to obey my command to move when I tried to shift to my side.

"... they usually are ..." The girl's shoulders twitched up and down.

Another attempt to turn flopped me round to face her. My head hit the ground with a hollow *thunk*, and my groan arrived as loud as a siren to my ears.

"... but you woke up, like, mega quick."

Her fingers wrapped around the bars that separated us. White-blonde hair hung in matted strands on either side of her narrow face. Amongst the tails that fringed her forehead, huge, pale green eyes stared out.

I tried bringing a hand to my face, but a gravitational-like force prevented it moving in the direction I wanted it to go. When I finally succeeded, a small grunt burst from me, and I realised I'd held my breath through the process.

A tentative finger-tour of my face revealed no further damage than what I'd already incurred. I went higher, checking over my head. The same injuries as before remained there, yet my skull continued its heavy metal drum solo.

"You sure you wanna do that?"

The drop of my hand brought the girl back into view. Her eyes looked bigger than ever, as she pressed her face between the bars like she could squeeze through if she only tried hard enough.

Maybe she could. What did I know?

"Do what?" A cough spurted out with my croaked words.

"Move." She shifted from the bars for a moment. Dust blew into the air like fireflies behind her shuffling body and clouded around her when she turned back. "I only have a little." Her hand thrust through the bars, a clear liquid sloshing inside the bottle she held, and my rusty inner cheeks contracted at the potential reprieve. "Take it," she whispered. "I don't mind sharing."

"Hey, little girl." The voice came from somewhere behind her and hit my ears like nails down a chalkboard.

The girl stiffened. Her gaze locked onto mine and held only dread.

"Share with me," the voice hissed.

I urged onto my front with a roll, tucking my arms and knees beneath me. A few grunts scratched my throat, a suppressed growl of frustration grating with the consistency of sandpaper. I finally made it onto my hands and knees, my limbs holding as much strength as those of a new-born giraffe.

When I turned back to the girl, I lifted so I could see beyond her. There, pressed against more bars on the far side of her space, a skinny male stretched an arm toward her, his black eyes swirling.

Vampire. My lips vibrated—I'd about had my fill of the damn race.

"You should have stayed down," the girl whispered.

I gave my attention back to her. An ache throbbed through my temples.

"It's safer to play dead." She dropped the water bottle, retracting her hand to her own side. "They don't come for you so soon."

"Who?"

Her eyes rose toward the ceiling. "Them. The ones who brought us here." She shrugged. "I think, anyway."

I made the mistake of inhaling, and a barrage of animal scents bombarded my sinuses.

"Only time they take me out my cage is for the bathroom," she said.

My nostrils twitched at odours that seemed to get sucked up from right beneath me. I had smelled cat earlier, but the array of feline odours stretched beyond one breed, as well as a canine stench that hadn't only come from wolf.

My lids slammed shut. Roiling started in my stomach, churning like a cement mixer, and a retch rocketed up through my throat until I dry heaved.

"You okay?" The girl continued to whisper, like no one else would hear if she only kept it low enough.

She had no chance at remaining undetected—at a guess, I'd have said the space held a host of supernatural abilities, and enhanced hearing would undoubtedly be one of them.

I gave as much of a nod as I could, caught sight of the water she'd left, and decided the time had come to brave the three-foot journey to get it.

One hand lifted, and I plopped it back down with the grace of a dinosaur, before raising the other to take its turn. The denim of my jeans snagged against the concrete floor beneath me as I nudged my right knee across. My breaths arrived deep, carrying a constant rumble with each movement, until a final one gasped from me upon reaching the prize.

Teeth came in handy as a bottle opener, and I made the final twist, unscrewing the cap and spitting it to the ground. The first glug battered my throat. A retaliatory cough sputtered it back out, and the girl dove aside.

I regained my composure with a few throat clearances and tried on a smile that in no way passed for one. "Sorry."

She sat back up. "Sure."

Up close, what had appeared to be a girl seemed more like a young woman—one not much bigger than Shelley.

Shelley. My jaw tightened at the thought of her still in the hotel, followed by the clenching of my chest when I realised I didn't know that she *had* been left behind.

Restraining my panic took immense effort. "So ..." While my voice remained controlled, my head screamed on the inside. "... you have a name?"

Her lips curved a little. "Lauren."

I sipped at the water and made another attempt to smile. "Can I ask you something, Lauren?"

Her eyes blanked, and her lips clammed.

Like that'd stop me. "Were you awake when they brought me in?" I coughed off the remaining hoarseness in my throat, keeping my gaze steady on hers.

She gave a small nod, but her lips didn't loosen.

"Did they ..." I winced against the words and potential answer before I'd even formed the question. "Did they bring anyone else in with me? Or was I—"

"Just one other." She glanced to her right. "Another man."

My pulse dropped down to third gear in its rhythm. "He have red hair?"

Her shoulders lifted. "Dunno. I can't see in the dark."

"What about a female?" I tried to keep the intense dread that thrummed through my veins out of my expression. "A woman?"

"No. Just you two." She turned back. "Why?"

I released my long-held breath, took another sip of water. "Did you see where they put the other ... um, man?"

She jerked her chin to her right again. "Two cages down on the other side."

"Can you show me?" Croakiness crept back in. I cleared it with a sharp bark. "Point it out?"

She gave a small nod to her right. "You're gonna need to crawl that way ..." Her eyes tracked the lift of my hand, and her shoulders gave a small jolt, as I wrapped my fingers around bars close to her left arm.

"I'm done crawling." Every muscle in my upper arm and shoulder yelled at me to quit, before I'd even gotten my feet firmly planted and passed some of the strain to my calves and thighs. With a little hauling and shoving, and a whole lot of grunting, I found myself upright.

My breaths panted from the exertion the manoeuvre inflicted. Forehead pressed against the bars, I closed my eyes as I steadied my body against the whir of my pulse.

"Oh, please let them put me up against you." The high male voice held only derision.

My lids lifted to the vampire. About an eight-foot gap separated us—in the form of Lauren's cage.

His lips pulled back, fangs slid out, and a high peel of laughter rolled over me. "You're so big. I'll bet you're full of juicy goodness." A line of phlegm trailed over his lips and marched across his chin in a procession of spit.

At a guess, I'd have said he hadn't fed in a while, but that brought him no sympathy from me. Gripping the bars harder, my lips pulled back to release the snarl his nearness induced.

"Oh, fudge." Lauren stumbled to her feet. Her palms lifted, to me more than the vampire. "No, no ..."

All amusement vanished from his face. Only a cold hardness confronted me in its place. "I shall look forward to bleeding you dry."

At the threat, and his tone, a small spasm tugged at my shoulder muscles.

"Ignore him." Lauren's voice came out a hiss.

The prickle at the base of my skull warned me I'd yet to regain full control.

"Please ... don't wind him up." Lauren's words carried a tone of desperation.

I forced myself to focus on the young female.

"It's not worth it," she murmured. "*He's* not worth it. Let me show you where they've put your friend."

My gaze flicked to the vampire one more time, before I urged away the tension in my jaw.

I studied my space while I moved along the iron rods, my awkward and slow inching allowing ample time for it. To my right, the stone of the ceiling extended into a solid wall—exterior, I presumed—but only bars held me in on the other three sides.

In a cell behind me, another female sat huddled into a ball. Although her arms cocooned her entire body, she stared up toward a spot in a corner of her cage, and words that couldn't even be classed loud enough for whispers tumbled past her lips.

I swung my gaze back to Lauren.

She lifted her shoulders at my raised eyebrow, mumbled, "Witch, I think."

Nine paces to my left brought me to the front of my own cage, where peering out did little to alleviate any concerns I had about our predicament.

Beyond my bars, about seven feet of empty space separated my cage from another. To its right, stood another cage, with a third next to it, and a fourth beside that. Even with my face pressed against my barrier, I couldn't decipher how many enclosures stretched off to the right.

To my left, I figured there had to be two or three more cages, before they altered course, shooting off at a right angle, stopping at a steel double doorway almost straight ahead.

"That cage over there," Lauren said.

My head swung back round, and I followed the point of the finger she'd extended through her own bars, toward a cage beside the one across from hers. Even with nothing more than metal columns to block my view, I couldn't make out Kyle within.

I searched harder through my gritty vision. "You sure?"

"I saw them drop him down, right before they put you in yours."

A quick check of the cage in front of me showed nothing but a pair of yellow eyes glowering back from the shadowed depths of the lined cube. "You know what's in that one?" I asked, inclining my chin.

"She's a shifter."

"A ... shifter?" *Jesus*. I rubbed a hand over my face. "She? *She's* a shifter?"

Lauren's head bobbed in my periphery. "Keeps shifting all the time, though. From human to panther, then back again"—her finger did a circling motion—"then back again."

Panther? I guessed that explained why I couldn't see her in the darkness. "What about in there?" I indicated the one between her and Kyle's cage.

"Werewolf."

The whip of my head toward her jarred my neck, and sparks flashed at the back of my eyes. "Have you seen him?" I blinked the light show away.

She turned toward me with a defiant lift of her chin—the kind that came naturally to teenagers. "'Course I have."

I tried to control my pulse as it attempted to surge. "He wouldn't happen to have blond hair, by any chance ... would he?" I peered across the aisle again, straining my eyes to see the ball of male, but looked back as Lauren's head shook.

"He's got dark hair." Her gaze rose to my head. "Darker than yours."

My eyebrows scrunched together. "Have you seen any blond werewolves here?" I switched from clutching the front of my cage, to clinging onto the bars between me and the young girl as I stared down at her. "Any at all. Young. As blond as you."

"You can't see him from here."

Needing to check for myself, I clanged back against the bars, a small growl rolling out of me when my eyes proved to lack periscope abilities.

"He's all the way down there." Eyes wide, Lauren pointed behind her. "'Round that corner."

I forced calmness into my tone. "Do you know if he's still alive?"

"Define alive." Her mouth opened and closed at my glare. "Sometimes he looks alive. Other times?" She shrugged. "I'm not so sure."

I let out a low groan and brushed up my hair, ignoring the ache in my shoulders at the lift of my hands.

"He wasn't supposed to be taken upstairs."

My head pressed back against the bars, as I thought of Shelley and what it would do to her if I didn't get Gabe back home in one piece.

"They only kidnapped him as bait."

"Bait?" Still leaning into the iron rods, I tipped my face to bring her into view.

"Apparently, they only took him to get the attention of another werewolf."

I pushed up and straightened. "Another wolf?"

With a nod, she curled her hands around the barrier between us. "A werewolf's been training him, they said."

"Who said?" I asked.

Her eyes rose toward the ceiling again. "Them. They've been after the one who mentors the blond wolf, but couldn't get close enough."

My frown spread across my brow like an infection, as my pulse gave a small lurch. "Why?"

"Dunno. I just know his name's Ethan something-or-other."

My jaw tightened again. Hands rubbing at my face, I blew out a breath, trying to organise the spiralling thoughts that revolved around my sudden wash of guilt.

Goddammit! They'd only brought him there to lure me.

"So ..."

At her voice, my gaze flicked back, but didn't remain on her.

"You have a name, if you're gonna be living next door to me?" she asked.

Blowing out a heaved breath, I lowered my face down to hers. "I guess you could call me Ethan something-or-other."

"Holy fudge!" Her eyes widened, and her mouth hung open for a second, or two. "I really don't think you should let them"—her gaze darted upward—"in on that."

"I doubt it will make a difference." I tracked the same route as she had. "Something tells me they already know."

14

Minutes of watching Kyle's cage didn't alter the fact that I couldn't see him, yet I refused to change my focus. "You been here long?"

Leaning back against the bars lining the front of her enclosure, Lauren had sunk to her rear, her folded knees gathered in her arms. "'Bout seven weeks ... I think." I caught her shrug. "Only two others were here then, besides me."

"That why you know so much?"

"I guess. Plus, I listen ... a lot. Mostly when *they* think I'm not." Her tone altered as if she smiled. "I pretend to be asleep, and they talk around me. Or I pretend to take longer on my bathroom breaks and press my ear to the door." A blown out breath drifted up. "Sometimes, they just talk around me, anyway, like they think I'm too dumb to understand. They're the dumb ones."

I lowered my chin, bringing her into view. "Why's that?"

Her gaze lifted to mine. "Because they can't figure out what I am."

"So, what race are you?" I cringed the second I'd outright blurted the question at her. Subtlety could have earned me more points—confirmed when her eyes chilled and she looked away.

"I'm not anything." Her words came out a quiet mumble. "I'm just me."

"If you weren't a race, they wouldn't have taken you ... right?"

She shrugged, but didn't turn back to me.

"You have ... abilities, Lauren?" I shifted around to face her.

"I'm nothing special." The sulk in her tone betrayed a youthfulness I struggled to evaluate. "I shouldn't be here."

My thigh muscles twanged when I dropped into a squat, taking myself down to her level. "How old are you, Lauren?"

No response other than a hitch of her deep breaths.

"Lauren, look at me." Although gentle, my tone held a firm undercurrent.

Chin dipped, she turned and peered up at me through the straggles of hair that flopped over her brow.

I ducked down a little more. "How old are you?"

"Sixteen."

"Jesus." I kept my whisper below her radar, but the lowered dart of her eyes told me she'd spotted the movement of my lips. "Lauren? You might not think there's anything special about you. And you might think you pass for human." I worked against the tightness in my jaw to keep my voice even. "But your scent tells me otherwise."

The slight widening to her eyes revealed her surprise. She hadn't known?

"And if I can smell it?" I pointed an index at the ceiling. "Chances are, they can, too." *Whoever 'they' are.*

She lifted her wrist to her nose and sniffed. "I don't smell of anything but me."

I kept my inhalation discreet as I drew her fragrance deep into my nostrils. Human definitely greeted me, so I understood her frustration, but an undertone of something I couldn't decode hit my senses with far greater strength. That struck one of the alien aromas off my list of detected but unidentified. I saw no point in pushing on that angle right then, though.

"Well ..." I allowed a smile to creep in, hoping to keep her calm enough to continue talking. "For someone who claims to be just me, you seem to know a lot about supernatural races."

She dropped her arm. "I read a lot."

"And you believe everything you read?" My eyebrow lifted.

"No, but I got eyes, don't I?" Her arms folded as her lips compressed. "When you've been here for as many weeks as I have? When you've seen what I have? Try telling me you don't believe after that." Her booted foot kicked up dust as she shoved a leg out straight. "It's not like I wanna believe all this stuff. I'd ... I'd rather be home ... and still flipping confused about ... stuff." Her chest heaved beneath a shuddered sigh.

I knew absolutely nothing about teenagers, less so about the female variety, but even I could recognise the onset of a stubbornness they all seemed to possess. Although her comment suggested she knew more about herself than she shared, I figured I'd do better waiting before I prodded her some more.

"Can I ask you one more question?" I asked. "If I promise it's not about you."

Her eyes did a huge roll. "Sure."

My lips twitched. "Is food ever brought down?"

"Define food."

"Morsels of edible substance."

Her eyes flicked to the side. "Define edible."

My chuckle arrived deep. "That bad, huh?"

"No." Her lips spread into a smile, the attitude back as she met my gaze again. "Worse."

A metallic clang reverberated through the space, attacking my ears as it bounced from one bar to the next, and from wall to ceiling. The double doors hit the stone walls on their in-swing. Through the opening, two males barged in.

The one on the left, with his dark hair framing even darker eyes, had to be vampire. His hip-swinging swagger showed an air of cockiness. What looked like bundled clothing trailed from his hand, and dragged through the dust coating the concrete floor.

A naked limp body that held the fine curves and scent of a female swung over the shoulder of the one on the right, concealing the second entree. Scratches and welts created a striated pattern across the flesh of the body's legs, and something akin to teeth marks had left puncture wounds in the hip visible to me.

I inhaled and, through the stench of blood, recognised werewolf and something else in the visitors. The something else smelled distinctly feline.

Lauren's head twisted around, and she glared behind her. Beneath the defiance, an element of fear peeked through. "Two go up." She sent a rapid glance my way. "Only one ever comes back down."

Pushing aside the urge to ask her to elaborate, I returned my attention to the two males striding toward my cage.

The vampire's black-filled eyes appraised me on approach, and he smiled as the duo veered to my left, to what had to be the corner cell.

Keys jangled. Metal clanked. The mechanics of a disengaging lock rang out. At my rear, the heavy thud of the carrier's feet sounded again, followed by a swing of motion cutting through air, a thud, and a barely-given grunt.

Beneath those sounds, quiet footsteps came my way.

I kept my focus on the ground, as the steps halted outside my cage. Leather shoes that had been polished to a high shine glimmered back at me. Above those, the cuffs of grey tailored trousers hung. I didn't have to lift my head to know the vampire studied me. The heavy weight of his scrutiny drew the hairs across the back of my neck to attention.

Clicks, clanks, and scuffling arrived from the cell his companion had visited, telling me he exited and locked the tossed body within. I followed his passage, made easy by the irritating squeak of his left shoe with each step, until he reached the vampire's side. A slight eye shift to the left showed scuffed white trainers beneath the hems of frayed denim. One set of breaths, and one shallow, rapid heartbeat emanated from the duo.

Although my squatted position burned through my weary tendons, I didn't give them the satisfaction of knowing my discomfort by moving.

The quiet stretched into a minute, maybe longer.

"Is this him?" The gravelled voice, and unmistakable scent of werewolf, came from the trainer-clad male.

"That's what Catherine said." More refined than the first, the speaker held a slight Irish lilt in his tone.

"This is who all the hype's about?" The voice held disbelief.

A delicate chuckle followed. "Apparently so."

The white trainers kicked up dust as the wearer shifted his weight from one foot to another. "Doesn't look like much to me."

Lauren fidgeted a little. A sideways flitter of my eyes showed me hers faced forward, and even beneath her shirt, I couldn't miss the high line of her shoulders as she sat rigid.

"Appearances can be deceiving," the Irish voice said. "Besides, I'd bet on him out-bulking you, Andrew."

"Size is irrelevant. The bigger they are, th—"

"The harder, blah, blah."

A quiet growl rumbled from the werewolf.

"Down, boy." The vampire's tone held only amusement, yet it seemed to calm his other half. "Are your legs working yet, wolf?"

My head twitched as I wondered if the question had been directed at me. I didn't look up, but it made no difference, when the vampire dropped to his haunches and brought his face to my level. I clenched my fists—my only movement besides the shift of my gaze to meet his.

The angle of his head matched my own, and a small smile tugged at the corners of his lips. "Ethan ... Holloway? If I'm not mistaken."

Other than a slight tightening to my eyes, I gave no response.

"Your reputation precedes you."

More shuffles from the white trainers exposed the one called Andrew's restlessness.

At the risk of later aches, I straightened my legs and forced myself upright, turning my attention to the werewolf. "Hey. Andrew, right?"

His head jerked back, taking his body back a step with it, before he squared his shoulders and peered up the four inches to meet my stare. Grey eyes roofed a prominent nose and a narrow chin that could have used a good razor. The vampire had been right. The wolf, in no way, competed with my six-five for size.

My lips curved into a smile, though I doubted they shared any humour with my unblinking eyes.

The appraisal I received from him in return travelled the length of my body, before heading back to my face. "You don't look so big without your shoes on."

The black dissipated to two solid balls of iris as the vampire gave an eye roll big enough to compete with Lauren's. "Idiot," he muttered. "That means he actually *is* that big."

"The bigger they are ..." Andrew said.

"Yes, ye—"

"Better make sure you're not in my way when I go down." My eyebrow lifted as I dipped my head to his level. "You wouldn't want to get squashed."

A low rumbling chuckle drew a twitch from my ears. I leaned sideways to see past the vampire and verify the source.

Lauren had been right about Kyle's quarters. From behind the bars of the third cage along, his smile beamed white in the gloom as his quiet laughter continued. "Making friend's with the locals, as usual?" A cough erupted from him as his forehead pressed to the bars, his white-knuckled grip no doubt contributing to his vertical bearing.

The vampire spun and glanced from me toward Kyle, as did the werewolf.

I shook my head at Kyle as my fists came to settle on my hips. "It's about time you stirred, sleeping beauty."

"Well ..." Hoarseness affected the volume of his voice. "I heard the party you had going on ..." He gave another tiny cough. "... wondered why I hadn't got my invite."

"You should check your junk mail more often." I ignored the avid interest we'd gained from our observers. "That's where the trash usually ends up."

His temple rolled across the metal that supported him as he swayed on his feet. Once steadied, only his gaze lifted. "You're pissed at me."

"Not yet." Maybe I'd let him in on the knowledge that I'd been their target all along—once he'd stewed a little.

"Joseph, we should go back up," Andrew said.

Kyle and I turned our attention to the werewolf, with his hand on the vampire's shoulder. So did the vampire—Joseph, I presumed.

He dipped his chin a touch. "You're right." Joseph glanced toward me and Kyle. "It's been interesting, gents. Now you're awake, I'll arrange for a meal to be sent for you both." He took a few steps before peering back. "We'll have to do this again sometime, though. You two are a hoot."

I didn't watch them walk off. My gaze remained on Kyle's. Neither of us spoke until the slam of metal sent a ringing echo through the space.

"Exactly how much shit did I get us into?" Kyle asked.

"Honestly?" I shrugged. "I'm still trying to figure that out."

With spoon poised, I stared down at the food in my bowl.

"You weren't kidding, Lauren."

"Eat around the lumps," she said.

I glanced across to Kyle, who stared at his own meal with the same kind of enthusiasm.

"It's not so bad if you avoid those," Lauren continued. "I choked on one last week."

Delivered by Andrew, the brown slosh seemed to be a cross between porridge, stew, and quite possibly vomit. As a beggar, though, I didn't get to choose, and knowing I'd need all my strength to get us out of there, I stuck in my spoon, and scooped some up.

Sniffing at it, I detected warmth that bordered on mugginess, pulses, and maybe something that could have been beef. My tongue tip took the first sample. Salt disguised the bland quality of the meal, as the soggy mush rolled around inside my mouth with the consistency of wallpaper paste.

Another peer at Kyle almost had me choking on the gunk. His screwed up expression was pretty much how I expected my own must have looked. His Adams apple made some serious dance moves as he forced a swallow.

"Mm-mm." Kyle smiled as he lifted his gaze to mine. "This is almost as good as your cooking, buddy."

I managed my own swallow before my chuckle burst out. "Be sure to eat it all up now. Or you might not get dessert."

A groan rolled from the panther's cage, and my attention shifted that way, to the flash of pale amongst the shadows. I cocked my head to the side, like it would give me a better view around the bars. Eyes narrowed, I stared harder and captured the altered form toward the back of the cell.

What had been black fur and camouflage had become flesh and visible. The very-human-looking female pushed to her feet from the floor in one fluid movement, like watching a spilling drink on rewind.

My curiosity over the race piqued my interest enough for my meal to be discarded, as I clambered up with far less dignity than she had and continued to stare.

The pale outline of her back curved into a stretch, her hands reaching to the ceiling, and her face angled upward. With the grace of a ballet dancer, her arms flowed down, and the slow, deliberate steps she took toward me lent her an air of exotica. She seemed unperturbed by her nudity as she stopped at the bars. Through loose tendrils of hair that matched the deep brown of my family and tumbled like waterfalls across her shoulders to conceal her breasts, amber eyes met mine.

To describe her as beautiful seemed a huge understatement, and as much as I wanted to show her my friendly people skills, any words of greeting clogged in my throat as I achieved nothing but gawping admiration—until my inhale caught the undesirable whiff of cat.

I snapped from my trance, rolling shoulders that had finally begun to loosen.

The shifter's lips curled into a smile, and she gave a slight jerk of her chin. "Food's getting cold, dog." Her words didn't hold the hostility I'd expected, but only a warm tone that smoothed like honey over toast.

I went to bend for my bowl, but paused at the shimmer that embraced her body as she turned away.

She took one step, two, and by the time she'd taken the third, only a black panther stalked through the cage.

Eyebrows arched, I glanced across to Kyle, who'd moved to the dividing bars. "You see that?"

"Yep." He shovelled in a spoonful of mush.

"You see how fast she—"

"Yep," he said around his full mouth. He swallowed, shifting his eyes toward me. "Cool, no?"

I wanted to shrug my indifference, but my head defied me and nodded in agreement. "Very."

As I retrieved my meal from the floor, the metal doors opened. I scooped up a spoonful, aimed it into my mouth, and watched Joseph and Andrew's approach.

Andrew's lips seemed to remain in a permanent grimace, while Joseph once again managed to look somewhat amused by me. They reached the panther's cage, turned the corner. One smile, and one scowl were tossed my way as they passed, like a poor rendition of a good-cop-bad-cop routine. The duo didn't stop walking until they reached Kyle, where they turned their backs on me.

Kyle's spoon-hand stalled mid-lift as he turned toward each of them.

I wanted to ask what they were doing, went as far as opening my mouth, but closed it at the entrance of a second pair of goons. The mousey hair and wielded dart gun identified the one who held part responsibility for my and Kyle's entrapment. Lack of fresh scents and tell-tale eyes branded the other as vampire.

With a low rumble claiming my chest, I watched them halt outside a cage on the right of the steel doors. I didn't know where I needed—wanted—to look more, and my hand came to rest around a bar as I tried to keep my focus on both parties at the same time.

The jangle of keys decided for me, and my head whipped to the right in time to see Andrew step toward the door of Kyle's cage.

Kyle lowered his bowl even farther, as I dropped mine to the floor with a clatter. "Overstayed my welcome already, have I?"

The cage door swung inward with a boot from the werewolf. He nodded his head to Kyle. "You're up."

I sensed, rather than saw, Lauren climb to her feet and turn to the happenings outside her bars, but my attention remained on Andrew and Kyle. "Where are you taking him?"

"Upstairs," Joseph said over his shoulder.

My pulse lurched as my panic almost clouded my vision. "What for?"

Andrew brought a gun that matched the vampires around in front of him—from where, I didn't know. Although he kept it pointed down, he aimed the barrel Kyle's way. "Walk." The deepness of his voice made the command sound more like a growl than a word. "Now."

Kyle hesitated less than a beat before complying. His gaze locked onto mine as he stepped out into the aisle, a million questions screaming at me from his too-calm stare.

"What are you taking him upstairs for?" I asked again. "He's barely woken." I pressed into the corner of my cage, like being closer would enhance my chance of answers. "Take me—"

Kyle's quiet snarl cut off my words—a warning that I'd been about to cross an unacceptable boundary. He probably still thought he'd gotten us into the mess, and he'd see my offer to take his place as nothing more than an insult. His gaze stayed on mine as he walked past with the two males at his back.

I clenched my fists, and my jaw tightened. I followed him alongside the bars, willing him with my stare to reconsider. Whatever they wanted him for, it couldn't be good. Stalled by the left corner of my restriction, I let out a low growl as Kyle turned away and headed off toward the doors.

Although my gaze didn't waver from my pack-mate, the spectators that gathered at the forefront of each enclosure didn't go unnoticed—not by me, and not by Kyle, if his head turns gave any indication.

The nearer he got to the exit, the more my frustration mounted, and the harder my soaring heartbeat forced the blood past my ears. My mind filled with static energy. I pushed my fisted hands against my temples like I could somehow stem the noise.

Within seconds, Kyle had stepped through the doors, and they swung shut behind his departure. Just as quick, the two vampires left behind pulled out keys. They unlocked the cage they'd stopped outside, and the occupant joined them without complaint. Beneath his chestnut hair, his black eyes swirled as he sought me out, and the chuckle he shared held only menace before his fangs shot down and he turned with his guards.

I dropped to my haunches, arms bunched tight around my pounding head as Lauren's earlier words filled my every cell with dread.

Two go up. Only one ever comes back down.

15

The surge of my pulse slowed enough for me to function, but didn't stay that way with the leap to my feet. I paced to the back corner of my cage, pressed my forehead to the wall. The rough stone scratched at my healing head wound until the scent of my blood announced its reopening. I closed my eyes, pushed harder against the surface, like something else to focus on would help me deal with the pounding inside my chest.

"He might be okay," Lauren said behind me.

I whirled to face her, swallowed the snarl attempting to break free. "No offense, but you wouldn't understand."

I strode back to the front of the cage, skidding when my left sole hit gunk that had spilled from my bowl. I kicked out at the steel as I righted myself with a growl, and the clash of metals, when the booted bowl hit the bars, rang like an alarm through the space.

The witch in the next cell jumped, jerking aside as the remaining dish sloshed through to attack her, before scuttling back to cower in the rear corner of her cube.

I should have apologised, wanted to, but rationality seemed a little out of grasp right then. My right shoulder slammed into the front of my barrier as I lifted my arms again to envelope my head—another attempt to block all the shit, as well as every face that had been turned my way since Kyle walked out.

"It's my job to look out for them all." My murmur tumbled from my lips.

"Why?" Lauren asked.

I dropped my arms, frowning down at her. "Who else have they got to watch their backs?"

"It's not your—"

I whipped away, and another disjointed walk returned me to the wall. Culpability pumped through me at the speed of a tornado, and the temptation to pummel the solid structure overwhelmed me, but I'd be no good to anyone without my fists.

I'd knowingly let Kyle go into that hotel room with a stranger. "I should have paid closer attention, dammit!"

Instead, I'd been too busy feeding my own needs.

Hands bunched so tight the tendons of my forearm threatened to snap, I stalked to the front of my enclosure again, and stared out at those still watching.

The werewolf occupying the cage beside Kyle's showed himself for the first time. Beneath almost black hair, his eyes aimed my way, while his toe kicked against the base of his bars. Sympathy gleamed from him—whether for Kyle's possible demise, or for me as Kyle's pack brother, I couldn't be sure.

I turned away from him, skimmed over the glowing eyes peering out from the realms of the panther's enclosure and onto the far row of attention I'd attracted.

In the cage beside the feline who'd been discarded by Andrew, a werewolf—judging by his scent—stared back through curtains of dirty blond. The high glisten of his eyes, while offering understanding, revealed relief that someone other than himself had been chosen to venture upstairs.

Orbs the shade of freshly cut grass shone from the next one along, as another male appraised me from beneath pale ginger curls. Canine undertones emanated from his body, yet lacked the familiar essence of werewolf, rendering his race unrecognisable.

The neighbouring cage stood empty, a reminder of the vampire who'd evacuated his quarters to accompany Kyle.

Ignoring the raging storm in my mind, my gaze flitted past and fell upon a slight female. *Witch?* She stood far enough away to provide distance for herself from the vampire who leaned close to their division.

With exception for the latter, every pair of eyes held the same concern, a unified show of empathy.

For me?

Why?

What the hell did they do with them upstairs?

I pointed a finger at the werewolf across from me. "Tell me what we're doing here." My hands slid around to grip the bars when he didn't respond. "What have they taken him up there for?"

His hands slid into his pockets as he averted his eyes. A step back merged him with shadow.

I turned to the other watchers. "What are they doing up there?"

Headshakes preceded the shunning bodies as they one by one skulked to the recesses of their pens.

What the hell was wrong with them? Were they not in the same situation as me and Kyle? My hands and jaw tightened as I verged on loss of control. "Anybody?"

Evidently, their compassion only extended so far. With a growl I made no effort to rein in, I whipped my hands free of the metal rods and took two paces to Lauren's cage.

"Lauren, if you know why they've taken him upstairs, now would be a really grand time to tell me."

"Taking it out on the girl will help no one," a voice said to my left.

I spun to snarl at the female, who'd once again shifted from her panther form.

My warning seemed to have little effect on her, as she continued to study me through her tumbling hair. "And losing control will not help your friend, either." Even her tone held the same smoothness it had earlier.

"He might be all right," Lauren said.

My glare kicked back in at her repeated words.

Her fingers twisted in the buttonholes of her shirt. "Your other friend was."

"My other ..." I marched across to tower over her. "Gabe? I thought you didn't—"

"He went up four times." She held up her left hand to show the number with her tiny fingers. "Came back down four times."

"In bad condition, you said."

She nodded. "But I think that was only because of the bites. Once they give him the stuff, he seems to wake up again after a while."

"Bites?" My brow scrunched until it hooded my eyes. "What bites?" I looked from her to the shifter, panic stoppering my throat. "What ... stuff?"

"Vam ..." Lauren's voice trailed off, when the shifter's glowing eyes flickered toward her.

My teeth risked shattering with the pressure I exerted upon them. I blinked away what I thought I'd heard and hoped I'd been wrong. It took only moments to realise I hadn't.

I slid my hands to the nape of my neck and linked my fingers as I paced away. My raised elbows hit the wall. I squeezed my eyes closed. "No, no, no, no." The words spilled out on a jumbled whisper. "It's not possible." I dropped my arms, spun back to Lauren. "That's not possible."

My imploration had to be clear in the stare I sent to the shifter. "She must have it wrong. A were can't survive a vampire bite. Any race knows that."

The female held my gaze steady. "They appear to have created an anti-venom."

What the—? "A cure? Against ... vampire bites?"

Her head dipped a touch.

"Wh ..." My arms flipped up with my shrug. "Why the hell—"

"Maybe the answer lies in your young friend." As the cat tilted her head a little, her dark hair brushed lower against the right side of her abdomen. "The pup is the only one they've used it on."

Crashes invaded my mind with the ferocity of a storm, as I absorbed her words. "So ... Gabe is getting bitten ...

and then they're sticking needles of some kind of anti-shit into ...." My hands fisted against the tremble that emanated from my spiralling incomprehension. "What the fuck kind of crap are they sticking him with to achieve that?"

My slipping control vibrated through me and hit my ears at the volume of a swarm of killer wasps, yet the feline never once looked away. "I don't have all the answers for you."

"It's probably made with their blood," Lauren murmured.

I broke free of the shifter's focus and turned to her, restraining myself enough to ask, "Why?"

Her fingers continued to fiddle with her buttonholes, and she still tapped the toe of her left boot against the concrete floor. "That's how they usually make antiviral stuff, right?" Her eyes darted away before she looked back to me. "Use some of the disease ..." She shook her head as though to clear her thoughts. "Use the blood of a carrier who isn't affected by the disease because it contains the antibodies ... right? Isn't that what they teach us in science?"

My eyebrows battled my deepening frown as they attempted to lift. I turned back to the shifter. "They've created an anti-venom from vampires' blood? How the hell—"

"Look around you, wolf." The feline's chin did a delicate inclination to the left and right. "It's not as though they have a short supply. I see two from my position alone—three, if the one they took returns."

I let out a low groan. "Fuck." The overnight bristles peeking out from my chin scratched as I rubbed my palms across my face. "But ... why? To what purpose? And why Gabe?"

"The purpose is obvious. To keep him alive."

"But, why the hell would he be getting bitten to begin? How? What reason could they have?" Another groan announced my mounting frustration. My fists tapped together as my thoughts rampaged but conjured no plausible explanation.

I threw my hands up. "I don't get it. I don't fucking get it. Not what we're doing here. Or why Gabe's being bitten, only to save him—"

"He's no good to them dead," Lauren said.

I scowled down at her, but tried to curb the expression, when she kicked at the floor again.

Her huge eyes lifted back to me when I didn't speak. "They used him ... remember I told you that? He was only brought here to bait you. A dead lure is no good to anyone, right?"

Another mystery I couldn't solve. What the heck did they want with me? All their talk about my reputation, and shit, and I had no idea of their motive, or reasoning, or even what bloody standing they referred to. Despite my silent questions, no answers screamed back at me. Would venturing upstairs provide enlightenment?

"If they never intended Gabe to go upstairs, why do so? What changed their minds? Why? What the—" I leaned in close to the bars as I pushed aside pride, ready to plead with the cat if I had to. "Tell me, have you been upstairs?"

She stared back at me for seconds, an unreadable expression within her amber eyes, before she gave a single nod.

"Then, you must know why we're here."

Further moments of quiet preceded her second nod. "That doesn't mean I understand it." For the first time a small crack showed in her tough exterior as her irises flared to a rich gold. "There can be no reasoning for this ... abomination."

"Abomin—" I blew out a breath. "What abomination?"

"Behave, on occasion, as animals ... and they believe that earns them the right to treat us like animals." The fire continued to burn in her steady stare.

"Who?" I rubbed at my brow like I could iron out the creases that enhanced my headache. "Why? How?"

"Think about it, wolf. Those upstairs do not need to kill us. As nature insists, we do a fine job of that, ourselves."

"What the hell does that mean?"

"You see a vampire, what happens?" Her eyes seemed to plead with me for comprehension, as though willing me to grasp her meaning without further words. "You attack, no?"

"I'd never met one until"—*when?*—"yesterday. And he attacked me. My retaliation was self-defence."

"Instinctual dislike and distrust works both ways, though, wouldn't you agree?"

I shrugged—lack of experience meant I didn't have an answer.

"What about the one over there?" Her eyes flitted to the right, toward the one beyond Lauren's cage. "What do you feel when you look at him?"

I followed her stare until my own hit the fugly male in his cell. My eyes narrowed, the hairs across my neck bristled, and a low rumble began in my chest. I told myself his earlier threats held responsibility for my reaction and tore myself away to look back at the shifter.

A small smile curved her lips, like I'd given her confirmation, but only for a split second before her golden orbs hardened again. "Now, imagine being face-to-face with that level of natural animosity. Even confronted by me, you feel somewhat repulsed, yes? Would you be so happy to communicate if forced to be nearer?" I went to shrug, but stopped as she said, "I think not, wolf. Just as I have no inclination to be closer to you." Like a water current travelling beneath her surface flesh, her body rippled, and tightness possessed her face. "What they're feeding us here is barely suitable for consumption. Few have managed to eat. We are all hungry—beyond hungry. Even the vampires here have not been fed. Those who have eaten conquered their own meals." Her hands lifted, and pale fingers encompassed the bars before her, her face coming to rest between one of the gaps. "Bring two starving, opposing supernatural races together, and the outcome can only go one way."

Two go up. Only one ever comes back down.

My pulse picked its tempo back up again. "But ... why? What can they get out of it?" *Apart from to reduce the supernatural population?*

"Do you really need me to spell this out for you, wolf?"

Apparently so. "Tell me."

A few beats passed before she responded. "They're pitting us."

"They ..." I frowned, rubbing at the dangerously fast thud of my pulse beneath my ear. "Oh, Jesus."

She nodded.

I stared hard at her as the solidity of her form wavered and altered, watched her spin away from me to stalk into the gloom as a cat, and as my mind caught up, it took my breaths along on a ride that could have given the rapids a run for their money.

"They're making us fight." My panicked body turned toward Lauren. "But ... why?"

Lauren provided no further answers, and my rationality kicked in, demanding I cut her some slack. With the shifter's incommunicado language barrier preventing conversation—I'd never been too good at translating meows—I skulked to the rear of my cage to try and figure some stuff out on my own.

At the same time, I needed to stem the too-loud timpani speed of my heartbeat. Regulating my breathing would have help with that, too, I guessed.

The scratchy surface of the wall dug into my shoulder blades as I leaned back against it and prodded my head where it had met with the pavement. A deep chill emanated through my body, but whether the cool concrete beneath my butt caused it, I couldn't be sure.

I'd spent as much of my life with Kyle as I had my own family—Kyle *was* kin, dammit, no more, no less—and far too much time had passed since his summoning.

Face tipped up, I closed my eyes, taking slow breaths in and out. My bare toes curled against the coarse floor. Too many thoughts, scenarios, emotions tore through me, hindering my self-calming efforts—as did my hands that clenched and unclenched in response, where they hung over my drawn up knees.

I could no longer bring myself to look at the double doors. Fear that it might not be Kyle who returned constricted my chest—like a part of me would be torn away with him should he come to a bad end.

Another flex and un-flex of my fingers drew the tendons taut through my forearms. I blew out a slow exhale, my nostrils flaring wide with the following inhalation.

As much as I believed in Kyle's abilities concerning self-preservation, the strength of the vampire in the Witchurch gulley still burned hot. The idea Kyle didn't match me for power came not from stubborn pride, but from fact. Nobody in the pack could beat me in a one-on-one—probably not even Dad since he'd hit his fifties—so I knew, without doubt, Kyle would offer little problem to the vampire.

Yet, his opponent hadn't returned, either.

Vampires held the advantage in speed, pure power, and an unnatural focus—from what I'd seen of them, anyway. Hunger would, undoubtedly, lend the beings determination, also. Adrenaline could be added into the mix, but would an absent heartbeat allow its production? Surely, with no pump, the hormone would be unable to surge through the vampire's bloodstream.

Unlike in werewolves.

Could the force that powered us in times of need be our upper hand against them?

For the first time since Kyle disappeared upstairs, I allowed an element of hope to creep in, until I recalled the other problem that came with vampires: their fangs, and their venom.

I gave a low growl at myself. Tried to tell my negativity to fuck off. Did werewolves not have decent dentals? Could we not cause serious damage ourselves?

Hell, yeah. I'd picked up more than a few pieces of leftovers after one, or another, of the pack had conquered in a fight.

My breathing hitched to a temporary halt as I processed that information, as I decoded the detail to find what had faltered my stride.

Dad and Connor had killed a vampire. Why would they not have faced the struggle I had when confronted by one?

Because there were two of them? I didn't see that to be it.

My mind clicked as the cogs shifted into position, and my retained breath seeped out past my lips.

Had vampires evolved in strength over the years?

The wall snagged at my hair as I shook my head. I preferred my first explanation.

All I knew for sure was they *could* be beaten—somehow. Dad and Connor had proven that.

With renewed optimism, my fists tightened. Each one jigged with small pumping actions as I mentally spurred Kyle on. My lips moved to the rhythm of *come on*, like my will alone could bring a better result.

About a billion mantra mumbles later, the scuff of shoes hit the floor on the other side of the steel doors.

My lips paused in prayer. My steadied breath hastened, as did my pulse. Every muscle in my body tensed.

The doors slammed open.

An inhalation would have told me who returned—just one—yet my brain refused to relay the action, as if afraid of the discovery.

One set of steps on the right, another on the left. The first held density that the other pair lacked, like they accommodated an additional burden.

My mind flashed to the feline who'd been carried in earlier, her lifeless body slung like a sack over Andrew's shoulder. That told me whoever they'd brought back had to be in bad shape if they warranted the assistance.

Open your eyes, chicken shit, and find out.

Stalling my breaths, I lifted my lids and scanned over the entrees. Andrew on the left had his scowl firmly in place, as though pissed he'd run out of toilet tissue. The still sharp creases in the grey trousers of the one on the right identified Joseph as the carrier of the body.

When understanding kicked in, that they hadn't paused outside the vampire's cage, I allowed my gaze to shift higher.

The sight of the russet-coated wolf hanging from Joseph's shoulder hit me with the impact of a bulldozer.

I may have pleaded with any higher god that happened to be listening for Kyle to return, but I hadn't prepared myself for seeing him look as dead as if he'd failed in the fight.

Time slowed down, the movements of the approaching men decelerated, and for just a split second, my body ceased to function.

No pulse patterned my ears.

No breaths lifted my chest.

I may well have blanked out.

As though I'd moved on autopilot, I found myself at the bars with the cold iron pressed against my cheek. "Kyle." The word scratched at my constricted throat on exit, sounding like it had been spoken by a distant stranger.

"Aww, you've been worried about him." For the first time, I received a smile from Andrew, though his eyes held only a harsh glint of chilled mirth. "You hear that, Joseph?"

A low thunder-like rumble filled my ears, but I gave Andrew no response.

Each of Joseph's steps brought Kyle nearer. I attached my sights to the unmoving form, searching for any sign that he breathed, or for the pattern of his heartbeat.

With the thickening of vocal muscles, my throat knotted until my breaths came short.

"That's sweet, Ethan." Andrew rounded the corner, passing the first couple bars of my cage before halting. "Do you ... do you two guys have something going on?" His laughter bounced off the stone walls.

Joseph turned at the shifter's cage, and the twist of his body brought Kyle's muzzle into view.

The rolling storm in my chest heightened in volume. Vibrations spread through me like something possessed.

His jaw hung slack, as did his tongue through parted teeth, and his forelegs even lower than those. Rocking from side to side, Kyle's head swayed in time to the rhythm of Joseph's gait. His auburn coat appeared lank and matted. Redness accentuated his natural colouring, and I knew from the smell it had come from the weeping of his own wounds.

"Oh, Jesus." My whisper portrayed the panicked desperation my body warned could soon become rage. "Kyle?" Deeper, louder, my call received no reply.

"What is he to you?" Andrew ducked in to soil the visual of my pack-buddy. "Your mate, or something?"

A low growl escaped as I sidestepped to lose his mug and recapture Kyle.

Another humourless laugh rolled from him. "Goddamn, I'm right."

"Andrew." Joseph stopped outside Kyle's empty cage. "Do you think you could open this door sometime today? This wolf is no lightweight."

"Sure, sure." His face bobbed in front of mine, and he sent me another smile before turning away to unlock Kyle's cell.

I moved as close as my restriction would allow. "What happened to him?"

Although I'd aimed the question at Joseph, Andrew pushed the door open and headed back my way. "You really are worried about him."

I kept my eyes on the vampire, as he lowered Kyle to the floor and placed my pack brother into shadow. A low thud signalled the hit of his head against concrete.

"Did he get bitten?" I asked.

Joseph left Kyle way too blended with darkness for my liking, and stepped from within the cage.

Held by some kind of invisible force, I couldn't look away from where my mind knew the prone wolf to be, as the too familiar drum of my heart beat out its panic again.

Seeing Kyle across the shoulder of the vampire had been bad enough. Not being able to see him at all hitched my breath until sweat beaded my brow.

"How badly is he injured?" Hoarseness revealed my emotions, yet I didn't care.

"This is just too cute." Andrew moved across, blocking my view of Kyle's cage, his lips twisted into a sick interpretation of a smile. "You've seriously got some strange kind of soft spot for him, don't you?"

I tried to look around him, to Joseph. "Tell me. Is he going to be okay?"

"Hey, Joseph." Andrew glanced at the vampire as he tossed him the keys to Kyle's cage. "Maybe we should do some switching around." He turned back to me, took a step closer. "You'd like that, wouldn't you? Arrange for your mate to move in next door? I reckon the bars are wide enough." His chin jerked to the side, before his eyes resettled on me. "You could keep each other happy, no?"

My shoulders stiffened at the taunting tone of his voice more than the words, and I squared to stare back at him. "I asked what happened to him," squeezed past my clenched jaw.

"Which part would you like to know?" Although he had to lift his face to meet my gaze, he still ducked his head a little and peered up. "The bit where he refused to change, so we helped him along?" He shifted forward a little.

I ground my teeth, as I willed my lips not to retaliate. Flames of fury licked faster throughout me, but my eyes never once strayed from his. *Come closer. I dare you.*

"Or did you want me to tell you about how he got his butt kicked by the vampire until he lost consciousness?"

The tightening of my hands stretched the muscles through my forearm to elbow, and higher to my shoulders, while my unwavering focus absorbed every slight movement he made.

Andrew's chuckle bubbled out like air trapped in a drain. "Or did you mean how we watched the vampire chow down on your pal like he was the best damn meal he'd ever tasted?" His right foot shuffled his body nearer, as he twisted and glanced over his shoulder. "Hey, Jo—"

My arm launched for him through the bars.

I gripped the back of his neck.

His head spun back around as I hauled him toward me with the power of an overwrought gorilla.

I snarled as his face smashed against the bars separating us.

Shock registered in his wide eyes before his expression rumpled.

My lips drew back, and my roar rolled free as a rough shove of my hand urged him backward.

He opened his mouth, and a small protesting squeak burst out.

Like my arm held the tension of a powerful bungee, I dragged him forward again.

The crash of his face vibrated a hum through the entire enclosure. Cartilage exploded like a firecracker. Andrew's nose collapsed. Blood sprayed to decorate the bars.

A high sheen of nothingness took over the agony his eyes had portrayed.

Another thrust off the metal rods, another yank toward me—again, and again. The third collision ruptured the flesh covering his snout. A fourth, and the iron gouged into his cheek. By the fifth, his body kept upright only by my hand, his forehead impact rendered him definitely screwed.

In some primal need to be certain, I drove my other hand through and grasped him by the throat. The rapid and sharp twist jerked his head to an unnatural angle. I'd thought his nose bridge breaking to be loud, but it paled beneath the boomed crack of his neck.

My hands whipped away from him like contact for longer than necessary could taint me somehow.

Gravity took him straight down.

His landing sent a *thunk* around the underground chamber like a message to any who listened. I'd no hard evidence, no facts, but the clawing guilt that they'd gone through someone I cared about to get to me for a second time screamed all the truth I needed inside my mind.

Only once dense stillness settled around me did I register the harsh rise and fall of my chest as my breaths battled within, and the ripple of my lips releasing my snarls. Only then did I focus past the haze of tunnel vision through which I'd seen nothing but the one who spoke of Kyle's plight with such mocking.

I stared down at what I'd done, at the crumpled and bloodied mess on the floor. What had been his face had already begun a slow spillage, and it appeared garish against the grey concrete. The hoods sheltering my eyes pulled back a little, yet my pulse continue to rocket my blood through its pipelines.

To say I'd never killed would be an outright lie. Before Andrew, though, not one of those deaths had been caused by anything other than self-defence, preservation of the pack, or protection of one my pack brothers, or sister. Never had I snapped over a mere taunting. Dad had taught me better than that, and the loss of control, however momentary, terrified the shit out of me.

I tore my gaze away and lifted it to Joseph.

He studied me with interest in his eyes, a hint of amusement in his lips. "It would appear Catherine was right about you, after all."

My hands restarted their flex-un-flex game.

Joseph stepped a little closer—not too close. "If you can do this from in there." His hand gestured toward the dead werewolf before pointing at me. "Imagine what you could do unleashed."

The drowning racket within my chest subsided a little. I watched him take a round-about route to Andrew's feet, where he stooped down and wrapped his fingers around an ankle.

"Of course, Catherine's bound to be a little peeved. You just killed one of her men." Joseph straightened, elevating Andrew's leg with the rise of his body, and sent me a smile that could be considered nothing short of conspiratorial. "I like you, though, so I'll put in a good word for you. Tell her he provo—"

"I need no favours from a vampire." My voice arrived too level—a damn sight more even than it should have, considering the tremors racing beneath the surface of my flesh.

If I'd offended Joseph, it didn't show. His smile broadened before he turned and walked away. Behind him, the corpse I'd created painted a crimson trail in its wake.

Even once they'd reached the doors, the scent of blood remained strong. I inhaled, and followed the path my senses paved, until I discovered the werewolf's DNA coating my forearms and clothing. As the doors clanged their departure, a quick swipe of my hand found more of Andrew on my face.

"Congratulations, wolf." The shifter's soft tones seemed out of place in the blackness of my mind.

I raised my gaze from my palms.

"Not only have you just shown them exactly what you're capable of." She jerked her chin to the left, toward where I knew Kyle lay. "You have just revealed to them your biggest weakness."

When I first absorbed the shifter's words, an invisible substance found home in my oesophagus and blocked any comings and goings my body attempted through there. On top of that, the horror in Lauren's eyes every time she sent a fleeting glance my way pierced my heart.

I guessed she had every right to look terrified. In her mind, I must have gone from somewhat friendly and approachable, to a monster who'd killed with his bare hands.

I'd had better days, for certain.

Wallowing, however, didn't fit well with me, so I put myself to a more constructive task: ridding my body of dead werewolf remnants.

Using my T-shirt as body cloth left me with only half my attire, but I'd nobody to blame other than myself. Besides, I had a strong preference for shirtless if it cancelled out my gory appearance.

Andrew's blood stank up my shirt. With each wipe, the grey jersey altered to resemble tie-dye. Once certain I'd removed every last trace, I tossed the cloth into the far corner and crossed to the front of my cage.

Lauren gave a small shoulder jerk. I frowned at the effect my closeness had on her, and how drastically my behaviour had provoked her change. I wanted to look at her, to somehow placate, or reassure, but my mind insisted she wouldn't thank me if I did either.

Instead, I focused on Kyle's cage, until a murmur from Lauren drew me from my self-shaming thoughts.

"He hasn't moved yet."

A dip of my head showed her facing the same direction as me. "Thought you couldn't see in the dark, Lauren."

Movement beneath her shirt suggested stiffening, or a shrug—I couldn't be sure which. "I can't. I just know he hasn't moved."

I frowned. "How?"

"Just do." She continued facing forward.

I went back to staring at Kyle for minutes, until my frustration crept back at seeing only dimness. "Wake up, dammit," I muttered, fingers curling around to grip the bars. In a moment of idiocy, I grappled with the bloody metal, grunting as I hauled, tugged, and shoved, as though I held the power to pry them farther apart.

"You won't move them."

My chest heaved beneath my efforts, as I stared back down at Lauren.

She didn't turn to me. "They're too thick. I already tried." With her own hands wrapped around them, she pulled a little, as though to prove her point. "Too strong ... see?"

"You ... already tried?" My gaze skimmed over the puniness of her arms even her clothing couldn't disguise, and I almost laughed. "You tried to bend the bars?"

"I just said so, didn't I?" A shift of her head brought her eyes around toward me. "So, you can quit wasting energy on something that's not gonna happen."

The moment broke my plummeting mood, and my lips curved into a smile. With a rough double-handed rub at my hair, I turned back toward Kyle and spotted shadows dancing in his neighbouring cage, while a scuffle announced motion within.

"Hey," I said.

The werewolf in there stepped forward a little, his gaze boring into me, as though he struggled to figure out my intent. Either that, or he had speech problems.

"Hey," I said again. "Can you see him from there? Can you see my friend?"

His eyes flitted to his left then back toward me, and he gave a slow nod.

I urged my face between the bars, though not far before the too narrow opening stalled me. "Is he breathing? Are you close enough to see that?"

He responded with a shrug. I thought that all I'd get, until he turned toward the division and lowered into a squat. His head pressed against the rods. What I assumed to be his hand nudged through into Kyle's space.

The wolf straightened, and held up a finger. "Gimme a minute."

My eyebrow lifted at his heavily accented voice. At a guess, I'd have placed him from somewhere toward Norfolk way.

He blended with murkiness, and I peered harder, wishing for even a sliver of light to see.

"I can't reach him." Two deep breaths followed, putting strain on his words. "He's too far." Footsteps followed and his face bobbed through the gloom. "Sorry. I tri—"

A jerked dragging sound from his left took both our attentions, and my heart thudded when Kyle appeared from the shadowed depths of his enclosure.

Lauren gave a small gasp, but I couldn't tear my eyes away from Kyle while his body shuffled across the concrete as though wound by a winch. "Kyle?" No response.

The dark haired werewolf stooped low, slid his hands between the bars, and patted at Kyle's rump. "Hey." Another prod. "Hey, you okay?" Still nothing. The wolf peered at me. "He's out for the count." He pushed to his feet, scratching at his head as he frowned. "How'd he move?"

"He's breathing, right?"

"Yeah, he's definitely breathing." His fingers continued to riff through his hair. "I just don't get how he moved."

I rubbed my hands across my own head and closed my eyes for a second, as I allowed my relief a chance to wash through me.

"I do not wish to intrude upon your moment," the shifter said.

I lifted my lids, my eyes narrowing as I studied her, back at her bars. "But ..."

"But, you are getting ahead of yourself."

"Meaning?"

"You smell his wounds." Her chin lifted toward her left. "What if the wolf you killed told the truth?"

My jaw tightened. "Then, Kyle's been bitten."

"How long do you think that gives him?" She blew at hair hanging across her features, seemed irritated by it for the first time. "I would imagine, not long."

"But ..." I tried to peer around far too many bars, toward the end of the underground chamber, with thoughts of Gabe. Would they treat Kyle as they had him? I turned back toward the feline. "Do you think—"

"I wouldn't begin to make guesses, if I were you." She smiled, and the expression lent a honey tone to her eyes. "The only thing I know with certainty is they have a different set of rules for you and your friends than they have for all the others in here. So, tell me ..." Her lips remained curved, her eyes holding an intensity that seemed to see through to my soul. "What is so special about you all? Or more to the point, what is so special about ... *you*?"

"Nothing."

"Bullshit!"

Her expletive caught me off guard enough for a small laugh to escape. "I'm no different to him." I pointed to the werewolf beside her. "Maybe they've made a mistake."

She shook her head, and her hair brushed either side of her abdomen like two halves of balance scales. "They've brought nobody in here, *yet*, that they didn't need. As soon as one is killed, it takes only days—sometimes less— before another takes their place. They know what each of us is ... with the exception of the girl." Her gaze moved to Lauren and back to me. "And the girl has no cause to lie to you. If they sought you for a reason, that reason has to be a good one. So, if I were you, I'd start thinking long and hard about what their motive might be."

My amusement nudged aside with each of her words.

"I'd also start praying for them to bring the anti-venom for your friend—however much the idea might repulse you. Without it, I don't like his chances."

The female's soothsayer-ish ways grated on my nerves a little. I could only take so much continuous enlightenment, and I'd already filled my quota for the day.

She stared at me, like the answers to her questions would appear within my features if only she looked hard enough. I repaid her scrutiny, while hunting through my brain for what kind of appeal I held for the ones upstairs.

Given the nature of what seemed to be happening, it had to boil down to my physical abilities. Had I been in that many fights to warrant the interest? Sure, I'd been attacked, and retaliated to the point the instigator wished they'd never bothered—mostly by other werewolves who'd tried their luck when trespassing in our borough. Maybe the fact I'd never lost a fight before I got accosted by that damn vampire had somehow reached their attention? Who the hell knew?

Who the hell knew *how*, seeing as I'd not been brought up as a bragger?

As though joined by a powerful psychic connection, my and the shifter's head turned toward the double doors at the same time, as the werewolf spun to face that way. A split second later, the scuff of a foot landed beyond the steel, and in half that time again, the barrier swung open to reveal the blonde who'd deceived Kyle.

Hands fisting, I tilted my head a little to the left, as she paused in the backlit doorway like she awaited applause.

In limpet jeans, and a shirt that came with the same clingy effect, she placed her hands on her hips. She scanned our area, and once her gaze landed on me, her face lowered slightly.

The werewolf receded into the rear of his cube, although he couldn't possibly have seen who'd arrived—maybe my body language had tipped him. Even the panther showed her willingness to leave me to my own demise as she mirrored his retreat.

Ahead, one dainty pump-clad foot lifted. The vampire seemed to be choosing a spot around the dried river of blood before placing her sole down. Her other foot received the same consideration, and she hopped across to the other side of the dark crimson trail. Once she had a rhythm going, her gaze locked back onto mine for the remainder of her approach.

She came to a stop beyond my bars, her proximity telling me I offered her no concern, and her eyes did their crazy shit.

My brow twitched. *She looks really pissed.*

"You killed one of my team." She slid a hand through the bars, poked a finger into my bare chest. "Now you owe me."

I stared down at her, and my lifted eyebrow up a little higher. "Lady, I owe you nothing."

"Lady?" The roiling of her eyes and curl of her lip suggested I'd offended her with a title common amongst humans.

I reined in my smile, ducked my head a little. "Trust me, the term was not meant as any kind of endearment."

Her eyebrows did a jig. "So, tell me. What do you intend to do to repair the damage you've caused?"

"Are you for real?" I loosened the tightness invading my jaw. "You kidnap a young kid I know, and treat him like crap, pitting him against vampires ..."

The black of her eyes reformed into their solid circles, and she glanced along the cages toward where I knew Gabe lay.

"He's barely even an adult, for fuck's sake, and you allow him to be bitten ..."

Her eyes held surprise when she returned to me.

"Then you do exactly the same to him,"—I jabbed a finger in Kyle's direction—"and have the nerve to ask how *I'm* going to repay your fucking loss of one man?"

"But your men are not dead, Ethan. I have allowed them to live—*assisted* in young Gabe's case."

"Kyle's been bitten. He won't live much longer with vampire venom in his bloodstream."

She smiled up at me as her hand slipped to her rear. When she brought it back around, a syringe balanced between her fingers. "What if I had the power to prevent his death happening, too?" A step forward pressed her chest against the bars. "What would that be worth to you?"

The urge to snatch through the bars and grab the medicine made my fingers itch, but I knew she'd whip it away before I even got near. Instead, I folded my hands around the bars and leaned in close to her face. "What is it, exactly, that you want from me ... *Catherine*?"

"So eager to please." She caught her bottom lip between her teeth. "Bet you like to please in other departments, too."

"Not with a vampire, no."

Her eyebrows flickered up, down. "You never know. You might enjoy it." She turned toward Kyle, but only for a split second, before she reclaimed me with her eyes. "Your friend didn't seem to mind."

"He would have, if he hadn't been tricked into thinking you were something different than what you are."

"And he wouldn't have been tricked if he hadn't been so gullible. You males are all the same."

The grind of my teeth vibrated through my ears like a power tool. "Are you going to tell me what you want so Kyle can be helped, or do you plan to just talk dirty to me all night?"

"Night?" She smirked. "You have no idea how long you've been here, do you?"

I kept my eyes in check as they went to roll. "Do you see any clocks?"

She laughed—a sound I recognised from my dazed stupor in Kyle's hotel room. It irked just as much as it had then. "So ..." With her gaze still on mine, she took two steps to her left. "Say I give this to Kyle." She held up the syringe like she'd been watching too many hospital dramas, and tapped the cylinder with her fingernail. "Will you comply?"

A right step brought me back in line with her. "Comply with what?"

"My requests, of course." She shifted closer to Kyle again—a move I matched.

"You're not my type. I prefer my females with a pulse."

Amusement tugged at the corners of her lips. "What if I promise my requests will be of a non-sexual nature? Would you, in return, promise to comply?"

"Help Kyle, and then ask me."

A small laugh preceded an even smaller shake of her head. "It doesn't work that way, darling. In case you didn't notice, you're in there, and I'm out here. Guess who's calling the shots?"

My growl rumbled through the back of my throat, as she turned away.

The vampire worked keys from her rear pocket and unlocked Kyle's cage. She pivoted back to me, fixed her gaze onto mine as she entered and crossed to where Kyle lay in the corner. "So ... last chance. Will ... you ... comply?"

Before I could stop myself, I nodded, while wondering what the hell I was doing.

Her drop to her haunches looked more like a glide than plummet. She folded her fingers around the syringe, held her thumb poised over the plunger, brushing through Kyle's shaggy hairs coating his rump. With hand and needle in position, her gaze met back with mine. "No promise, no anti-venom."

Don't do it, my mind screamed. *It's a trick.*

"Choice is yours," she said.

My focus fixated on the needle—relief for Kyle. "You have my word," the oath uttered past my lips. *Shit!*

I kept the self-aimed groan an internal one, as she stuck Kyle with the needle and applied pressure I hoped sent much-needed medicine into his bloodstream.

She withdrew the empty syringe and slapped Kyle's flank before she straightened. "There. He should come around in a few hours."

"Does he have to stay in there alone?" I swallowed down a lump that tried to stopper my throat. "What if something goes wrong? What if the serum doesn't work?"

"It will." She headed for the door.

"It might not."

With a clink, the door slid back into place. "It will."

"You should have him transferred into here." My hand fisted, pumped toward the floor. "With me. He needs watching over."

"He'll be fine." A twist of her wrist turned the key, and she rammed the bunch back into her pocket before spinning. "You wouldn't be thinking of backing out on our deal, I hope?" Her steps barely made a sound as she crossed to my bars. "If you did, I'd have to kill you."

I gave a low growl. "I never renege on a promise."

"Good." The curve of her lips turned her from psychotic to almost charming. "Then, I'll be seeing you very soon, Ethan Holloway."

"I can hardly wait."

As if something had tapped xylophone bars in her throat, her laughter tinkled out like disjointed notes. "Funny *and* cute," she said as she walked away.

The doors banged like a death toll on her exit.

18

"You are an idiot!" Panther-girl glowered at me through her bars, like my moronic behaviour over Kyle caused her severe offence. "The vampire played you. And you made it easy for her. Idiot!"

I couldn't quite make the 'yeah, I know' admittance a verbal one.

"If she didn't intend to let that one live,"—she flung her arm out to her left and pointed toward Kyle—"he'd never have made it back down here, at all."

My jaw tightened at her snappy tone.

"She used him ... to get to you." Her finger swung around, and she jabbed it toward me. "And you let her." A growl vibrated past her lips.

My eyebrows winged up at the first feral sound she'd made. "What's it to you, anyway, puss?" I winced at my barked tone, as well as my words. "Why do you care what I do, or don't, agree to? Or what might happen to us? You don't even bloody like werewolves, remember?"

"Well, maybe I quite like you." She spun and strode away from the bars until submerged in shadow. "Though, goodness knows why." Her disembodied voice flew out to me. "You're an idiot!" She re-emerged from the gloom. "And my name is not puss." She spun and marched away again, her dark hair lashing the air like a string whip.

My expression tugged in all directions as my mind struggled to decide if I should be mad or amused. "So ... what is it, then?" When she didn't answer, I turned my focus back to Kyle, resting my head against the bars as the onset of weariness crept in.

"Brook."

Only my gaze shifted toward the female, who'd returned to the forefront of her enclosure.

"My name is Brook." Her tone held insistence, like she thought I hadn't understood her first utterance.

I couldn't help but smile. "Nice to meet you, Brook. I'm—"

"Ethan. Trust me, we know."

A chuckle rolled past my throat.

"And I happen to think you're okay ... for an idiot. And for a dog."

"Brave words, said from the protection of her cell." My smile remained, and hers reflected back at me.

Returning to Kyle, I folded my arms across my chest to assist with propping me up and leaned my entire body into the barrier. My nostrils flared, my chest rose, and a yawn juddered out on my exhale.

"You should get some rest," she said.

I shook my head. "I'm on sentry." I gestured with my chin toward Kyle.

"I can watch him for you," Lauren said to my right. "If he wakes, I'll ... poke you, or something."

"If I were you, I'd take the girl up on her offer," Brook said.

Maybe I should have given the suggestion deeper consideration, but the preference to go under by choice, rather than through an inability to remain awake, won out. I turned to Lauren. "He moves ... you wake me."

She nodded, her stare unwavering.

"The slightest sign that he stirs, and I want you to let me know."

Another nod—slow and exaggerated.

"Even if it's something small like a change in his breathing—"

"I get it," she said. "I'll wake you."

Just the idea of taking my focus off Kyle induced a throb in my temple, but my own body had needs—ones I couldn't neglect for much longer. My teeth ground even as I complied.

In the corner nearest Lauren and Kyle, I spun to face inward. The metal chilled my flesh as I slid my back down the barrier until my butt met the floor. "However small his movement ..."

"I *know*," Lauren said through clenched teeth. "Dude, you're a worse nag than my mum."

With a low chuckle, I closed my eyes.

Although my mind woke, my lids remained lowered. An inhalation drew in every surrounding smell, but filtering took immense effort. The familiarity of Kyle's scent gave him an immediate pass to the forefront, and brought with it the knowledge that he'd changed forms.

"What happened to waking me if he moved?" I murmured.

"You said I had to wake you if he looked like he was waking up." Lauren's quiet voice came from my left. "He didn't wake. Just turned into a man."

"No, I said to wake me if he so much as moved. It's impossible to change without moving." I opened my eyes and twisted my head to bring her into view. On her knees, she stared forward toward Kyle's cage. "Even unconscious," I added.

"Sorry," she muttered. "But your snores kinda made me think you needed the sleep."

My eyes narrowed. "I don't snore."

"Do, too."

A whisper of a growl vibrated across my lips. "How about you? Don't you ever sleep?" I asked as I turned to check on Kyle.

"I've learned it's safer to stay awake." She shrugged. "As you're only the second neighbour I've had who didn't look like he wanted to eat me, I taught myself to survive on less downtime."

I stared across the aisle until my sleep vision lost its blurred edges, and the outline of Kyle's body sharpened in my view. "That bad, eh?" I caught her acknowledgement—a fuzzed movement—at the corner of my eye, rubbed my hands across my face in the hope of clearing my sight further. With a yawn extending my mouth to cavernous proportions, I surged to my feet and worked out my kinks—shoulder rolls, a few neck rotations.

Upon lowering my chin for the fourth time, my gaze fell on the entrance to my cage.

What the—

The metal-barred door stood ajar. Not wide open—nothing quite so obvious as that—but just enough to reveal an inch-sized gap.

Afraid it might be an illusion, I stayed firmly fixated on it. "Lauren?"

"Yep?"

"Someone been down here from upstairs?"

"Nope."

I peered through the slit like I'd find something different than what rationality insisted had to be there. Within the inch, the metal stripes of the deader than dead vampire's empty enclosure solidified in my focus. "You sure?"

"Yep."

"Maybe you fell asleep for a while?" I took a step toward my door. Pure instinct insisted I inhale, yet only the same delightful bouquet from earlier greeted my senses.

"I didn't. Just like I told you I wouldn't."

Another step, followed by a third, and impatience drew me the rest of the way in two strides. I slid a finger into the sliver of air, raised it up, and dropped it back down. *What you checking for? Booby-traps?*

"So, how did my door get open?"

Without waiting for her answer, I folded my fingers around the frame and gave a gentle pull. The door swung inward, creating a bigger gap.

I peered across to Lauren. "What's going on?"

Without sparing me a glance, she scrunched her shoulders up and gave a reply that sounded like, "I-unno," which I interpreted to mean she didn't have a clue.

I twisted back to the door, from the opening to Kyle, and back again. Once more, my gaze flittered between the two points.

"Why the hell am I just standing here?" I muttered.

A gentle nudge took the door the rest of the way with no more noise than a sighed squeak, and I stepped from my cell into the aisle.

Static tugged at the hairs across the nape of my neck. Natural suspicion kicked in, and my pulse thrummed a little faster.

To the left, nobody appeared. The same to my right. Ahead, the bars to the feline's cage separated me from her.

Moving forward, I spotted Brook curled against her rear wall. The black glossy coat she'd adopted made her almost invisible. With the deepness of her breaths, and the absence of golden orbs to pinpoint her eyes, I presumed her to be sleeping.

My padding soles produced a quiet slap on each contact with the concrete, as I paced from her bars, past the werewolf's cage, to Kyle's.

He still lay in the corner. A rapid check told me his cage remained locked. I sank down to my knees beside him.

His rear faced me. Slashes decorated the muscles either side of his spine—fingernails at a guess. A still raw wound left a gaping hole in his shoulder, the flesh there torn as though savaged by teeth.

"Jesus, Kyle."

At my whisper, a twitch affected his right shoulder beneath the gnaw marks. A groan murmured from him—a sound so quiet, I couldn't be certain I'd heard it at all.

Almost afraid to hope, I waited to see if he'd wake.

Catching the flex of his toes, my face spun that way, gaze skimming over more bites across his right hip.

Another groan—no more audible than the first—sounded.

As much as I wanted grab him by the shoulders and shake him to consciousness, some inner voice insisted I wait it out, that he needed to come round on his own. My fingers fidgeted beneath the brushing of my thumbs where my hands hung over my knees.

Contracting muscle beneath his shoulder blade preceded a jerked shift of his right arm. With great slowness and deliberation, as though suffering from stiffness or pain, Kyle reached his hand up toward his neck. His fingers hovered above the wound at his shoulder before he lowered them the final drop and prodded there.

"Fuck." Deepness affected his tiny whisper. "Must be dead." His temple scraped against the concrete with the slight move of his head. A gasp followed. "Bollocks." Grunts suggested he tried further adjustments to his position, as did the tremulous up-draw of his knees. "Must be in hell."

My chuckle snorted out and, along with it, a gush of relief.

"If I'm not mistaken, the bastards have killed my bud, and sent him along with me." Each word adhered to the next to form the sentence—a mumbled jumble that made him sound drunk.

"Maybe you were in hell to begin," I said. "And they just sent you back down here."

Kyle's body rolled toward me until his shoulders slapped against the concrete. He swung his head round, blinking like he struggled to bring me into focus.

Further open cuts, gashes, and punctures patterned his chest and hips. My jaw clenched as I studied them, crunching beneath the exerted pressure.

"I feel like shit," he whispered.

"Really? 'Cause ... you look a lot worse."

He breathed out a laugh, chasing it with a wonky smile cut short by his wince.

We remained quiet a moment. Kyle's fingers made a slow tour across his torso. His knees lifted, sliding his bare soles over the rough flooring, and he peered down, assessing the damage, I figured.

Each time his hand traced a wound, he paused and craned his neck toward it. With each new discovery, the fondling of his fingers seemed to increase into manic twitching.

"Fucker bit me."

Although sure he didn't really need the confirmation, I said, "Looks that way."

His expression sobered completely as something akin to fear crept into his eyes. "Why the hell am I still alive? How—"

"Later." I reached in and squeezed his arm. "Need to see if I can find Gabe."

Still poised for speech, his mouth hung open, and his eyebrow lifted. "Sure ... but ..."

My thigh muscles bunched as I straightened and turned away.

"Ethan?"

I glanced back.

Kyle lifted his head from the floor, the movement drawing tightness to his eyes. "What ... are you ... You're not in your cage. How the hell did you get out?"

"No idea. Woke to find my door open. That's all I know."

"But ..." Grunts and groans accompanied his manoeuvre to his knees. "It could be a ... um ..." He held his hands out in front of him, flexed and un-flexed his fingers. "Could be a trap," he mumbled, turning his palms up and staring at those.

Something about his self-scrutiny seemed off—his actions, too.

To anyone else, he'd appear to be checking himself over. To me? The tense set of his shoulders told me he'd found something wrong.

I watched his visual scouring of each arm, of each hand, each individual appendage.

Had the venom or anti-venom had an adverse effect?

His gaze came back and latched onto mine. "Watch your back." He cocked his head, side-to-side, linked and tugged at his fingers. The crunch of his neck action matched the crack of his knuckles. "You going, or not?"

I moved away.

"What the hell?" The voice of the vampire beside Lauren screeched even in a murmur.

I ground my teeth to withhold the retaliation and kept going.

"Hey, how'd you—"

I glared at him, growling through gritted teeth. "Shut ... the fuck ... up." I resumed my journey before he could continue the discussion.

Hunching over and trying for stealth seemed like a waste of time, especially in a chamber filled with enhanced hearing, vision, and senses of smell. Still, I bent at the waist and baby-stepped my way along the aisle as though it would be enough to conceal me from the watchful eyes either side.

My nostrils flared as I made short, rapid inhalations en route. I discovered scents that smelled the closest to human as I'd come across since arrival, as well as shifter and were.

Amongst those drifted one as easily recognisable to me as any of the pack: Gabe.

19

I followed the beckon of Gabe's familiar scent. Two more steps along the aisle, a left slant of my head, and I spotted what my senses insisted had to be him—even if his physical appearance had diminished enough for me to question his identity.

Three cages down from the corner, the naked werewolf possessed the small cube. His side-to-side pacing from bars to bars lent him the manic air of a trapped animal, as did the jerked pump of each fist at his hips.

I moved across to his enclosure, my head twisting with each of his turns as he marched side-to-side, like watching a pendulum driven by rocket fuel—one bulked by the power of a fully grown werewolf on a teenager.

Filth coated his body and mingled with sweat, adding staleness beyond pungency. Grease and blood matted his blond curls. None of those disguised his unique aroma.

Another pace. Another turn. Two strides.

He froze.

The flare of his nostrils revealed his intake of air. A shake of his head showed his uncertainty, as did the couple steps he took before he halted again. More inhalations, deeper, longer—an obvious need to be sure—and a slow pivot of his body brought him around to face me.

His gaze met mine. He squinted, every muscle in his face seeming to tighten, and his lips formed an indistinguishable mumble.

The heavy beat in my chest broke into my focus, and a sigh eased out past my lips as I smiled. "Hey, Gabe."

"Eth—" His shoulders heaved beneath erratic breathing. "Eth-Ethan?"

I nodded—a gesture he matched as though realisation sunk in that I really stood before him.

"Ethan." One step, two, another stall. More tension claimed stake upon his features. "Aw, shit!" Three strides brought him to the front of his cage, and his face pressed to the bars. "I knew you'd c-come," he whispered.

The tremor in his limbs lent vulnerability to his tough façade, exposing his youth and fear. I slipped my arms through and ruffed up the scraggy mop his hair had become, before offering an embrace I believed he needed.

"How'd you g-get in?" He continued to mumble, as though normal speech had left his abilities. "I c-can't believe you got in. You f-fight your way through?"

I frowned as it dawned on me that Gabe had no idea Kyle and I had been captured. "Not exactly."

"You need to be c-careful." He pulled back, lifting his gaze the couple of inches to meet mine. "They c-come down a lot. If they c-catch you down here ... You have the keys? To get me out? You g-got the keys, right?"

I took his face, peered at him. The dart of his eyes, an agitated left and right flutter, worried the hell out of me—as did the dull grey, which had replaced the brightness of his blue irises. "Gabe, I don't have the keys."

"Wha-wha-wha ..." His mouth opened and closed with each sound in rapid succession. "Wh-what you mean? You c-came to get me out ... that's wh-why you're here, right?"

His stuttering speech creased my brow. "Yes, I'm going to get you out, but ..." I frowned even harder, when his eyes went back to flittering. *Just tell him.* "But ... I'm here because they got to me and Kyle."

His wide stare froze in position. "No." He gave a small headshake. "No, no, no. No, not you. Not Kyle." His head shook again until his curls flopped about. "Oh, man, we're fucked."

"Mind your language." I gave a mental eye roll at the admonishment I'd heard Shelley say too often.

"Sorry." More eye darts.

"And we're not fucked, yet," I said. "I'll figure something out."

"Like how to get me out from these bars."

"Sure." I tilted my head for a better view. "How badly have you been hurt?"

"I'm sweet." He stepped across to his door, tugged at it a little. "You ... um ... have another way to g-get me out, or something?"

"Sorry, no—I'm working on it." I shifted right to bring him back into my sights. "How badly are you injured, Gabe?"

"Why aren't you in a c-cage?" Confusion clouded his fidgeting eyes. "D-didn't they put you in one?"

I hesitated for only a beat before nodding.

"But you g-got out?" He nodded and didn't wait for an answer, striding away toward the rear of his enclosure. The turn of his body revealed similar wounds to Kyle's across his back, but already forming into scars—some to white, others red and raw, most of them raised welts. "Of c-course you did." His murmured words held deepness. "This is you, right?" His grunt arrived with a spasm that twitched his shoulder muscles until taut. He slapped his hand over the twisting flesh, his fingers kneading there. "How?"

I frowned. "How what, Gabe?"

He dropped his arm as he spun. "How'd you get out your cage?"

"The door was unlocked when I woke."

"That's not g-good." His eyes went back into shifty mode. "That's really bad. Has to be a trick." His utterance sounded more like he spoke to himself than to me. He marched back over. "You need to get back in your cell. Now. Right now."

"I don't think they're respons—"

"You have no idea who you're d-dealing with." His fingers curled around the bars separating us.

"Nobody had been down when I found it op—"

"You have no idea what they're c-capable of."

"And nobody has been down here since I stepped from my ca—"

"You d-don't get it." His eyes stilled.

"Yes, Gabe, I do." I ducked my head in the hope of holding him steady for longer. "I get it."

"How can you?" he whispered, a pained expression twisting his face.

My jaw tightened, my eyes, too, as his desperation spread to me like a virus. "Because Kyle's already been summoned by them upstairs. I know what's going on."

"K-K-Kyle." Each sound punctuated with a jerk of his shoulders.

What the hell had they done to him? "Yes."

"Aw, shit." His eyes flashed to the left, to me, to the left and back again. "He return? Is he okay?"

I nodded.

"Did he make it? T-Tell me he did."

I reached in to take his face again, drawing him close. "He's back. I just spoke to him."

"But you think everything's all right when it's not," he whispered. "They fucked me up, good and p-proper."

In the high shine of his eyes I saw only terror, telling me a hell of a lot more about his condition than any words could, and controlling my breath took immense effort. "Soon as we get you out of here, Gabe, we'll get you fixed up."

He lifted a hand, tapped a finger against his temple. "C-can't fix up what's screwed on the inside."

Murmuring started up somewhere to my rear. I ignored it, keeping my attention only on Gabe. "How much do you trust me?"

"With my life." He met my eyes. "'S'how I knew you'd come."

"If I tell you I'm going to make sure you're okay, would you believe me?"

More words to my rear, a little louder, the scuff of movement. As long as I had Gabe's focus, I couldn't look away.

A few seconds passed before he nodded. "I believe you. You never lie." His gaze wandered away again. "But I don't think we're getting out ... don't see how we—"

"I'll get you home. I have to." I waited until his gaze swung back and smiled. "I made a promise to your mother."

His teeth flashed with his returned expression. "You never break your promises to her."

Pain bubbled inside my chest as thoughts of Shelley threatened to explode into something greater. "I wouldn't dare."

"Ethan?" Kyle's hissed call rolled along the corridor.

Gabe's attention darted aside, as I whirled to look behind me.

The aisle remained empty.

"Ethan?" The second call arrived in the smooth voice of Brook. Both tones held insistence that prickled the nape of my neck.

"Something's wrong," Gabe said.

"Get back in your cage." The order arrived in a duet of deep and honey.

"Now," Kyle said, followed by Brook's, "Get back in, now."

"They're coming," Gabe muttered.

The boom of the double doors reverberated through like an invisible Kraken seeking its prey.

I spun back toward Gabe. His lips moved with whispered utterances, and the evident panic and fear sent the jig of his eyes back into overdrive. I reached in with my hand, drew him forward until an inch from my face. "Listen to me, Gabe. I need you to hold it together for me, okay?"

Footsteps marched through the far side of the space—two sets, at a guess.

He gave me a jerked nod.

"Let me sort this, then I'll figure a way to get you out of here. You will not have to go back upstairs for them. I swear."

More up and down head bobs answered—an action his eyes joined in with.

The footsteps grew nearer. I thought them still far enough away, but then the curses began.

"What the—"

I blanked them, as well as the demands being made to those surrounding my deserted cage, kept my steady stare on the young werewolf. "Trust me?"

The pounding of feet hit the concrete like a ticking countdown to the shit about to fly. Thud, thud, thud, coming in my direction.

I turned toward Joseph and the vampire who'd shot me in the hotel room. The latter had his stun gun, or whatever the hell it was, trained on my torso, evaporating any idea I'd harboured to fight. My palms lifted in an attempt to placate, and I shifted forward.

They grounded to a halt. Mousey, on the right, lifted his weapon higher to his shoulder, peering at me through the lens.

Beside him, Joseph gave the smile I'd grown used to seeing on him. "Ethan?" A pleasant tone mixed with an underlying strain of tension. "What are you doing out here?"

"Perusing the neighbourhood." My left sidestep matched a shift in the other vampire's stance. "How about you?"

Joseph's quiet laughter rolled past his lips, yet I didn't relax the set of my shoulders or lower my hands.

"How did you get out?" The one on the right kept his viewfinder on me. "More to the point, who the fuck let you out?"

"Nobody."

"Bullshit." His tone didn't reflect his words but held only calmness, like my lack of restriction offered him no stress. "I know that door was locked. I took care of it, myself."

I raised and lowered a shoulder. "I have no answers for you."

"You expect me to believe you have no idea how you got out?"

"I don't expect you to believe anything, just as I doubt I'll believe anything you have to say." I turned my attention to Joseph. "Did you come to speak to me specifically? Or can I go back to being bored shitless now?"

He smiled, flashing the points of his half-extended fangs as his eyes performed for me. "The tedium getting to you, is it?"

"Not yet."

"Well, you're in luck. We come to offer reprieve to your boredom." His dialect thickened for a moment. "Catherine wants to see you."

This can't be good. I rolled my shoulders. "Why didn't you just say so, then?"

Another musical laugh from Joseph coincided with the tightening of the other vampire's hand on his gun.

Keeping the tension from my face took effort as I peered back over my shoulder. Only Gabe's outline showed from his skulked-to position at the rear of his cage, but I still sent him a wink in the hope he'd receive it, before turning back to my escorts. "Let's go, then."

"Stay in front." Vamp number two gestured to his right with the barrel pointed my way.

"Whatever you say," I muttered.

Joseph came to my left, keeping up with my strides.

I sent him a quick glance. "You sure I don't need to grab anything en route?"

His smile glowed in the dimness. "Like?"

"Oh, I don't know. My handbag from my room." I folded my arms across my chest. "A bottle of wine, maybe?"

He laughed. "Just yourself will do."

"Ethan?" Kyle pushed against his bars, panic in his eyes. His arm snaked out, and his fingers folded around my upper arm. One yank from him slammed my chest into the bars, as his stare penetrated me with a concern I made effort to control. He leaned in closer until only his breath filled my senses. "Promise me one thing, buddy. Can you do that for me?"

Despite the urgency in his voice, I nodded. "Sure."

"Promise me you'll swallow your pride."

What the hell does ...

"There's stuff you don't understand." His voice dropped to a whisper. "Stuff you won't understand. About who's behind this."

My heart gave an irregular thump against my chest. "Who?"

"Move along." Joseph's fingers clamped onto my arm, dragging me away from Kyle's stronghold, and jerked my feet back into action.

I strained to look back. "Who, Kyle?"

"It's not what we—"

With the rammed butt of his weapon against Kyle's mouth, Mousey cut off the words before Kyle finished.

I went to stride back at Kyle's grunt and wavered balance, but managed only two steps when another sharp tug from Joseph returned me to my path.

"Don't want to keep Catherine waiting," he said. "She'll only get pissy if you do."

Lauren's green eyes seemed the diameter of saucers as she stared out at me. I tried to smile, but couldn't quite get my mouth to obey as dread weighed heavy on my shoulders, and sent her a half-assed attempt instead.

From within Brook's enclosure, only her eyes showed her position.

Promise me you'll swallow your pride. What the hell had Kyle meant?

I halted, pivoting to bring him back into view, his bleeding face pressed against the iron rods, arms stretching through while his swollen eyes held the plea his split lips couldn't form.

Although I had no idea what the agreement meant, I said, "Promise."

20

Leaving the underground chamber didn't exactly instil me with optimism. Beyond the double doors, two brick shithouses stood guard at either side.

I squinted against the blinding light and surveyed the duo.

Elongated and completely black eyes above high cheekbones suggested oriental descent for the one on the left. His companion, also of vampire origin, had the stockiest body I'd seen on any of their race. The broadness of his shoulders almost matched Kyle's, which made them not much less wide than my own.

Both of them stood to attention on our exit, protruding fangs providing backup for the guns they pointed at me. My brain could have argued as much as it liked that dart bullets would do no more than put me to sleep, but it didn't stop my shoulders stiffening at the affront.

On passing the goons, we turned right, twice, bringing us to a staircase. The stark, drab stone matched the décor of the space I'd just left.

I paused at the bottom and stared up, but could see only the first landing illuminated beneath a single strip-light. A harsh jab to my shoulder blade came with Mousey's grunt, to, 'Move', and I caught up to Joseph on the third step.

"We underground, down here?" I asked.

"You work that out on your own?" Joseph laughed.

Refusing to bite, I slid my hands into the pockets of my jeans. Tiny traces of gravel bit into my soles and saved me slipping on stone polished to a smooth finish. Odours assaulted my senses en masse, of all those who'd passed before me, but the high stench of blood held less potency—a result, I guessed, of the cool breeze that wafted through.

I lifted my face toward the freshness of the chilled air. "How many floors are there?"

"There's the ground floor." Joseph took my elbow at the first landing, steered me left around a U-turn, and gestured for me to continue. "Then, there's a higher mezzanine level. That's where you're going."

"What's up there?" The next landing stood thirteen steps up, the space ending with a door that looked like it had been shipped in from the set of a medieval film. "On the mezzanine level?"

"Catherine's up there ..."

And what's on the ground floor?

"... and that's all you need to know."

Another prod to my shoulder knocked me forward. Fists clenched, I swung to confront Mousey with his poke-happy barrel, a growl rumbling out before I could stop it. I barely took a step before a set of fangs shot out from each vampire.

For seconds, I glowered at my assaulter with thunder in my chest and thoughts of ripping out his oesophagus whirling through my mind.

His expression never wavered. "Turn around and walk."

He stood close enough that I could have knocked his stupid weapon aside and grabbed hold of him before he even got a shot in. Where would that have gotten me, though? His pal on my back, and me returning to my cage in the same condition Kyle had?

Pick your fights, Ethan. Choose your moment.

My attention remained on the idiot as I cleared my throat against the lingering growl. "Quit poking me. Or you *will* be sorry." Jaw tight, I dragged my arse away and resumed my climb.

Joseph stepped onto the top landing as I did and reached out for the huge, bronze, knocker-type handle of the door.

The moment the thick oak panel swung inward, my pulse lurched to speeds of Olympic standards beneath the bombarding stench of blood and death.

Bile rose in my throat. My eyes watered. I slammed the back of my hand to my mouth against the retch, just managing to retain the digested slops.

"You okay?" Joseph patted my shoulder like he gave a shit, while the amused twinkle in his dark stare told another story. "Maybe it's too much for you?"

My cheeks constricted each time my gag reflex tried to push forth another bout of vomit. I switched to shallow breathing through my mouth, and speaking through clenched teeth, said, "I'm good."

Brown stone greeted us as we ducked into a shaded corridor that stretched east and west.

Joseph rounded my left side and tipped his chin to my right. "That way ... for now."

The domed stone passage reminded me of the gulley in Witchurch and offered an oppression that didn't come from fetidness alone. Tightness consumed my throat. I didn't consider myself claustrophobic, but I'd never craved open spaces more than I did in that moment. The band of pressure spread to my chest, my unease expanding with each step I took.

Sconces bearing church candles adorned the walls either side, none of them aflame, yet light spilled into the upcoming curve. Upon rounding the bend, the corridor opened up on the right, and huge floor to ceiling windows explained the light source.

I lifted a hand to shade my eyes, and stared through the glass, searching for clues to our location. The bright solar glare could have made it any time during autumn sunlight hours, but the deep terracotta blush bathing the lawn beyond the glass hinted at late afternoon.

"You sure that isn't the way we need to go?" I nodded with my head and took a step toward the warm glow.

Joseph clamped a hand around my arm and steered me back with a chuckle. "Maybe if you ask Catherine very nicely, she'll allow you to pee in the yard."

"Amusing," I muttered as I fell back into line. "You have many dog jokes?"

"Enough to keep you entertained for a very long time."

The welcoming, open space disappeared with a few more strides, to be replaced once more by the asphyxiating low-domed ceiling.

"This is us." Joseph grabbed the bronze ring handle of another heavyset door, in the right hand wall of the stone tunnel, releasing the catch with a twist. "Please." He inclined his chin. "After you."

The way led to more steps, winding up and round and disappearing from view. The spiral design reminded me of turret cases in old castles.

"Go on," Mousey said. "Up."

After climbing a few steps, a slight turn of my head and shift of my eyes showed Joseph a few notches below. Behind him, Mousey and his weapon.

A backward kick would send them both sprawling. Five ascended leaps would take me from their visual range, before they'd have the chance to retaliate.

I smiled to myself as I took three steps in succession.

My hands unclenched in my pockets, and I adjusted them enough to ensure a quick-draw release when needed, while my hearing absorbed the two footfalls in pursuit.

I took a deep breath, long and slow—enough to regulate my pulse.

One.

The muscles across my shoulders bunched to twanging. My breaths almost ground to a stop.

Two.

My left foot hit the next level. The cogs of my brain shut off their motors, idling to a speed that allowed time to slow down alongside them.

Showtime.

Muscles taut, I whipped my hands from my pockets, shoving against the upcoming steps for additional thrusting power, and swung my right leg back. The full-bodied boot of my sole impacted with Joseph's too-pretty face.

With the crack of bone vibrating through my foot, Joseph's head snapped back. His eyes opened wide. He threw out his arms, but the cylindrical centrepiece of the staircase offered no traction to save his flail.

A *thud* arrived with the collision of the two vampires' skulls, and the knock-on effect of my attack sent the duo falling like a bodied domino run.

With a chuckle, I spun back to face the way I needed to go, and two upward leaps took me around the next curvature, while grunts, curses, and the clatter of the dropped weapon, all resonated up from below.

The staircase went two only ways—up, or down. I had no idea where up would take me, but down didn't appeal, not with the pair of pissed off vamps lying at the base, so I made another upward spiralled circuit.

Feet pounded the stone and echoed up, bouncing off the solid structure. With one hand pressed to the outer wall for guidance, I went higher, each propulsion of my left leg sending an ache through my muscles as it contrasted against each short hop of my right.

Thuds. More grunts. A shout of, "Bloody catch him, you fool!" The pursuing beat of movement grew louder, faster, nearer.

Don't look back. Keep going.

Lack of sustenance brought weakness that hindered my ascended race. The volume of my breath and my soaring pulse thrummed like a windsock during a storm.

Further climbing ensued, until a hint of light invaded the shadow. Straight ahead, I saw only a dead end. With a shift to the left, my eyes found an arch leading away from the dimness.

One final leap took me onto the inadequate landing. The momentum crashed my shoulder into the cul-de-sac wall. Breath expelled from me with a grunted wince.

A backward glance showed nothing of the two vampires. Only the sounds of their frantic passage exposed their positions.

To the left, I caught a glimpse of a room through the doorway. Like the open space downstairs, sunlight filtered in from somewhere, showering every surface with golden warmth. A walnut desk. High backed seats. A sofa that looked pretty inviting after the concrete bed I'd been kipping on.

I ducked inside. Inhaled.

Nothing.

My feet hit a rug that coated the floor in symmetrical design, and the all too familiar tickle taunted the base of my skull.

Five strides in, I halted.

Another inhalation found no scent.

"Do not move." At Catherine's quiet voice, I tensed for attack, but a sharp piercing into the flesh at my carotid artery dictated I remain motionless.

My entire body stiffened. Only my chest moved, pushing forth and releasing beneath the effort of breathing.

"In the syringe is ten mil of liquid wolfsbane. Do you know what that means?"

Fuck! Of course I knew—as plant, it held the potency to induce uncontrollable changes. I didn't even want to think about what it could do in its concentrated liquid form.

I went to nod, until common sense told me to quit fucking moving, and I froze, all moisture evacuating my throat, leaving only an arid pathway for speech not even a swallow could cure. "Yes." Hoarseness deepened my whisper.

"Good."

The slap of feet suggested her backup joined us, confirmed by Mousey's imaginative curse of, "Bastard!"

"Maybe you shouldn't have underestimated him, Chad." What I presumed to be Catherine's knee nudged the back of my leg. "Walk, please."

With little choice but to obey, I skimmed one foot across the carpet, followed by another.

"Any chair will do. Take your pick."

The needle remained in my flesh. Her hand against my back held the temperature of an ice cube. Arching my neck seemed a natural reaction, as I shifted forward a little more.

"I do not wish to kill you, Ethan."

"Then, you'd better be sure you have good control over your appendages while you're threatening to stab me with that shit." Afraid of moving my jaw, each word forced past my gritted teeth.

"I have excellent control. A skill you could do with learning." The hand at my back switched to take my arm, and she steered me around and into the nearest seat. "This is the second time you have attacked one of my men."

My rear hit the springy cushion of the chair, as Catherine's chilled fingers slid to rest on my shoulder. With each beat of my heart, my flesh seemed to throb around the inserted tube of metal. "You have me secure," I said. "You want to remove that needle now?"

"Are you afraid, Ethan?" Her words irritated the drum of my ear with her nearness.

"Of dying? No." I just had to rescue my family and save the world from psychos like her before I could let anything happen to me.

Mousey—*Chad?*—rounded the seat I'd taken. My gaze lifted, locked onto blackness that swirled with erratic energy—what I presumed to be a vampire's show of fury. Chad took a place beyond the desk in front of me and realigned his dart gun scope to my chest. "The wolf was not in his cage when we went down for him, Catherine."

A slight quiver affected the invasive syringe, as Catherine's head brushed the side of my own. "Who was responsible for securing his door?"

"Me." Chad's brow scrunched above the scope he peered through. "I can assure you, the door was locked. He did not exit through any negligence on my behalf."

Quiet fell upon the room before a sigh hit my ear. "Relax, Ethan. You're no good to me dead." The pressure in my neck slipped out as smoothly as it'd entered, replaced by a gentle pat of Catherine's hand.

Releasing my held breath, I straightened my head.

Joseph moved beside Chad, his cheeks either side of his nose affected by swelling, though no bruising advertised the blow he'd taken. Only humour pumped from his smirked expression—whether at my predicament, or my ballsy attack, I couldn't tell.

Fingers trailing across my shoulder as she passed, Catherine glided to the far side of the desk. Reaching Joseph, she leaned in close, and he ducked, offering his ear. The communication that passed between them sounded on par with the false whisperings kids often do when pretending to share a secret—no matter how much I strained my hearing, I couldn't decipher their words.

Catherine took a step toward the desk, placed the hypodermic on the surface. "You spend much time talking to the others downstairs, Ethan?" Her gaze locked with mine. "I mean, two days is a long time to spend somewhere with no company, wouldn't you agree?"

Two days? Jesus. Shelley would be spewing. I frowned as the fiery female entered my thoughts and winched further tightness into my chest, but sent a shrug in response to the vampire's questions.

"So ... tell me ..." Catherine leaned across the table, resting upon her forearms, and the blackness of her eyes evaporated from the whites to form two solid orbs. "What have you learned about young Lauren?"

21

Although my lips remained sealed as I stared at Catherine, thoughts collided through the riot within my mind.

The loudest one of them all came in the form of: How the hell had being out of my cage led to questions of Lauren?

"Want to enlighten me?" I finally asked.

"On what, Ethan?" Her expression hardened to an iced fury, and for a moment I saw what kept her ranks in line. "The question was simple. Answer it. What do you know about the girl?"

"Nothing." My shoulder lifted.

"You left your cage, yes?"

I rolled my eyes. "You know I did."

Her eyebrow ticked up as she thrust her face a little closer. "How?"

"Is that a trick question?" I lifted my palms. "I opened the bloody door and stepped out."

"Yes, Ethan, but how did you open a door that was locked?"

"It wasn't locked. It wasn't even closed."

She pushed up to stand. The muscles of her jaw tightened, and she rounded to my side, slid one butt cheek onto the desktop at my knees. Her left hand reached toward me, the proximity confirming what I'd come to suspect. Her perfume consumption had been no more than a disguise for her lack of scent.

I gritted my teeth and held my position, when her fingers came to rest at the thrumming beat below my ear.

She smiled. "You have a steady pulse."

My eyebrow twitched. "Shouldn't I?"

Her hand shot down between my knees.

I jolted backward, went to jump up, but the forward jerk of my chair slammed my arse onto the seat, as Catherine grasped the wood and drew me closer with shocking ease.

She shuffled her rear fully onto the desk and lifted her bare feet, nudging her toes to settle on my seat ledge. If I shifted forward, her pink painted nails would have been poking my crotch.

I followed the line of her denim-encased legs, and met her gaze as she brought her elbows to rest on her knees.

The curl of her finger beckoned me closer. When I didn't move, her lips upturned at one corner. "I'm not going to bite, Ethan. Come closer."

Leaning a little to the left showed me Chad and the unwavering focus he had on me with his weapon; to the right Joseph's irritating smile beamed back. I looked to Catherine. "I'd rather not."

As she breathed out a quiet laugh, her fingers once again stretched forward, her other hand mirroring on my other side, until they rested against the beat of my pulse. "If you lie? I'll know."

"I've nothing to lie about."

"Then, you have nothing to worry about, darling." She wiggled a little, and her eyes shone like two polished onyxes when they locked onto mine. "What happened right before you noticed your door was unlocked?"

"Nothing. I stretched. I yawned. That's it."

"Did you see anything?"

"Actually, yeah." I nodded, pursed my lips. "I saw the inside of my eyelids."

Her stare hardened, and a flash of temper sparked a glower into her eyes.

I blew out a breath. "I was asleep and woke to find the door that way."

"When you awakened, did you notice anything about Lauren? Where was she looking?"

Back to Lauren. Why? I shrugged. "She wasn't looking my way."

"At all?"

"Didn't I just say that?"

"Now's not the time to get smart with me."

"No, it would appear it's the time for pointless questions."

Her fingers tapped against my pulse points for a moment. "Did Lauren say anything when you noticed your door was open?"

Back to the door. Back to Lauren. "No." Did they think Lauren somehow opened my door?

"Nothing at all?"

My left eyebrow winged up. "We're going around in circles, here, Catherine."

"I'm just trying to figure out Lauren ... and how your door came to be open." She smiled.

She does think Lauren opened my door. Which would make Lauren what? "I have no answer, to either, for you."

"So"—another smile, a flash of fangs—"your door's open with no idea of how ... yet you step out of your cage with no consideration?"

"What can I say?" My shoulders hitched up with my shrug. "Curiosity got the better of me."

"Curiosity killed the cat, Ethan."

I chuckled. "Just as well I'm not one, then, I guess."

"I guess so." She didn't speak for seconds, didn't move either, except for the smoky blackness in her gaze and the further lengthening of her fangs.

My lips vibrated with my expelled breath. "Is this why you invited me up here? To ask about my social relationships downstairs?"

"No. Not even close."

"Well, if you're done with the questions, would you mind removing yourself from me?" I lifted my hands and grasped her forearms, but a tug at each didn't budge them.

"If you weren't so arrogant, you'd save yourself the humiliation you seem so intent on self-inflicting." Her half smile reappeared. "You're no match for me, wolf."

"That's a big assumption." With a grit of my teeth, I forced her fingers from my neck. "One only a fool would make." The muscles in my arms protested against the force I exerted to return Catherine's hands to her lap. "It's also one I intend to prove wrong in the very near future."

"Tough talk." Her smile extended to the other side of her mouth. "Now, I'm really looking forward to seeing you in action."

"It's not going to happen—not in the sense you mean."

"Really?" Her eyebrows arched up. "Why do you think you're up here, Ethan?"

I released my hold on the vampire, leaned back in my seat, folded my arms across my chest.

"It's your time to shine, darling."

"Then ..." I frowned. "What am I doing ... here? None of the others—"

"None of the others have shown disrespect, or misbehaved."

Disrespect? Misbehaved? She made me sound like a naughty kid who deserved a clip 'round the ear for scoffing all the cookies behind the garage. "Disrespect is as much a two-way street as its opposite, Catherine."

She surprised me by nodding. "You're right. Which is why I'm showing you a little courtesy by telling you exactly what will happen if you refuse to comply with my requests."

"And those requests would be what?" *Do I really want to know?*

"I put you in the cage against whatever opponent I've chosen for you. You change, without question, and fight, without inhibition."

Cage? I narrowed my eyes beneath the scrunch of my brow. "Or?"

Another of her smiles arrived to fill her face. "Ordinarily? If one of our weres or shifters refuse to change? We make them."

"How the hell—"

"It's amazing what results come from a sharp electro shock, or a decent shot of adrenaline into the bloodstream. Of course, there are the ones we leave to their own demise. They have only themselves to blame, if they don't change and aren't strong enough to defend themselves, right?"

Well ... fuck.

"But for you, the option is much simpler." She slid off the desk and crossed to a bureau on the other side of the office. With her back to me, she pulled down the desk and extracted a decanter from within and poured the dense red liquid from within into a wine glass. Small glugs forced it past the narrow opening. Once she'd replaced the stopper, she lifted the glass to her lips and drank, her eyes closing for a moment before she turned back to me. "You." She pointed a finger my way, and her tongue darted out, capturing a rogue trickle of what looked and smelled like blood. "If you don't fight, like I ordered, I will cancel the fight and substitute you with one of your friends." Black filled her eyes as she sent me a smile. "And they will be made to change however we choose."

My teeth ground at her words. "You know what I don't get?"

"No." Another sip on her refreshment painted her lips a bright crimson before she did a little self-cleaning. "But I have a feeling you're going to tell me."

"Why?"

"Because you like to ask what—"

"No." I shook my head. "*Why* are you doing this? What's the point? What the hell do you get out of this kind of bullshit?"

A spark entered her eyes. "Wouldn't you like to know?" After lowering her glass to the open bureau, she headed across to the doorway. "You're a smart cookie, Ethan— I'm sure you'll figure it out soon enough."

She paused in the archway with a smile. "I'll escort you. It's time."

***

Down the spiral staircase, Catherine led me by the hand, while Joseph hung on behind by the syringe they'd stabbed back into my neck. Upon re-entering the corridor, we took a right instead of left, and followed the curve of the circular path in silence.

Like I'd seen the other way, windowed coves ducked off at intervals, and arch-shaped doors that probably led to other rooms. While we'd been upstairs, someone had set each of the wall candles aflame, and their lambent flickers created dancing shadows across the stone.

The rumbling hit me first—about ninety seconds before the stench crashed down on me with the impact of a forty-foot wave. My gags kicked in. The clench of my jaw to restrain them lest I knock the hypodermic in my neck sent an ache through both sides of my skull.

Like a potent hum of electricity, the noise levels escalated with each step and vibrated through the building. My chest rose and fell to a rapid beat. Soreness infected my throat, each shallow breath scraping at the raw pathway. Blood rushed to my head, and my eyes almost lost sight as the vile and stale odours of destruction consumed my every sense.

About then, the natural defence system of my body kicked in, and my mind began a slow shutdown until I had a vague awareness only of placing one foot in front of the other.

The corridor became a blurred continuation of glowing grey. Filtered noise arrived as no more than the thrum of a trapped moth. Numbness infiltrated, blocking the sensory receptors at each of my contact points with the vampires, and at every coiled muscle.

A clang and a whine penetrated my mind as though arriving from a great distance.

Even the forceful shove of my shoulders and the forward stumbled stride of my feet struggled to register within my brain.

At the same metallic screech and clank behind me, I snapped alert.

The fuzzed and dancing shadows I'd followed in the periphery of my tunnel vision brightened. I blinked against the visual attack, lifting a hand that didn't want to obey the command to shield my eyes.

Buzzing lengthened in tempo, until the noise evolved into spoken words and shouts. Voices of anger, excitement, anticipation, filled my ears—none of which held familiarity.

A quiet chant of 'wolf' should have set my pulse soaring, alongside the barely recognisable call to 'place your bets'.

Only once my nose got its act together and dissected the decay from all the surrounding and very much alive forms did panic lay claim to my body.

My head whipped up. My eyes focussed.

No longer in the corridor, no longer escorted, I stood inside a cage that made mine downstairs look like a rabbit hutch.

I spun on the spot, staring at every viewable angle in disbelief.

From beyond the heavy duty mesh, faces stared at me, their lips moving and producing the sounds my mind had initially muted.

I blanked them once more and took a deep inhalation in the hope my senses had it wrong.

They hadn't.

I stood in a cage.

Surrounded on three sides.

By humans.

Lots of them.

Oh, fuck!

22

I spun in the centre of the cage, fast enough to induce a wave of nausea, until my gaze fell on Catherine and Joseph, both beaming at me from the other side of a door.

Hands fisted, I strode over to them. "What the fuck is this? There are humans in here." The clenching of my jaw scarcely allowed the words to pass through.

Behind me, a thrum of impatience took over my audience. The order of 'change already' shouted out in a deep bass.

"I never said this was my enterprise, Ethan," Catherine said.

Had that been what Kyle tried to tell me?

"You've sold us out? To humans?" I went to pace away, but whirled back to her before I'd even taken the first step. "Are you fucking insane?"

"Very far from it, darling." Her smile dimmed and only malice made home in her features. "Now, change."

Others joined in with the demands, until the cries of 'do it, wolf' merged with the more insulting yells of 'freak'.

"Screw you!" I stormed away. Upon realising that only took me closer to the bellowing people on the other side of the mesh, I turned back. "I'm not playing your game, Catherine."

Her expression remained the same, eyes hard, mouth unsmiling. "You get five minutes to change. If you don't, we fetch Gabe."

"Fuck! You!" I raged back to the bars, pressed my temples against the steel.

"Rules are rules, Ethan. I did tell you before we brought you down."

With their limited vocabulary, the callers returned to their favoured shout of 'change'.

"This is bullshit!"

"Five minutes—"

"Five minutes is not long enough, dammit!"

"Make them enough. And one of those has almost passed."

With a snarl, I lunged through the gap with my hand, my chest smashing against the metal.

Catherine shot backward way too fast for my fingers to find purchase. She seemed unbothered by my attempted attack when her emotionless face lifted back to mine. "Four minutes, Ethan."

I withdrew my arm to my own side, and backed away from the two vampires. While my gaze remained on the female, the continued chant of 'change' from the watchers beat inside my head.

How the hell could I change? In a roomful of humans? Packs had spent years—hundreds of years—keeping our existence a secret. To change in front of one human—let alone a roomful— went against everything I'd been taught to believe in.

Obeying would be a betrayal to my race.

My hands fisted and un-fisted at my hips. The bulge of my chest heaved with each inhalation.

Catherine moved back to the door. "Three and a half minutes until we go for Gabe."

Promise me one thing, buddy. Kyle's words boinged around inside my mind. *Promise me, you'll swallow your pride.*

One face after another peered at me through the mesh. Every set of eyes held a hunger that made my skin crawl.

The meaning of Kyle's plea became so clear when mixed with Catherine's words from upstairs. *It's amazing what results come from a sharp electro shock, or a decent shot of adrenaline into the bloodstream ... then there are the ones we leave to their own demise.*

Swallow my pride and change of my own free will, or suffer a forced change and provide even further entertainment for an already sick crowd.

Not swallowing my pride would bring worse consequences than that, though. It'd bring suffering for my brothers.

I gulped down the phlegm sitting in the back of my throat. My fingers unclenched, and I reached down for my stud and zipper, tugging them both loose.

Catherine's eyes took on a high shine, when I shoved my jeans over my hips and legs, and kicked them aside. With my eyes focussed entirely on her, and my mind on plans to slaughter her the second I got the chance, I blanked every sound in the room, every scent, every presence, and hunkered down to all fours.

Through deep breaths, I concentrated, until a prickle teased at my skull and spread backward to bleed into my spine. My fingers caught the tingle, followed by my toes, and the sensation itched at the joints in its attempt to infiltrate my limbs.

My lids lowered at a tug of flesh in my thigh. I forced them open, kept my eyes on the vampire before me—a reminder to myself of who needed to pay for the fuckup I'd been hauled into.

I didn't need to watch to know how every affliction affected my body. I knew the stretch of my flesh to be necessary for the deformation of bone beneath the surface. Just as I understood some parts needed to break before they could restructure into my new form.

Muscles and tendons went into spasm, condensed and strengthened, to accommodate my bulked mass.

Grunts passed my lips to the beat of the humans' shouts, while cramps attacked every inch of my body—flexing appendages and twisting limbs from man to canine, contracting my rippling cheeks before the warping began. My breaths huffed past my rusted throat as each new wave of pain stabbed into me.

Another distortion drew my muscles taut either side of my spine, solidifying them into a duet of ridges, a split second before my vertebra cracked.

One. Two. Three. All the way down to the thirty-third—
a gasp arriving with each crunch and the arching of my
body.

The order reversed, and each realigned into place.

Growls rolled up from my chest, when the high line of
my back plummeted to bow against the agony, and the
growth of my hair hit my periphery. Each strand
thickening and sprouting through my pores provided a
rich, brown shaggy coating, as the surrounding flesh at my
coccyx protruded to a throbbing extension, and my breaths
panted from me throughout the delivery of my tail.

The agony ceased, but I knew it to be nothing more than
trickery of the mind. My transformation hadn't completed.

I tensed. My breaths came short.

The splitting of my skull boomed through my mind.

Feral grunts erupted up through my throat.

At the elongation of delicate facial bone, quiet whimpers
took over my vocals.

Through the sharp stabbing to my head, my cranium re-
knitted, and with a rippling snarl, I thrust forth from my
change with the power of a missile.

Victorious cheers filled the room.

I grounded to a halt. Inhaled.

Powerful sweetness invaded my senses, its sickly odour
worse than any of the remnants of past battles.

I sneezed—sneezed a second and third time.

Mocking laughter overtook the cheers.

Another inhalation resulted in a second round of chuffed
breaths spurting past my nostrils.

I lifted my gaze in search of the source, and it fell on the
two vampires before me.

Dad's insistence over the stench of vampires flashed
through my mind. *Damn thing blocked my sinuses up for
days after I killed it.* Was that the big why? We had to be
changed to detect them?

I certainly smell you now, bitch.

My lips drew back to reveal my teeth. I lowered my rear, tensed my hind muscles, sprang for the duo with a roar and collided with the barrier.

Breath gushed from me as Catherine and Joseph took a hasty step back. I poked my muzzle through the bars, instincts urging me after them, despite rationality telling me I attempted an impossible task.

With each effort, the cheekbones of my face crashed against the metal.

I didn't care—not while consumed by the vampires' scent.

A squeak tugged my ears up. Whistles from the humans hit with the same effect. At a shout of 'that's one pussy I'd love to stroke', I paused long enough to take notice.

Catherine squatted down to my level. Her lips curved into a smile. "Showtime." Her chin lifted as her eyes flitted to something at my rear. "Watch your back."

I whirled round.

Cat essence mingled with vampire before I'd made the full turn.

My gaze lifted the full length of her body, past the long dark hair brushing each breast, until it met with the golden gaze.

Shit, no!

Before me, Brook's lips held a thin line of determination. Although her usual elegance refused to leave her, tentativeness affected her step forward. When she dropped into a crouch, regret showed in the fluttered frown that creased her brow. "Ethan, I'm sorry," she said in a warm tone.

For what? I wanted to ask, although I already knew the answer.

Every fight had been a battle to the death. I had no right to believe Brook would allow me to win. Just as *I* didn't intend to be the one carried out in a body bag.

Her head lifted, yet she didn't fully straighten as she took a few steps back. With her stare locked upon mine, she leapt with the grace of a gazelle. Mid-flight, a shimmer rippled the length of her body and the beauty of her fresh midnight silkiness held me rapt.

She'd barely landed as panther, when a whip of her paw sliced scalpel-sharp claws through my shoulder.

A loud yelp burst from me. I staggered to the left.

The watchers cheered out their approval for the cat, along with their disgust for my weakness.

With a harsh shake of my head, I spun. Thunder grumbled within my chest.

My hackles rose as I brought the circling feline into my sight, and I matched her round route with a smaller one of my own, following every one of her movements.

Five more paces, and she halted.

So did I.

Her body revealed its flexibility in her change of direction. Muzzle low, shoulders high, I turned to stalk the same direction as her.

The lack of sound from her steps told me her claws had retracted. Quiet descended upon our audience, no more than whispers crossing their lips.

Each clockwise move I made took me a fraction closer to the feline. Although she showed no concern, I doubted my manoeuvre went unnoticed by her.

She paused, turned to face me. Altering her path, she slunk to the left.

My shoulder wound stung in my sudden switch of course. I took one step, two.

Before my paw regained its third contact with the concrete, she'd pushed from the ground.

A heartbeat behind, I dived for her with my jaws already open and aiming for her gullet.

The enthusiastic shouts arrived loud enough to endanger the foundations.

Brook's spurted breath bristled the hairs of my face on impact. Stomping feet enhanced the humans' cries of encouragement.

Snarls tore from both of us. A scream of 'come on' vibrated through my mind.

Brook's head whipped side to side—as did mine.

The cage rattled beneath the onslaught of bodies, as if the spectator's bottlenecked to get closer to the action.

Claws slashed through my flesh, and my internal roar arrived loud enough to drown out every other sound as I swung for her. When my teeth located her throat, I locked on with full strength and drove her to the ground.

Pinned by my jaws, she wriggled and bucked. Feline-like whimpers screeched out, their pitch irking my ears.

I growled in warning, pressed down harder.

Her head tossed side to side. Each jerk heightened the risk of my teeth piercing her flesh.

I willed her to calm. Tried to meet her eyes. Her thrashing rendered the attempt a failure.

Please, Brook, don't do this.

With the kick up of her legs, she sliced the underside of my belly.

Agony poured outward and into my limbs. My grip slackened, as did my stance. I stumbled sideways as my forelegs gave way.

A second boot against my chest sent me sprawling. As my chin smacked against concrete, Brook rolled to her paws, and slunk off to my rear.

Calls of, "Get up, mutt," flew from the crowd of humans.

I forced myself to rise and shook my head with a disgruntled growl.

I shouldn't have misjudged her. I wouldn't make that mistake again.

Another headshake, and I turned to face her, but I'd taken no more than a step, when the black blur flashed into the corner of my vision.

My claws scratched against the smooth surface before I found enough traction to thrust myself forward. On collision with the mesh barrier, I expelled a grunt.

From a few inches behind the fencing, the stench of humans intensified. I sent them a growl, and they scrambled backward, almost falling over one another as I pivoted.

In my vacated space, Brook tumbled and skidded across the uneven flooring.

Without waiting for her recovery, I pounced, landing hard along her spine. Finding her throat, I took hold and used my entire body to bind her movements.

Beneath me, she bucked.

Growls rumbled from within my mouth, past her black satin coat, and lent vibrations to my lips.

Another thrash of her body almost lifted me, until a shove down rammed her head to the ground.

"Ethan?"

At my name, my brows knitted together. I lifted my gaze to Catherine's solid blacks beyond the door.

She smiled. "Finish her."

Had my vocal chords been available, I'd have told her to fuck off. My snarls increased, and my attention on her clarified for whom the warning was meant.

"Play the game, Ethan." She dropped to a crouch, wrapped her fingers around the bars. "You win."

Play the game? Over my dead body.

I closed my jaws around Brook's windpipe, throwing every ounce of control I had into the action.

The panther's struggles knocked me up with each jerk. Whimpers burst out with each effort she made.

I tightened my grip. Applied more of my bulk to restrain her.

Mumbles arose from the spectators.

From her position, Catherine's smile widened until her fangs extended to the longest I'd seen them.

As Brook's thrashing lessened to wiggling, I kept my jaws rigid around her throat.

Her whimpers faded. Gasped breaths took their place.

My own chuffed from my nostrils to steam the cool air, while saliva trailed over my chin.

The twitch of her limbs arrived next. Her breaths no longer held substance—a pathetic intake followed by a pitiful exhale.

I counted down from thirty in my head, the estimated seconds she had left.

At ten, a final flutter affected her right foreleg.

At five, she stilled.

Only once I reached zero, did I release my hold.

23

Silence whistled through my ears at a much higher pitch than any of the shouts had. Those around me appeared to be waiting for something, as though poised on a pivotal moment in time.

I removed my muzzle from Brook's throat and sniffed her face. At the soft breaths that warmed my nose, I let out a sigh and lifted my gaze to Catherine.

Something within her expression told me my charade hadn't gone unnoticed, and the small pump of her fists at her waist sent an unspoken urge I struggled to interpret.

I risked looking to the left and caught the stares of the watchers—every one of them directed on the innate panther at my paws.

Did they suspect?

With little other option, I let the rumble brew within my chest. Like an overheated volcano, it vibrated through me, until a howl of victory erupted from my throat.

Gasped complaints responded. Hands slapped over ears. Feet shuffled the humans back in one big stumbling unit of movement.

As my call faded to a low growl, I stepped over Brook's body to disguise the shallow rise and fall of her chest. While my thunder continued to roll, I took in the faces around me.

One by one, my mind absorbed them: from hair the colour of a Red Setter, green eyes and sweaty scent, to golden blond with blue eyes and the aroma of mint. I made a personal promise to return for each of them the second I got the chance.

At the choking waft of vanilla smoke, I lifted my gaze upward.

The cigar dropped from mouth to waist with the wave of the human's hand. With the meaty fingers of his other hand, he slapped the shoulder of the companion who shared his balcony. The duet of almost bald heads shone beneath chandelier light I hadn't noticed before. Each dome held nowhere near the brightness of their teeth when they flashed smiles my way.

The resonation of my snarls escalated.

Whistles loud enough to compete with the howl I'd provided came from the audience.

My focus remained on the two men, on their paunchy stomachs I already knew would hinder them when they ran. Back to their faces, I committed them to memory.

I'll be coming for you, fuckers.

I dropped my face to Brook's. Her breaths continued to ease past her parted lips. With as much care as I could muster, I enclosed her throat with my teeth. My jaw locked into place and a gentle tug slid her along the floor between my legs.

Mumbles rolled from the watchers. "Hey, you see any of the others behave that way before?" The deep tone held disbelief. I distinguished it as the one who'd made the lurid comment at Brook's initial entrance.

Other than ensuring I could recognise that last voice again if I needed to, I ignored them and headed for the farthest spot from them all.

Brook weighed a lot more than I expected for a panther—no doubt a result of solid musculature. Each haul of her limp form risked puncturing her with my teeth. My waddling made the manoeuvres awkward, but I reached a spot in the cage the spectators couldn't get near and laid her down. Once an inhalation of her neck revealed no wounds had come of my mauling, I settled back on my haunches to wait for the farce to be over.

After they'd gotten over their amusement at my protection of the conquered 'meal', the watchers dispersed. As if the degradation of being made to fight for the despicable humans hadn't been enough, Catherine and Joseph left me in the cage while winnings were collected, losses mourned over, and hands shaken—a final slap to an already splintered soul.

Throughout, I kept my attention on the two bald guys peering down from their self-imposed pedestal. Once or twice, I stalked side to side in front of Brook, but my gaze stayed fixed on those I believed responsible for the outrageous setup.

At one point, the steel grey stare of the one on the left met my scrutiny. Vibrations curled my lips with a growl I restrained. The guy's expression gave no indication he'd noticed. Maybe he believed I offered him no threat.

I intended to put him straight on that matter.

The spectators thinned, and the noise levels dwindled as, one by one, they left through double doors in the back wall.

I peered through the stragglers to get a glimpse beyond the circular room that confined those of us left, yet saw nothing to suggest a way out of the building. No windows. No other doors. Only a chandelier that hung above the departing crowd and illuminated the differing shades of hair as they passed beneath.

Once the doors had closed behind the last of the humans, a quiet hum fell over the space, and my gaze swung upward, toward the half-moon balcony.

Empty.

Where had my thoughts drifted to that I'd missed them leaving?

"You can change back, now."

At Catherine's voice, I whipped my head to the right, chuffing my scoff at her smiling face.

"Change back, Ethan."

I sent her a growl—my only way to communicate the curses inside my head.

Her smile diminished. "If you don't, I'll make you." She glanced over her shoulder at her shadowing friend.

"Joseph, go fetch the adrenaline shots." Back to me, her smile returned. "Or maybe you'd prefer wolfsbane."

My shoulders tensed, body coiled tight and ready to spring, until rationality took control and reminded me I'd already accepted enough needless bashes for one day.

With a snarl of disgust thrown at the vampires, I stalked away and prepared to change back.

"Bet you think you're clever, don't you?" Catherine said.

"I don't think I'm anything." I strode over and snatched my jeans off the floor, tugging them over my left leg. "Let us out." I fed in my right leg and slid the denim over my hips.

"I'll let you out when I'm ready, Ethan."

My growl escaped as I went to button my jeans.

"Oh, quit with the dramatics." She lifted a forearm above her head and leaned into the door. "Would it help if I said you impressed me with your skills?"

I left the top two studs undone to allow air to the still-seeping wound below my navel. "Sure, because impressing you has been my number one aspiration since I got here." I pivoted away and padded across to the prone panther.

"You showed excellent control," Catherine said. "I'd heard that about you."

I looked back to her. "From who, exactly?"

"You can't build up a rep and not expect word to spread."

I could have argued I'd gone to no effort to build up a reputation, or that I had no idea how word could spread when most of my fights finished with the other party no longer breathing. Instead, I shrugged—wincing beneath the tug to the gashes across my shoulder—and dropped into a squat beside Brook.

"Funny, though," she said

My head tilted.

"You never struck me as the kind to show mercy."

"I don't." I shuffled my arms beneath Brook's torso and hefted her off the floor with a grunt. "But I choose who I do and don't kill. Not you. I told you I wouldn't play your games, and I meant it." My thigh muscles bunched as I straightened my legs, and a jiggle of the panther settled her into the crook of my arms above my stinging injury.

Catherine's expression could have set stone when I turned to her. "What exactly do you think you're doing?"

"Taking her back down with me."

The blonde waves surrounding her face followed the shake of her head. "Not your job."

"My supposed kill. My clean-up." I angled back a little to accommodate carrying Brook's mass on my walk to the door. "Untidiness isn't my thing. Now, let us out."

Her eyebrow lifted. "You think I'm going to simply allow you to walk out of there?"

I rolled my eyes. "What are you afraid of, Catherine? You have your weapons. And your backup. I have my damn arms full. I'm good, but even I have limitations." I adjusted my grip on the feline, stepping closer to the exit.

Neither Catherine nor Joseph moved. Only two blank expressions stared at me.

I let out a low growl. "Open the door, already. It stinks in here."

Catherine sent a small nod Joseph's way. "Let them out."

From his pocket, he withdrew a bunch of keys and showed no hesitation in choosing and inserting one, and a twist of his wrist unlocked the catch holding me and my feline hostage. The keys returned into his pocket, and his hand reached behind his back, revealing a dart gun.

Where the hell did they keep hiding them? Down the back of their pants?

Catherine kicked in the door, and I stepped back as it swung toward me, and forward to enter the passage. In my arms, Brook's length filled the corridor. Unless they wanted to flatten themselves to the walls, the vampires had little choice but to take the lead.

More relaxed than Joseph, Catherine turned her back on me and trailed her fingers across the stone as she wandered ahead. Her guardian, or whatever the hell Joseph could be considered, walked backward along the route. One black eye stared through the small glass lens of his weapon, while his lid concealed the other, as though he struggled to keep me in his sights with both eyes open at the same time.

About twenty yards into the passageway, an iridescent glow drew my attention down at the same time as Brook's body alterations tickled the flesh along my forearms. Even up close, I couldn't comprehend the ease with which she shifted—couldn't follow it with my eyes. Within seconds, her rump in my one hand had been replaced by a butt cheek, and her shoulder blade nestled into the palm of my other.

I paused to adjust, nudging her higher, attempting to find less invasive spots to grip. The motion rolled her, flopped an arm to dangle below, and the twist of her head tangled her hair around her slackened features.

Battle scars decorated her flesh, paled to paint a map of injuries past, and I couldn't help but wonder how long she'd been held captive, in how many fights she'd been made to perform. I also wondered if she'd leave with me, given the chance, because I doubted my conscience would allow me to walk away and leave her behind.

"She's truly beautiful, don't you think?" Joseph asked.

I lifted my gaze from the panther, found Joseph's smile aimed my way. "Sure." *'Cept she smells like a cat.*

"You want her?"

At Joseph's question, Catherine made a slow turn toward us.

I shook my head, and the small movement sent a sting shooting from my left shoulder to the side of my neck—another panther scratch located.

"You sure?" Joseph smiled, raising his eyes to peer over the scope. "Could make arrangements for you."

"Very accommodating." I met his gaze, yet I doubted any humour warmed mine. "First, I'm offered Kyle to keep me company. Now, you try to give me a cat. Your room service sucks, you know that?"

"Give him a week, maybe two." Joseph's face half-turned toward Catherine. "Once the frustration kicks in, he'll lose his pickiness."

The smile that crept across Catherine's features chilled me— and not simply because of the quick draw of her fangs.

I suppressed my shudder. "I very much doubt that."

Joseph continued to share his smirk, and Catherine ran her tongue across each sharp bicuspid before whirling to walk forward again.

Once it seemed as though we'd trekked full circle, Catherine swung open a door on the left. From the freshness of the atmosphere within, I recognised it as the staircase to the underground chamber.

The same two goons guarded the lower doors. They didn't appear to have altered their ready stance from earlier, at all. Their eyes flitted from me to the limp form in my arms.

Stocky vamp's brow quirked up. "What's going on?"

"We got ourselves a new breed of predator, it would seem," Joseph said.

"Two never come back down." His voice held a deep gruffness, like his words had to sift through gravel to reach us.

"I know." Catherine moved forward, patted him on the shoulder. "Apparently, Ethan doesn't like to kill his prey. Imagine that. No more unnecessary corpses. No more finding replacements for decent fighters." Excitement tinged her tone, and her eyes danced when she turned them on me. "With a few more Ethan's, we could evolve."

I'd refused to play their game. To bow to their demands. To kill at their will. All I'd succeeded in doing was giving them ideas. "You going to open the doors?" I stepped closer to the entrance, biting down on my growl. I'd rather be back in my cage than listening to their bullshit.

With a high-pitched laugh that grated through my jaw, Catherine broke from Mr Shithouse and leaned into the chamber doors.

As every scent from earlier drifted out, I took a deep breath, a final intake of clean air, and forced my feet to carry me back inside.

Eyes peered out from behind bars. Whatever their thoughts at the two of us returning, they didn't verbalise them, and nothing but the life-sounds of bodies met my ears.

Joseph strode ahead, whipped out his jailer's keys, and ducked around the corner before me. He halted outside the door to Brook's cage, as I headed for my own. "Nuh-uh, in here, for the lovely puss."

"Thought you offered her to me." My gaze fell on Kyle. At my subtle nod to let him know I was okay, a half smile curved his lips.

"I did." Joseph slid in the key, unlocking Brook's door. "And you turned the offer down. Now, bring her in here."

My mind raced through the injuries I knew patterned Kyle's body, the damage to Gabe's mental condition, the promises I'd made, and I hesitated.

To keep Brook in my own cage would make any future plans for escape so much simpler—especially if Catherine's questions about Lauren had provoked the right suspicions into my head. All I had to do was talk to the girl, try and get her to open up to me, and convince her to help us get out. I had no intention of sticking around to see who they made me fight next.

"Now, Ethan!" Catherine's voice bore no room for dispute.

With a growl, I whirled and marched toward Brook's cell, but not before I sent a glance in the direction my thoughts had travelled.

My step almost faltered, my pulse lurched, and the tightening of my jaw shot pain into my skull.

The cell beside mine stood empty.

Lauren had gone.

24

I forced myself not to look back at Lauren's empty cell, made demands of my head not to turn that way. Eye contact with Kyle pled for him not to give the watching vampires an inkling of my concern, though the thudding beat inside my chest might well have already alerted them.

Joseph offered a smug smile, as I passed him into Brook's cage. I halted near the bars at the front, and lowered her where I'd be able to see her when she woke.

"Ready?

A twist of my head brought Joseph's face back into view. With a nod, I exited the space, and crossed to my own enclosure.

Catherine didn't speak. She hadn't since she ordered me to return Brook to her cage, yet her scrutiny could have pinned even the strongest of fighters.

Pretending I hadn't noticed, I stepped into my cell, and rolled my shoulders while waiting for Joseph to lock me in.

With my back to them both, clinking told me when he secured the panther, and the quiet tap of his shoes announced his walk to my door, where the keys jangled once more.

"Just so you know, I'm not done with you, yet, darling," Catherine said. "We need to ... get together. There are things we need to discuss."

"Thing is,"—I stretched my neck side-to-side, without turning—"I never much enjoy our little chats."

Her laughter tugged the flesh tight around my eyes. "Always the entertainer. I'll let you recover, first, before I send someone down for you."

If not for Lauren's absence altering the course of my plans, I'd have smiled at the near certainty that I'd no longer be there. Instead, I shrugged. "'Sup to you."

"Yes, it is."

Her pump-clad feet made next to no sound beside Joseph's hard soles on their way to the exit. Once the double doors had whooshed back into place, I spun and marched across to the corner of my cage, where Kyle's gaze already aimed my way, and prodded a thumb toward my neighbouring pen. "Where'd she go?"

His shoulders hitched up a touch. "No idea." His chin flicked toward Brook, back to me. "How was the fight?" His eyes seemed to search for so many more answers than the question asked. "Looks like the cat has more moves than I thought, judging by the marks she left on you."

"Fight was fine." My voice arrived flat—an absent reply with my mind only on the young girl. "How long's she been gone?"

Another jerk of his shoulders. "Maybe an hour. Maybe a little more. You okay?"

"I'm peachy." I met his swollen eyes, frowned at the wedge cut from the bridge of his nose.

"We need to get out of here." His voice deepened. "This is some kooky shit they've got going on."

"I'm going to get us out of here. Just as soon as I figure a few things out." *And as soon as Lauren gets back.* I rubbed at my face. "Who came down for the girl? Did they say why they wanted her?"

"Bathroom break, he said ... one of the vamps on guard out there." He gestured toward the double steel doors. "Been a long time for a bathroom break, though. You think something's going on with her?"

Drawing in a deep breath, I nodded. "Very much so." And it couldn't be good.

Time ticked by—or it would have had there been a clock. The cold iron of the bars dug into my back, and my arse lost all sensation once the chill of concrete took effect. I didn't move, though. What little energy I had needed preserving. Just in case.

"How bad is Gabe?" Kyle's voice came out low.

"I already told you. He's holding up."

"That tells me nothing, and you know it."

I peered over my shoulder. Kyle's intense stare, as it met mine, and the tightness around his eyes, told me everything I needed to know about his fear for his own health. "He's fixable." I gave a slight nod, hoping I'd told him the truth, but my frown crept in, when he began to self-study—a repeat of his earlier behaviour.

With his fingers splayed out before him, Kyle seemed to be staring down at them as though looking at parts belonging to somebody else. He flicked them over, giving the same scrutiny to his palms, before curling his flexed fingers into tight fists. Another finger straighten, another clench, and his focus travelled the length of each forearm, the tendons drawing taut with the exercise. A lift of his head brought his narrowed gaze to mine, and like he'd been caught doing something he shouldn't, a sheepish smile curved the corners of his lips.

His expression did little to ease my concern, or the tripled pace of my pulse. "Everything okay, bud?"

His smile widened, yet not far enough to warm his hazel irises. "'Course."

"You must have expected some side effects." Brook's soft voice arrived on a drowsy cadence.

I twisted round and met her golden orbs. "Hey."

"Hey," she whispered, her gaze remaining on mine. "I did not expect to be waking up."

"I didn't like the game they wanted me to play. So I made up a few of my own rules."

"I am grateful you did." She gave me a small nod. "Thank you."

"No worries." Pointing, I drew her attention to Lauren's absence. "They took her."

"Why?" She rolled up to sit, and leaned against the bars. "After all this time?"

"How long have you been here, Brook?"

Her slender shoulders lifted in a dainty shrug. "Maybe four weeks. Maybe more ... or less. The only time the girl has left her cage is for the bathroom."

"According to Kyle, that's what they said they wanted her for. But she's been gone a hell of a long time already."

"That isn't good."

Ours gazes locked as panic fluttered through me. I couldn't have agreed more.

More time passed, as did more murmured conversation about how our situation could have been better. The longer Lauren didn't return, the further convinced I grew that she'd never come back. When the steel doors swung open, I didn't bother to glance up, so resolute in my mind that it wouldn't be her.

Only once her subtle scent drifted to me did I check.

Red blotches coated the skin of her cheeks, matching the bright rims of eyes still moist from evident tears.

The strong set of her shoulders had gone, along with any ounce of teenage attitude she'd clung onto. Only a broken girl remained as her entire body appeared to shrink in on itself.

Each step toward her cage seemed to take immense effort, as she swayed from side to side, and her feet slapped down with lack of elegance.

Jaw tight, my body tensed to thrust up and confront Chad beside her, before my brain sent a silent order not to react. I dropped my attention back to the ground.

Her door squeaked closed once she'd stepped into her cell. As soon Chad had her secured and had tugged the double doors closed at his rear, I swung my head round to face the young teen.

She'd moved only a foot from the entrance. Her hands trembled at her sides, and a quiet sob erupted from her as she chewed at her lower lip.

I sent a quick glance toward Kyle, to Brook, both of them facing the girl. Back to Lauren, I asked, "You okay?"

Her shoulders shuddered, but she didn't speak, didn't turn my way.

I climbed to my feet and moved closer to the separating bars, ducking my head in the hope of making eye contact through the blonde tendrils hanging across her face. "Lauren?"

An indistinguishable mumble passed her lips. The tiny wave of her right hand hinted she'd said something I was expected to interpret.

My eyes screwed up a little as I tried to figure it out. Failing, I asked, "Where'd they take you?"

Another murmur, higher in pitch than the last, accompanied the upward point of her finger to the ceiling.

"Want to tell me why?"

Her headshake whipped her hair side to side.

"Maybe I can help you."

"How?" That one, although it arrived on a banshee-type howl, I caught. Her delicate hands fisted, and she reached them toward me. "How you gon—"—a hiccup hitched her voice—"stop 'em putting me"—a shuddered breath—"in the cage."

Oh, Jesus.

Her chin inclined until her gaze locked with mine. A desperate plea shone through her tears. "How?" As though the bones had evaporated through her entire frame, her legs crumpled beneath her, and she landed with a thud. More squeaked incoherency pushed past the fingers she spread across her mouth and cheeks, and her shoulders wracked beneath an onslaught of violent sobbing, to the point I had no chance of deciphering anything she said.

I stepped back from the bars and raised my face to the ceiling, sending a mental cacophony of threats and curses in the direction of those who'd treated a young girl so fuckishly. I sent a glance toward Kyle and Brook.

They both stared back.

Blowing out a long, slow breath, I dropped into a squat. "Lauren?"

Her mumbles, which had lessened a little, crescendoed again to wailing proportions.

I ignored the tic that kicked in below my left eye. "Lauren, I'm going to help you, I swear. But I can't do that unless you talk to me."

The operatic crying dropped a notch, as did the shake of her body. Green glistened out at me through hair fallen forward again. "Whacayoodo?"

My cheeks puffed out as I restrained my heavy sigh, and I let it out on a slow release while trying to think how to calm, how to approach what had to be discussed, how best not to set off any more tears than those already spilled. "Okay ... I'm going to start by telling you what I think the vampires think they know about you."

Although her shoulders continued in irregular judders, she moved her hands from her face and brushed her blonde straggles aside.

"I think, they think, you can do stuff."

Her head shook—a tiny, almost imperceptible action.

I pursed my lips. "I think they think you have the ability to move or manipulate objects."

A breath shuddered from her, but she didn't deny my orated thoughts.

"They also think you opened my door." I held her gaze steady for a moment, before continuing, "Just like, if they'd been down here to witness it, they'd think you moved Kyle's unconscious body across his cage."

Lauren's lower lip quivered.

"Telekinetic?" Surprise carried across in the feline's whisper.

An upward tilt of my chin answered Brook's question, while my eyes remained focused on the green ones before me. "But ... do you want to know what I don't get?"

Lauren stared at me. Her shoulders lifted in a shrug.

I paused to gather my thoughts, to convince myself I wouldn't lose her by opening my big mouth further.

"What?" she mumbled when I still hadn't spoken.

I relaxed teeth I hadn't realised I'd begun to grind and pointed a finger toward Lauren. "If you can really do what they suspect, if you really did open my door ... what are you still doing here? Why the hell haven't you made a run for it?"

Her lips popped beneath her blown out breath, and she asked, "Would you?"

25

I couldn't decide whether to be happy I'd got the girl to inadvertently admit her ability, or alarmed that she hadn't tried to make a run for it. "Actually, Lauren, I'd take any opportunity I could to get out of here."

"So, why didn't you, then?" A quiet sniffle tacked onto the end of her words. "You got out your cage." Snot bubbled from her nose. "You could have gone. But you didn't."

"Because I have more to consider than simply what's best for me." I shrugged. "No way on earth would I be able to walk away and leave my pack brothers behind. Just like I now won't be able to walk out of here without taking you along, either. I'm overprotective—it's just who I am." I stared at her a few moments. "What's your excuse?"

"So, you're saying, they're the reason you're still here?" A couple of judders affected her breathing. "Otherwise, you'd be gone?"

Lips pursed, I gave a slow nod. "I'd have given it my best shot, sure I would." Even without guaranteed success, I'd have tried. "Wouldn't have had the advantage you have, though."

"Wotchoo mean?" She tucked her fingers inside the sleeve of her denim shirt and wiped it beneath her nose.

"How'd you know Kyle was breathing, Lauren? Before he'd woken up?" I stared hard at her. "I know you couldn't have seen him ... so, how'd you know?"

She didn't answer at first. I thought she wouldn't, but she shrugged. "I don't know," she mumbled, bringing her index fingers to her temples and wagging them like antennae. "I felt it, I guess."

My eyebrow quirked up. "In what way?"

Her shoulders lifted again, drooping on a deep sigh. "Dunno." She walked her fingers through the air. "Kinda like feeling my way round, or something, and then feeling over stuff when I find an obstacle."

With no telekinesis experience, I had no idea if what she said rang true, but I still nodded, impressed by her potential. "Anyone else in your family have this ability?"

She hesitated before shaking her head. "I hoped my mum had, but when I tried telling her, she didn't believe me." She tugged at her snot-covered sleeve. "So, I tried to show her." A quiet laugh breathed past her lips. "She hunted for the string I'd used to move the cup, and then got mad at me for tricking her when she couldn't find it. I never bothered to tell anyone else—'cept Jackson—"

"Jackson?"

She nodded. "My friend from school, but he said it sounded like I had a brain tumour, so I kinda stopped doing stuff ... just in case." Her lips squished to the side, and she rubbed her face using her sleeve.

I peered away for a moment and considered the best way to address her situation, finding zilch help in the uncertainty hooding Kyle's eyes.

Common sense told me fear played a big factor in why Lauren hadn't made a break for it. Getting Lauren's agreement to aid our escape would take some tact, yet I had no option but to try—especially as I had no idea how long I had before Catherine would decide she wanted to 'chat' with me again.

Blowing out a breath, I gave my attention back to the girl. "If I ask you a couple questions, for good reason, will you answer?"

The momentary confusion in her eyes suggested I'd thrown her. "For what good reason?" Hesitancy slowed her words.

Go for the jugular, or beat about the bush? "To figure out our chances of getting out of here."

Even if I hadn't heard her swallow, the movement along her throat showed her nervous response. "Okay." Her voice arrived at barely more than a whisper.

I smiled in a hope to reassure, as I mimicked the finger dance she'd done at her temples. "How far a distance can you feel with your mind?"

Her shoulders twitched, before her tiny hand pointed toward the steel doors. "I know there's two of them outside ... that there's pretty much always two of them. I know this place is never left unguarded, which makes us screwed as far as getting farther than those doors are concerned."

That's why she's still here. Doesn't believe there's a way out beyond this basement. "Another question ... how hard is it for you to unlock doors ... like you did with mine?"

"I never said I di—"

"Please, Lauren." I wanted to sugar-coat, but my mental ticking clock had been counting down since her return. "There's no time for messing around. Not any longer."

"It's hard." She twisted her skirt hem in her hands. "Working through the mechanics takes a few minutes. But even if I get you out, you won't get past them. They're too strong." Her huge eyes widened. "And they have guns. They always have those."

"Let me worry about the guards." I waited a beat, before asking, "How long would it take you to open five doors?"

The whites of her eyes showed as she stared at me. "You mean ... we're not letting everyone out?" Something that sounded like disbelief heightened her whisper. "You're gonna leave them behind?"

"For now." I scanned through the shadows at the surrounding cells. Too many held beings whose behaviour I couldn't predict once released. "Unless you fancy handling them all?"

She shook her head.

"That's what I thought." I smiled. "So, how long for five doors, Lauren?"

"It should be faster after the first." When she stared upward and ticked off her fingers, I realised I had her. "Ten minutes."

"Narrow it down to five, and I swear I will do everything in my power to get you out of here." Keeping the urgency, the plea, out of my voice took a lot of effort when all I wanted to do was demand she open our five doors that instant so we could get going. I fed my hand through the bars until it hovered before her. "Do we have a deal?"

She stared down at my hand but didn't take it. "They'll kill us if we're caught," she said.

"I won't get us caught."

"He won't," Kyle said, and Lauren twisted toward him. "I should know." Kyle pointed between himself and me. "We've been friends since birth. I've never seen him fail at anything."

Though I wanted to tell Kyle not to make uncertain promises, I kept my mouth shut. Self-doubt needed to vanish if I intended to succeed. It could show its face later.

Lauren continued to stare toward Kyle, like she was trying to work out if he'd merely told her what he thought she wanted to hear.

I watched her, waiting for her to speak. When she didn't, I thought I'd failed, until her head leaned to the left, her eyes screwed up as though in concentration, and a quiet click arrived from the direction of my door.

I turned toward my exit. Just as it had done so before, the barred way out of my cage stood slightly ajar. My lips curved as I straightened to stand, and I marched across my enclosure. "Time to roll," I muttered as I swung open the door.

Lauren's cage came as my first stop, to assure her I had every intention of keeping my word. When she didn't look up, I figured she concentrated, so I kept my mouth shut. I didn't have to wait long—less than a minute of her eyes narrowing and brow creasing—before the quiet disconnection of metal announced the opening of her door.

A prod of my fingers sent it on an inward swing. "Ready?"

She scrambled to her feet, but moved no closer to me. "I think this is a bad idea."

"I think staying here is an even worse one." I hesitated a second. considering whether to go for the blow low enough to get her to comply. "And neither of those are anywhere near as bad as going in the cage upstairs will be for you."

She chewed on her bottom lip, her eyes flittering away to the side. "I'm scared."

"Of what? Me? Getting out of here? Going in the cage? Figure out which you're most scared of, and try facing the other two." I reached a hand out toward her. "Please, Lauren. Show me a little trust."

She took a deep breath and stepped forward. Her skinny fingers held the iciness of shock when they slid into mine. "Who next?"

"Kyle."

"Okay." Her whisper accompanied a small nod.

I stared away while she worked, figured she'd be more comfortable without my scrutiny, and kept my focus on the vampire in the cage beside Lauren's. At the rear of his enclosure, the only detail that led me to believe his closed eyes didn't mean he slept was his vertical posture, yet no tension claimed his shoulders or features. His entire body appeared relaxed. Still, I studied him for a sign of movement. I didn't want to imagine the ruckus he'd likely cause if he spotted our antics.

Head tilted, I caught the light pad of Kyle's steps and the low squeak of his door, before his hand grasped my upper arm. "Go, get Gabe. I'll take over here."

Without a word, I ducked off to the left, Lauren's hand still in mine. When she tugged back a little, I peered down at her.

"What's wrong?"

"It's too dark round there," she mumbled. "Can't we do it from here?"

"And risk you opening the wrong door?" I drew her in front of me to shepherd her along. "I'd rather not."

Lauren allowed me to guide her without further complaint, but her boots plonked against the concrete as though making a statement of protest with each step. Small tremors vibrated through my palms when I placed a hand on each of her shoulders.

I bent down to her ear. "You're safe with me."

"I know," she whispered back, yet her scent held a strong redolence of fear and anxiety.

I searched the dimness for disturbance from the surrounding beings, all of them in varying stages of distress—footsteps in the far corner identified the pacing of one, but only slumped or defeated felines, canines, vampires, and whatever the hell the unidentifiable scents were, filled the other spaces.

I kept my attention on my goal as we passed along the passage, my body instinctively curved around Lauren's the closer we got to Gabe. If she noticed, or if it bothered her, she showed no indication above the unease she'd already portrayed.

As though he'd heard us coming, Gabe's eyes already aimed toward our approach.

I sent him a smile of reassurance and kept my voice low to avoid unnecessary detection from the surrounding enclosures. "Hey, Gabe."

He narrowed his eyes, and his nostrils flared as he took a deep inhalation. "Wh-who's this?" The stammer somewhat killed his toughness aura.

"Her name's Lauren." I watched him as I spoke, unsure about the way he studied the young girl.

"W—" His jaw tightened as did his fists at his sides.

"Lauren's our skeleton key." I caught his gaze with my own, until his steadied, and hoped he received the unspoken order to play nice. He backed down with a nod, and I assured him, "She's going to let you out of your cage."

His head whipped up. As he took a couple strides toward us, a tiny jolt of Lauren's body knocked her back against my chest. Despite the nervous energy pumping from him, hope emanated from his gaze.

"You ready to get out of here?" I asked him, when he reached the bars.

"As ever." Something resembling a smile spread across his face beneath his jittery eyes.

"Okay, Lauren. Work your magic."

Other than the rise and fall of her chest, her body stilled. For a few moments, only her breaths filled the stagnant air.

Gabe sidestepped to his door. His eyes bored into it, like he could somehow join forces with Lauren's mind to get the job done quicker. His muscles drew taut across his shoulders and through his arms. Even his thighs bunched tight—ready for springing.

"Where's K-K-Kyle?" he asked.

"On sentry."

Gabe pressed a hand against the door. The second it disengaged, he yanked it open and nigh on dived from his cell. "Let's g-g-go!" His body gave tiny jerks in time with his speech impediment.

I twisted to follow him, but not faster than Lauren, who leaned around my torso. I tracked the path of her focus, finding it on Gabe making his way down the passage to where Kyle waited. It took me a second to realise she must have been staring after his naked butt.

With a twitch of my eyebrow, I nudged her to get going.

Her chin lifted as she walked, yet her head didn't turn away from whatever had her attention. "Who's number five?" she whispered. "The shifter?"

"Yes." *If she'll agree to come.*

Kyle ruffled Gabe's hair, as the younger werewolf sniffed at his wounds. Lauren and I headed straight for Brook's cage. I half expected her to have shifted to her panther form, considering the inconsistency of her changes, yet she stood at the door as though confident I'd never leave without her—shoving any doubt I'd had about that out the window.

I moved close to her bars. "You with me on this?"

She answered with a chin inclination, adding, "And you'll watch my back, yes?"

"If you'll watch mine."

A scuffle in the adjoining cell preceded the emergence of the werewolf from the shadows at the rear, drawing my and the feline's attention that way. "Take me with you." An underlying desperation dominated his whisper.

One captive requesting to join us was a minor issue. If others caught on and started calling an SOS, it would become problematic pretty fast.

I leaned in close to Lauren's ear. "Tell me you're working on Brook's door, already?"

Without speaking, she nodded, and around thirty seconds later the lock clicked.

Brook exited her enclosure, but hadn't even stepped through the doorway when the other werewolf's hand shot out, and he grabbed hold of her upper arm.

Beneath my palms, Lauren's shoulders stiffened. I rubbed at them to help me focus on controlling my brewing growl.

"Please." Although the wolf held onto Brook, his eyes were directed to me. "I can help. You won't regret it."

Famous last words ... "Think you can manage one more?" I asked Lauren, because letting him out would draw less notice than arguing against it.

The speed at which his door unlatched hinted she'd already begun working on it before I'd given the okay. Maybe she wanted to attract unnecessary attention even less than I did.

With mostly bare feet, our group made little noise, as we congregated outside Brook's cage, just out of sight of the double doors.

Lauren twisted within my grasp, and she turned to Kyle, to Brook, to the other wolf and to Gabe before she stared up at me. "Tell me you have a plan for the dodgy clothes situation."

26

Lauren had a point about our clothes situation, given three of our six-member party wore nothing, but the bigger issue of getting past the double act beyond the steel doors took precedence.

We turned away from the bothersome vamp, after a last check assured us his eyes were still closed. How we hadn't disturbed him puzzled me. Something told me the beings' hearing held as much acuteness as my own, yet not even an eyebrow twitch affected his features. It took a lot to turn my back on him when so much rode on us getting to the exit unhindered.

With each additional step, we drew one supernatural after another to the front of their cage, their knuckles white as they gripped the bars—the could-be-witch, shifter, wolf, shifter, another possible witch.

Those who spoke kept their voices low. The ones who didn't emitted a quiet rumble, probably of frustration.

As much as I wanted to swear I'd return, to ensure justice would be carried out, and to set them all free, I clamped my lips shut and ignored them as best as I could. I'd always been taught not to make promises I didn't know I could keep.

Admittedly, I hesitated outside the wolf's bars. No more than a kid, his rigid jaw and shining stare offered up beseeching his lips didn't vocalise. His being a kindred kind almost urged me to take him with us, but our party already had more members than I wanted.

Only the vampire in the last enclosure failed to come forth.

Like the one who resided beside Lauren's cell, he stood with an unnatural stillness that prickled the nape of my neck.

Did vampires sleep standing up?

Damn beings gave me the creeps.

Silence carried through from the other side of the double doors when we reached them. I didn't know whether to take it as a good sign, or not. Even the mumbles from the cages dwindled, until only breaths and heartbeats remained.

I steadied my own breathing, tried to lessen the pound of my pulse whirring through my hearing, and took my lips down close to Lauren's ears. "They out there? You feel them?" She nodded, and I turned to Brook. "I want you to look after Lauren, whil—"

"Stupid idea," Brook hissed.

My hackles rose, as my eyebrow twitched up.

"Do not try to protect me for being female." Fire blazed in her golden eyes. "And do not underestimate me for that reason, either." Her levelled tone did nothing to disguise her fury. "In case you had not noticed, other than the girl, I am the only one here unaffected by vampire venom. Would you care to risk your friends being bitten at this point, Ethan?"

I'd been chauvinistic without even realising it. Blame it on my responsibility to Jem and Mum, and my natural instinct to look out for them. I'd not even considered that Brook should make up a quarter of the fighting pairs—two of us against each vampire.

"Sorry," I muttered, before looking to Lauren. "I want you to stand over there,"—I inclined with my chin— "beside the door on the left." That way, she'd be behind it when it opened. "I want you to face this way. And I do not want you to move until I come tell you it's clear. Understand?"

Her nod arrived as a jerk, and she took her position in silence, grabbing a fistful of denim and dropping her gaze. As she twisted her hands in the fabric, sweat drenched her scent to the point I questioned how she'd cope with the breakout.

I swung to the right and found Gabe's attention already on me, and a subtle point of my finger drew it to the girl. "Stay with her." He opened his mouth, to protest no doubt, until my hardened stare cut him short. "Not a request, Gabe."

Although his jaw tightened, he gave a curt nod and padded behind me to join Lauren.

Her head whipped up as soon as he stood in front of her, and her eyes fluttered toward the ceiling as her fiddling fingers went into overdrive on her shirt cuffs.

"Plan?" Kyle mumbled to my right.

Damned if I know. "Take them out."

His quiet chuckle rumbled from him. "Good plan."

"I thought so."

"Do you two never take serious issues seriously?" Brook's harsh reprimand dragged a 'Sorry', from Kyle and me.

I scanned from the shifter to Kyle, to the young wolf with his flexing hands and ready posture, and tried to make a rapid assessment of who to pair with whom. Given the choice, I'd have opted for Kyle at my rear any day. If not him, I'd have gone for Brook, but leaving Kyle with backup whose abilities I hadn't witnessed offered too much concern—at least I'd seen first-hand that the panther could hold her own.

I switched position until I met the wolf's side, and sent a nod to the other two. Kyle wouldn't need telling of my game plan, but Brook's at quizzical expression I offered her a smile. "I'm counting on you to hold his hand."

Amusement brightened her eyes, as Kyle's growl grumbled in my direction.

Without waiting to hear what he had to say, I took one stride forward, grasped hold of the door handle, but hesitated at a whimper to my left.

Lauren stood with her face turned as far toward the wall as it could go, and I realised the sound had come from her—just as quickly as I recognised Gabe's proximity had to have been the cause.

With one hand braced against the wall over her shoulder, his flared nostrils followed the curve of her neck.

My heart stuttered a beat. "Gabe!" I thrust toward him a step with my barked command.

As though unbothered, his face made a slow twist my way. One corner of his mouth quirked up. "Sorry," he said with a lazy drawl.

Even beneath my glower, his expression didn't alter. At least he pushed away from towering over the girl. I guessed I still had an element of control over the pup.

At a hiss behind Gabe, my head whipped up in time to catch the very awake vampire's lunge of his arm through his bars—toward Lauren.

Gabe twisted before I'd even growled.

I pounced forward for the vampire at the same time as Gabe, and would have reached him if the damn doors hadn't shot open and smashed into my side.

The power of the collision knocked me sprawling through the air. I hit concrete with a grunt. Roughness tore at the skin of my shoulder as I skidded along the ground.

"Look out!" The warning arrived from the caged werewolf.

Following a pop, a dart soared toward me.

I rolled just in time to avoid sedation, flicking over onto all fours and kicking out at the missile before it could ricochet off to affect anyone else.

My head snapped up to see Gabe grabbing the caged vamp through the bars.

He twisted his neck with a force I'd never seen in him before. The body dropped to the floor with a heavy thud.

My gaze flitted to the right, to both guards in the open doorway, their weapons directed on me.

Bollocks!

"You're starting to become more trouble than you're worth," the stocky one said.

The curl of his companion's lip suggested he held me in the same regard.

"Only just starting to be a bother?" Gabe's stance altered to the side, but I kept my attention on the threat before me, blanking out the frozen bodies of the other four of my party. "Damn, I must be losing my touch."

Spotting the tightening of the Eastern vampire's finger against his trigger, I bounded to the left a second before another dart homed in on my vacated spot.

I whirled back into a crouch.

How many rounds did a dart gun hold? Impulse told me one, but I couldn't be sure.

Without waiting for the vampires' next move, I thrust forth into a dive that smacked my shoulder against Stocky's torso.

He stumbled backward, taking me down on top of him, and his head hit concrete with a solid thud.

A growl rolled free behind me, as I scrambled to my knees.

Scuffles brushed the floor at my rear.

Fingers clutched like claws at my shoulders for a brief instant before vanishing.

A shout rang out from Gabe, but before I could catch the words, the doors crashed against the stone walls behind me, echoing with enough resonance to bring the two vampires reinforcement.

If we didn't get a move on, we'd end up back behind bars.

I drew back my fist. Drove it down. Aimed for Stocky's nose.

Cartilage splintered and blood sprayed on impact.

At a grunt and bump to my right, a quick glimpse showed Kyle tussling with the other vampire. When Kyle flipped onto his feet, my instinct to pounce in and help him dulled, and I focused back on my own issue by ripping my arm back for another hit.

"Goddammit!" Another roar came from Gabe—one that merged with the crunch of bone on bone as I punched Stocky.

The second spurt of blood coated my forearm in a gory tattoo.

Around me, the sound of flesh smacking flesh, of heavy breaths and rapid heartbeats, of Gabe yelling whatever the hell he kept yelling seemed to represent a bongo drummed alert that had to be pounding through the walls like a Morse code.

Kyle stumbled past me.

I tensed to pounce after him—until the outside wolf hauled him up on his way to toss a punch at Mr East.

As Kyle righted himself, Brook's glossy black feline coat slithered across my periphery. Her jaws clamped around the vampire's shin at the same time that a second throw from the outside wolf took the undead dick back another step.

Pain exploded through my jaw with enough sting to vibrate my teeth.

When I blinked my eyes into focus, the ceiling stared back at me around the leering glower of one pissed off Mr Stocky. His fingers grabbed my throat. His arm yanked me upright with enough force to cripple a human.

"Their necks!"

The shout seemed to come from Gabe, but the ringing in my ears made pinpointing his location difficult, as did the lengthening of Stocky's fangs.

His body jostled right before he could duck in for a bite, and his face twisted in what looked like pain. As he dropped his gaze, I followed and found Brook hanging off his left thigh, feline growls humming through her as she tugged at the flesh.

Joining in while she had him distracted, I struck my right fist against his torso—one, two, three—before switching to jam my left into his jaw.

"Their necks!" Gabe's voice bellowed again. "You have to snap their necks!" Gabe flew past toward the other scrap in the corner. "Get out the way!"

Stocky kicked the leg Brook had latched onto and thumped his fist on her head while his fingers dug deeper and deeper into my throat and each judder of his body rattled my skull against the solid wall at my back. As he booted and punched himself free of Brook's teeth, and turned his smiling attention back to me, hands grabbed his jaw and forehead from behind.

A rapid jerk of Stocky's head resulted in a neck crack. His hold on me slackened. He dropped to the floor.

Gabe stood, chest heaving, sweat coating the pup's body. The grey of his eyes had darkened around his dilated pupils. He pointed at the supine body beneath him before bringing a finger to tap at his own neck. "S-s-cerebral s-severance." He nodded, blew out a breath. "Seems to w-work."

My gaze shot to the other corner, where Mr East lay in a similar state of sorry-end to his comrade. I stared hard at Gabe when I turned back to him. Instead of allowing any concern over what he'd just so easily done, I gave him a nod. "Good to know."

With the first threat out the way, the volume of interest from the other captives increased in the form of murmurs, growls and banging.

How long would we get away with that kind of noise before someone arrived to investigate?

I looked toward the outside wolf, where he stood poised as though still ready for action, and at Brook, her sleek black body prowling left and right. "I doubt we have much time," I said.

Brook came to a standstill, a shimmer tugging at her coat for a few seconds before her flesh and long dark hair moved in to surround her golden eyes. "Then, let's get out of here."

"We are. Just as soon as we have some clothes for you guys." I pointed to the Eastern vampire in his crumpled heap across the hallway. "Strip him, Kyle." I prodded Gabe away from Stocky and unfastened the buttons on the vampire's jeans, twisting to look at the outside werewolf. "You have a name?"

"Samuel." He stepped forward and began yanking at the dead vampire's shirt.

I worked the jeans over Stocky's thighs, the name prodding at my brain for a few seconds before my brow winged up. "Samuel Toulsen?"

His eyes widened a tad. "Yes."

The vampire's arms stretched over his head as his shirt was hauled up and off.

I stared harder at the wolf. His matted hair, the filth across his face, and the hollowed expression to his eyes had altered his appearance way beyond the image Jack Brosen had shared of his missing pack member, but the resemblance beneath all that was strong enough for me to accept. "Your Alpha's been worried about you, Samuel."

He blew out a breath, his shoulders deflating with the expelled air.

"Jack's son here, too?"

Returning home with only half the cargo would not bear well for the amicable relationship between our two packs. No way could I take one without the other.

Samuel's headshake told me everything I needed to know—just as the dart away of his eyes told me he didn't look forward to explaining that to Jack.

I patted his shoulder before tossing the vamp's jeans to Gabe. "Dress."

"But—"

"Not asking, Gabe. It's an order." I glanced across at Kyle holding Mr East's trousers against himself. "Not a chance." I turned to Brook. Her body was way too slim for the narrow waist. "Here, swap," I said to Kyle, exchanging

Stocky's shirt with Kyle before handing Mr East's to Brook.

She shook her head. "I cannot shift in clothing. I would prefer that option not be taken from me just yet."

"At some point, when we get out of here, you'll need to get dressed, Brook." I tucked the jersey T to hang from my back pocket. "It's there when you're ready." I didn't wait for Kyle's face to pop out of his T-shirt before I told him, "I'm going for Lauren. Head up and see what you can hear through the upper door. We'll meet you up there."

He nodded and made for the stairs, as I stepped across to the steel double doors.

The noise level, though not quite as extreme, seeped through the opening at the first opportunity. I ignored it— just as I refused to meet any of the eyes I knew would be aimed my way.

Rounding the door brought me directly to Lauren. The girl had curled into a ball, arms enfolding her head. If she realised I'd entered, she showed no acknowledgement.

I dropped to my haunches before her, tapped her arm, and waited until her eyes peeked through a gap between her forearms. "Time to go."

The tremble of her tiny frame seemed to hinder her movements as she unwrapped herself at the speed of a geriatric. When her eyes fully appeared, they held the circumference of an eagle owl's—without the focus.

Not good.

"Okay." I wriggled my arm beneath her bent knees and slid the other around her back. "I've got you." She didn't protest as I drew her close to my body and straightened. "Let's get you out of here."

The others had waited in the hallway, when I ducked back out with Lauren. As soon as the doors closed at my rear, the noise from within the cages diminished to a more bearable level.

I didn't speak—didn't see the need. When I rounded the corner and started up the stairs, three sets of footsteps trailed behind.

On the landing, I made the full U-turn and mounted the second set of stairs. At the top, Kyle leaned into the doorway—one he held open with his head stuck through.

"Thought I told you to listen *through* the door," I whispered when I reached him.

"I did." A twist of his head brought his eyes into view, as the following scuffles of the others came to a halt at my rear. "And I heard nothing, so thought I'd check if it was because the door was too thick, or if I really couldn't hear anything."

"And?"

"Nobody out there," he murmured. "Which is a little concerning, don't you think?"

"Let's hope not," I said, a jerk of my chin telling him to move. He stepped aside, nodding at Lauren in my arms. "She okay?"

I bobbled my head in a maybe-maybe-not gesture. "You bring up the rear, if I take the lead?"

"Sure."

Lauren made peering around the doorframe awkward, but a quick glance and inhalation in each direction brought no concern—not that I'd have smelled anything above the ever-present stench of rot and gore.

Just like before, shadows dominated the curved walkway as I stepped out and headed off to the right. My bearings insisted the main exit had to be on the opposite side of the building. No matter. I had no intention of staying in the place that long.

It took possibly less than a minute with my rapid-tiptoed pace before I spotted illumination ahead.

Good.

Daytime.

Not that it made that much difference. Even in the light, I didn't seem to be a match for vampires.

I picked up my speed. As soon as the space opened up to the looming windows, I ducked off into the alcove. Striding across to our exit, I scanned the outline of the panel and almost groaned upon locating the catch—fifteen feet up. I could have reached it, if I jumped, but I couldn't do that without some kind of collision with the window, which would have resulted in more noise than any of us dared make.

Lauren's eyes still held their roundness—not what I'd hoped to see.

"Lauren?" I kept my voice low, and a tiny flutter of her lashes told me she'd heard, but I received no further response. "Lauren?" I tried again, a gentle prod despite the voice in my head screaming at me to hurry up. "How you feeling?"

Her eyes flickered off to the side, as a shiver raced through her rigid body.

I lifted my head to Brook and Samuel, both staring hard at the girl like they could drill her brain into snapping out of it. Behind them, Kyle and Gabe aimed their eyes and flared nostrils toward the corridor we'd left.

Peering back down at Lauren, I deepened my voice: "Lauren, come on."

Samuel took a step forward, his hands on his hips. "What's the matter with her?" He strode round the small space, coming back full circle. "Lauren?"

"You will frighten the girl further, growling at her that way." Brook nudged him aside, and moved in to lean close to Lauren's level. "We could really use your help right now, Lauren."

A breath hitched up from the girl's chest—a tiny reaction, but one all the same.

"The windows are our fastest way out of here," Brook said, as Samuel paced left. "And you are our best chance of getting those windows open."

Samuel spun back. "Let me jump for it—or maybe we should just find something to break the glass."

"Too noisy," Kyle said.

"Please, Lauren." Brook drew a straggle of the girl's hair back from her face and tucked it behind her ear. "Time is not on our side, and I would prefer not to see ourselves back behind those bars, so if you're listening ..."

"I can't stand here doing nothing," Samuel said.

Brook sent him a glower before turning back to the young girl. "If you are listening to me at all ... you must not want to go ba—" A screech drew all eyes toward the window catch as it made a southward click.

My lips funnelled with my expelled breath. "Nice job." I nodded to Brook, inclined my chin toward the window. "You want to do the honours?"

Her eyes deepened to pure amber as a smile curved her lips. "It would be my pleasure."

27

Kyle's frown creased his brow while his eyes scanned left and right. "Um ..."

Standing outside the castle-like building, beside the other four in our party, including a semi-alert Lauren, I mirrored his search of the landscape.

To the left: green.

To the right: green.

Straight ahead: more bloody green.

Supposing, of course, we looked beyond what appeared to be the remnant, empty ditch of a moat—around seventy feet away—which seemed to circle the entire building. If I screwed my eyes up just right, browns and oranges offered the occasional punctuation. Whichever direction we chose to travel, I figured we had some walking ahead of us.

"I want you to switch places with me and take the lead." I took in Kyle's face—shadowed by the stone walls of the castle and full of concern. "Just get as far from here, as fast as you can, until you come across a bush ... or something ... anything to duck behind, where we can scour again for any signs of life that don't involve vampires."

His gaze swung to me. "And you?"

"Gabe and I'll be right behind. If we lag, I'll sniff you out."

"Yeah, 'cause you'll have no chance of finding us out there in that maze."

The twitch of my eyebrow let him know I didn't appreciate his sarcasm.

His expression sobered. "The ditch is going to be a problem."

"It's around ten feet wide, at a guess—not much different to the forest river at home. Maybe fifteen, twenty feet deep ..." I pursed my lips, offered a shrug. "Not a problem for you. I'm not so sure about Brook, or Lauren. You might have to go into-and-out of it, instead of over."

"Just what I was thinking." Kyle nodded. "Good job it's empty ... but, with Lauren having no physical abilities, it'll still add time on getting her across."

"Then, quit wasting it talking to me."

Kyle breathed out a laugh and waved Lauren closer. "We're going that way." He pointed across the endless moorland. "And I want you to stick near me, so I can help you. Okay?" Lauren gave him a nod. "Good." To me, Kyle said, "Send the others behind me." He strode off, covering a few metres before backtracking to take Lauren's wrist, when she failed to shadow him.

They crossed the unshielded lawn, and when they'd gone over halfway to the moat without interruption, I nodded to Samuel to follow, and he took his turn.

Less than a minute later, Brook's pursuit left Gabe and me alone.

After watching her take a few elegant bounds across the grass, I patted Gabe's shoulder. "Come on, kid, let's go."

His long-loped jog matched mine. With nothing but dusty concrete and grime to walk on for days, the soles of my feet welcomed the moist grass, and my toes curled over to embrace the blades with each union.

Ahead of us, Kyle and Lauren made the descent into the moat until only Kyle's shoulders remained visible. Samuel had less than fifteen yards to pass before he joined them.

"Wh-what d'you think's g-g-gonna h-happen?" Gabe pressed a fist to his skull—over his stutter giving him grief, I figured, as much as anything else.

"To you?"

"No." He aimed his thumb in a point behind us. "This lot."

Ahead, Samuel had vanished from sight, and Brook neared the moat. "First things first. We get ourselves home. Then we come back with reinforcements and clean this mess up."

"Wh-what if they up and go? Wh-what if you come back and everything's already been cleaned up." His voice grew deeper, revealing his emotions. "Who-whose gonna pay for this fuckup then?"

"Don't worry, Gabe. I've already thought of it. I need to ask you a question, though."

"O-k-kay." A frown accompanied Gabe's guarded response.

"The other kid—your friend you were with when ..." I trailed off, as he faced me, pausing a beat before asking, "What happened to him?"

Gabe's eyes darted off to the side as a twitch of flesh lingered in his shoulder. "I d-didn't stay awake long ... w-w-with what they pumped in me. I was out p-pretty quick." His stare came back to mine. "But I st-st-stank of him ... when I woke up." He winced but kept moving. "I had C-Colum's blood on m-m-m-me. And his p-piss ..." His jaw tightened, the sudden blankness to his face telling me I'd prompted him to remember something he'd rather not. "Sick, too ..." His nod arrived as a jerk.

"Okay, Gabe." I squeezed his shoulder, to calm as much as reassure. "It'll be okay."

Nearing the huge ditch, I slowed to a stop.

With one hop, Gabe landed at the bottom in the middle of the void. He slammed to halt, glanced back my way. "Aren't you c-coming?"

"Tell Kyle I'm heading back in to do what needs to be done," I said, squatting on the grassy ledge.

"Then, I'm c-coming with you."

"No." I shook my head.

"You c-can't ask me to—"

I held up my hand to stop him. "I'm not asking you. I'm telling you, Gabe."

"B-but ..."

"I vowed to get you out. I've done that. Now I need you to do as I sa,y so I can uphold that promise and keep you there—because I will not have the alternative on my conscience.”

Reluctance coated his nod as he blew out a heavy breath.

“Tell Kyle where I’ve gone,” I said. “Tell him to keep going forward, and I’ll find you. And, Gabe, once you’re all regrouped?” I waited until I had his full attention again. “Promise me you won’t scare the girl.”

Something akin to pain entered his eyes. “I ... I didn’t m-mean it. I didn’t—”

“I know you didn’t.” I flicked a finger toward the far side. “Now get going.”

Though his downturned mouth told me he was far from happy about my order, he turned away, and a two-step run led him into his leap for the far side.

Only once his feet pounded grass toward where the others had headed did I turn back, and I matched his action in the opposite direction—toward the building where we’d just escaped.

I knew exactly where to go, knew exactly what I was going in there for. I just hoped my assumption would turn out to be fruitful. The more of us there were, the more conspicuous we’d have been, and no way on earth would I have seen any of them back in a cage.

Upon reaching the window, I stood to the side and peeked through.

No movement met my scrutiny.

I pried my fingers into the sliver I’d left ready for my return and swung the huge pane open until wide enough for me to pass through.

I paused just outside, inhaled, studied.

A twitch of my ears caught the rapid pace of running behind me. The breeze swirled the scent around my face, exposing who approached. I gritted my teeth against the curse balancing on my tongue tip, and made a slow turn toward the panther racing across the grass.

Her black coat glistened like silk in the natural light of day with each muscular thrust toward me. Five metres away, paws became feet and hands, fur departed in a tidal wave as flesh moved in, and her running frame heightened to vertical without a glitch to her stride. "You are the biggest pain in my behind I have ever met." Her words spat out in an enraged whisper, as she marched forward pointing at me. "And your idiotic ... *unselfish* attitude"— her fingertip prodded my chest—"will more than likely get you killed." I went to speak, but she shoved past to the opening I thought I'd done a good job of blocking. "Going back in there is a *stupid* idea." Once she'd pushed the pane closed, she turned toward me. "So, how about you tell me what is so important you would risk going back in for it?"

My growl of frustration tried to escape—almost succeeded. "We haven't time for this, Brook." I took her arm, slid her to the left of the opening. "That we got out of there at all with no more than the Blues Brothers to oppose us is a damn miracle. I doubt our luck is going to hold out for much longer."

Her mouth set in a line I'd come to recognise as determination. "Then, condense and spit it out."

I tilted my face to the sky, let out a low groan, and looked back at her. "Okay, listen. This operation is run by humans." Somebody had pulled Catherine's strings throughout, and my money was on them—especially with the number present during the fight. "You agree?" When she didn't, I elaborated, "*Funded* by humans, then? This is *their* enterprise the vampires are running *for* them."

She gave a small nod. "I believe that, yes."

"In human law, even underground fight clubs involving their own kind are highly illegal. That's why they're underground." I leaned a palm against the stonework, using my other hand to brush sweaty hair from my forehead. "Usually mob-type folks are at the wheel of the enterprise. No one crosses them. Most people are afraid to open their mouths."

"Okay."

"It's a tight run ship. Those who are in on it, or have exclusive membership into those kinds of clubs, are hand selected. Or they come by referral, or recommendation."

"How do you know all this?"

I stared off across the grounds, eyes squinting a little when the sun poked its face through a break in the clouds. "I watch a lot of films."

Her sultry laugh drew my attention back down to her. Although her curved lips straightened, the sparkle remained in her eyes. "You have a point?"

"My point is that I doubt any one of the humans who come in here to watch these pit-fights are permitted entry without producing ID as some form of insurance. And I'd bet each and every one of them are filed away somewhere on record—again, as insurance—should one of them talk and blow the whistle on this." Eager to get moving, I rushed through each word to get the explanation out quicker. "Even with who—what—they have fighting, they would not want the authorities to find out about something this illegal—especially not when the level of entertainment probably brings in a way higher income than a regular underground fight club."

"So, you came back in to look for the records?"

"Yes. If I can find those records, I should have a complete list of anyone who's ever witnessed the werewolf changes, and your shifts, the vampires' existence and abilities. This is a fucking mess, and no way can any of us risk this level of exposure." I unclenched hands I'd unconsciously fisted, relaxed my tightened jaw. "Sooner or later, one of these power hungry bastards will talk to the wrong person, even if only by accident. Don't forget, they have each of our names, too. It won't only be exposure for our races, but for us as individuals. I'm not going to take the risk of that happening."

"Where do you think they'll be—the records, that is?"

"Only place I can imagine them being. In Catherine's office." I pushed away from the wall, but dipped my face to her level. "Now you know that, you sure you still want to come?"

"Of course."

"You're insane." I ducked aside to the window. "We're so going to get caught."

Back inside, I stopped where the wall of the open space curved round to join the passageway, my outstretched arm bringing Brook to a standstill.

Sticking my head out, I peered both ways. I'd already learned the hard way that my olfactory wouldn't detect all threats. If anyone loitered, the thudding inside my chest would have given us away, but no one jumped out at us. No one attacked.

All's quiet on the Western Front. Too quiet.

Breathing out through barely parted lips, I motioned for Brook to follow, and we slipped from our spot.

She peered back over her shoulder as we walked. *Where is everyone?* she mouthed to me.

I shrugged, though the hairs across the back of my neck stood high. We'd not only got everyone out, but had managed to slip back in without deterrence, so what holes had everyone disappeared into?

More to the point, what holes would they all jump out of?

Straining my ears for any sounds, I kept going. Nothing but our duet of padding feet reached me, until the opening of a door rang out somewhere to our rear.

I grabbed Brook and swung her back against the wall.

Upon the impact, she burst out a grunt, and another when I pressed against her. I whipped my hand up, smothering her mouth to prevent further sound like that'd be enough to hide us.

Turning away from her wide eyes, I stared toward the sound, Brook's rapid breaths coating my palm in condensation.

Shoes tapped against the floor of the stone walkway, each one sending a quiet echo that seemed to boomerang from one side to the next.

I tried to suppress my own breaths to avoid being heard, yet my chest still rose and fell hard against Brook's cheek.

The volume of the steps lessened. I didn't move for a few beats. Only once they'd faded out did I allow myself to relax.

My exhale fluttered Brook's hair. *Keep moving,* I mouthed as I released her.

Twenty more paces. No more disturbances. Still, the lack of interruption made me uneasy.

Nudging my concerns aside, I halted outside the entrance Joseph and Chad had accompanied me through earlier.

My gentle tug of the door revealed the spiral staircase, and I leaned in close to Brook's ear. "Catherine's office is through here." I turned away to poke my face into the cool turret, listening for any signs of overhead movement. Brook's breaths hit my shoulder, her fingers folded around my arm. When no sounds drifted down, I chanced a step inside, pausing to listen again.

"Anything?" Brook murmured.

Placing a finger to my lips, I twisted to enable her to see, before using the same finger to point toward the stairs. At her nod, I padded forward to the first step and continued up a few more when still no noise offered concern.

Brook's body heat and hair swishing across my lumbar told me she'd spun and opted for a back-to-back position. Made sense with all the blind spots on the staircase—cover all angles, less chance of being taken by surprise. Her fingers grasped onto the denim of my jeans legs, and we started the climb.

Less than two minutes later, almost overheating from Brook's constant contact, I came to a halt and stared up at the opening into Catherine's office.

Brook's hair tickled my hip, as she released her grip of my jeans legs and leaned round me. She didn't complain when I took her arm and swung her back to the wall beside me and signalled for her to stay put.

After all, both of us striding into potential disaster would be suicide. I preferred to go in knowing I had backup the vampires hadn't spotted.

Four more elevations took me to the edge of the top step and adjacent to the archway. I peeked around the frame so only my eyes and forehead would be visible to anyone within, but I needn't have worried. The desk sat unoccupied, and no actions stirred the air. Of course, someone could have been hiding just out of range— again—but I'd never know if I didn't venture farther inside.

Holding my breath for fear of being heard, I moved into the doorway, giving myself a wider view of the room.

Still nothing.

If the room held someone, they were doing a mighty fine job of remaining concealed, but I couldn't wait any longer—not if I didn't want Kyle performing a search and rescue.

I stepped into the room.

A rapid left and right twist of my head showed no hidden surprises, and my held breath seeped out past my lips.

At my beckon, Brook joined me in one soundless leap.

"It's empty?" she whispered. When I nodded, she asked again, "Where are they all?"

"Beats me."

"Do you not think getting in here has been a little too easy?"

Yes. Definitely. "I'm not going to complain, when it means we should be in and out of here faster."

"Where are we looking?"

"Drawers. Shelves ... under loose floorboards." I pointed to the nearest corner, where an alcove provided the only part of the left wall not made up of glass. "I'll take those filing cabinets."

"It is duly noted that you took the easy spot," she murmured, as I strode off.

The top drawer slid over runners at the volume of a freight train. I froze before I'd even drawn it out four inches, my brows scrunching as I winced. I glanced back at Brook, who stood frozen with wide eyes aimed my way.

The lift of my hands and shoulders sent a silent apology, and I turned back to try again. Five, scarily-loud seconds later, I peered into the contents.

As I'd hoped, dividers kept everything in some sort of order, each tab across the top a label of explanation.

I flipped through them. Accounts, by the looks of it, or the bookkeeping files for the tabs and placed bets. I slid out a thick bound book, leafed through the pages.

Each and every wager listed inside had the date of placement, followed by a singular name—surname, I presumed.

"Found something?"

At Brook's whisper, I held up the book. "Betting records."

"So, we can go now?"

I shook my head. "It's not enough—not without addresses to accompany the names. Keep looking."

I placed the evidence on top of the cabinet and reached down for the middle drawer, cringing once more at the noisy opening, but too impatient with the time ticking away to bother with subtlety.

I held my breath a moment.

The quieting of shuffled items at my far right told me Brook did the same.

When no footsteps approached, I reached in and dragged out file after file, placing them on top of the book with the intent to check out their importance later.

On the verge of closing the drawer, a dark blur waltzed into my periphery.

I snapped my head around in time to see what the lack of scent made me miss.

A vampire—one I didn't recognise.

Pale chestnut hair, tall and slender frame, he halted on the huge patterned rug, his attention on the shifter. If he knew of my presence tucked away in the alcove, he showed no sign of it. "Brook?"

Brook whirled toward the new arrival.

Slowing my breathing, and hopefully my heartbeat, I stayed as still as possible.

A dark glower entered the cat's stare, rendering her golden eyes a rustic bronze, but no verbal acknowledgement arrived from her—only the fisting of her hands.

"What are you doing up here?" Suspicion dripped from the intruder's tone.

When Brook still didn't speak, the vampire's head twisted to his right, toward the opposite corner I stood in, before making a slow return as though he searched for answers elsewhere.

Brook stared at him in silence. I expected his attention to stay on her once they reconnected, but when his head continued toward the left, my heart nearly galloped at the realisation that, if he looked far enough around, he'd spot me straight away.

I tensed, waiting for the inevitable. My knees bent ready to spring as my fingers curled to form the only weapons I had.

Three more inches, and he'd see me.

"I was summoned," Brook said in a harsh murmur.

He halted, turned back to her. "She speaks." He folded his arms across his chest. "Not quite sure I like the tone, but it's a start."

Brook's jaw bulged beneath the grind of her teeth. "What do you expect?"

My eyes narrowed at the venom in her tone. *What the hell am I missing here?*

"You're still annoyed with me. I see that ..." He couldn't have sounded more condescending.

Ducking lower, I took a tentative step forward and hoped like crazy Brook could keep her poker face in place.

"... but how else would I have gotten you away from your clinging posse of Tomcats, otherwise?" he continued.

"The very role of those Tomcats is to protect me from scum like you, Paul."

Another step forward took Brook's expression of fury from my view. I didn't think then was the time to ponder over the fuel behind their discussion, especially when I had a chance of reaching 'Paul' undetected.

"Well, I guess they aren't very good at their job, then ... seeing as you're here." His head tilted to the side, and I paused with my right foot lifted in mid-step. "Speaking of which ... who exactly summoned you?"

Without hesitation, she answered, "Catherine," the name spitting from Brook like the vampire had trodden on her tail.

Paul's head straightened, as did his entire posture as he stood tall. "When, exactly, as Catherine has been with me for the past two hours ..."

Three more tiptoed steps took me directly behind Paul.

"And more to the point, why the hell would you be in here ... alone?" His right hand shot out to grip Brook's arm, and his yank shook her entire body.

She didn't resist, simply accepted his mauling.

I strode the last two paces until Paul had no choice but to acknowledge the body heat at his rear.

The jolt of his shoulders preceded the whip up of his head, and his forward shove sent Brook to the floor an instant before he started to turn.

I didn't wait for him to see me before reaching around, grabbing his head in both hands, and twisting it in a rapid jerk to the right.

With the crack of bone, his body went limp.

After lowering him to the rug to avoid unnecessary thuds, I stepped over to help Brook up. "You okay?"

Her eyes shone with what looked like suppressed tears as she nodded and took the hand I offered.

"Good. Then, let's grab what we have and get the hell out of here before somebody stumbles across your boyfriend."

28

Luckily, we made it back downstairs and to the window undeterred—over which, I didn't know whether to be elated or concerned. Brook climbed through first, and I handed her the bundle of files bound with a rubber band as I followed.

"What now?" she asked, as I straightened. "Do you have any more antics you want to try before we make our escape?"

"Nope." I cocked my brow at her. "Now we're going to run like crazy. You ready?"

In response, she slammed the roll of papers against my abdomen and bolted toward the moat, leaving me no option but to pursue and try not to get lashed by her trailing dark strands.

The parting air bristled every hair on my face as I cut through it. Each muscle in my legs groaned in complaint over the sudden demands placed upon them. Brook's erupted speed had given her a head start, but it didn't take long for me to gain the ground she'd made, and the moat sat less than fifty feet in front of us by the time I reached her shoulder.

At thirty feet to go, I tucked the papers into the back of my waistband and glanced her way. "You like to fly, Brook?"

"Sometimes," she said with her gaze still on the path we ran. "But only first class." She covered a few more paces, her breaths showing the initial sign of strain. "Why?"

"Because ..." I double checked my estimation of fifteen feet to go. "... that's the quickest way to get you over this moat."

"What?"

I whipped my arms to the right, grasped hold of her hips, and yanked her in front of me. "Hurt me later." I pushed off the dry embankment with my left foot, and with a forward thrust of my arms, sent Brook sailing in front of me.

"Etha—" Her quiet screech fizzled out into a trailing hiss, and her arms wind-milled for a second before she gathered control. She hit the other side in a crouch, diving upright into another run, as my own feet slammed down beside her vacated spot.

Another couple hundred metres whizzed by before our paces slowed to a jog. I folded my fingers around Brook's arm and drew her to a halt.

She bent at the waist, breaths heaving, hands resting on her knees, leaving me wholly grateful the length of her hair did a fine job of covering key parts of her body. "Do we ... even know ... which direction the ... others have gone?"

I shook my head and rubbed a hand across the back of my neck, where sweat had begun a slow saturation of my skin. "That's why we've stopped," I said, scouring the land, "so I can take a moment to pick up their scent."

She dropped down to all fours, her nostrils flaring, eyes closing as she pushed her face forward in a very feline gesture. I squatted beside her, more than able to detect earlier scents without nuzzling my nose into the ground, inhaling as I searched every rise, every shade other than green, any potential trees.

"Anything?" she asked.

With the subtle concoction of the rest of our party detected, I said, "We need to go west a little because that's where their scents are drifting from."

She pushed up as I did and reached around to my back pocket, coming away with the T that still hung from there. "Should be safe for me to put this on now, yes?"

"Let's hope so," I said before setting off.

***

I could only guess the others had hit the far side of the moat, then reconvened and ran like hell, because they'd covered a lot more ground than I'd anticipated. Either that, or we'd spent far longer in Catherine's office than I thought.

The rolled up proof we'd collated stuck up from my jeans waistband and scratched against my back with each step I jogged. Every once in a while, we paused and hunched down to be sure we still followed the trail. Around twenty-five minutes of tracking later, once we'd hit the first signs of vegetation and the landscape had begun to change, gurgles and bubbles entertained us and a stream came into view.

Grey rock jutted out, and weeds stood high and proud as though in protection. To our right, trees and brush grew in greater abundance on the far side of the stream. A glance to the left showed the slow upward rise of a hill, down which the stream gushed.

Coming to a pause at the six-foot-wide obstacle, my nostrils flared.

"Do you smell them?" Brook asked from a lowered position. "I don't smell them beyond a foot, or two, before the water."

"Me either." I peered down at her. "How far can you jump unassisted?" My energy had waned, and I doubted I'd get Brook over with the same ease as earlier.

"You think they crossed the river? All of them?"

"Well, it stands to reason if all of their scents end here."

She glanced across the river and walked backward a dozen steps. "Six, seven feet is not a problem. Nor would the moat have been, had you given me a chance to prove it."

I joined her for the run up, and with a race for the edge, we made our second leap of the hour.

Pain jolted through my weary limbs, on impact with the opposite bank, and forced a grunt from my throat. Brook stumbled forward before regaining her footing, managing gracefulness even for that. Still close to the ground, knees bent from absorbing my landing, the scents that had vanished on the other side hit me with full force.

I turned to Brook with a smile, as she faced me with one of her own. "Definitely came this way," I said, as she murmured, "It smells as though you were right."

Our heads snapped up at a whistle to the left. I followed the sound along the incline of the hill, through rocks and boulders, until I found Kyle's ginger mop atop his grinning face.

Gathering a burst of energy from somewhere deep inside me, I climbed up to his spot faster than I'd have thought possible. Catherine said we'd been captive two days, and that had been, what? The day before? One meal—if it could be called that—in no way sufficed to fuel a werewolf over that time period.

Hell, a human male would have struggled without more sustenance than we'd had.

My chest heaved beneath laboured breaths, and the first waves of dizziness had kicked in by the time I rounded the apex to the others.

Gabe halted his frantic pacing and turned on me, his hands fisted in his curls. "Wh-what took you long?"

"We were interrupted."

Kyle, as well as Samuel, stared at me. "They know we're out already?" Kyle asked.

"We don't think so—at least, not when we left." Brook brushed past me and sank onto the grass beside Lauren. "Pau—one of the vampire's ... caught us searching Catherine's office, and I ... distracted him, while Ethan crept up behind—"

"Tell me you broke his neck instead of rolling around like a couple of lovers," Kyle said, his eyebrow raised.

"I did." I slid the thick bundle from my waistband, waving it toward him. "Before you ask, I went back in for these. Records of the fight spectators." A glance through them had confirmed my hopes. "So we now know who everyone is, and where they live. Should make cleaning this mess up a whole heap easier."

Kyle's grin returned, and even Gabe produced the closest I'd seen to a genuine smile. "Well, we have some good news, too," Kyle said. "Which is why we only came this far and paused for you two to catch up."

I lifted my hands in impatience, when he didn't spit it out right away.

"Civilisation." He poked his thumb at the air over his shoulder. "A cottage around a mile away in the valley."

Drinking from the natural spring offered enough refreshment to get us down the other side of the hill, and our exhausted and staggering party trailed through feathered brushes that hit my ankles with a sharpness their appearance belied.

Beyond the farmhouse, the low rumble of an engine droned away. The glances I received from Kyle assured me he'd caught it, too. We continued, though, if only because a property would undoubtedly have a road leading from it, which I hoped could give us an indication of our location.

Outhouses decorated the barren ground up to the main property. The doors stood open on the first one we reached. Within, tools lined the left wall, on hooks or shelving, and stall after stall stretched opposite them. Although it obviously had the setup to house livestock, the oil patches that dotted the un-uncluttered floor led me to believe we'd stumbled across a tractor shed, and that maybe said tractor held the deep engine we heard.

From there, we squat-ran across to building number two and slipped inside the partially closed doors, yet backed out just as fast when the goats in there kicked up a screech of alarm as though they'd smelled the predators in our group.

The third barn lacked the wooden sides of its neighbours, but in their place, walls of haystacks enclosed the interior, providing us with invisibility from the farmhouse, and also warmth and shelter with somewhere semi-comfortable to sit.

We rounded the front, and I ushered Lauren before me with the intention of settling her barely-standing body down for a few minutes. At the opening of a door at the main house, all six of us froze.

The small woman that stepped outside halted the instant our gazes met. She stared for seconds. I didn't like to think about how the hell we must have looked to her. Less than half of us could be consider fully dressed, and only one of us had shoes. On top of that, apart from Lauren, who couldn't have looked any more terrified if a bull charged toward her, we all stood poised as though ready to pounce.

"Can I help yeh?" the woman asked at last.

"Want me to sort this?" Kyle asked out the corner of his mouth.

"Sure, swing your oscillating dick over there, and see how long you last before she runs screaming for the authorities." I turned to Samuel—the least battered and best presented of us all, besides Lauren. "Show's yours."

"No problem." He marched forward, leaving the rest of us huddled together like goodness knew what, and sent chickens scattering from the yard like the Red Sea had parted for Moses. A few feet in front of the female, he stopped. "Hey, sorry to trespass, but ... we're hikers, and we ... got lost—you know how it is." He shrugged, tucking his hands into his pockets. "Couple of my friends are ... the worst for wear."

The woman's face appeared as she leaned and peered around him at us. "Yer friends all look a lot worse than that, lovey. What on earth happened to all their clothes?"

Samuel's hand withdrew from his pocket, and he rubbed it across his matted hair. "Rocks 'round here are sharper than they look."

If I hadn't been so tense, I'd have laughed at his ridiculous explanation.

"Yeh're not from 'round these parts, are yeh?"

"Er ... no." Samuel glanced at me over his shoulder, like he could use a little guidance on what to say to the woman. I spiralled my finger through the air, telling him to wrap it up, and he turned back. "You couldn't tell us where we are, I suppose?"

"Aye, yeh're in Winnedown."

Samuel scratched at his hair again. "And ... that would be ... where?"

A small cackled laugh resonated from the woman. "In Yorkshire, lad."

He nodded. "So, if we follow the road from here, where will that take us?"

I motioned for the others to start forward, ensuring Gabe and Lauren took the lead with me, to hide what a human would consider indecent when it came to Brook's and Kyle's appearance.

"If yeh follow the road out 'til yeh hit the main road, yeh'll eventually wind up in the town of Huddlesbridge."

"Is there a phone box on the way?" I called, as the woman came into my line of sight. The sooner I called Dad, the sooner we could get home and start organising the clean-up.

Light danced in her eyes as she sent me a smile. "Well, if yeh wanted to use the phone, why didn' yeh just say?"

We didn't actually walk *on* the road out from the farmhouse. If any vehicles chose that route, no way would we have gone unnoticed, so we stuck to the fields, using hedgerows as cover.

The call home to Dad had gone as expected. His heavy sigh had revealed his relief, followed by his single question of, 'Do you know where you are, Son?' Despite a suggestion from the farmer's wife to await collection in the hay barn, I'd given Dad details of the road and direction we'd be following. I couldn't afford to place the family in danger, if the vampires decided to come searching. As soon as I'd relayed the size of our party, he'd responded with, 'We'll be there as soon as we can'.

Although the generous offer of the woman had gone unaccepted, she'd refused to let us leave without filling us up with hot drinks, cake and bananas. She didn't say a word, when we polished off a coffee cake, as well as a carrot cake, and worked through three pots of tea—nor about our non-attire, which left me questioning just how many strange occurrences went on in what I presumed to be the Yorkshire Dales.

Our refuelled energy reserves showed in each step we took, in the way we held our heads higher as we strolled across grass that spread off to the south like a rustic patchwork quilt.

Brook hogged my side, as I led the party, a slight limp to her left leg where she'd trodden on a stinger the size of a savoy cabbage. "I should explain," she murmured.

For some reason, the low volume of her voice had me glancing behind to check the proximity of the others before I asked, "Explain what?"

"About Paul."

"What's to explain?" The interaction between them had become pretty clear. "He seduced you into thinking he gave a shit, so he could get you alone and spring his damn trap. Catherine used the same trick on Kyle."

"But how long for?" she asked.

I peered down at the hurt in her eyes, and wanted to say something to ease it, yet didn't have a clue what that something could be.

"For weeks, Paul fooled me into thinking he was ..."

Special? "An okay guy?"

She nodded.

"You shouldn't feel bad about it." Fury roiled beneath the hurt in her eyes—an emotion I guessed she aimed at herself more than the vampire. "You probably weren't the first person Paul pulled the stunt on, just as I doubt you were the last."

The firm set of her mouth told me she wanted to argue, to beat herself up over it some more, but instead she nodded. "Thank you."

"No worries. How's the foot?"

"I have had worse injuries and survived."

I turned to walk backward, taking in the others. "How's everyone else holding up—you okay?"

Mumbled words of affirmation and nods came from Samuel and Lauren, who'd taken middle position. Gabe nodded, too, behind them, but beside him, Kyle's eyes flitted between Brook and me before I received his nod, and he murmured, "Just fine and dandy."

An estimated hour later, figuring it wouldn't be that much longer before the convoy showed up, I brought us all to a halt at a field gate that overlooked the main road to Huddlesbridge. Gabe got the job of gatekeeper, as someone without open wounds and a familiarity with the pack, and Samuel propped forward against the bars next to him. The rest of us flopped onto the grass either side of the rutted wheel tracks that led to the field exit.

"You shall be home soon." Brook's voice drifted across as she spoke to Lauren. "Your mother will be relieved, yes?"

Knees drawn up and tucked beneath her chin, the young girl gave a small bob of her head as emotion glistened in her eyes.

"So ..." Kyle murmured beside me. "You and the shifter seem to get on pretty well."

I peered down at Kyle, lying on his front with his chin wedged between his fists. "She seems okay."

His hands stretched the skin across his cheeks. "Thought you had a thing for ..." His attention flickered across to Gabe for a split second. "... someone else."

"What's that got to do with ..." I followed his gaze to Brook, where she sat passing daisies to Lauren, for the girl to weave into a flora-chain. My brows shot up. "It's you who has a thing," I whispered, staring back down at Kyle. "For a damn cat."

"No, I don't." His focus snapped back to me. "That'd be moronic."

"Yeah." The notion of feline and canine united in such an alien sense refused to gel inside my brain. "Yeah, it would."

Engines growled in the distance. It took mere seconds to establish they were coming our way. I looked up at Gabe, to see if he'd heard, but he'd already climbed onto the gate and leaned far enough forward to hang over the road. Kyle bolted up to a seated position, telling me he'd heard them, too.

My shoulders tensed, my breaths stalling as I unconsciously held them.

As first one, another, then a third familiar rumble grew louder, and I recognised the pitches of Dad's, Connor's and Daniel's trucks, I blew out in relief.

"Cavalry's here." Gabe leapt over the gate.

Connor's truck rolled away first, with the two females in the back. Lauren's wide green eyes stared through the rear window a bit before she turned around. In Daniel's Toyota Hi-Lux in front of us, I could make out Kyle in the front seat, his red hair sticking up all over the place, while Samuel's almost-black hair made a dark contrast beside Gabe's blond on the rear bench.

Ordered by Dad, he and I shared his newly-bought Ford pickup, and his hands tightened around the steering wheel as he followed Daniel and pulled away.

I figured he had a whole heap to say to me, despite the relief etched into his features since the second he'd drawn alongside the gate.

Rather than wait, I blew out a breath and dived straight in. "How's Shelley?"

"She's not doing too well, Son. Hasn't been since she had to tell us you'd gone missing. Something she only figured out once she realised you hadn't taken your mobile or shoes ... from the *hotel room*"—his voice deepened to a low growl, and the steering wheel groaned beneath his crippling grip—"which she apparently shared with *you*."

"I'm sorry," I muttered.

"For what?" He glanced at me before returning his attention to the road and manoeuvring us around a harsh bend to the right. "For lying to me about where you'd be? For disobeying a direct order and splitting up with Kyle, which placed the two of you in a danger we didn't know you'd be able to walk away from? For your dishonesty over your relationship with Shelley?" He paused, and I opened my mouth to speak, but shut it again at his glower. "Or for the tears that have spilled from your mother and Jem since Shelley's phone call?"

I cringed. "I said I was sorry, Dad." My jaw clenched. "But don't ask me to apologise for anything that happened between Shelley and me ... because I won't—I'm ... not."

"I never said what happened between you and Shelley was wrong." On the approach to a T-junction, he followed Connor's and Daniel's lead and flicked his indicator up. "But you shouldn't have lied about it."

"I didn't."

A low rumble preceded his growl. "Withholding information from your Alpha does not un-constitute it as a lie, Ethan."

I twisted in my seat to stare at him. "I didn't withhold anything from you, either." As arctic frostiness in his eyes revealed his fury, I rushed on. "I didn't, Dad. None of what happened was planned. We ... *I* made a bad choice with regards to staying at the hotel—which I'll take full responsibility for—but me and Shelley? We just ..." ... *finally got our act together*. I sighed and leaned my head back against the seat.

Minutes passed with only the engine's low grumble as the soundtrack. Hedgerows whizzed past, their natural shades darkening as the daylight showed signs of making way for night. The smell of leather, saturated in the pack's body odours, permeated the truck's cabin, as did a discarded sweater of Jem's in the backseat, and for the first time in days, stiffness began its slow seep out of my shoulders.

"You're hurt." Dad spoke without taking his attention off the road. "How badly?"

"It's nothing," I mumbled.

"Last time I heard those words from you, you had a hairline fracture in your skull. So, how badly are you hurt?" His voice held more force the second time. "And don't tell me it's nothing. I see in your eyes that something bad has gone on, Ethan."

"Just scratches, Dad. They'll be healed in a day, or so." I lifted my right foot to the seat and hooked an arm around my knee. As I shifted to lean against the door, the glass offered a coolness that soothed the ache affecting my entire body. "It's not me you need to worry about."

When his lips pursed, I thought he'd argue some more. Instead, he said, "Kyle stank of blood. You want to tell me about his injuries, as you obviously don't want to talk about your own?"

I ignored his insistence that he have the last say. "Kyle got messed up pretty bad. The worst of his wounds are beneath his shirt ... not as bad as Gabe's, though—except Gabe's are all healing already."

He turned to me, eyebrow raised. "They happened before you got there, I presume?"

I nodded, peering off across fields turned bottle green, as long shadows stretched out to claim them. "They've well and truly screwed the kid up." I rubbed a hand across my face, sensing Dad's eyes on me as the truck slowed for a stop sign. "And I don't know if we can fix him."

"The doc should already be at the house. I called him before we set off." He meant our family doctor, who Dad paid big sums of money to treat us without questioning his discoveries. Doctor Monkton—Craig to us—had been treating the pack since before I was born. "He'll sort him out."

"What if ..." I clenched my jaw, tapping a fisted hand against my raised knee as I drew in a long breath, my exhalation rushing past my lips. "What if he can't, Dad? What the hell am I supposed to tell Shelley?"

"We'll tell Shelley everything. As his mother, she deserves to know. And if she's important to you,"—he aimed a probing stare my way before facing forward again—"she's owed your honesty."

The skin tightened around my eyes as I considered what outcome my honesty could bring, but I shoved the thought out as fast as it entered.

Dad accelerated and shifted the gearstick into fifth, as we hit a straight stretch of road. "In the meantime, you can tell *me* what you know."

I raked my fingers into my hair, fisting them in there. "I don't even know where to start. It's a mess. A huge mess."

"Just start at the beginning."

I lowered my hand. "Can I call Shelley first? I should at least let her know we have Gabe."

"Wouldn't you prefer to just collect her and take her home with us?"

My father—the sage. Even when furious with me, he never lost sight of how I felt, or what I needed. I sighed. "Yeah, I would."

"Good." His twist of the lamp lever spilled light across the road in front of us as more shades of darkness affected the land. "Now, fill me in."

Clouds dominated the sky, light washed across the pavement from the streetlamps, and specks of rain decorated the windscreen, as Dad secured the truck's handbrake outside Shelley's home. I stared at the distractions until they merged into an incomprehensible pattern of nothingness, while trying to figure out how to word my apology to her.

"What are you waiting for?" Dad kept his voice quiet, yet it still carried over the idling engine.

"Nothing." I looked past his profile at the house, my heart banging around like a mutant moth pumped with steroids at the thought of seeing Shelley again.

"Faced with a deranged wolf and you're fearless." When he turned to me, I expected humour to mark his features, but only a deep concern lined his face. "So, why do you look terrified about going in there to speak to Shelley?" His eyebrow lifted. "Would you like me to go in and ask her to come?"

I shook my head, peered away. "How mad is she ... with me?"

"She's furious. Apparently, you broke a promise to her."

I wanted to argue. It hadn't been a *promise*. The wordage didn't matter, though. I'd told her I was going nowhere and did the exact opposite. Leaning forward, I rested my elbows on my knees, brushed a hand across my sticking-up hair.

"How much do you like her?"

I tried to blank out his curiosity and deep breathed in preparation for stepping from the truck.

"When did this happen?" Dad asked.

At his hand on my shoulder, I glanced up. "What?"

"When did my boy fall in love without my noticing?"

An obstacle the size of a plum lodged in my throat. "He didn't." I opened the door, climbing out into a cool breeze and drizzle against my torso before spinning back to him. "Shelley and I just ... gel."

"Denial won't solve a thing, Ethan." His serious gaze locked onto mine.

"I'll be back in a minute."

I ducked away and rounded the pickup, mounting the kerb to the pavement. I'd only taken one step onto Shelley's path, when the front door to her house swung open.

"Ethan?" Her whisper drifted along the walkway, and the sight of her froze me to the spot.

I wanted to avert my focus, to take a moment, if only for composure, to better prepare myself, but my mind refused to allow the action to happen. Not even the falling rain offered distraction.

Instead, my right shoulder lifted in a stupid half-shrug. "Hey."

Her eyes shone as she released her hold on the door and shuffled forward. She paused for a beat, or two, before stepping outside.

Unable to read her expression, I waited—truly unsure for the first time ever what to do. With each foot of path she covered toward me, my heart beat harder, my breaths came shorter. The streetlamp illumination burned her hair to a fiery red, which matched the heat in her stare, and all I could think about was the taste of her on my lips.

I forced the thought aside. "Shel, I'm so—oomph."

Her punch into my solar plexus stole my breath with a force I wouldn't have considered her capable of. She followed up with a second from her left hand, thankfully swinging a little wide to hit with full impact.

"You"—she smacked against my shoulder—"bloody"— a thump rippled through my chest—"arse. How could you?" A triple pounding hit the other side of my chest— each one knocking me back an inch. "How could you lie to me?"

The second accusation of the day. "Shelley, I didn— agh." My jaw vibrated beneath another blow as it resonated across my chin.

"Bastard!" Another thump landed against my chest.

"Shelley, will you le—ugh." I choked on the word beneath her jab into my throat, and with a growl, I thrust out my arms to grip her hips.

"Bastard!"

More pummels rained across my upper arms, as I strode forward with her squirming body between my palms.

"Put me down!"

Her feet kicked at my knees hard enough to bruise.

"Now, Ethan!"

A smack against my ear banged my head against the doorframe, as I pushed inside the house. I gritted my teeth against any retaliation and ducked against another blow.

Three more steps took us to the wall, where I pinned Shelley with my chest. Nuzzling my nose against her throat, I inhaled the scent pulsating from her.

"Please stop," I murmured, when her fists started on my shoulder blades.

Each fresh hit arrived with a grunt or a sob and less strength than the last. Her body wriggled beneath mine, her knees knocking against my thighs.

I released her hips and took her arms, urging them down to her sides, then folding my own around her tiny frame.

Her deep breaths heaved her chest against mine. Closing my eyes, I pushed my face into the hair teasing her neck. "Shelley, I found him."

Her entire body went rigid, except for the flexing of her fingers brushing against my waist. "Say that again," she whispered.

"I found Gabe."

Her body shuddered beneath an erupted sob. "Where is he— why isn't he here?" Her struggles kicked back in. When I lifted my face, the high shine of dread in her eyes matched the spike of fear drenching her scent. "Why haven't you brought him home?" Her voice pitched high with anxiety. "He can't ... he can't be—"

"He's *alive*."

Her body went limp in my arms, as though weighed down by relief and the exhaustion of fighting. "Why isn't he here, then?" Even as a whisper, her tone held a deep demand to know.

"The family doc's going to check him over. He got ... injured."

"How bad is he?" Still, she whispered.

"I don't know. Not until the doc's looked at him." Certain she'd stopped her attacks, I slid my hands back down to her hips. I had every intention of telling her the full story—as soon as I had her in the truck and us on our way. "He's walking, and he still has his strength ..." *and then some.* "He's a fighter ..." *stronger than me, with whatever the hell they've done to him.* "He'll be ..." I couldn't bring myself to voice what could be a lie— couldn't force myself, even, to tell her Gabe would be fine.

She sighed, and her eyes cleared a little, skimming over me as though seeing me properly for the first time since I'd shown up. "You're hurt." She trailed fingers over the slashes across my shoulder. "What happened to you?"

"Will you come with me, Shel? Come back to mine, see Gabe for yourself, and I promise I'll tell you everything I know on the way."

She gave a nod, the action a little jerky. "You're going to have to put me down first."

"Just don't hit me again, okay?"

Her fingers slid around to my nape, and with a gentle tug, she drew me closer. Her eyes continued to glisten when her soft lips pressed against mine, and it took every ounce of will power I had not to race up the stairs with Shelley and show her exactly how much I'd missed her.

In no way rushed or urgent, the kiss ended with as much tenderness as it started. Her breaths warmed my face as she continued to gaze at me. "Thank you."

Rather than ask her 'for what?', I set her down, tucking strands that had fallen forward during her outburst behind her ear. "Get some bits together, okay?" As she ducked around the corner to the stairs, I turned away, rubbing hard at my face as I blew out a breath of relief. When I peered out the front door to check for witnesses to our altercation, I found Dad staring my way through the open window of the pickup. "She's coming," I told him.

His lips curved up into the faintest of smiles. "Of course she is."

From disbelief, to denial, to distraught shuddering sobs, Shelley's emotions had filled the cab almost to the point of suffocation.

"How dare they?" Her fists thumped against the seat either side of her legs. "How bloody dare they?" Her gaze darted from me beside her, to Dad in the rear view mirror, and back to me. "Who are these people? Give me their names."

"Shelley, that's not goi—"

Her hand thrust toward me. If I'd been wearing a shirt, she'd probably have grabbed a handful and yanked me forward. Instead, she jabbed a finger into my chest. "You *will* give me their names, Ethan Holloway. And I will hunt them down, because I will not let this go until I get some damn answers as to why someone would take my Gabe and treat him this way. Do you hear me?"

What answer could I give? *Actually, Shel, you're looking at the why.* Once more, guilt tore through me with all the finesse of barbed wire. I faced away, floundering in my mind for something to say that wouldn't land me in future trouble for not sticking to my word.

"Fine." Her curt tone drew me back round. "Protect the human."

"Damned right, I'll protect you. You should never have been involved in this in the first place, Shelley, so if you think I'd let you, in any way, sort this crap out, you don't think as highly of me as I thought." She probably wouldn't, anyway, if she knew the truth. I rubbed at my face, irritated by the ever-expanding length of the bristles coating my chin. "Gabe should never have been dragged into it, either."

"You say that like it's your fault." At her fingers on my arm, I lowered my hands. Her almond-shaped eyes gazed up at me, full of concern, full of sympathy, and full of something I couldn't decipher but that drove my pulse to soar. "Why do you always have to beat yourself up over stuff? You can't hold yourself responsible for every single problem that crosses your path, Ethan."

Yes, I can, my head demanded—especially when the blame did fall on my shoulders—yet the expanding bubble of common sense and self-preservation made a stand in my throat to stop the words from departing.

"It's nobody's fault," Dad said, his voice firm. "Ethan'll realise that once this mess is cleared up."

Dad was someone else I'd have to come clean to. Only difference there? I had a way better chance of walking away unscathed from him.

The sight of home should have been enough to send my tension packing. Maybe it would have—if not for the bodies highlighted through three out of four illuminated windows. Although I'd been expecting the presence of so many, what my natural instincts insisted had to be an invasion of territory irked me enough that my virtual ruff puffed up in defence.

In the top window on the left, Jem's profile filled the rectangle in silhouette, backlit by the ceiling bulb. A spilt second later, she vanished. Four seconds after that, the front door flew open.

The truck rolled to a stop, as Jem bounced down the front steps in her waddle-hobble. Sean chased after her, hands reaching, panic on his face like he had no idea where to grasp her. "Jem, wait!" He made another grab for her, but failed when she twisted and snatched her arm away. She could move damned fast for something resembling a Weeble. "Please, Jem. It's no good for you, getting yourself so wound up. Take it easy, will you?"

Pushing open the truck door to her growled comeback of, "I'll take it easy once I've seen for myself he's okay," I jumped out with borrowed energy and caught her mid hop as she threw her arms round my neck. "I'm fine, Jem."

Trying to hold a bundle whose bulge separated us took a whole heap of effort. Her nose nuzzled my ear, her sobs shook her body, and her tears tickled in their run down my skin, stinging the slices in my shoulder.

At my rear, doors opened and closed on the truck, and the heavy footsteps I associated with Dad strode toward the house, as I peered over Jem's head at Sean.

His wild eyes and flexed hands told me exactly how much trouble Jem had been to placate in my absence. It also told me her emotions must have rocketed right off the scale.

"You get bigger, or something?" I asked, hoping regular chatter would help calm her down.

Her nod soaked my throat with what I hoped were tears rather than snot. "And you got thinner." She lifted her head at my chuckle, and her dark sapphire eyes glistened. "I didn't think you were coming back. Should have listened to Sean. He told me you'd never miss being an uncle."

"You mean his thick skull actually said something sensible?"

She laughed on her exhale before angling her head as though she'd spotted something behind me. "Shelley's here?" Jem wiggled her legs until I lowered her to the ground, taking my arm in a death grip as she swung round me to Shelley. "Gabe's with the doc. He's doing okay." She pointed toward the house, her composure in place despite the moisture still coating her cheeks and lashes. "You want to come in?"

"Thanks," Shelley said.

With one massively round female hanging off one arm, and a miniature one clutching onto my other, I headed for the fuller-than-usual house.

Connor's roar vibrated the windows before I'd even reached there. *"Kyle!"*

I almost knocked Shelley and Jem off their feet in my leap up the steps. The front door crashed into the hall table as I forced past it.

Following the choking gurgles and the violent bangs, I took the stairs three at a time. My breaths gasped from me, as the panic I'd heard in Connor's voice affected my frayed nerves.

I swung right into the guest bedroom and halted, chest heaving.

"Kyle, come on." Connor reached out, backed away, over and over, as though he needed to do something, yet didn't know what.

On the bed in front of him, Kyle's body jerked and thrashed. His legs kicked out in spasmodic contraction. His arms flailed while his fingers flexed to the point they looked like they might snap. The whites of his eyes stared out at the lilac walls above his twitching features, and his mouth froze in perpetual grimace as thick white froth bubbled past his lips.

Footsteps thudded up the stairs like a stampede. I identified the rest of the pack by scent, as they arrived on the landing outside the room.

Craig stood at the foot of the bed, hypodermic in hand, his wide eyes fixated on Kyle like he couldn't quite believe what happened.

Connor turned his accusing glare toward the doc. "What the *hell* did you give my son?"

30

Craig stared at Connor through his glasses and the strawberry blond hair hanging low over them. He gave a small headshake, dropping his focus to the syringe in his hand. "It's just antibiotics," he said, his tone one of utter disbelief.

A snarl built deep within Connor's chest. With teeth bared, his lips rippled as the sound roared from his throat.

"Oh, Jesus." The doc dropped the needle and staggered back, his hands flying up.

Dad rushed in, slapping one arm across Connor's chest, using the other to push him back by the shoulder. "Calm yourself, Connor."

"I only gave him antibiotics," Craig said. "I swear I did."

"Then, *why* is he convulsing like he's overdosed on some serious shit?" Connor knocked Dad back a step, but Dad regained his footing and control.

"I-I don't know." Craig's grey eyes held only pleading. "For goodness sake, you know I wouldn't do anything to harm your family."

Connor's hands fisted. The tendons strained throughout his neck.

"He knows that." No amount of tightness in Dad's voice could hide the quiet warning in his tone. "Don't you, Connor?"

On the bed, the froth ceased to spill from Kyle's mouth, and gut-wrenching, zombie-like groans took their place.

Dad's head whipped to the right, Connor's to the left, and the stiffening throughout their bodies matched my own as we all stared toward Kyle.

The stench of urine, without fluids for days to dilute it, arrived strong enough to wrinkle my nose, before dampness seeped into the bedding from Kyle's groin.

"The medicine must be reacting," Brook said.

I spun, finding her just inside the room, the rest of the pack right behind her. Brook's eyes, a deep glowing gold, fixated on Kyle.

Kyle's spasms slowed, the mattress ceasing to squeak with the lessening onslaught, until each of his limbs slumped to the bed as though liquefied. Muscles relaxed in his face. His head rolled to the side. Deep, deep, breaths took over his groans, each inhalation sucking at his lips, each exhalation vibrating past them.

As the feline's words sank in, I turned back to the doc, my heart bouncing like a possessed space hopper. "Please tell me you didn't give Gabe any of this shit."

"I didn't." He held out his palms. "He's doing fine."

I glanced from Craig to the door. "So, where is he, then?"

"I'm in *your* room, where I was ordered to stay put, or *else*," Gabe growled out.

"He spend a lot of time with you?" Craig asked, and I nodded. "He complains as much as you about being treated."

"I very much doubt that," Dad muttered.

I ignored him. "So, Gabe's had no antibiotics?" I asked Craig.

He shook his head. "His wounds were all closed over. I only gave them to Kyle because his looked inflamed, and I didn't want to risk infection." He rubbed a hand around the back of his neck, above the collar of his green polo shirt. "Never seen anyone have that kind of reaction before, though."

"Why would antibiotic react with ..." Brook's focus lifted from Kyle to me, but it seemed to take immense effort.

"React with what?" Craig stepped forward with a frown. "If he's been given, or taken, something, I need to know."

Brook slipped from her spot and farther into the room, wearing a pair of Mum's sweats. "How much does the human know?" she whispered as she passed me.

I shrugged. 'Nothing' would have been my answer of preference, but I refused to be that naïve. Common sense told me—*us*, the pack—he must have made discoveries he'd never voiced.

"Is somebody going to tell me what's going on?" Craig made a slow focal tour across the four of us standing in the room, toward Josh and Daniel crammed against the opening with Jem peering between them, and Sean behind her. When none of us spoke, he bent for his syringe, his eyes aimed at Dad and Connor. "How can you expect me to treat him like this?"

Neither of them spoke, only folded their arms across their chests in some kind of united front. I willed them to say something, barely daring to open my own mouth, knowing the reprimand it would bring.

The loaded glare Brook sent me seemed to question my muteness, beseech me to spill the details, and bollock me for not doing so. Her breath snorted from her nostrils as she turned to Craig. "Venom. He was infected by venom." Her hands flicked back and forth. "Although ... technically, it was anti-venom."

"After he'd been infected with venom." I avoided Dad's stare as its weight settled on me.

Craig frowned. "Do I want to ask what kind of venom you're talking about?"

"The better question is should you," I said.

"Okay." He said the word slowly. "Should I ask what kind of venom you're talking about?"

Three resounding 'No's responded from Dad, Connor and Brook, as I shook my head.

Craig opened his mouth; it hung there a moment like he considered arguing, but he nodded. "Okay, then, the best I can do for him is put him on a saline drip to ensure he doesn't dehydrate any more than he already has, and keep an eye on his vitals. Which means, I'll have to hook him up to an ECG. But"—he turned to Connor—"if he goes into seizure again, I'll need to administer an anticonvulsant, which I'll have no choice but to take him in for as I don't have any with me." He shrugged. "With the limited information, that's the best I can offer to do."

Connor nodded, as Dad said, "Do it."

The doc released a long exhale. "Anyone care to go to my car for me?"

Dad pointed to Josh, waved him in, and Josh pushed forward, hand already held out. "What do you need?"

"It could be a long night," Craig said, dropping his keys into Josh's palm. "You'd better bring me everything."

Josh paused as he turned for the door, his green eyes skimming over my body before settling on my face. "You look like you pissed off a cat." When my eyes darted to the left, landing on Brook's gaze aimed at me, Josh chuckled and nudged me with his shoulder. "Good to have you back."

After he ducked out the room, Jem stepped into the gap he'd created, a bowl of water sloshing around in her hands. "Make way for the wide load." She paused beside Brook. "You hindering, or helping?"

"I would very much like to help. It may work to take my mind off the discomfort of being the only ..." Her eyes flickered to the left, where the doc cleaned his glasses like he pretended not to be listening. "... one of me in a houseful of ... you."

Jem smiled. "The bathroom's at the end of the landing. Washcloths are beneath the sink, if you'd like to grab some."

Brook nodded. "Of course."

"Better bring some towels, too," Jem called after her. "You'll find them on the shelf below."

"How about you?" Craig asked me. "Those gashes of yours could do with stitching—especially the one you think you're doing a good job of hiding beneath your waistband."

"I don't need stitches." I followed Brook's apologetic stare, as she waltzed past me with the towels for Jem, and tried to convey with my own eyes that I didn't hold her responsible. Catching Dad's disapproving expression, and the fold of his arms across his broad chest, I turned back to Craig. "I'm fine. Kyle needs you more than I do. Gabe, too."

Craig sighed. "Gabe is not in any immediate danger. Though, I could run tests to find out exactly—"

"No," Dad said.

Craig met Dad's stare head on, though only for a split second. "Then, the best treatment he can currently receive is rest, rehydration, and fuel for his body, which is the job of the drip I've set him up with." He sent me a small smile. "And some good old fashioned TLC."

And hope for the best, my mind finished. "I'll go check on him." *For myself.*

In my bedroom, familiarity greeted me in the coffee walls, the crisp freshness of clean linen, the view of the forest through my window, and Shelley ... on my bed.

Stood to reason she'd be with Gabe, but the sight of her sitting somewhere I never thought I'd see her faltered my step and sent me in a sideways stagger. I righted myself before I shoulder slammed the wardrobe, going for cool and collective as I tucked my hands into my pockets.

Gabe sat in the only chair, with way more worry lines than should have been present on a nineteen-year-old face, and a tube that connected the back of his hand with a bag of clear liquid on the window ledge beside him. "W-what's up with K-Kyle? He okay?"

I went to nod, but stopped myself when I realised I didn't have that positive an answer. "Hopefully." Shelley staring up at me drew my eyes her way. "How you holding up?"

"Better," she said. "Thanks."

Giving a half-nod, I twisted back to Gabe. "You been fed?" The aroma of some kind of broth told me Mum had been busy prepping for the troops.

His eyes brightened as he smiled. "K-kitchen was my first s-stop."

I chuckled. "Of course it was." Mum probably talked everyone into eating. "Lauren—she about?"

Gabe pointed his thumb toward nowhere in particular. "Beth t-talked her into helping out in the k-kitchen."

"I'd better go check on her." I swung back toward Shelley, mouth open for far too long as her green eyes captured mine. "You need me, I'll be downstairs."

Sean stood propped against the doorway to the guestroom, when I strode back down the landing. I glanced into the room, caught Connor perched on the windowsill, looking far more composed, and Josh helping the doc on the far side of the bed. Daniel sat in the wicker seat, his forearms resting against his thighs. No Dad, though.

Tossing soiled bedsheets to Brook, Jem pointed to the corner. "Drop them there. We can take them down once we're done here."

I continued past and down the stairs. Rounding the bottom newel post, I spotted Samuel through the living room doorway and swerved that way. "How you doing?"

His face lifted from its resting place in his cupped hands. "Be better when I get home."

Any werewolf would have been on edge while smack bang in the middle of another pack's domain—surrounded by them.

"You made your call, yet?"

He shook his head. "Your father asked me to wait."

No doubt an order made to sound like a request. "It shouldn't be much longer before we start formulating a plan." *Hopefully.* I jerked my chin to the right. "I'll be in the kitchen."

Figuring he'd be more comfortable alone, I left him and padded along the hallway to the kitchen entrance at the end. The second I stepped in the room, I found Lauren in Dad's regular seat at the end of the table.

Her chair scraped back as she stood. "You were ages."

"I had a detour to make." I waved at her to sit back down and moved across to my chair beside hers. My entire body groaned with the relief of relaxing into a spot of my own. "Mum been treating you okay?"

The female in question came in from the dark conservatory before Lauren could answer. Mum stopped short. More lines than I remembered marked the skin beside her eyes, though they smoothed slightly when her face relaxed into a smile. "You must be hungry."

Food couldn't have been farther from the top notch on my priority list, but knowing Mum wouldn't stand for excuses, I nodded.

"I'll fix you something."

Dad stepped in behind her, as she crossed the kitchen, his eyes searching mine—for what, I didn't know.

A mug appeared beneath my nose, steam spiralling upward from its contents. I scooped it up, smiling my thanks at Mum. The coffee smelled like strong chicory, as well as brandy—Dad's no doubt. I took a long, slow sip, my lids lowering.

"Can I go home soon?" Lauren asked.

I opened my eyes. Hers held so much hope, they risked overflowing, and I'd never wanted anything more than to tell the girl exactly what she needed to hear.

She must have seen the despair I knew my face displayed, because tears arrived to coat her irises with glistening moisture. "Can I?" she whispered.

"Lauren?" Dad dragged out the chair on her other side and sat. "There's no reason for you not to go home, but there are some things we need you to be clear on before that can happen."

She sniffled and wiped her cuff beneath her nose. "Like what?"

Liquid bubbled on the hob Mum tended to, the steam carrying rich flavours to all four corners of the kitchen.

Saliva coated my tongue, despite my brain's rejection of the idea of food.

"Well ... for one, I think it would be wise if you remained here until we know it's safe for you to return home." Dad leaned forward, his expression radiating trust with an ease that came naturally to him. "I need to be certain the people—"

"Vampires," Lauren said.

Dad's eyebrow arched up.

"They weren't people, Mr Holloway. They were vampires."

Dad dipped his chin. "I need to be certain these ... *vampires* aren't in a position to come back for you. We also need to come up with a plausible story for where you've been." He paused, as if to ensure she followed, and although Lauren didn't speak, her finger shuffling kicked up a gear. "Because an explanation of, *I was kidnapped by vampires and caged next to werewolves and shifters,* probably won't cut it with everyone who'll have been looking for you."

"Not unless I want to be locked up, right?" she mumbled.

"Right." Dad nodded.

Mum placed a bowl on the table in front of me. "Eat." She folded my fingers around the spoon like she used to when I'd been a kid. Her hand stroked across my hair as she brushed her lips over my cheek. "You'll be no good to anybody if you collapse from exhaustion."

I responded by scooping up the spoon and feeding it into my mouth. My taste buds perked up as the liquid spilled over them, but the initial swallow sent it to my stomach with the subtlety of a dropping slab.

"So ... what am I supposed to tell everyone?" A tear spilled over Lauren's lashes. She swiped at it with her forearm. "What am I supposed to tell my mum? That I ran away, or something?"

Smart girl. I sent her an encouraging smile before trying a second sample of the Scotch broth.

"That is the line of thought I've been leaning toward." Dad nodded. "You see, I'd be willing to bet your mum contacted the police as soon as she realised you were missing. Any story you go home with will more than likely be passed onto them. Do you understand what I'm saying to you, Lauren?"

"Keep my mouth shut."

Dad shook his head, somehow managing to make it look as though the concern emanating from his eyes was all for the girl, rather than for the pack's exposure. "Let me try and explain it better, okay?" Once she'd nodded, he continued, "If you made an announcement like that? It would hit the news within minutes. Every news-watching person across the nation would hear about it and know who it came from. Some of those who catch wind of it could very well be of supernatural origins. Most of them will not be happy about their secret existence no longer being secret."

"Your own secret would be out, too, Lauren. Folks would want to know more about you." I slurped my broth and swallowed. "You ready to be studied through a microscope? Treated like a test subject?"

Her head jerked side to side. "But how am I supposed to go back and act like everything's normal? Nothing will ever be the same. I won't ever be the same. Not after ..." She twisted toward me, seemed to make some sort of imploration with her eyes and the wringing fingers she set on the table by my elbow. "How am I supposed to deal with this ... on my own?"

"You won't have to." Mum walked across to Lauren, all mother, one hundred percent reassuring—a trait in her that had earned the pedestal I'd stuck her on for as long as I could remember. "I'll ensure you have a way to contact me. If you ever feel the need to talk to somebody, all you'll have to do is call."

Lauren's frightened yet intelligent eyes locked onto Mum's for a few seconds before she swung back to me. "You'll give me your number, too, right?"

"Sure." I gave her a smile. "Just don't be texting me every time you buy a new pair of shoes."

Her eyebrows and lips set in straight lines. "Bet you can't text, anyway."

I matched her expression. "Can, too."

"Not with those fingers." A hint of the teen-girl attitude I'd first met peeked through. "They're too podgy." The humour faded almost as fast as it arrived, and a small tremor affected her shoulders. "But you'll be around ... if I need you?"

I doubted the girl would sleep easy for a long time—not with the sights she'd witnessed, not with her harsh reality call and her new understanding of the world she lived in.

I met her gaze. "Any time. Every time."

"Right," Mum said, drawing Lauren from me. "You ready to take that bath, now?"

Lauren nodded. "Thanks, Mrs Holloway."

One arm extended, Mum waited for Lauren to stand and folded it around her like the wing of a bird around her chick.

Opposite me, Dad's bright blue eyes bored into me like a drill trying to penetrate the exterior to my soul.

Evading him, I watched Mum and Lauren from beneath lowered brows, sticking another spoonful of soup in my mouth that I didn't really want. Once they'd left the kitchen, I pushed to my feet to avoid the bucket-load of questions I sensed coming.

"Do not leave that table before you've finished your meal, young man," Mum said from the hallway.

Half-standing, I froze.

"Sit back down ... and make sure he eats, Nathan."

Dad's raised eyebrows seemed to mock me when I turned back to him. "You really want to argue with your mother?"

And lose? I shook my head, lowering into my chair like I'd made the choice to do so myself, and picked up my spoon as though I'd never intended to leave the bowl half full to begin. "So ..." I deposited almost cold broth into my unwilling mouth.

Dad relaxed back into his seat—an act I'd have bought, if I didn't know him so well.

"... when are we going to organise the clean-up?"

"Soon." Dad sighed. "That the only thing on your mind?"

I frowned. "Isn't it enough?"

"A question isn't an answer, Son. You're distracted." His head tilted. "You're never distracted."

I dropped my spoon into the bowl and nudged both away. "There's a lot to do."

"I agree. But it's a clear-cut problem. We know what's going on. We have all the evidence and documentation we need to locate those responsible. It can be wrapped up in a couple of days—maybe sooner, if I get Jack on board." He took a deep breath. "But you know that. Whatever's bothering you has nothing to do with all this." Laying his forearms on the table, he leaned forward until I had no choice but to meet his gaze. "Are you going to tell me what's really on your mind?"

My teeth pressed together until my jaw ached. I wanted to look away, but couldn't—either that, or my pride wouldn't let me.

"Well?" he asked.

"It's my fault."

"What is?" No dispute, no coddling, which I'd expected.

"Us—this ... *mess*, and us getting dragged into it. It's all down to me. *Because* of me."

"Care to elaborate?"

"I was set up. Set up to be taken." I brushed a hand over my hair, back to front, laying strands flat across my brow. "I have no idea why."

Dad's brow creased a little. "No idea why you were set up?"

"No idea why they wanted me that badly."

"Modesty has always been a quality of yours." He half-smiled. "But I still don't understand why that makes this your fault."

"Because if it wasn't for me, Gabe would never have been kidnapped and fuc—messed up the way he has been, and Kyle would never have been used as a trap."

Dad gave a small headshake. "Not following."

"For goodness sake, Dad. What's not to get?" My right hand fisted on the table-top. "If I'd just kept my nose out of other peoples' lives, Gabe would have stayed safe, at home with Shelley. I thought I was helping him, and all I managed to do was put the kid in danger. It's my fault." I banged my fist against my chest. "My fault Kyle's lying up there on that bed. My fault Gabe's infected with something we don't know can be healed. I should never have got so involved with him." My brow dipped low. "They took him as *bait*, Dad. If not for me, Gabe would never have been taken."

Dad's focus darted to the doorway, and a quiet groan left his throat.

I twisted—already knowing what I'd see.

Beneath her shock of red hair, Shelley eyes burned with way too many emotions to separate, but amongst those, blazing way hotter than any other: betrayal.

31

Shelley's hands fisted at her sides, as red bled into the cheeks of her face. "You lied to me?" The grind of her teeth reached my hearing—a split second before she bolted into the hallway.

I shot to my feet, my chair clattering back. "Shelley, wait!"

Her shoes slapped along the floor tiles. "Gabe!" A moment later, rapid pummels hit each step on her run up the stairs.

I swung into the empty hallway.

"Yeah?" Gabe called from my bedroom.

Shit! I reached the bottom step, as she leapt onto the landing above. "Shelley, give me a chance to explain."

"Why?" she snapped, spinning to glare down at me. "So I can be lied to some more?"

I ascended a few steps and peered up at her. "I never lied to you."

Footsteps crossed the landing, and Gabe's face appeared over Shelley's shoulder. "Mum, wh-what's wrong?"

Shelley's blazing stare remained fixated on me. "We're leaving."

"Wh-what?" Gabe's eyes widened before his brows knotted. "Wh-why?"

"Please, calm down, Shelley," Dad said from behind me. "You're misinterpreting what you think you heard."

"*Think*?" Shelley's glower shifted to Dad. "I *know* what I heard, thank you very much."

"Will you please come back downstairs?" he said. "Let me tell you why you're wrong about this."

Shelley's mouth set in a grim line. "Why would I want to hear more lies?"

Dad's foot hit the step behind me. Nudging me aside, he climbed higher. "Believe me, Shelley, nobody has lied to you."

"I know what I heard." Shelley folded her arms across her chest.

Dad's shift to the right blocked my view of her. "Yes, and I understand your reaction to it." As I went to duck to the left, he reached behind and grabbed my forearm, forcing me back. "However, I'm pretty sure you, in return, understand Ethan is his own worst enemy when it comes to self-blame. He'd shoulder the responsibility for global warming and every tsunami that hits the planet, if he thought for one second there was a possibility of him having contributed to them."

Shelley stared hard at Dad as though absorbing his words. Uncertainty arrived with the flicker of her eyes. I thought he'd succeeded in getting her to see sense, but then she said, "Can you honestly tell me that Gabe being taken had nothing to do with him being close to Ethan?"

"Wh-what?" Gabe stared down at me over Shelley's head. "Wh-what's she t-talking about?" When no one answered him, he tugged on his mum's shoulder until she gave him her attention. "Mum, wh-what's g-going on?"

"It's not safe for you here, Gabe." Her gaze swung and locked onto mine behind Dad. "I made a mistake."

"Shelley, I'm ..." My words sizzled beneath the inferno in her eyes.

Gabe's focus flitted between me and his mother, his irises dulled to a dark grey. "Wh-what are you t-talking about?"

"Him." Shelley's chin jerked toward me.

I shook my head, mentally pleaded with her not to say anything.

"He bloody got you kidnapped."

Gabe frowned, mouth puckered in frustration. "Wh-where would you g-get a stupid idea like that from?"

"From him." Turning back to me, she said, "Or are you going to deny it?"

How could I? Shelley *had* got her information directly from me, and surely, to dispute that would make me look worse than I already did.

My eyes darted aside as shame heated my cheeks.

"Ethan?" The confusion in Gabe's deepened tone far outweighed that claiming his eyes.

"She's right." I lifted my gaze back up toward his towering form. "It's because of me you were taken."

"Bullsh-shit!" Gabe's teeth ground as he scowled down at me.

"I couldn't agree more," Dad said.

"It *is* my damned fault," I said, turning on him. "I know they took him as bait. They knew who I was from the off. They knew who Gabe was when they targeted him. They've probably hand-selected each and every bloody being they've taken from day one. If Gabe hadn't spent time with me, then the chances are, he'd have slipped beneath their radar."

"How the heck can you go from dampening your worth beneath modesty to placing tickets on yourself?" Dad gave a low growl. "You have no proof that they hadn't already spotted Gabe prior to targeting you. They could just as easily have gone after him and *then* realised how they could use his kidnap to their advantage, and—"

"And I played right into their hands? Dad, these ..." Sending a quick glance toward the room that held Craig, I lowered my voice. "... vampires—as much as I hate to admit it—are smart. If they went after Gabe, they did so because they'd already planned to. They've done their research. They know who each one they've taken is, and what they are—with the exception of Lauren. Gabe has spent his life beneath the radar—proven by the fact Jack didn't even realise he had a pup in his territory. And he'd have stayed that way, if I'd just refrained from sticking my damn beak in, drawing attention to him. Tell me, Dad—how the hell does that make me blameless?"

"It doesn't," Shelley said as she grabbed Gabe's wrist. "Come on." She stomped down three steps, her hold on Gabe dragging him behind her in a stooped plod.

He tugged back, sloshing the liquid in the drip bag he still held. "Mum, st-stop."

With her entire body braced, Shelley hauled Gabe until he complied and stamped onto the next step down.

He looked to me, as she yanked at him again. "D-d-do something."

"Shelley ..." I veered round Dad, went to climb higher, but his fingers grasped hold of my waistband. When he forced me back down three steps, a low growl brewed in my chest, but I kept my focus on Shelley. "I get you're pissed at me, but what about Gabe? You're not thinking straight, Shel."

She slammed to a halt. "How the hell would you know what I'm thinking, or feeling?"

Gabe's body jerked forward again, when Shelley descended a step. "Mum, please."

"Don't *please* me, Gabriel." As Shelley went to round Dad, I pushed up to block her. "Move!" she snapped through gritted teeth.

I shook my head, beseeched with my stare for her to cease when I caught the despair in Gabe's eyes behind her.

She shifted to the right, her shoulder brushing my chest with the twist of her body. "Move, Ethan."

"Mum, stop," Gabe said. "Wh-wh-what the hell's g-g-got intto you."

"This!" She whirled on him, moisture in her eyes. "This is what the hell's gotten into me. He's bloody messed my son up. He messed you up, Gabe." She spun back, glowering at me. "And if he doesn't move out of my way, I swear I'm going to knock his sorry arse down these damn stairs."

"Go away, Son." When my head whipped toward Dad's almost whispered command, his cool blue eyes met mine in a level stare. "For goodness sake, go away and leave me to handle this."

I wanted to tell him *I'd* handle it—*my mess, my problem*—but clamped my teeth against retaliation and backed down the stairs, my movements jerky, thunder in my chest beneath the sting of the order.

Shelley squared her shoulders to Dad, instead, like no height difference or rank existed. "Now, *you* are in my way."

Dad made no move to step aside. "Where will you go, Shelley?"

"Home." She said the word as though it should have been obvious.

"That's not an option right now."

Her eyes narrowed. "Are you threatening me?"

"Of c-course he isn't, Mum." Gabe turned to Dad. "Wh-why can't we go home?"

"Because your friend is still missing, Gabe," Dad said, his voice calm. "And because his parents reported your absence to the police."

Gabe seemed to process Dad's words, then he groaned and rubbed at his face. "W-with him still missing, I'll b-be their prime suspect if I show b-back up alone." He twisted back to Dad. "Right?"

Dad gave a slow nod.

Shelley's brows drew tight, her lips, too, as I watched the realisation of their situation sink in. "Then, we'll find somewhere else to stay." Her tempered stare once more latched onto me. "You've all already done more than enough."

"Stay ... please." I stepped forward, lowered my arms. "I'll go, instead." Dad spun round, warning in his glare, but my chances were close to running out. "I'm obviously the reason you're leaving. If I'm not here, you'll have no reason to go."

The fire in Shelley's eyes lessened to lambent flames. Gabe's hopeful glances alternated between the two of us, like he could get his mum to concede through the power of wishful thinking alone, but Shelley seemed oblivious to them.

After agonizing seconds, during which my breaths ceased and my pulse slowed almost to a halt, she murmured, "I can't."

Mum materialised at the top of the stairs and took three steps down, the creaking of wood beneath her feet wrenching Shelley's attention from me. "Will you allow me to help you?"

"I don't ..." Shelley raked fingers into her hair.

"I understand your instinct to protect your son," Mum said. "Trust me when I say I've gone to great lengths to do exactly the same thing. But I can't see you out there on your own, Shelley—not with nowhere to go. If you'll let me, I can drive you somewhere you'll both be safe. Somewhere none of the pack will bother you." Mum paused, imploration clear in her dark eyes. "Please, let me help you."

I suspected Mum's secret venue would be the flat she'd lived in when she'd needed someplace incognito to hide out—one only three of the pack knew the whereabouts of. Outsiders had caused more desolation for my family than we'd ever brought on ourselves, and yet again, they held responsibility for someone I cared for deeply being driven away.

With my gaze on Shelley, as I willed her to agree, all of those to blame spun through my mind in a tornado of wrath. Fists clenched, notions of violence colliding with the identities I conjured, I silently vowed to make sure each and every one of them paid.

Shelley nodded after a long minute, snapping me back to the moment. "Okay," she said. "Thank you."

I blew out a breath, relief flooding through me, until it sank in that Shelley and Gabe would be gone any moment.

They'd also most probably never return, or call—not me, anyway.

Pain lanced through me like a spear to the heart.

I barely heard as Mum offered to get her keys. It scarcely registered when Dad padded down the stairs, allowing Mum past. My focus refused to shift from the female who'd taught me what I could have. Only the excruciating tightness of my jaw stopped my true emotions from erupting.

Mum reappeared. "Ready when you are, Shelley." At Shelley's nod, Mum reached around me for the door catch. "Please, Ethan," she whispered when I didn't move. "Don't make this more difficult on yourself by creating a scene."

Dragging my feet to the left took immense effort, yet the success of the action beat that of removing my focus from Shelley. I hoped beyond hope that she'd read the screaming apology in my expression.

"Gabe, let's go," Shelley said as she began her descent.

The pup didn't budge. "I don't w-want t-to."

She gave a tug with little effect. "Now."

He turned to me, his frown cutting deep lines across his forehead. "Ethan? T-tell her."

The weight of Shelley's gaze drew me back her way, to the defiant tilt of her chin as she dared me to overrule her. "Do as your mother says," I mumbled to Gabe.

Shelley's feet hit the hallway tiles, followed by Gabe's and his exasperated sigh. My eyes remained aimed at the floor, as Shelley squeezed around the door to exit the house, and would have stayed there if Gabe didn't halt in front of me.

Disappointment saddened his features when I lifted my face. "Y-you c-c-could have said f-for me to st-stay. She w-would have listened t-to you."

I shook my head. "Not this time she wouldn't, Gabe." *Probably never will again.*

"My p-place." He peered away, the skin beside his eyes taut with tension, before looking back. "In the p-p-pack."

"Now's not the time, Gabe." Mum's hand at the small of his back nudged him forward a step. "Come on now, your mum's waiting on you."

He lifted a hand, fisted it in his filthy hair. "You p-p-promised."

I could think of nothing else to say besides, "I'm sorry."

Gabe stared at me a moment longer, his right hand intermittently contracting against his temple. With a headshake that yelled volumes of frustration and hurt, Gabe ducked outside and followed Shelley.

I stared after their retreating backs, as the trio crossed the driveway, the muscles in my face drawn so tight they created a tic beneath my left eye.

Footsteps tapped the tiles behind me, and I turned to Dad in the kitchen doorway. He opened his mouth, but I shook my head before he could say anything, and spun away.

Up the stairs, past Sean, past the blur I caught in my periphery of all those in with Kyle, I strode into my bedroom. The slam of my door rattled the photograph of the sun shining through the forest trees that hung on my wall. Fists pressed to my forehead, I released a groan that bubbled up from my throat as a deep growl.

A quiet tap sifted through my door. I crossed to my bed, flopped down on my back, and drew my pillow over my face.

"Ethan?" Tender concern coated Jem's tone.

I lifted the pillow, considered answering, if only to ask her to leave me alone, but on realising whatever left my mouth in that moment would be far from polite, I clamped my lips shut and rammed my concealment back firmly in place.

Jem's feet padded away again, but no reprieve arrived. Only aggravation, frustration and confusion coursed through me like the expanding bubble inside my chest, growing with each breath I took, just waiting to burst.

I managed to remain motionless for about three minutes before slinging the pillow across the room. It collided with a wooden sculpture I didn't even like, sending it from the dresser to smash against the wall with enough force to chip plaster. I flicked my legs over the side of the bed, rolled up into a stand, and paced to the window.

The light from my ceiling bounced my reflection back at me.

Filthy. Sweaty. Hair all over the damn place. For the first time in my life, I'd experienced an epic failure, and it showed—in my hollow eyes, in the sag of my shoulders, my inability to remain stationery, and in the heave of my chest as each additional breath I took required more effort than the last.

The outline of the treetops in their midnight dance drew my focus beyond what I didn't want to see, calling to me to go out there and burn everything off.

My yank of the door almost dragged it off its hinges. I ducked right onto the landing, halting as Sean stepped out from the guestroom.

A low growl arrived before I could stop it. "Now is a really bad time to be blocking my path, Sean."

He shifted aside, and I resumed my journey in the same erratic manner with which it began.

My feet thudded the stairs.

My fist tapped against the newel post in the hallway.

My shoulder rammed the kitchen door wider.

When Dad pushed to his feet from his chair, I blanked him and headed for the conservatory.

"Where are you going?" he asked.

I paused in the doorway, but didn't look back. "Out."

"It can wait. I want you to round everyone up so we can start strategizing."

"You don't need me to formulate a plan." My teeth ground as I marched into the conservatory. "You can just tell me what to do when I get back, I'm sure."

I snapped down the door handle and stepped outside into drizzle.

"God knows, you've had enough practice, tonight," I muttered as my feet hit the sodden lawn.

With each step, spray soaked the hems of my jeans, just as with each step, my muscles coiled tighter in anticipation of my run. By the time I'd ducked beneath the arches, the forest swallowing me whole, the rumble had become a constant within my chest.

Fingers fumbling, I unfastened my jeans and shoved them over my hips without breaking stride. The denim bunched around my knees, and I lifted one leg, and the other, stumbling as I kicked the jeans aside.

Naked, and eager to encourage pain as a blockage for pain, I broke into a jog.

Through foliage covering the overhead branches, the partial moon allowed brief offerings of light along my path.

In less than a minute, I'd crouched beneath its illumination in *my* spot. We all had them, each of us in the pack—tiny circles of the forest we favoured for our changes, small patches of land we held territory over, the border marked with our scent.

Shoulders hunched high, head hung low, my breaths arrived deep as the initial ripple washed through me from crown to toe tips, and the skin prickled across my scalp.

I closed my eyes, concentrated.

The first tug of flesh stretched the wounds wider across my pelvis, shoulder, and thigh. At the biting sting that accompanied the splitting skin, I grunted and pushed myself into the change harder.

Sweat popped out across the surface of my body, began a steady trickle along my spine. When my outer layer twisted, and the inevitable ripping arrived from each wound, I emitted a quiet groan, and forced into the change faster.

Only once the first contortion began the snapping of bones, with an agony powerful enough to temporarily smother that within my heart, did my mind switch off.

Growls rolling from me, and with no attempt made to curb them, I handed myself over to the change.

Blood fogged my left eye, where it had trailed from a gash caused by a low hung branch, yet it left me no more blind than I'd been on first take-off. The canine-induced muteness of colours had long vanished beneath the haze of red in my mind, as frustration and anger became fuel to surge my legs faster.

The pummel of my front paws against dirt sent jolts to my aching shoulders. Each land of my hind-quarters and upward thrust of muscles sparked a blazing infliction, which reverberated through my flank and travelled the length of my spine.

I welcomed them all: every wave of pain, each course of agony—using them to distract from that which hurt the most.

A chilled breeze swirled through the trees like a heat-seeking missile—my already weary body its only goal. On it carried the aroma of rodent, and I altered course, my body leaning into the wind as I rounded a trunk broader than even myself.

Ahead, the small creature scurried, its tail taunting as it darted left and right. The stench of fear pumped from the critter. Small crumbs of dirt clouded the air behind the bobs of its body.

Thunder rolled through my chest and arrived as a roar, as I threw my jaws down and snatched the squirrel up.

A clicking cry squeaked from it, until a sharp snap of my head to the left broke its neck. Legs still pumping me onward, only a tiny trail of blood hit my tongue before I tossed the creature aside.

I didn't want food, just as I hadn't wanted the last six morsels I'd thrown down like a disgruntled werewolf's interpretation of a bread trail.

Only my soul lacked nourishment—my heart, too.

"Ethan!"

Rain drummed against the sparsely-coated treetops, almost masking the shout. I told myself I hadn't heard and raced off to the north.

"Ethan! I know you can hear me!" The second shout arrived louder, more desperate.

Without intending to, I slowed and swerved toward the location of Jem's voice.

"Ethan, please! Come back!"

Breaths ragged, ears pinned back, I picked up speed, forcing my limbs into a frantic sprint.

I pivoted left around a silver birch. In my leap over a bare brush, branches scraped at my underbelly, irritating my wound there. I growled against the smarting, pounded my paws into the earth, and lunged back into my run.

Jem's scent reached me before the view of her did. Following it, I burst into a clearing, mud spattering my forelegs as I stopped dead.

Jem knelt within the small circle of barrenness. Desolation dominated her expression beneath the hair plastered over her forehead by the fine rain. She'd have heard my approach—I'd made no attempt to disguise it— yet the second her gaze latched onto me, she let out a gasp of obvious relief.

"Thank goodness." Her breath hitched as her hand swept over her swollen mound in a manic spiral. "I didn't think you'd come."

I breathed out a whine, as I padded closer, and nudged her extended hand with my nose. *What's wrong?*

She combed her fingers through the fur at my throat until I pressed into the embrace. "I need you to change back." She scratched behind my ear, pushed her face against my ruff. "I know you won't feel like it, but I need you to."

The quiet plea in her voice set my nerves on edge, and I whined again.

"They're leaving already."

I lifted my face, my brows knotting as I studied her.

"Sean's going with them. He has to. I knew he would. It's who he is." Her hands cupped my face as she rubbed her nose across mine. "But I need you to be there, Ethan. I trust you to make sure he comes back home in one piece. And I really need that reassurance right now." Her gaze connected with mine. "Can you do that for me?"

32

No way did I want to face the rest of the pack right then. That didn't mean I'd in anyway allow that to tarnish my decisions. My brother intended to head out and clean up a mess I'd been part of. I'd never let that happen without being there to watch his back.

Besides, I owed the vampires an arse-kicking. Someone had to pay for the shit hand I'd been dealt.

Dressed in fresh attire Jem had brought out for me, and with my mobile tucked into the jeans pocket, I strode back toward home.

The rumble of engines reached me before I'd emerged from the forest. I shoved aside my pissy mood, which had worsened on realisation that Dad would order the others to leave without me, and picked up speed through the arches.

Jem stood in the kitchen window, the worry lining her face smoothing out as she gave me a small wave upon my jog across the lawn.

I nodded, kept going until my trainers hit the block paving in a rhythmic beat, and rounded the house. Two trucks idled on the driveway—Dad's, with its nose peeking out the gates, and mine in line behind.

I headed for my own black Ford and yanked open the door to find Sean behind the wheel.

He blew out a breath as he turned to me. "Had me worried for a minute, there."

"Yeah, well …" I grabbed the handle, hauling myself into the passenger seat. "You worry too much. You want me to drive?"

"No. Only things you need to do on the journey are eat and rest."

I grunted. "I've eaten."

"Not enough, according to Mum." At rustling, I twisted back, as he plonked a plastic bag down on the centre console. "She said I had to make sure you eat the lot."

"She's back?" *How long did I run for?*

Sean nodded. "And she said to tell you she did what was best for everyone." He patted the bag before his honk of the horn set Dad's truck into motion in front of us. "Now, eat."

As I belted up, Sean engaged first gear and followed Dad out the gates. No traffic interrupted our turn onto the road, though I guessed not many folks travelled lanes at two-fifteen in the morning.

Inside the bag, I found four crusty rolls, a peek beneath the lids revealing thick ham and sliced boiled egg. Under those, lay a two-litre bottle of water with a yellow sticky label attached to it that read: drink me.

I wedged it on the seat beside my thigh and chose one of the rolls to bite into. "What did I miss?" Crumbs sprayed from my mouth as I chewed. "And who's in with Dad?"

"Samuel and Josh. Dan's been ordered to watch Connor's back, while Connor's watching everyone else's. Dad thought it best to have reinforcements at the house, as the vamps who took you seemed to know so much. So ... simple planning is all you missed." Sean shrugged. "And Dad got Sam to contact his Alpha."

I wiped the back of my hand across my lips. "What did Jack say? Is he willing to join forces?"

"He just found out he lost his son. What do you think he said?"

"He's in." I shoved the remaining chunk of cob into my mouth. "He'd have to be." *Just like I have to be.*

Sean nodded. "Yeah, he's in. Dad's given him directions to a spot near the site. We'll meet them there."

"How many?"

"Four, including Jack."

I swallowed the last of the first roll and opened the water, gulping down a swig. "So ... plan of action?"

"We go in. The best points of penetration can be decided once we arrive. Split into two groups—maybe three. Only half of each group changes, to detect any vampires by scent and prevent being snuck up on. We take out the threat. Check out any captives still caged and decide what to do with them. Then, we'll work our way through the list of names you got until we've eliminated anyone with knowledge of us."

"Working straight through until the entire job's done?"

"Yep. No loose ends left untied to go blathering to anyone."

That made sense to me. I drew out two rolls and passed one to Sean. "You want one?"

"Nope."

"I won't tell if you don't."

"Well, in that case." His fingers wrapped around it and guided the bun straight to his mouth.

I tore a hunk off my own and waved the remainder toward Sean as I munched. "Dad tell you about the wolfsbane?"

He stopped chewing, his gaze met mine, and I didn't need words to know the answer.

I could understand his response. Sean had been one of the pack members kidnapped by witches eight months earlier, and he'd been exposed to the plant as a form of torturous control—for days.

"It's liquid," I said. "Vampire who threatened to stick me with it had it in a syringe."

"Well ... shit," he mumbled around his mouthful before turning back to the road.

"Yeah, that was pretty much my thought at the time, too."

Quiet settled over us for a mile or two. With our chewing and swallowing and chugging out the way, only the engine or whoosh of displaced air each time we passed a tree or high hedgerow entertained us.

Sean glanced my way. "You eating that last roll?" When I responded by passing him the bag, he fiddled around inside it until he'd engaged his prize. "Okay, now rest up."

"I still haven't got all the details."

"You've got as much as I do." He shoved his roll into his mouth and stretched over, knocking the stereo on. The local rock station blared out, and Sean sent me a grin, his head jerking back and forth to the beat.

My half-hearted argument arrived as a pathetic growl, and did little to stop Sean in his stupid antics—he sang over the top of me with lyrics that had nothing to do with the song playing and everything to do with ordering me around.

Realising I wouldn't win—or that I didn't have the energy to try—I kicked my feet up onto the dashboard and let nothing but the brain-numbing tunes fill my mind.

Intermittent blinks of light infiltrated my closed lids, flashing a pink Morse code at my aching eyes. I had no idea how long I attempted sleep—an hour, or so, at a guess, but no matter how much I begged the spiralling thoughts to depart my mind, no reprieve arrived.

When the truck slowed and bumped to the crunch of gravel, I rubbed at my face. "We there?" Even my voice sounded exhausted, as though it hadn't the strength to arrive louder than a mumble.

Sean's seat creaked beneath the shift of his weight, and the thumping beat from the radio died away. "You say something? You awake?"

Was never asleep to begin. "I said, are we there?"

"What are you—a damn Sat-Nav?"

"I'll take that as a yes." Opening my eyes, I straightened in my seat and peered through the windscreen at the dark expanse of shadow beyond. The only illumination came from our headlights and the red taillights on Dad's truck in front.

Dad veered to the left, and his high beam cut through the night, exposing a BMW.

"Jack's here, already," Sean said, following Dad in a wide arc. He braked, sliding the gears into reverse. As he tucked us beside Dad's truck, the doors on Jack's Beemer opened and spilled an additional hazy glow across the dirt trail.

Taking Dad's lead, Sean and I climbed from the pickup, and all three parties stood illuminated by their vehicles. The slam of nine doors in quick succession boomed over the wind, followed by the quiet slop of wet soil as Jack Brosen strode our way.

He rounded Dad's truck, passed Sean and me, and pointed toward Samuel. "Tell me what happened to him."

Samuel took a step back, palms up. "I don't know."

Jack grabbed Samuel's shirt front, his hands fisting in the fabric. With a spin to the left, he yanked Samuel from the ground and body slammed him into Dad's truck, letting loose a snarl. "Tell me!"

"I swear I don't know." Samuel rapid blinked, as though dazed from the impact. "He wasn't there by the time they took me." His words tumbled over each other, as Jack pushed into his face with his teeth bared. "I never even saw him. Believe me, I'd have done what I could, if I had."

A deep growl drew my attention to the left. "Just words," said the one I'd presumed to be Jack's son from the Battleground.

Jack continued to glare at the younger wolf, his bunched shoulder muscles visible even through his polo shirt, as frustration and fury pumped from him in a palpable heat.

"You know I'd never have come back without him." Voice dropped to a gravelly murmur, Samuel's own grief surfaced in his tightening jaw. "When have I ever been unfaithful to the pack? Dead or alive, I wouldn't have left him behind."

An aura of tension seemed to charge the surrounding air. Samuel just hung there like he'd been rendered mute, before Jack's shoulders drooped a little, and he blew out a breath. "I believe you." With the lowering of his arms, Jack slid Samuel's body down the vehicle until his feet hit the ground, shifting his hold to grip Sam's face. "Are you hurt?"

Samuel shook his head.

"Okay." With a tight smile, Jack turned to Dad. "Are we ready to clear this mess up?"

Dad nodded. "But let's walk and talk. We're wasting time." He set off, leaving Jack to catch up.

Nothing could quite set the tone for the night like the dismissal of one Alpha to another in a display of superiority. Either Jack didn't notice the intention of Dad's body language, or he figured we all had bigger issues at hand, but his long strides took him to Dad's side in ten steps, which left the rest of us to decide who'd shadow whom.

Like some weird homing pigeon, Dad walked us over mounds, into dips, across a stream that relieved the night quiet of its eeriness. The thick dark clouds obscured the moon until only a suffocating blackness surrounded us, yet no stumbles arrived from Dad's direction, only the steady pad of his footsteps led the way.

Rain continued to fall, and had spread a slow saturation across my shoulders and hair by the time we rounded a craggy corner about a half hour later.

"Does that look right to you, Son?" Dad asked, slowing to a stop.

I stared beyond his vague outline toward the only distinguishable shape ahead—the points of turrets, linked by solid blocks of what I guessed to be walls, and three windows glowing out their rooms' engagement. "Yeah, that's it."

"Sammy?" Jack's rumble carried from beside Dad.

"For sure, that's the hellhole."

"What information do we have on the interior?" Jack asked.

"Nothing," Samuel said.

I turned to him. "They didn't pit you?"

"Your friend took my turn. Apparently, he had more to offer them." Samuel's tone arrived as blend of disappointment and relief.

"You should count your blessings," I said, pushing forward to stand beside Dad. "I'm unclear on specifics. But from what little I saw, there appears to be some kind of central hub— that's where the fighting takes place. Circling that is a corridor. Whether that's one singular corridor, or there are others leading off it, I don't know. But all ground level rooms seem to be accessible from there—maybe the entrance hall or foyer, too. The place is built like a miniature castle." A brief cloud break lent moonlight for a half second, beneath which I caught the intensity in Dad's pale eyes, telling me how closely he listened. "The turret I went in had a spiral staircase leading to an office on what one of the vampire's described as the mezzanine level," I continued, "so I'd place bets on the rooms on that level being somehow linked, too. I only saw the one, though, so it's another guess."

"And you left which way?" Dad asked. "Front, or back?"

"Not front." I gave a small headshake as I ran a mental inventory of the side of the building we'd exited from. "Definitely not through the front. But other than that, not a clue."

He slapped a hand against my shoulder and turned as though to include everyone in what he had to say. "We should start at the main entrance, and split into two to work our way around the outside until we find a way in or at least a weakness. You agree with that, Jack?"

"Sounds logical."

"Good. Then once inside, we do the same circling in separate groups again. Now ... as for the groups—"

"Two packs—the split is an easy one," Jack's son barked.

My lips vibrated beneath my warning snarl. For me to cut in over Dad was one thing. For an outsider to have the audacity to do so was an outright affront I couldn't accept.

"Manners, Darrell," Jack said, his tone hard. "What kind of division did you have in mind, Nathan?"

"I agree that remaining with our own would work best. We each know the strengths and weakness of those in our packs, and if we stick with our own wolves, we won't have to second guess anyone's potential."

Jack nodded. "You happy with the number you have?"

"Yes, I am." No hesitation—Dad always trusted in our abilities and teamwork.

After crossing the moat bridge to the front entrance, we found it locked as anticipated. Staying in the shadow of the building, we took the clockwise route, Jack's team anti-clockwise.

We passed the first, second, third window—all of them secured too well to be opened.

Dad had Josh hoisted high over his shoulders, to check for spots to pry the fourth window open, when running footsteps squelched the wet grass toward us from the left.

Sean and I pressed into the stone wall, at the same time as Dad swung Josh down to the ground, and they joined us.

The footsteps halted. Deep inhalations followed. "It's me," Samuel whispered before appearing.

"Find a way in?" asked Dad.

"There's a window open." He sent a smile my way. "And as it smells familiar, I'd guess it's the one we used to get out."

"Lead the way," Dad said, though I couldn't help but frown. As we all went to march forward after Samuel, Dad reached out and grabbed my arm. "What's wrong?" he asked, when I looked back to him.

"Something's off," I murmured. "But maybe I'm just being paranoid."

"What's your instinct telling you, Son?"

"It's a trap."

"You're basing that on what?"

My sigh came out heavier than intended. "No way could we have been missing this long without them noticing. I already told you they're smart, so I'm one-hundred percent certain they'd have scoured the damn place to figure out the how and where of our vanishing act. If that window's still open, it's because they want it to be—not out of negligence. They're too focused for that."

"Do you think we shouldn't go in?"

"I think we have to go in." I brushed both hands over my hair, stretching out my shoulders muscles in the same action. "But we can't go in blind, thinking we got lucky, because we haven't."

"Okay, then." He started off in the direction Samuel had led Josh and Sean. "Let's go give the others the heads up."

33

The rain had lessened into a light drizzle that weighed down my clothing and invaded every layer of my skin, even though I squatted against the protection of the looming stone structure.

Beside me, Sean peered out toward the dark. Neither of us spoke. Focus always came easier with a clear mind. I only hoped the vampires wouldn't be expecting the numbers we'd brought—because optimism had to be in my thoughts somewhere.

A few metres to our right, back and forth mumbles mingled with the wind, as Samuel filled in Odder— another from the battleground—and his Alpha as to what he'd witnessed while inside, and on the difficulties of killing vampires.

The rest of each team had disappeared into a shadowed alcove to prepare for infiltration, and after waiting for almost ten minutes—during which my calm exterior threatened to crack and reveal my true anxiety—four wolves rounded the corner.

They snorted into the dark, breath fogging the air in front of their faces. Dark brown, dark blond, nondescript brown, and chestnut—the colours of the fur coats bristled by the breeze.

When Dad stepped forward and huffed my way, jerking his chin to the left, I pushed up from my hunched position and walked across to the window. The second I pried it open, Dad hopped through and into the dim space, halting just inside.

A chestnut blur flew past my shoulder, and Odd, of the Odd and Odder duo, landed on the other side of the huge window, taking Dad's example in his cautious advance. Josh followed suit, with Darrel the last to bound through.

At Dad's low snorted command, the rest of us climbed inside to join them.

Uncertainty showed in the high set of everyone's shoulders, as the party split in two. Brosen went to the left, Holloway to the right.

Protectiveness and possessiveness warred with each other as we slunk our separate way. Watch Dad's back, or Sean's, which would let me also keep an eye on Josh? My promise to Jem won out, and I nudged my brother in front of me, letting Josh, with his wolf senses, fall in line at my rear. Besides, I already knew Dad had even better fighting capabilities than me. He'd taught *me* to fight.

From hugging the inner stone wall like a lost lover, I crossed the corridor at the first door. As I placed my ear to the thick wood, Dad dropped his nose to the sliver of air seeping out from below. Only sounds I'd heard by then had come from our invasion. Even opening the door and checking within bore no discovery.

Three more doors encountered, and we found little else, other than the stale odour of old blood within the second room.

The fifth door led to the spiral staircase to Catherine's office. As we'd no intention of venturing up until assured the ground floor was clear, we continued past.

After checking out more empty, useless rooms, we finally stumbled across one that held something of substance. On a row of industrial storage shelves sat supplies. Not anti-venom—nothing quite as useful as that—just fresh darts, syringes, and a handful of guns.

"Why the hell would they leave these lying around?" I muttered.

Sean peeked around my shoulder, as I grabbed a dart gun and begun loading it. "Maybe they've forgotten they're in here?"

I grunted. "Maybe." *Or maybe it's all just part of some sick game.*

Still, I couldn't ignore the potential of having a firearm. The time for fair fighting and following our usual ethics of 'our bodies are our weapons' had long passed. I no longer gave a shit how we took them out, just so long as we did.

Sean frowned down at the gun like I'd handed him a live grenade before looking back to me. "Must we?"

"If I'm telling you these bastards are meaner and stronger than us, you know it's the truth, yes?"

He rubbed a hand across his lower stomach, as he nodded.

I studied the grimace lining his face. "Problem?"

"Just indigestion, or something."

Though he still looked unhappy about it, he tucked his gun in tight to his side, as I grabbed one of my own, and we headed for the door where Dad and Josh stood sentry.

It didn't take long to hit the main entrance and the huge chandelier-lit foyer I'd spied through the doors after my fight with Brook—the point from where we'd planned to double back.

"Still nobody about," Sean murmured from ahead of me, as we re-trod our route.

They were probably hiding from us and waiting to jump out, but I didn't voice my thoughts.

The vampires seemed only part of the worry, though. I'd spent the past ten minutes frowning at the alteration to Sean's gait and the slight awkwardness that seemed to affect each of his steps, especially as it'd slowly worsened the more he rubbed at his stomach.

"What the hell's up with you?"

"Rolls must have been dodgy, or something. They make you bad?"

"No." *Nothing bloody wrong with them.* "You should have said before we came in if you were ill ..." *instead of giving me more crap to fret over.*

"I'm good. Nothing I can't handle." His hand went toward his abdomen again, but he stopped as though realising his action. "We heading up a level, or what?"

"Yup."

I slid open a door we'd already passed once, leading to a turreted staircase like the one to Catherine's office, and allowed Dad through first with his vampire-detecting nose.

At my nod, Sean slipped in behind him, but shoulder slammed the doorframe as his step skewed to the right.

My hand shot out to steady him.

When he twisted back toward me, a frown showed his confusion over the unbalance. A thin layer of perspiration dotted his upper lip.

Shit! Throat tight, I questioned him with a jerk of my chin.

"I'm good." He nodded as if for emphasis.

The room we found at the top held the same dimensions as Catherine's office, except with plush sofas and a flat-screen instead of the desk and chair.

In the opposite wall, a door I must have missed in the other space stood closed.

Rising hackles tugged at the skin coating my nape, and a sense of foreboding settled across my shoulders like a death cape.

And still not a freaking soul in sight.

The vampires had been in there, though. If the headshakes and wrinkled noses from Dad and Josh were anything to go by, they'd been there recently.

At the opposite exit, I strained to listen.

Nothing—*still.*

The hairs across my neck sprang up even straighter, as a shiver tickled its way along my spine. I shrugged them both off, unaccepting of jitters when I needed to focus, though I couldn't help but half-wish I'd been chosen to change into wolf, too.

At a huff from the left, I peered down at Dad, and he bobbed his head as though telling me to get a move on. I twisted the handle and pushed. "Dad, I'm starting to get a real bad feeling about this." I stepped into the space that held no more than a single cot, bedside table with lamp, and a chest of drawers. "Maybe we should have checked the cells first?" I aimed for another door that lay directly ahead. "What if they've already moved them all out to a new venue, and we're searching an empty shell?"

Or what if they've killed them all and abandoned their enterprise, only to vanish into the stratosphere?

A low growl rumbled from Dad, and his head jerked up and to the left—werewolf code for 'get going'.

With muscles tense enough to play squash against, I sucked up my unease and did as ordered.

Throughout the second floor, one room led to another, and to another, until we eventually reached a door that didn't yield.

Dad scratched at the wooden barrier.

Josh whined, his nose lifting as his nostrils flared, his eyes widening a little more with each inhalation.

I didn't need either of their responses to tell me something bad lay on the other side. The stench of sickness, filth and blood blasted my senses, too.

Beside me, Sean's cheeks had turned an unhealthy shade of puce, as small gags contracted and expanded them. We'd smelled enough blood and gore in our lives to not be so affected by it, and the sight of him sent my heart into hammer mode. "You okay?"

"Nauseous, is all." He gagged again, his eyes bugging. "Bloody stinks."

"Guess that means I'm not sending you in to investigate, then." I turned away, angling my shoulder into the door for a forced entry, but spun back at a mewling groan.

A sound pretty close to air squeaking from a balloon eked from Sean's lips, as purplish-red colouring broke out across his face. From his tightly-scrunched eyes, I followed the tense line of his shoulders, down his arms, to his damn hands clutching once more at his stomach as he bent forward.

"Jesus Christ." I took a step toward him and grabbed his shoulder. "What the hell's up with you, Sean?"

Dad and Josh fidgeted, quiet whimpers accompanying their manic ear twitches.

The noise Sean made grew in pitch, tickling my ears, and the longer it spilled from him, the further over he doubled—until a breath gasped from him, his hand flew out to clutch at my arm with enough vice to bruise, and he staggered sideways. "Fuck." For seconds, he panted, before he lifted his face and opened his eyes. "Thought my bowels were going to lose it for a second, there."

Irritation got the better of me at the state of my brother. "What the hell were you thinking?" Even as I barked at him, my pulse whirred at the pain still evident in his eyes. "You had no damn business coming in here as my backup if you're sick."

"I wasn't bloody ill when I came in." His voice held conviction, yet panic still fired my temper.

"I have enough shit to focus on, don't you think?"

Straightening, he wiped a hand across his mouth like he had a bad taste in it. "You don't need to concern yourself over me. I can take care of myself."

"You'd better be right." I spun for the door again. "Now get a grip."

The lock on the barrier couldn't have been a strong one. With a snap of my wrist and a barge of my shoulder, wood splintered, and the catch broke free.

As the stench we'd detected intensified, Sean retched again, and the click of Dad and Josh's claws made a backward retreat at my rear.

Switching to shallow breaths through my mouth, I nudged the door farther. Only shadows stared back. If the room contained windows, they'd been covered over. After a handful of blinks to adjust my vision, I stepped inside, halting at a fluttering vibration that stop-started from somewhere within.

I peered harder into the dimness.

Straight ahead stood another door. Two ways in. Two ways out. Front and rear—meaning I could keep an eye ahead of me, and the pack had my back.

To the left appeared to be only wall. At a tiny whimper, I twisted to the right until my gaze fell on the outline of a cot.

The raised shape of its upper side looked very much like a huddled body. It also seemed to be the source of the blood and dirt smells.

Small sporadic tremors shook the bed, identifying the noise I'd heard. Whoever lay on there must have heard my entrance, so I saw little point in covering my presence.

"Hey," I murmured.

The trembling intensified until a steady rattle bumped the bed against the wall.

Palms out, I chanced a forward shuffle. "It's okay." *Please do not let this be a fucking trick.* "I'm not going to hurt you."

Another whimper, louder than the last, came with a jerk from whoever lay there.

I risked an inhalation and weaved a path through the undesirable odours, until I'd wheedled out the musk of male—human male.

Crap.

I strode the distance to the cot, and it became clear the human had some kind of blanket over their head. Only breaths and heartbeats carried in from the rest of the pack, as I pried sweaty fingers from around the hem and eased the fabric down.

Two huge eyeballs peeked out, the dark irises appearing tiny amidst the showing whites. They darted to the left, back to me, to the left again—a back and forth flitter that seemed out of his control.

"You okay?" I continued pulling the blanket away, revealing a bare torso that looked bruised in the gloom, before his jittery arms folded over as though to defend. "My name's Ethan." When I tossed the blanket to the foot of the cot, only a baggy pair of cotton boxers preserved his dignity. "You have a name?"

He didn't answer, but his face tilted as he peered up at me, and with the movement came the exposure of his neck.

I tried to hide the jolt of shock.

Shit, shit, shit!

I dug my fingers into my hair, fisting the strands for a second before my breaths and pulse returned to a more regular rhythm.

"Who the hell did this to you?" I reached out a hand, my conscience willing me to touch him while my mind yelled at me to run. He flinched a little, when my fingertips brushed over the ragged mess of flesh near his collarbone, but he didn't pull away, and I traced the outline of merged bite marks that had torn his body from one shoulder to the other. In a rapid scan, head to toe, I spotted dark crusted patches across his inner thighs, too.

"Can you speak?"

His eyes darted, like he tracked every one of my movements.

I dropped down onto my haunches, and his gaze followed my path. "Can you walk at all?"

A high shine visited his eyes, though the whites remained just as big, and his head gave a singular nod.

"Good. That's good." I looked across to the doorway for a moment. When I turned back, the kid's gaze followed the action. I returned the scrutiny, filtering through the filth. His hair held grease, stiffening strands that would have otherwise been over his eyes. He couldn't have been any older than a teen. Big for a human, though small compared to wolves of the same age. "You ready to give me a name, yet? You have mine. Seems only fair to meet me halfway, right?”

Another unhinged nod responded, before his tongue pushed free and licked at lips in dire need of fluids. “Colum.”

Like I’d gotten blasted by wind, static rebounded inside my mind and filled my hearing at the raspy-spoken word. “You’re ... Gabe’s buddy. Colum ...” *Man, what was the kid’s name? Colum ... Colum ...* “... Delaney?”

The nods that followed held more enthusiasm than the last two.

“Okay.” I blew out a breath. “Well ... I’m a good friend of Gabe’s ... and we have some stuff to do, me and my family.” I jerked my chin toward the door and hoped he couldn’t see the couple of hulking wolves around the frame. “But I’m going to leave someone to guard over you ...” Sean could have probably used the rest, anyway. “... and, as soon as we’ve finished, I’m going to get you out of here. How does that sound to you?”

His brows scrunched like he made effort to hold his emotions in check, but no amount of suppression could disguise the relief in his eyes.

“Just hang in there.” Muscles bunching, I pushed up to stand. “I’ll be bac—”

A crash boomed through from the adjoining room where I’d left the others, and my head whipped round toward the opening that stood too far right for me to see out there.

“Gentlemen.” I didn’t recognise the voice. “Nice of you to join us.”

Beyond the partially open door, rumbles of aggression rolled through—Dad’s and Josh’s. To my left, shakes claimed Colum’s body until the bed sang like a tambourine.

An inhalation told me nothing. I needed to know how many had come. Needed to understand the shit that had dropped on us. I also needed to get Sean the hell out of the firing line when he didn't seem to be in any position to fight.

I strode for the door, but the panel slammed shut as I reached it, and I glared down at the kid, where he leaned in my path against the wood.

His chest heaved. His heart bounced so loud, it competed with the escalating snarls next door.

The vibration of a growl brewed beneath my sternum. "What the fuck are you doing?"

He shook his head—a manic side to side. "Don't ... don't let them come in here."

A roar carried through from the next room.

Another thud.

Snarls—the desperate kind that came when a wolf tried to clamp hold of its prey.

Scuffles. Thumps.

A grunt, followed by a moan of pain.

Sean!

I snatched for the handle, prepared to shove Colum aside if I had to. "Get out the way!"

Another bang came from somewhere behind me—and light spilled over the wall I faced, along with the dark shadow of my body.

I spun to find the opposite doorway wide open and filled with three bodies.

Catherine. Chad. Joseph.

She laughed. "Looks like we got the consolation prize, boys."

Just fucking brilliant.

"Just can't help yourself, can you?" Catherine took a step inside the doorway. "I should have guessed sooner that this would be where you'd get stalled with that hero complex you have going on."

My mind held too much weariness to conjure a witty comeback. Instead, I reached behind for the whimpering kid and began a slow shuffle across to the bed.

"Of course, I'm glad you came back," Catherine continued. "It means I won't have to hunt you down."

Beyond the closed door at my rear, scrambling feet, snarls, and thumps still continued. If not for the density naturally installed into old fortress-type buildings, the walls would probably have shaken beneath the onslaught of blows.

Once my knee bumped the mattress, I risked turning my head to the side, though my focus stayed on the vampires. With a push down on Colum's arm, I murmured, "Get under the cot and stay there."

He ducked down, the quieting of his scuffles telling me when he'd immersed himself, and I gave my full attention back to the threesome.

"You can't save everyone, Ethan," Catherine said.

Joseph raised a dart gun, fiddling with it as though checking the round.

"No," I said, keeping an eye on him, "but I can certainly give it my best shot."

She smiled up at Chad. "Don't you just love an idealist?"

Though Chad's lips barely cracked a smile, Joseph sent me a satisfied grin. "Good to go."

I slid a hand around to my back, to the waistband of my jeans where I'd tucked a pistol of my own. Three fingers folded around the grip, the fourth finding its way to the trigger.

Catherine nodded, all humour gone from her face. "Take him down."

I lunged to the left.

The faint pop of a releasing dart reached me just prior to my shoulder slamming into the far wall.

I dropped straight into a crouch, whipped my gun-wielding hand around in front of me, aimed for Joseph, and fired.

Nothing. No pop. No expulsion of dart. Just an annoying click. As I stared down at the weapon, Catherine laughed.

"Oops. Surely, you didn't really believe we'd leave live ammunition lying around?"

Hot rage burned through me.

Beside Catherine, Joseph slid another dart into the chamber, his smile still plastered across his smug face. "Only so many times you can leap side to side." He snorted out a laugh. "Would be amusing, though—like those old Westerns where the bad guy shoots at the cowboy's feet to make him dance."

Over my dead body, shithead. I drew my arm back a little. Tension wound the muscles tight through my shoulder, down to my forearm, my thighs.

"If only we had more time to pla—"

With a forward thrust of my arm, the gun bulleted through the room and bounced off Joseph's skull. His eyes widened for an instant, then he stumbled back.

Both Catherine's and Chad's head twisted to follow Joseph's heavy drop, and I launched myself at Chad, ramming my shoulder into his stomach.

His body halved. Breath I didn't expect blasted the nape of my neck.

An upward shove took his feet from the floor, and I fisted my hands into his shirt and rammed him down onto the rug of Catherine's office.

A few metres to my left, Joseph scrambled for his stupid lifeline of a weapon, his fingers trembling as he fiddled with it.

He snapped the round into place, and his arm made the lift.

I shot forward. Kicked out. Booted the blasted gun from his hand and sent it hurtling into the far corner.

He spun toward its flight path, mouth open like he couldn't figure out how he'd lost it, and I brought back my fist and pounded it into his temple, the impact spiking through my arm.

He let out a grunt, but I didn't wait for him to land before lunging upright in search of Catherine.

From the head of the spiral staircase, she sent me a smile. Her fingers lifted in a delicate wave.

A moment later, she whirled away and vanished.

I knocked a chair from my path and raced forward. On my dive for the archway, a force crashed into my right ribcage with the power of a Trojan horse.

Breath whooshed out of me.

The window sped toward me.

"Shit!" I threw my arms up to protect my face.

The collision resulted in a brain-buzzing crack that left the glass patterned with an internal spider web of splinters, and my body slid south.

On hitting the deck, my grunt burst out.

The backward jerk of my body jarred so hard my teeth chomped down, and the metallic tinge of blood spread across my tongue. It took a couple of blinks to register the hand gripping the back of my neck, as it hauled me upward and held me in place like a damn puppet.

Joseph stepped into my field of vision, fangs fully extended, eyes completely black.

I tried to twist and look behind, tried to throw my fist round for a shot, but the fingers squeezed harder against my pulse points until dizziness invaded, and my arms would barely lift, no matter how loud my mental demand.

"I always told Catherine you were more trouble than you're worth." Chad's voice identified him as the one holding me up.

Through wavering focus, I watched as Joseph yanked a drawer open on Catherine's desk. While my feet made unimpressive kicks in search of the floor, shuffling and clacking arose from his search before he whipped up his hand.

In it, he held a syringe.

My heart powered up until it sounded on par with a sports clacker. Grunts forced their way out as I struggled and my legs flailed harder.

The totally selfish urge to yell at Dad to get his act into gear and bloody well save my hide overwhelmed me, yet my conscience forbade me to make the plea.

"Catherine should have let me kill you from the off," Chad said, as Joseph rounded the desk toward me.

Fuck, fuck, fuck.

My cheeks contracted as I sucked in breaths, puffing back out on each erupted exhalation.

Do not let me pass out.

I tried to lift my arms. Wading through a damn bog would have been easier.

I tried to kick back my legs. All coordination had vanished.

The bloody vampire had arms of steel and a grip cast from titanium that knew exactly which pressure spots would manipulate me into submission.

Joseph stood before me and tapped at a syringe I suspected held wolfsbane. "This is probably going to hurt."

My hands curled into fists—that much I could control.

"Nothing he doesn't deserve," Chad said.

My teeth ground beneath the clench of my jaw. The whir of my pulse marred my hearing.

"Where?" Joseph asked.

"Neck." Chad's grasp flicked to the right and took my head along with it.

I sucked air through my clenched teeth at the stretching of my throat.

The needle came closer, and a quiet joy illuminated Joseph's eyes until they shone like polished onyx. A sharp scratch against my skin. A prick. A hint of pain.

Panic insisted I do something. It screamed at me for just hanging there, for allowing them to better me, and erupted through my head as a roar until I saw only white.

My neck snapped to the right so hard pain splintered through my spine.

My legs whipped out to left.

My entire body seemed to spiral—*whump, whump, whump*—through the air.

What the he—

I plummeted—fast. Hit the floor like I'd run into a man-sized baseball bat.

"Urgh." The groan sounded as though miles away, though I knew it had come from me.

Something squeezed my arm, and its yank over my head burned through my shoulder, matching that throbbing through my neck. The heat spread across my entire back, like I was being dragged.

"Ethan." Sean's voice—definitely Sean's.

Tingling bled outward from below my ear, across my collarbone, and down into my chest.

"Dammit, Ethan, open your bloody eyes."

I shook my head. My brain seemed to slosh with the movement, left to right.

"Now!"

Cramps clawed through my calves.

My knees shot up.

An inferno raged through the muscles in my thighs.

Growls. Snarls. Clashing. Thudding. Some alien kind of hissing.

I heard every sound, but as though through the throes of a tornado—one happening inside my head.

"He okay?" *Jack?* "Did we get up here in time?"

"No." Sean's voice again—filled with ... *dread?* "It's spread already."

My body shook, rolling from side to side.

A sharp sting vibrated my cheek. "If you don't open your bloody eyes this second, I'm going to beat you senseless," Sean barked.

I forced my lids to comply. Almost closed them again when the brightness penetrated the shadows lingering within my vision.

I blinked. Blinked again.

Somehow, I managed to focus on the dark eyes in front of me, on the utter terror etched across every one of Sean's features. A few more blinks, and the doubled over position of my brother registered with me, as well as the diving and flying bodies beyond him.

My senses sharpened to the twisting and breaking of my skeletal structure and the foetal position I'd curled myself into.

My arm shot out. I grabbed Sean's shirt.

My teeth ground, and my lips welded shut, though a scream gurgled along my throat until my oesophagus tore, and I swore all the blood vessels erupted across my face.

Agony coursed through me with the speed and strength of a tidal wave, setting my back arching against the attack. It hit my toes, torching the nerve endings there, before it switched direction and blasted back up, through my legs, across my lumbar, along my spine—crunching each vertebra into alignment along its route, until it hit the base of my skull with enough punch to crack it.

"Ethan, breathe."

I tried to part my lips. My jaw refused to budge from its locked position. The trapped snarls blocked my throat.

"Breathe, damn you! Use your bloody nose, for God's sake."

Somehow, despite the frying of my brain, a signal pushed through. As the sensation of knitting bone travelled the length of my newly-forming muzzle with the effect of painful popping candy, a gushed breath snorted from my nostrils.

My whine broke out the second my jaw unclamped.

Sean's blown sigh mussed the hairs across my face, tickling the longer ones around my ears. "Okay, I think you're through it."

I may have made it through the fastest and most incapacitating change I'd ever experienced, but every nerve in my body still buzzed and frazzled like the lit end of a sparkler, every muscle ached as though they'd been linked up to a twelve-volt battery for kicks, and the weariness trying to stake a claim on my brain had the potential to induce a damn coma.

He twisted, peered over his shoulder, and spun back. "Just rest up. Don't be a hero." He ducked his face lower, brought his eyes in line with mine. "You listening to me? Just stay where you are."

I huffed out my compliance.

He nodded. "Goo—" Sean grunted as his body shot backward, and he crashed into a bureau.

The horrid sickly tell-tale scent engulfed me, a moment before Joseph stole Sean's vacated spot and smirked down at me.

Rumbling brewed in my chest, as he dropped to his knees. I tried to lift my head—though it seemed anchored by a ton weight—and rolled onto my front.

"I'm going to enjoy this." Joseph's fangs slid down.

My claws dug into the rug as I beseeched my legs to straighten and get me the hell away. When his face neared, his smirk growing into a smile of anticipation, a bubbling snarl discovered its outlet, rippling my lips on exit.

The black in Joseph's eyes did an impressive swirl before solidifying again. "You're not as big, or bad, as everyone says."

My limbs forced me upright. They trembled like a damn leaf in the wind as my hackles puffed up, my shoulders hunched high, and I sent Joseph his final snarled warning.

He only laughed, and as he darted forward, I rammed my lids shut and thrust toward him.

My front paws hit rug. My legs gave out. My chin slammed the floor.

I grunted and opened my eyes, shaking my protesting head to sharpen my focus, and spotted Sean throwing one punch after another at Joseph's face and ribcage. Each connected, sending the vampire back a step, blood hanging from his chin like crimson drool.

Blinking against the fuzzy edges of my vision, I observed the room.

The chestnut coat of Odder lay still in one corner, except for the shallow rise and fall of his chest. Jack Brosen crouched beside him, a hand stroking the wolf's ruff.

In another corner, two vampires batted what looked like stakes at Dad, Josh and Darrel. All three wolves prodded their muzzles forward around the brandished sticks, nipping wherever they could, before withdrawing and trying again.

The stench of the undead seemed to fill the entire room, strengthening with each wafted movement. Nausea threatened to spill the contents of my stomach and sent my brain into a dizzy spiral.

Wood panelling blurred, merging with the red of the rug. I shook my head clear and absorbed the room's other occupants. Chad lay supine with enough of his body-exterior missing to be a problem, though I knew his dodgily-angled head would have been the cause of his death. Another I didn't recognise by sight—but by scent knew to be vampire—had what once must have been intestine spilling from a trench dug into its stomach while the twitch of fingertips warned the job hadn't been completed to the end.

Above him, Odd gave a cry and drove down a fire axe with enough force to slice bone and split the weave of wool beneath the vampire's decapitated head.

A grunt tore my attention back to the left, though my slowed mind struggled to keep up with the speed of my motion.

Sweat dampened Sean's hair, gluing it to his brow, dual southward trails competing to reach his jaw line. His T clung to his chest, also dampened by his body's secretions. Despite Joseph being the one who took step after step backward, resembling a steak attacked with a meat mallet, Sean's face held lines that screamed of unapparent pain.

As Joseph's back met with stone, determination showed in the tight line of Sean's mouth, and in the sharp focus of his eyes as he continued to hit—left, right, left, right, jaw, ribs, ribs, jaw.

I hadn't seen my brother look that seriously fucked off since another pack had tried to take his mate.

Amongst the red mush left of his face, Joseph's fangs bared long below solid ebony eyes, and a keening from his throat pitched high enough to leave my eardrums humming. Another blow to his ribs knocked his entire body to the floor. His left knee seemed to refuse support on landing, and he stumbled forward.

A final punch from Sean snapped Joseph's head back against the wall.

The vampire stilled on impact, his body slumping to an unruly heap.

Sean staggered back a few steps. He swiped a forearm across his forehead, leaving a smudge of blood that bridged his eyebrows, and half-turned toward me, revealing dark spatters staining the front of his shirt. The instant his gaze settled my way, he frowned. "You okay?"

I snorted the affirmative, urging my trembling limbs to turn back toward the growls in the corner, where I'd last spotted Josh and Dad.

I needn't have worried.

With snarls rippling his lips, Dad savaged one vampire from existence. Beside him, Josh bit down on the other vamp and jerked back, bit down and jerked, while Darrell mirrored him as though synchronised. Each movement of the wolves tore flesh and incited low groans from the duo on the receiving end. Like a dozen idling engines, only growls responded.

A gasp came from Sean's direction, followed by a groan.

I pivoted back to the left with enough haste to blur my vision, but even that couldn't muddy Sean's form hunched upon the floor, his arms cocooning his stomach.

His twisted features and the strained tendons throughout his neck should have convinced me he was mid-change, and I'd have considered the idea, if not for the lack of contortion to his body. Even the hand he flattened against the carpet seemed braced with tension.

I whined at him, took a step forward, growling at myself when I listed to the right.

His eyes, full of pain, met mine. "I'm ... okay." The fact he spoke through gritted teeth said otherwise.

I padded a couple more doddering steps toward him, until close enough to check for myself. My nose nuzzled into his neck. That he didn't push me away spoke volumes of his distraction. A dozen snorted inhalations checked how much of the blood decorating his front belonged to him.

"None of it's mine." His nod ruffled the fur behind my ear. "I'm good."

I backed up a little, intent on a visual for confirmation.

Rouge showed in his cheeks even through the blood spatters—cheeks that contracted and puffed with his breaths. A high gloss still affected his eyes. Despite the additional nod he offered me, he still grappled with his abdomen like he had an alien roaming around in there.

I growled at him to cut it out. His behaviour had me on edge.

"I'm trying," he murmured, telling me he understood.

I growled again, nudging him with my muzzle to get himself straight. To get back on his feet. To quit rolling around like a pussy and giving me shit to stress over.

"Okay." The word came out a bark. "I'm on it, okay?"

His supporting hand left the floor, he pushed up onto his knees, and his eyes rolled up into his head a split-second prior to his body slumping to the right.

Behind him stood Joseph, the dart gun held in his hand by the barrel.

I saw only red.

Somewhere in the recess of my brain, it registered that every muscle throughout my body flexed. It acknowledged the weightlessness of flight. It accepted the instinctual reach of my maws for the throat of my enemy.

Not one of those actions seemed within my control.

Neither did the snarls, the grunts, the growls, the rips, the slashing, the whip of my head.

From somewhere beyond all of those, beyond the white noise of autopilot violence, the shouts and snorts and huffs and screams arrived as no more than a muted buzz.

Something sliced the length of my right shoulder, though I couldn't see what—not with single-mindedness blinding me to all but the endgame.

A kick knocked my flank sideways, though I had no idea from whom—not with the scent of Joseph's syrupy blood seeping into my nostrils and masking all else.

Shoves at my stomach jolted me back the other way. A shout vibrated through my ear—my name, I thought, though it arrived as no more than a distorted echo.

When something nipped just below my right jaw line, I jerked that way. Teeth snapping. Lips rippling.

The snarl I received in response matched mine, the warning it carried far outweighing my own for superiority. Still, I bared my teeth, grumbled out an irrational response, until a jaw clamped around my throat and tossed me down.

The instant I met with carpet, I bucked and kicked, the roar inside my head erupting from me in a show of fury.

Whoever held me didn't budge. Their hold didn't slacken. Their stance refused to waver. The rolling growl thundered deep in their chest, tickling my flesh where they gripped me beneath the curl of their lips.

Who the hell? I inhaled, long and deep. Only vampire blood sucked into my nostrils, and I sneezed with enough force to sting. As I blinked to clear my watering, crimson-misted eyes, Josh's muzzle nudged against my face. He grunted at me, his eyebrows twitching as he glanced above my head, and I realised whoever had taken me down still pinned me there. I also realised it had to be one of the pack if Josh hadn't leapt to my defence.

Dad. Should have known only he would have managed it with such ease.

I tried to relax my body beneath him, failing when my muscles refused to un-tense.

He must have recognised the effort, as his grip loosened a little. Though, he didn't let go—not until I'd steadied my breathing, quit with the grumbling, and controlled my jerking legs that knocked against his like something possessed. Even then, he barely moved away, his breaths still rustling my ear tufts.

I twisted to peer up at him.

Intense concern and severe pissed-offness vied for dominance in his dark eyes. The snort of disgruntlement I sent him didn't help much with that, either. He nudged at me, his huff pretty much telling me to get the hell up.

I rolled onto my front, the action an ungainly one, as weariness and dizziness skewed my coordination. How I got from there to upright, I didn't know, because as I pushed tall enough to match Dad's height, all four limbs threatened to give up and collapse me back down with the grace of a busted deckchair.

Dad's head jerked to the left. A grunt burst from him. Like I'd spoken out of turn in class, he sent me to the damn corner. That stung even more than the evacuation of vampire scent from my nostrils. I let him know it with my snort before I spun away to oblige, wishing I hadn't when he followed my rhino-plods across the room.

Each step on the rug coated my pads in shit I'd rather I didn't have to walk through until we reached the corner, the only spot in the entire room seemingly unaffected by carnage.

I turned to Dad. His brows knitted together. For seconds, we stood there, eye to eye, neither of us moving, then he urged himself a little closer. He sniffed at my face, then his nostrils trailed to my ruff, where he pushed into the thick hair and his inhalations deepened—checking for damage.

My chest heaved beneath my sigh. I huffed at him to let him know I was fine, but he didn't quit with his inspection. Probably thought my assurance to be bullshit.

In truth, it probably was. I couldn't have been much farther from fine.

My shoulders, my flank, my legs—all of them went under his scrutiny before he butted me with a grunt to change back.

Could I, though? After the wolfsbane, would I be able to reverse what it had done?

At another grunt, a shove, and the hunkering down of Dad's head as he prepared to join me, I guessed I didn't have much choice but to try.

35

Sweat saturated my flesh. My entire body stank like a cesspit. Wobbling affected my arms and legs, and they wanted nothing more than to sink me to the carpet, where I could sleep for eons, but pride demanded they hold me up while the other pack still shared the room with us.

"Son?"

I twisted my hung head, bringing Dad's frowning, blood-streaked face into view beside my shoulder.

"You okay?"

I wanted to say no, that I felt about as grand as a steaming pile of shit. Like electricity, the after effects of the poison still hummed through my veins, fraying my nerve endings and leaving me twitchy as hell.

Instead, I nodded, my voice hoarse with my mumbled, "Peachy."

His gaze flittered over me. "You sure?"

No. "Positive. Why'd you change back?"

"Because we think everyone involved came to us. Jack's wolves are happy to scout and double check, but with any luck we already got all of them."

"Except Catherine."

"She was the only one who didn't show."

"Actually, she did. But her bloody goons covered for her, and she bolted before I could grab her." I lifted my head, peered about at the funky gore decorating the room, at Sean pacing in the other corner, his face and grappling hands no more relaxed than earlier. "Jack see her on his way up here?" I asked.

Dad shook his head. "Maybe we'll catch her downstairs somewhere."

"Maybe," I murmured, though I doubted it. Catherine had most probably scarpered.

"Come on." He gripped my shoulder, gave a small squeeze. "Let's wrap this end up."

On the thrust to my feet, the room's colours kaleidoscoped in my vision for a moment before settling into definition. Sean halted in his pacing, the quirk of his eyebrow private language for *You all right?* I gave a slight inclination of my chin and returned his expression, receiving the smallest shrug of his left shoulder in response.

I doubted either of us had been honest in our answer.

"Everything okay?" Jack asked, striding across.

"Sure." Dad nodded toward Jack's team in their restless hustle. "How about yours?"

"Lee'll probably have to be carried out of here, but he'll heal." I guessed he meant Odder. "Otherwise, we're good to continue." He turned my way, his gaze skimming my entire length. "You look worse than you are, I hope."

I bristled under his concern. "I'm fine." Maybe if I said it enough times, I'd begin to believe it myself.

He turned back to Dad. "We wrapping this up now? Assessing the damage downstairs?"

"Yeah. Josh and I will stay back and help with the releases. But I'm sending Ethan and Sean on ahead to begin the clean-up of the humans. This is taking too long. The sooner we get started on the outsiders, the better."

"Agreed." Jack glanced toward his pack. "I'll keep Samuel with us so we have his knowledge of the downstairs setup, but I can spare Darrel and Bobby to hit the road and start knocking some names off that list, too." He shrugged. "Seems unproductive to keep all our resources in one spot, when we could be covering more ground."

Dad nodded. "Then, let's get moving."

As Jack marched off, I reached for Dad's shoulder. "Do me a favour, and don't let any of the vamps out their cages."

He stared at me a moment. "We can't just leave them locked up, Son. However much they've pissed you off."

"I know that. Just trust me on this. I have an idea for how we can release them. But it won't be tonight. And it won't be with you and Josh there."

He gave another hard study of my face, though he eventually nodded. "Okay, I'll go with you on this. Now, clean yourself up, and get you and Sean on the road. Even in your conditions, you should manage a bunch of lone humans."

"You're not as okay as you tried to tell Dad." Sean peered at me through the darkness, as we marched back toward the waiting truck. "Are you?"

"Neither are you, Doctor H." When he stared at me, I added, "Right now, I'm counting my blessings the wolfsbane only forced one change out of me."

Though, I imagined the dose had been measured with accuracy for exactly that. After all, what good would an ever-changing wolf have been in the arena?

I squished a nostril shut with my thumb and blew hard in the thousandth attempt to lose the vampire stench in there, barely missing my jeans that Sean had managed to get off me before my change had taken over. "Now quit talking, and just walk ... unless you want to tell me what the hell's been going on with you all night."

Only our breaths created sound, alongside the whisper of the wind through grass blades, the bubbles of a far off stream. Fifteen metres later, he uttered, "No idea."

"You ill?"

"Feels worse than ill. Feels ..." He rubbed around the back of his neck. "Like nothing else. Like changing. But not. Because it's only in my lower stomach and round to my spine. Damn, I feel like someone's been ripping me open from the bloody inside out."

With each spilled confession, I stared harder at him. He looked like crap, though I doubted I represented much of an oil painting myself, and his cramps and nausea had grown progressively worse as we'd continued through the night. The haunted glint in his eyes, though, and the constant tenseness to the lines of his body told me it went way deeper than just a shit night of wrap-up and clean-up.

"Leave the humans to me for a while," I told him. "You can play lookout."

He opened his mouth, like he considered arguing. That he shut it and merely nodded told me he felt a whole lot worse than I'd evaluated from his exterior. I couldn't help but heave a sigh when the pickup finally emerged through the gloom, and released another the second I'd got Sean safely inside and we'd set off.

Barely ten minutes passed when Sean doubled over in the passenger seat, and his head vanished somewhere between his knees. As I peered across at him, he turned a scary shade of beet, the tendons popped in his flexed arm, and his knuckles turned white where they gripped the rim of my seat.

I hit the brakes and grabbed him, giving a slight shake. "Sean?"

He twisted until his face showed. His eyes looked glazed and about to leap from his damn skull, his cheeks bloated from clenching his jaw too hard. "Something—" He gasped. "Not ... right."

"You're telling me." I growled as my mobile rang and, snatching it up, checked the display before answering. "Dad?"

"Change of plan for the two of you. You're heading straight home. Jem's in labour."

"But ... I thought she still had a few weeks."

"She does—did. Not anymore. Baby's got fed up with waiting."

My gaze returned to Sean and the panted breaths he'd begun as I processed Dad's words. "Well ... shit. That explains everything."

"Ethan?"

"Sean ... he has to be feeling it. That's why he's been all over the damn place."

A quiet groan travelled the line. "Okay. Get your rears home pronto. I'll speak to Jack, explain that we'll need more time to cover our share. Then Josh and I'll be there as soon as we can with Colum."

"See you at home." I shut off the call. "Sean, you better buckle up."

"What's going on?" he asked through seething teeth, and I managed a smile.

"You're about to become a dad."

36

After fidgeting, groaning, and rolling around the entire journey home, Sean had the truck door open before we'd even stopped. He flung himself out, hitting the block pavers as his knees buckled beneath him, and threw himself up and into a sprint for the house just as fast.

Almost as eager, I ground on the handbrake and leapt out myself, slamming Sean's door closed on my way past.

Groans reached me before I'd hit the top step, and I followed them upstairs and into Sean's bedroom.

Jem's glower landed on me the second I rounded the doorframe, bringing me up short. Teeth bared like a rabies-infected mutt, she let out a high-keened cry and ended on a screeched whistle. "Where have you beeeeeeeeen?"

I held my palms out as I took a step closer.

Pretty much pinioned to the bed by her grip on his wrist, Sean already sat on her right. The bright red of his face didn't seem far off Jem's. On her other side, also restrained and with his beseeching eyes aimed at me, Daniel didn't look in much better shape.

"I'm here now," I muttered, moving forward a little more—like I approached an untameable beast instead of my brother's mate.

Craig nodded to me from the corner, blood-smeared gloves on his hands, a small twitch to his lips. "Thank goodness. She's been asking for the two of you."

I tried to smile, though even breathing through my mouth couldn't quite stem the stench of bodily fluids that had probably permeated the wallpaper, the brickwork, the roof—the entire fricking house. I also thought about bolting, until Mum bumped me forward from behind and sent me a step closer.

"Take over from Danny," she said, just as a fresh roll of mewling broke from Jem. "I think he may need blood transfused into his hand if he doesn't get his circulation back soon."

"Unh ..."

"Go on." Mum's hand hit the small of my back and nudged me all the way across to the bed. "You look like you could use a sit down, anyway."

Relief flooded Daniel's features as he practically dove out of my way. With him gone, Jem peered up at me, her face swollen with pain, lips a circular funnel as she expelled her breaths in small pants.

Seeing her in so much distress knocked my emotions off kilter. I reached down and unstuck the hair sweated to her forehead. "You're doing great, Jem."

"Here," Mum said, passing me a wet flannel.

I took it from her, the water in it a welcoming chill against my palm. For an instant, I contemplated sticking it on my own weary head, but the scrape of Jem's fingernails across sheets warned of another round of whatever the hell kept happening about to restart. Her eyes closed, as I wiped at her brow, lips relaxing to part for her sigh.

"Feel good?" I asked.

A tiny nod. "Un-hunh."

Still dabbing at her, my gaze skimmed over Sean's hunched form, his hand wrapped around one of Jem's almost as tight as hers was around his.

Behind him, Craig unwrapped one of the scariest-looking contraptions I'd ever seen from a sealed packet.

Did he plan to use that on Jem?

Holy. Shit.

I dislodged the gulp threatening to stick at the sight of the polished metal 'tool'. "How's Kyle?"

Craig peered up and gave a tight smile. "He woke. And he was talking, though he was still a little drowsy. Looks a lot better." He nodded toward the room on the opposite side of the landing. "His lady friend is sitting in with him and Connor."

Who? I glanced that way, and back again when I realised he meant Brook. "And Lauren?"

"I talked her into taking a nap," Mum said, bustling in with a shedload of towels. "She's in my and your dad's room. Now quit worrying over everything else and concentrate your efforts where they're needed."

"Arrrrrrrggghhhuuuununnnnnnneeeeeh!"

My head whipped back at Jem's unholy wail. "What's wrong?"

Sean jerked rigid, tears pooling in his eyes, his arm wrapped so far around his middle he almost enfolded himself.

"*Pushing.*" Jem's whisper shot out on a gasp. "Need to—" Another cry rang from her, uniting with a similar, deeper one from Sean.

As Craig shot to the end of the bed, nudging the covering sheet out of the way, Sean's head swung toward him, a low growl bubbling past his taut lips.

Craig met his glare head on. "The baby's head is showing already. You haven't time for theatrics. Now get a grip." He jerked his chin at Jem with her glassy stare aimed at the ceiling and her free hand grappling around for something to crush. "She needs you."

Cloth forgotten, I stuck a knee on the mattress and leaned across to grab Sean's shoulder. "It'll be okay."

He faced me, teeth grinding and his eyes wholly consumed by a mixture of fear and agony. At my nod, he blew out a slow breath and turned back to Jem, though as I released his shoulder, his hand shot up, and his fingers grabbed onto my wrist tight enough to incapacitate.

I tugged a little. His vice-grip didn't budge. I thought about asking him to loosen up, until Jem snatched hold of my other wrist with as debilitating a hold as my brother's and hauled me onto the mattress across from Sean.

Groans rolled from Jem, as deep as a bear's, before crescendoing into a deafening screech. From beside her, grunts arrived with each one of Sean's panted breaths, as every tendon across his body threatened to explode through his skin. Stuck between the two of them, the veins throbbed in my wrists beneath their crushing hands, and I could do no more than sit and accept it as I became a conduit for their shared agony.

"Good, Jem," Craig said behind my shoulder. "Now catch your breath before the next one."

Together, Jem and Sean sucked breath in and gusted it out, in-out, in-out—each one right into my face where they'd dragged me like some kind of canopy to Jem's contracting stomach. If the situation hadn't been so intense, it might have been hilarious.

Over my shoulder, Craig had his hands right down at Jem's crotch, that fugly metal device resting on the bed between her legs.

My vision wavered for a second, before I ordered myself to turn away, even if that did take me toward the duet of gales steaming my face to unbearable temperatures.

Mum popped up behind Sean, another dripping flannel in her hands. By that time, I *really* could have used it myself.

More groans. More cries. Gasps. Pants. Grunts. Wails. Keening. Not to mention the stench—oh, God, the smell.

At some point, I zoned out. Though, somehow, mumbles of reassurance still managed to make their way past my lips.

The sounds of pain became distant echoes. As did Daniel's footsteps across the landing, and Connor's when he emerged to join him. Movement rushed in and out of the room—to Jem and out, to Sean and out, as though they'd all finally acknowledged that both of them were in labour, not just Jem.

I simply sat there, trying my damnedest to ignore the burning sensation that crept higher and higher into my arms as numbness took over.

At some point, the front door slammed and feet pounded the stairs, followed by Dad's demand of, "How's she doing?" and Mum's even quieter response of, "Just fine." After which, the strides the length of the landing sounded on par with a marched parade.

"Okay, one more push, Jem!"

At Craig's command, the entire household seemed to still, noise suspended, until Jem's, "*Uuuuuueeeennnnn-nhhhhhhhh*," broke the spell.

Sean's body stretched toward the bed end, his intense stare one hundred percent dedicated to the point of delivery, despite the twisting of his features reflecting his agony.

I couldn't help but follow his focus. "Holy shit!" I whispered.

A tiny head stuck out from Jem. Hair thick and black. And gunky with something I didn't want to think about.

Craig's fingers pried at the entrance. "Another push, Jem. Not so hard. A gentle one. Come on, now. You're almost there."

Like I could loan strength to the female who'd gone through such an amazing ordeal, I twisted until my hand cupped hers and squeezed. Her next groan arrived quieter, as the muscles tensed in her thighs and stomach, and her hand clenched against mine.

Like a seal on an ice slide, the baby shot out.

Craig caught it as though he tackled childbirth every day, and he laid it down with care before lifting his smiling face to Sean. "Want to cut the cord?"

Sean's eyes widened, though he'd yet to shift them from the little being he'd helped create, his slightly parted lips lending him a look of wonderment, but he managed to unleash me and held out his hand.

When Craig wrapped Sean's fingers around the metal tool I'd tried to block from my mind, I spun back toward Jem, flexing my own fingers to work some blood back into them and freeing Jem's face of yet more sticky strands.

"How's your hand?" she murmured.

"Give it back, and I'll let you know."

I didn't realise she'd obliged until she touched my cheek. "Thanks for staying."

"Any time."

At the cutest and smallest cry I'd ever heard, I whirled back round to see Craig standing with the baby in his grasp.

All purply, browny, creamy and wrinkly as heck, what looked like an alien Sean spawn waved an arm, kicked a leg, screwing its face up as though the effort of the actions took its toll. I studied the fists, curled like the baby prepared to take on the world and then some, following the body down to the spindly legs, and as Craig went to turn away, I rocketed to my feet.

Sean bolted up also. "Wait!"

Craig twisted back, his eyebrows raised. "What's wrong?"

"Why hasn't he got a winky?" Sean's desperate tone merged with my, "Where the hell's his dick?"

Craig chuckled and held the baby up for quick inspection before sitting him on the towel draped across Mum's arms. As Mum wrapped the cloth round and carried the bundle off, Craig turned back to Sean. "He's a *she*. You have a daughter."

"I ..." Sean's mouth opened and closed. "I ... *what*?"

Jem giggled behind us, drawing all attention to the tired smile spread across her face. "Told you so," she mumbled before another laugh seeped out.

The next few minutes got taken over by Dad and the Larsen's stepping in to kiss Jem and slap the back of a shell-shocked Sean, before Craig cleared everyone away from the bed. The swaddled baby he held made adorable little coos, as he lowered her into Jem's outstretched arms.

As soon as she had her, Jem drew the baby tight to her chest, eyes moist as she gazed down at the new addition.

"Any idea what you're going to call her?" Craig asked.

Working her index into one of the delicate fists, Jem nodded. "Lia. Short for Natalia. After her granddaddy." She turned to Sean. "Okay?"

Warmth darkened Sean's eyes. "Perfect."

Dad's grin eclipsed all others in the room.

Getting some time alone hadn't been easy. I'd had to take my turn holding my new niece, and handing her back had been harder than I anticipated. Even once I escaped the excitement next door, I'd stepped in to check on Kyle and Brook, relaxing at Brook's insistence that they'd both be okay. After I'd found Lauren propped up reading in Mum's bed, her huge eyes wide as she asked about Jem, and reassured her everything and everyone was fine, I finally reached my personal space.

Leaning back against the door, I closed my eyes and took a deep breath. The first intake sucked up the remnants of Shelley's earlier presence, and my gut twisted at the reminder of my screw-up.

I rubbed at my face, my palms scratching across stubble, before reaching back for the neck of my shirt and sliding it up and over my head. A shower would have been an ideal option, if I'd the energy to stay standing, but weariness had long before kicked in and bled deeper and deeper into my bones.

My legs dragged me across to my dresser. Even the lift of each to exchange jeans and underwear for grey workout shorts seemed an immense feat. With a hoody tugged on to ward off the chill that had little to do with the temperature and a whole lot to do with the emptiness inside my chest, I trudged across to the window, snatching up a couple of pillows on my way.

Beneath a sky rife with cotton clouds, the forest waved its welcome from beyond the arches. I punched the pillows into place, sat my arse on the broad ledge, and swung my legs up. Opening the window a crack allowed the freshness to sift through, and I gulped it down as I wondered how my life could yoyo so drastically in a matter of days—hours.

Even as the historic event of the day settled over the house like an incense of joy, I couldn't help but ponder my own future and how barren it suddenly seemed.

The handle squeaked before the door clicked open. I didn't bother to turn, merely inhaled, relaxing when Mum's homely scent drifted across.

Her feet brushed the carpet until she came to a stop at my side. "Hey, you."

My lips curved for a second. "Hey."

"How you doing?"

"I'm fine."

"Liar."

I breathed out a quiet laugh, but sobered fast. "I'm tired, Mum, that's all. Just ... so bloody tired."

Mum's fingers combed through my hair, and my lids lowered as I swayed beneath the massage.

"Besides, I don't want to dampen their moment," I murmured. "I'm happy for them—I really am. I just ... don't have it in me right now to do any more."

"Honey, they know that." A few beats passed, with her fingers doing some amazing shit against my scalp. "When was the last time you slept?"

I shrugged, draping my arms to hang over my drawn up knees. "I don't even remember."

"You need to sleep."

"I can't, Mum. I bloody had to leave the job half finished ..."

"All taken care of," she said.

"Brook hasn't even been given the chance to contact her pack, or whatever she's a part of ..."

"She's refusing to go anywhere until Kyle's stronger, anyway."

"What about Gabe's friend we found? Where is he? Did the vampire's turn him? What's supposed to happen to him?"

"Being treated under Jack's care, as he's from his territory. He hasn't been turned—it's apparently more complicated than just being drank from. As soon as he's strong enough, he'll get to go home in exchange for a vow of silence."

I guessed it could have been worse. "Talking of home, what about Lauren. When's she going back?"

"Tomorrow. When everything has had a chance to calm down."

"And I have no idea if Gabe's okay. How the hell am I supposed to know now?"

"Don't pretend you don't know where I've taken them. All they need right now is a little time."

"But—"

"Quit trying to carry the world on your shoulders for five minutes." She pushed against my back, until I shuffled forward, and climbed up behind me. "Lay back."

"I'll crush you," I muttered.

"Don't be so ridiculous." Her husky chuckle vibrated against my shoulder blade, as she wrapped an arm around my chest and wrestled me down until I couldn't help but get hauled along with her attempt to lighten the moment. "Do as you're told, boy. Didn't your daddy ever teach you it's rude to disobey your mama?"

"Sure he did." I peered up at her as my crown settled against her lap. "But the mama I had to obey taught me to stand up for myself and never take any crap."

"She did that." She sighed, her fingers tousling the strands along my hairline. "And look what a fine specimen of a male you grew up to be."

Shelley didn't think so, not any longer—if she ever had.

I pinched the bridge of my nose as my eyes slammed shut against the emotions that threatened to spill, then I curled an arm around Mum's waist and buried my face in her fleecy sweater.

She didn't speak, merely stroked a hand across my hair as she cocooned me like she could protect me from the universe. For the first time since my childhood, I fell asleep in the embrace of one of my parents.

Lauren tapped my arm from the passenger seat. "It's next left."

I slowed Mum's Lexus and took the corner she pointed to like she thought me too dumb to get it without direction. "How far now?"

"Not far." She jigged a little in her seat, tucking her hands beneath her thighs, tugging them out again, under, out. "You see that grassland over there?" She jerked with her chin.

"Yep."

"My house is on the other side."

"We'll need to find somewhere to park up on this side, then." I slowed to a crawl, glancing at her between checking the road in front. "You recall how we said you'd—"

"Yeah, yeah, I got it," she said, rolling her eyes. "There's a massive tree if you keep going to the end. You can *hide* behind that."

I sped up again, kept going right on past the 'massive tree' until I found somewhere to spin around and double back.

On first pass, Lauren turned toward her passenger window, fingers pressed to the glass. By the time I made the manoeuvre and parked us up in the shade of an oak, she'd tucked her hands back between her thighs. Shoulders hunched over, she stared down at her lap, hair falling across her face.

I didn't bother killing the engine as I twisted to face her and studied her sudden shift in body language.

Getting her home had been like organising a major event. Mum didn't want me making the trip because she demanded I get more rest and had offered to make the journey with Lauren. Dad hadn't wanted me leaving full stop. He'd kept his reasons to himself, but I figured that his 'knowing how it could affect a werewolf to be parted from his mate' speech had something to do with it. 'Shelley isn't my mate,' I'd argued, but all I'd received in return was a pity-filled stare. Even Daniel and Josh had suggested they take Lauren instead of me and grab ice cream on the way.

Lauren had other ideas. She'd point blank refused to get in a vehicle with any of them. Her reasoning? 'Ethan got me this far. So I can trust him to get me home, too.'

How the hell could I argue with that? Especially as the doleful expression she'd aimed at me had dared me to deny her.

"You okay?" I asked.

She gave a small nod.

"So ... which one's your house?"

"The one with the white fence and the ugly bubble windows," she mumbled without looking up.

I traced the row of properties to the only one with a picture window, though the bubbles looked more like nipples to me. "You think your folks will be home?"

"Mum's car is out front."

I turned back. "What you so worried about?"

She shrugged.

"You scared about sticking to your story?"

Her hair flopped with her headshake.

"What, then?"

She withdrew a hand and scratched at her nose. "What if they're really mad at me? When I tell them I ran off, they'll be mad and might not forgive me."

"Maybe they'll be mad at the thought of you running off to begin. But I doubt it'll last once the relief at you being home kicks in."

She shrugged. Nodded. Tucked her hand back between her legs.

The car swayed a little beneath a wind blast that spiralled the first fallen leaves across the grassland. In the distance, a knee-high kid in wellies and shorts did a crap job of riding a scooter up and down a garden path, and I watched his chubby legs pushing and tangling, expecting him any second to end up with the wheels wrapped round his neck. A Volvo came toward us along the road. Though it didn't slow down to round us, I almost considered ducking. The longer I sat beside Lauren on her street, the greater the risk of being spotted with her grew, and that would only lead to questions she'd struggle to deflect.

I blew out a breath, prepared to suggest we go back until she felt certain she could handle it.

"Okay, I'm ready." Though quiet, her voice carried an edge of determination.

I turned back to her. "Sure?"

Even as she smiled and nodded, her eyes misted over. "Am I supposed to tell you how awesome you are and pay my debt with my soul before I go?"

"Nah, no need. I already know of my awesomeness, and I have no use for your soul. Besides, you'd only torture me with texts about snogging and popcorn."

She laughed, her smile expanding, before the worry and sadness crept back in. "I guess I'll catcha later, then." Before I could respond, she swung her door open. As she stepped from the car, she paused, her face reappearing in the opening, and her blown out breath arrived louder than the wind surrounding her. "Thanks, dude."

"No worries."

The door slammed closed, and she marched across the grass like she had purpose on her mind, though anyone watching close enough would see the tight clench of her hands around her shirt cuffs. Halfway across, she broke into a run, and only slowed as she met the pavement alongside the property.

Everything screamed at me to stay, to ensure her parents didn't hound on her for her absence, to be one hundred percent certain she crossed the threshold into her home.

I had orders, though. Ones that made sense. Ones that preserved the privacy of too many and deserved following.

As Lauren took the first step onto her path, I slipped into first gear and rolled away from the kerb.

The park I found to pull into had few visitors, thanks to the late morning hour of the weekday. Engine humming, I stared through the screen and sighed at my first serving of true solitude in days.

Crisped leaves lay in mounded rows either side of the footpath. A gull swooped down, far from its natural habitat, before looping back up again and circling the play area, where a woman sat on a bench with a young child.

What sun existed offered warmth through the glass, as I leaned back in my seat and rubbed at my face. Heaving a deep breath, I closed my eyes and willed myself to relax.

Beyond the vehicle, footsteps scuffed the ground, a kid squealed, a dog barked, the foraging gull squawked out its signature cry, and before I knew it, I'd straightened and reached for my mobile from the central console.

On any other day, under any other circumstances, with time to kill, I'd have just called Gabe. We'd have hung out together, or arranged a hunt, or eaten Shelley out of house and home.

My thumb hovered above the keys.

Quiet beats passed. People strolled along.

I located Shelley's number and hit dial.

The ring tone trilled through the earpiece. By the fifth sound, I realised how stupid I'd been to believe she might answer. On the seventh, it clicked, and the mechanical voice droned out with the option to leave a message after the tone.

I lifted the phone to my ear. "Hey ..." I brushed at my brow with my fingertips while I tried to figure out what the hell to say. "I'm ..." *sorry.*

As my hand fisted, I bounced it against the steering wheel. "I ..." *hope you're okay.*

I rubbed over my shoulder, round to the nape of my neck, and swept up and over my hair to my forehead. "Please, um ..." *don't stay pissed at me forever because I don't think I can take it.*

The high-pitched bleep hit my ear, signalling end of message space and cutting me off.

"Fuck!" I tossed the phone aside like it held blame for my screwed up attempt to let Shelley know how I felt. It bounced off the passenger seat and slammed the dashboard before nose diving for the foot-well.

When the vibration kicked in prior to ringing, I jolted and dived across the seat, grappling it from the floor. I rammed it against my ear at the same time as hitting connect. "'Lo."

"Son?"

I repressed my groan.

"Everything okay? You need me to send Dan and Josh to meet you?"

Since when had I become so big a concern? "No, Dad." I didn't exactly fancy the idea of sitting around, waiting the couple of hours it'd take them to reach me. *Unless ...*

I realised Josh and Daniel had probably tailed me the entire journey.

Suppressing a growl, I pushed up to sit and rammed the stick into reverse. "I'm just heading back now."

After assuring him I was on my way, and scraping at my scalp hard enough to leave trenches, I drove from the park and took my sorry self back home.

A light breeze wormed its way through the trees, teasing the mulched carpet of leaves, as well as the longer hairs of my ears. The dropped temperatures of late had set the ground to concrete-hardness, and each pummel of my paws sent shocks through my legs that jolted every muscle in my body.

The forest had become my retreat on a daily basis. After work in the week. At night on weekends.

I knew my excessive exercise fuelled the looks of worry I got from Mum and Dad, but I didn't care—not when it seemed to be the only place I could stem the swirling thoughts threatening to drive me crazy.

What had shocked me the most in the days following the clean-up had been the nightmares. I hadn't had a nightmare since puberty passed. Why I dreamt of the castle, of Catherine, the fucking cage, I didn't know—especially as I'd had to play no more of a role where the humans had been concerned. Dad had personally dealt with the head honchos of the operation, his fury over their treatment of us reason enough for him to ensure they suffered before he snuffed them—he made sure I knew they'd been treated just as they deserved. Apparently, Jack had shown his support of our family crisis and completed the elimination of every other threat on the list. I just hoped that didn't make us indebted to him, and that he wouldn't come calling for repayment at any point.

That had only left the still secured vampires.

Jess had been far from happy about setting up a meeting with the local nightlife of Witchurch—even less so when I explained my first encounter with them hadn't gone so smooth. However, with curiosity a strong enough motivator for the blond vampire to agree, I'd handed over directions to the castle, cage keys, and total responsibility to him. For some reason, my empathy had earned an ounce of respect from him—like I'd cared. Pity he hadn't a clue over Catherine's whereabouts.

As for Brook? I'd no idea what passed between her and Kyle during his recovery, but something definitely had by the time she eventually called home.

Her father had shown up to collect her like a shot. Stuck-up Tomcat had snubbed the lot of us, marching Brook off to where he'd parked at the roadside before he showed even an ounce of compassion for his daughter's ordeal. If given free reign, I'd have taught him exactly what I thought of his attitude, assuming Kyle didn't beat me to the task.

Annoyed at myself for letting my thoughts stray again, I shook my head hard enough to affect my entire body and raced off in hunt of rabbit.

Having gone almost full circle, I zoomed by scattered scents of the pack, where they clung to bushes and trees, or indicated their changing spots. Not much longer passed before the bob of a brown tail entered my periphery, and I pivoted after the rodent that had been too downwind for detection.

It took only the crush of a twig to alert it, and its bright eyes snapped round to me before it took off like a miniature furry basketball on whizz.

Driven by the stench of its fear, I surged forward, muzzle outstretched, ears flattened, legs pumping like the most powerful of pistons.

Within seconds, the gap diminished—only metres separated us.

Allowing it false hope, I stayed back a little, toying with it, enjoying the bouquet as it whet my desire like a good appetiser.

Another breeze blew through, stinging my eyes until I closed them. On opening, a trampling mass of brightness flew across my path at bullet speed.

The rabbit vanished from sight.

My halt clawed dirt up to cloy the air, as well as my vision, and I almost went sprawling from the violence of my sudden stop. A snarl rippled my lips as I swung toward where the trespasser had vanished, my muscles tensed for pursuit—until the masculine scent hit me like a mocking slap.

Gabe?

I stared along the downtrodden route he'd cut through, the soggy leaves, paw poised to take a step and head angled as my ears twitched to track the huge loop he seemed to be tracing all the way back around—to me.

I spun as Gabe skidded onto the path at my rear.

Head ducked, shoulders high, he stared at me from above the dead prey hanging from his jaws. An aggressive posture, though his eyes held only amusement.

Giving a low growl at him for the ambush, I padded forward a little.

As expected, Gabe flicked his head, and the rabbit arced, landing at my front paws in offering.

I lowered my muzzled to it, sniffed, looked back to Gabe as he settled onto his stomach—his show of respect while I ate.

The moment he dropped his chin onto his forelegs, I pounced. A half second too late, he thrust forward, meeting my attack.

Our chests collided.

We plummeted, impacting with the solid earth.

One over the other, we rolled, dust spraying up like a mushroom cloud, claws scrabbling for control. Despite the thunderous snarls, neither of us had intent to harm.

No more than our established ritual of greeting, we grappled until our tongues hung loose, and our breaths steamed the air.

When he squared his shoulders and sent me a grunt, jerking his head toward home, I knew he hadn't called round for a simple frolic.

Gabe had come to talk.

***

Changing as regularly as I had meant I'd increased the speed at which I could perform it, but not without a price. Arms rigid, muscles taut, sweat left my flesh glistening as I remained in my crouch and attempted to regulate my breaths. By the time I'd even a modicum of composure, steps crunched toward me from the east, and Gabe rounded a naked silver birch into my clearing.

As I reached for my clothes, he padded across to me, jeans slung low and undone, shirt hanging from his shoulder.

Eyes still bright from his change, he held out his hand. "Come on, old man."

"Show some respect, pup." I climbed to my feet and stared at the blueness of his irises, the colour in his cheeks, and the grin, noting that only a hint of perspiration tinged his scent. "You're looking good." Sounded good, too.

He gave a nod. "I'm okay. Had six weeks to heal."

I didn't need reminding of the time that had passed—the length of time I hadn't seen Shelley for.

"But you already know that." His head cocked to the side. "You probably know down to the last hour how long you've stayed away for."

I flinched at his phrasing as I stepped into my boxers and tugged them over my hips. I hadn't stayed away out of choice.

He kicked at the dirt, as though he'd caught my reaction, face ducked for a second, or two. "So ... what's the deal with you and Mum?"

"There is no deal." Jeans and shirt bunched in my hand, I turned to walk off.

His low growl pursued me. "Bullshit."

I halted, spun back. "Mind your tong—"

"You think I haven't noticed the looks you two've been sending each other for months?" He shook his head, eyes aimed at the treetops.

"I haven't—"

"Man, who're you kidding?" He delved into his pockets, tugging his jeans lower over his hips. "'Course, now you're refusing to even see each other."

"I'm not—"

"Something's gotta give." More toeing of the soil. Another headshake. "I can't take it anymore."

I shook out my jeans, bent to feed my feet into them, and yanked them over my thighs to my hips before straightening to stare at him.

He seemed uncomfortable as he met my gaze. "What're you gonna do about it?"

I hooked my shirt over the waistband of my trousers. "I know you're young, Gabe, but even you can figure out that it takes more than one participant to make a relationship. Your mother wants nothing to do with me. So just quit with the hassle, okay?" I turned away, took three strides.

"More bullshit."

Halting again, I gave a deep sigh.

"She's done nothing but mope about. Nothing but mope and stare at her phone like she's waiting on something important. For the entire six weeks since she last saw you."

I turned back to him, his expression intense like all I had to do was say the word and I could solve all his life problems—pretty much as he'd always looked at me.

"She's there now ... on her own. I'm here for a bit." He shrugged, the action taking his jeans up a notch. "Mum thinks I'm with Mia for the night, but I figured I'd come talk to Nathan about a place in the pack, seeing as I managed to get out the apartment without her shadowing me for once." His gaze flitted away before returning to me. "For fuck's sake, Ethan ... go and sort this shit out. Please. She's miserable." He drew in a deep breath.

She's miserable ... without me? I stared away, toward the town fifteen miles away, as though I could somehow bring to mind Shelley sitting in the apartment there. Nothing quite like a talking to from a nineteen-year-old to put everything in perspective.

Would she listen to what I had to say?

I'd never been too good at talking. I'd always preferred to just act.

Would she even let me in?

I swivelled back toward Gabe and his heavy scrutiny, the strong plea in his bright eyes, and found myself nodding. "I'll try."

His footstep echoed mine, as I wove through the trees toward the arches. Neither of us spoke. Maybe we both thought plenty had already been said. Or maybe I realised the thoughts inside my head would be best saved for Shelley.

By the time I reached the sparse patch linking brickwork and forest, Gabe's shoulder brushed mine, our bare soles crunching dirt to the same beat. Even his gait mirrored mine, with his hands buried deep in his pockets and his gaze aimed at the ground.

No one occupied the garden when we entered, though the conservatory door had been left wide and Lia's blanket decorated the lawn with a mauve square. Her three teddies sat alongside it, each one of them bigger than her, and I veered to scoop them up on my way to the house.

At the kitchen table, Dad peered up from his paper as we stepped inside, and Mum turned in her spot beside the chilli-smelling pot on the hob. Both raised their eyebrows, their attention flickering between Gabe and me.

Rounding the table, I dumped the bundle of Lia-Gear, as we titled it, on Sean's seat and headed to the rack for my truck keys.

"Going somewhere?" Dad asked.

I sent him a nod over my shoulder. "Some business Gabe needs me to take care of." Buttoning up my jeans, I shied away from the questions in Mum's eyes by reaching for my T-shirt and tugging it over my head. "I don't know what time I'll be home."

Without allowing them a second glance, I ducked into the hallway and strode for the front door.

"Ethan?"

I halted at Gabe's call and spun to find him in the doorway behind me.

He stared at me for a long moment, his jaw tight. "If you hurt her ... I'll ..." He blew out a breath, but his gaze never once wavered.

I sent him a nod. "I know."

Last time I'd visited the pack's 'safe' apartment had been to talk Jem into coming home after she'd walked out on the pack. Standing outside D3, hand poised to knock, shouldn't have seemed much different to then. After all, I'd come to find a female, one I needed to convince. So, why did I feel so much more concerned I'd never get Shelley to listen? Why did it feel as though my future rode on getting her to answer the door?

Because it does.

Taking a deep breath, I rapped a couple of times with my knuckles.

Silence preceded the faint shuffle of feet across carpet, the rattle of a security chain, a twist of the key and catch.

The door opened, and Shelley stared up at me, her green eyes unreadable, lips slightly parted.

My heart thudded just at the sight of her, banging out its approval as my gaze trailed south over her delicate frame encased in jeans, her aqua-painted toenails poking out on the ends of her bare feet, and all the way back up again to hair that had once been a fiery shade of red.

She reached up, tugged at the strands of blue and black, longer since I'd last seen her. "I changed the colour."

I nodded, swallowing the *no shit* balancing on the tip of my tongue.

Her brow creased a little. "You don't like it?"

"Sure." I almost went to touch where her fingers had slipped from, but dug into my jeans pockets instead. "You smell amazing, so ..." I shrugged.

She rubbed a hand around the back of her neck, the movement drawing her shirt up from her waistband and exposing her navel. "You want to come inside?"

"Yeah." The word tumbled from me before she'd barely finished asking, and she peered up at me for a moment before stepping aside.

Not much had changed since I'd last been in the apartment. The same neutral colours graced the walls in the living room I entered. The same furniture decorated the space. It didn't smell the same, though. The old combination of scents had faded, replaced by an infusion of Gabe and Shelley.

The door clicked shut behind me. "I'll put the kettle on," Shelley said

I tracked her as she trotted across the room and into the small kitchen. Running water sounded out, along with a click and the clank of cups. I moved across to the sofa, sinking onto the soft cushions, though my focus remained on the room where Shelley pottered. Maybe I figured staring that way would get me a faster glimpse of her.

Yeah, or emerging to my beady eyes'll creep her out.

I took a deep breath, forced myself to turn away, told myself I had plenty of time for absorbing what my senses had missed out on for too long. She had, after all, allowed me through the door. She hadn't kicked me to the kerb. Maybe she'd be prepared to listen.

To what?

What the hell did I intend to say to her?

"Here." Mug extended, Shelley scarcely made any noise as she brushed across the carpet toward me.

I took the offering and watched as she folded herself into the singular armchair with her own drink. "Thanks."

She nodded, sipping on what the aroma identified as coffee.

I mimicked her, sampling my own, while trying my damnedest not to stare at her like a freak.

Her left calf balanced on her right knee. She flexed the toes of her outstretched foot, her eyes aimed at them over the rim of her mug.

I rested my elbows on my knees, lacing my fingers around my drink. "How have you been?"

She lifted to me. "Okay." Sip, swallow, shrug. "I guess." Sip, swallow, sigh. "You?"

Out of it. All over the damn place. My shoulders bunched up. "Okay."

She nodded.

I peered down into the liquid beneath my nose. "You seem settled here." I raised my gaze to her green-eyed one. "You like it?"

"It's a bit small." She looked across toward the far wall that separated us from the bedrooms. "But it's better than facing the neighbours back home would have been. Better to be where no one knows us." She glanced back at me. "Fresh start, and all."

"I heard you're relocating the shop, too."

She nodded. Her little bookshop of oddness, with way more to it than what remained visible on the surface, had been where we'd first met, where I'd first met Gabe, too, and offered to lend a guiding hand.

I watched her, thinking she'd elaborate, but she dropped her gaze back to toes she wiggled about again.

Seconds passed, with only breaths and heartbeats as conversation, each one ticked off by the kitchen clock. Shelley never once took her focus from her foot, like she couldn't bring herself to look at me.

Or maybe she just had nothing more to say.

Resigned, I pushed to my feet and strode into the oak-fronted kitchen. My coffee splashed the stainless steel as I poured it down the sink before heading toward the exit.

"You're going?"

I nodded, continuing for the door. "It was nice seeing you again, Shel." *Real nice. Too nice.*

The creak of springs told me Shelley stood. "And there was me thinking you had something to say for yourself."

I paused in my reach for the catch. "I did."

One footstep crunched the deep pile of the carpet. "Like what?"

"Like sorry." I turned back around.

She stood beside the armchair, the fingers of her left hand gripping its back.

I raised my gaze to the ceiling. "I am sorry, Shel. Sorry for all the shit Gabe got dragged into. Sorry I didn't turn out to be who you hoped I'd be. Sorry that I'm a major fuckup." *Sorry my lack of focus let Catherine get away ...* I looked back to her deepening frown. "You know, I've thought it through so many times. Trying to figure out what I could have done differently. How I could have prevented it from happening. And the only answer was the impossible one of turning back the clock. But ..." I sighed, deep, heavy, my chest rising and falling with the effort. "... even if it were possible, I wouldn't do it, because it would mean I'd never meet Gabe. And I'd never meet you. Don't ask me to be sorry for that, because I can't." I gave the tiniest of nods. "That's what I came here to say." I turned back for the door, spinning the catch.

"Ethan, wait," she said as the door sprung free.

I rubbed a hand across my face, wondering how much more I could take when my head already felt on the verge of implosion along with my chest. When her fingers folded around my arm, I almost jumped, and as I twisted to look down at her, her eyes shone.

"I'm sorry, too." She sighed, as though taking a moment to collect her thoughts. "I'm sorry for laying all the blame on you. I had no right—not after all you did for Gabriel."

"You had every ri—"

Her fingers pressed to my lips. "I had *no* right. I should have listened. Given you a chance. I did neither. And I'm sorry."

As her scent drifted upward from her fingers, my lids lowered. "I missed you, Shelley."

Quiet followed, except for a couple of erratic heartbeats competing for unsteadiness, and I did dare open my eyes for fear of what I'd see.

Fear of the rejection her expression would show.

"I missed you, too," she whispered after a few beats.

When the door clicked shut, I lifted my lids to Shelley's glossy stare. "So ... what now?" I murmured against her fingers.

Her gaze flittered to the side, returning to me as her lips curved a little. "I think this is the part where you hold me."

My eyebrow twitched up. I hadn't been expecting that, and half expected her to announce the joke. When she just stood staring up at me, I ducked until my nose tucked beneath her ear and slid my hands down to her butt. Her hair tickled my cheek as I inhaled, and her fingers left my lips, sliding over my shoulder as I drew her up until my chest met with hers.

"Like this, you mean?" I murmured.

She nuzzled into my neck, her body moulding into mine. "Exactly like this."

As my eyes closed, I tighten my hold, snuggled a little deeper, and finally ... finally, I allowed myself to smile.

ACKNOWLEDGEMENTS

Huge thanks to:

my man, for putting up with my sulks every time I didn't think I could do it. Probably should thank the kidlets, too.

those who critiqued chapter by chapter at first draft and begged me to write faster when I couldn't keep up with their demands: Aimee Laine, Pam Bitner, Rebecca Hart, Jocelyn Adams.

my beta readers: Julie Reece, who took the trouble to leave comments throughout so I understood what needed work; my sister: Jennifer Turner, who found my HUGE boo-boo, which meant I didn't look a total tool when I subbed it to my editor; Elaine Hart, who loved it and cheer-leaded and helped me believe; Dawn Whipps, who has allowed me to convert her into a werewolf-loving-fiend; Carla Huxley—who should know why without me even having to say a word.

Lauren Pryke for being such a great model on which to base a young teen when I needed one.

the team at J. Taylor Publishing for 'getting' what I write, for giving me a Rocking!!! cover, for putting up with me, and for doing such an ace job of spit & polishing.

I should probably also take a moment to emphasise those responsible for Caged actually reaching completion. Because Caged was my most difficult assignment to date. I think I hit around the 60% mark when I first threatened to throw in the towel. Both Aimee Laine and Jocelyn Adams pleaded with me not to hit the delete button.

And for the final 40% of writing it?

You guys kept me going. Every single one of you. Every time I received a review on my other works, every time one of you sought me out just to say hi, every time one of you visited my blog … it spurred me into pushing through the tough times—for you!

Thanks for the encouragement, it made all the difference in the world.

ABOUT J.A. BELFIELD

Best known for her Holloway Pack stories and The Therapist, J.A. Belfield lives in Solihull, England, with her husband, two children, a spoiled dog and a cat who likes to vomit in unfortunate places. She writes paranormal romance, with a second love for urban fantasy. And now she writes erotic romance, too. Because she can. ;)

In 2016, Instinct [now part of Beginnings] earned J.A. Belfield International Bestseller status when it featured in the Paranormal Attractions anthology. J.A. Belfield now hopes to claim that same status solo.

To stay updated on everything J.A. Belfield, join her on Facebook in the Belfield's MotherBookers group.

TITLES BY J.A. BELFIELD

HOLLOWAY PACK

BEGINNINGS
CALLED
LURED
CAGED
UNNATURAL
CORNERED
HEREDITARY
ENTICED

EROTIC ROMANCE

THE THERAPIST

PARANORMAL ROMANCE

HER MANE ESCORT

www.ingramcontent.com/pod-product-compliance
Lightning Source LLC
Chambersburg PA
CBHW071153100726
47908CB00002B/354